ROCK ICON READY

Kella Campbell

TIED STAR BOOKS

Rock Icon Ready
CONTEMPORARY ROMANCE

TRADE PAPERBACK EDITION
ISBN 978-0-9921152-9-6

BOOK TEXT TYPESET IN ZAPF RENAISSANCE ANTIQUA BOOK
WITH HEADINGS IN INKED GOD PRO & LOVE LIGHT
COVER PHOTOGRAPHY BY TIFFANY JOHN
EDITOR TANYA OEMIG

TIED STAR BOOKS
VANCOUVER, CANADA

WWW.TIEDSTARBOOKS.COM

Once I met a boy and thought my summer would be fun;
twenty-seven years later, he's still the one for me,
father of my children, friend of my heart, love of my life.

KIMMY SAT ON ONE OF THE EQUIPMENT CASES, drumming with her fingers on the surface beside her, watching as Dice paced around twirling his drumsticks and air-drumming to the hype music playing in the green room and corridors. "Stressed?" she asked, softly enough that he could pretend he hadn't heard her over the music. They understood each other that way – always gave the other an out, a chance to ignore what they didn't want to answer. The big drummer and his punky little drum tech had been best friends from nearly the moment they'd laid eyes on each other.

"Just... burnt out," he said, and gestured with his drumsticks like *what can you do?*

It had been a hell of a long tour. Kimmy nodded, and patted the box where she was sitting. "Rub your shoulders?"

"Yeah." He sat down, and she got up on her knees behind him, strong hands working at least a bit of the tension and fatigue away. It was the second of three back-to-back nights in Los Angeles, all sold out, to be followed by a trek across the continent – a grueling 30 hours for the convoy of tour buses and semis, though only four hours in the air for the band – for a Fourth of July event at a huge outdoor festival in Milwaukee, then another show in Indianapolis the next day. Too much, especially a year and a half into what had been nearly unremitting touring to promote their third album, *My Tainted Baby*. Their label expected a lot of them.

Kimmy kneaded Dice's shoulders as she had before and after shows so often – not part of a usual drum tech's job, maybe, but they were close friends as well. And deep down, she found his muscular shoulders nice to look at and nicer to touch, even if she'd never do more than give him friendly massages and brush against him in passing. A good friendship and a good job were both hard things to find, and no way was she planning to jeopardize any of that. "The fans out there love you," she said. "Think of how happy you're making them."

"Yeah." He nodded, perking up. Forcing himself to perk up, maybe, but sometimes an entertainer had to do that for the fans. Kimmy understood.

"Five minutes," Mack, their stage manager, called down the hallway. "Ready to go, boys?" Voices echoed readiness. "Pyrotechnics on deck."

"You bet," Dice chimed in as he stood up, pulling away from Kimmy's hands. He adjusted the bandanna that kept his floppy chin-length brown hair out of his eyes, then pinged the elastic hair tie around his wrist for luck. She wasn't sure where *that* little superstition had come from – either the part about always needing to have a hair tie on his wrist during a show or the part about snapping it against his skin right before he went onstage, but it had been at least five years since she'd first noticed it. "I drum better with it," he'd say if asked. "It's lucky."

"Gather round!" Angel brought the band together as he always did, for a quick fist bump and a moment of eye contact, of gathering their energy into one connection. Then, nodding to each other, ready, they jogged down the corridor and up the ramp to the stage. An eruption of crowd noise greeted them.

Kimmy followed, taking her place – ready, if Dice should need anything.

♥

Smidge hadn't been so famous when she'd met them on a Saturday night six years earlier – popular, sure, filling up clubs and big enough to have graduated from a van to a tour bus, but nothing near what they'd since grown into. It was the beginning of the tour for *Skanky Treat*, their first album, just before it all started to blow up and go big, just before everything sold out and the tour was expanded and their songs were suddenly all over radio stations and streaming services and social media. Just before that.

It was still one of the best concerts she'd ever been to. Magic in the air, that kind of thing. She could feel in her soul that the band was going to make it big. Every song, every word of the front man's banter, every guitar pick tossed to the crowd was all charged-up potential. For Kimmy, the night had a strange foreknowledge feeling to it, a sense that they'd look back and say *we were there.*

Knowing that the event was general admission and the floor would be packed, she and her girlfriends had arrived hours early, lining up with the die-hards to get a place on the rail, reach-out-and-touch distance from the stage.

After the concert, their group split up. They'd come in two cars, so one of the designated drivers took the drunk and tired girls home, and the other stayed with the ones who wanted to keep the night going. But that group split up further, with some wanting to find food and others wanting to wait by the band's bus to see if they could get selfies or have their albums and t-shirts from the merch table signed. Smidge hadn't been big enough then for paid meet-and-greets or radio show prize winners, so if you wanted their attention, an uncertain wait out back by the stage door was the thing to do.

"You coming to Leo's, Kimmy?" Marisa asked. "I told Bryan we'd stick together." Bryan was Marisa's boyfriend and the eldest of Kimmy's four brothers.

"I really want to get my t-shirt signed, if I can."

Marisa grimaced, evidently torn. "Well..."

"Just go get your midnight breakfast. I'll be fine," Kimmy said. "It's not like I'll be alone, and we'll be along to meet you before you even know it."

And that was how Kimmy found herself outside the back of the Royal Oak Music Theater, where the big tour bus waited in the alley, wearing a borrowed blue denim miniskirt and a brand-new band t-shirt, on a summer evening that would change her life.

There weren't a lot of fans waiting that night, maybe a dozen, and as time slipped by and the band didn't emerge, some of them drifted away. Eventually the stage door crashed open and some men came out with amps and mic stands and loaded them into the underside of the bus before heading back inside. She didn't recognize them as band members, so they had to be either road crew or people belonging to the venue. "You want to just go meet up with the others and eat?" Kimmy's friend Angie asked after a while, shuffling her feet and wrapping her arms around herself. It wasn't cold, but the summer night wasn't entirely warm either, and they hadn't brought jackets.

"No way," said Gina, the other friend who'd stayed to try to meet the band. "I'm getting a selfie with them. They have to come out sometime."

"True," Kimmy agreed, though she thought the band might not want to be bombarded with fans, if it was taking them so long to get out of the venue. Their bus would be on a schedule. It might not be convenient. Her brothers' band had only played locally, so a tour bus schedule had never been an issue for them, but Kimmy read books like *The Musician's Guide to the Road* so she'd be prepared – she knew about schedules and load-out and how fans and delays could cause trouble. "Let's wait a while longer, but if they seem like they're in a rush when they do come out, we shouldn't be that kind of fan, right?"

Angie and Gina nodded. They'd seen desperate fans at other concerts, begging and badgering the performers for one more minute, one more signature, hands clutching at clothes and body parts when it was plain the musicians were out of time and needed to be on their bus and away. None of them wanted to be that kind of fan.

The stage door banged open and the same group of men as before came out with more gear, trundling everything over to the bus and fitting it into the cargo bays. Then back inside. And out again with more things. *Load-out time.* But the band didn't emerge.

Eventually the door opened again, and there was Easy, the bassist, his blond wave of curls glinting in the alley lights. Behind him came the guitarist, Blade, all in black with inky spiky hair. They stopped when they saw the cluster of fans, Easy with a sexy smile and Blade with a sort of diffident shrug. *He looks like trouble*, Kimmy thought in that instant, looking at Easy. *A heartbreaker.* Very attractive, no doubt, but not her cup of tea. And the word that came to mind when she saw Blade up close for the first time was *unhappy*. She got the silver fabric marker out of her purse and joined the line, and shortly had two of the four signatures she wanted, while the four guys who were probably road crew trundled around them getting the bus loaded, and a woman of about Kimmy's age with electric orange hair in a sleek inverted bob towed out a garment rack with one hand, lugging a giant makeup case in the other.

As soon as he'd signed the various items held out to him, Blade pushed off and boarded the bus. Easy stayed on, chatting to the fans who seemed happy to gather around him for as long as he was willing to talk with them, and Kimmy found herself gradually pushed to the edge of the group.

The metallic sound of the stage door opening echoed yet again, and this time she didn't even look over – until something clunked to the ground with a crash and frustrated voices flared up, an argument that had simmered down roiling onto the boil again. "That does it, Dyl," said a deep voice, smooth and rich as chocolate, that Kimmy had last heard shouting goodnight from the stage. "I know you think you can do it all, but fuck it, you need a drum tech. We don't have *time* to do after-show fan stuff and pack up our own gear and still make roll-out on schedule. This isn't just us in a van anymore."

Then an actual prickle of... something ran down Kimmy's spine as another voice, lighter, slightly hesitant and repentant, said, "You're right, I know. You always are. But I like my kit the way I do it. I don't want someone else messing with that."

Angel emerged, thin with drugs and his early twenties – he and Blade had both still been using back then – his bleached-platinum hair longer and in a ponytail. Then he turned back as another crash echoed in the hall behind him. "Ask if you need help, man."

And the lighter voice echoed from deep in the hallway, "I've got this. I'm coming."

Something about that voice... Kimmy couldn't look away from the stage door, *needed* to see the owner of the voice. Logic and the conversation told her it had to be the drummer, Dice. She'd seen him on stage, seen him on posters and websites and in magazines. She knew what he looked like.

"You waiting for Dice, babe?" Angel asked, pausing on his way to join Easy and the small crowd around him.

"Well, I–" She held out her fabric marker with a smile. "I've got two of your four signatures on my shirt and I'm hoping for the full set. Would you...?"

So Angel took the pen and signed her shoulder, with a flourish that swirled onto the sleeve in an artistic way, just as some of the fans around Easy caught sight of him and swarmed over. Once again, Kimmy found herself edged back, on the outside of the group.

And her eyes were drawn back to the stage door.

He's got a cute butt. She couldn't help noticing it, seeing as how he'd hip-checked the door open and was backing out butt-first, dragging a wheeled hardware bag *and* a multi-tom drum bag while carrying – Kimmy's eyes assessed the load – his snare, bass drum, and cymbals, plus a handful of drumsticks that hadn't made it into any of the bags. These weren't the hard-sided ATA cases he'd have in the future, but a battered set of padded soft bags he'd probably had since Smidge first started playing shows. Faded blue denim hugged that cute butt, and she couldn't stop looking – not a view one got from the audience, that was for sure! Fortunately, he had his hands too full to notice.

She jumped forward and grabbed the door to stop it crashing back onto him while he worked his big load through the opening.

"Hey, thanks!" he said, looking over his shoulder at her. Much taller than she'd expected, taller than his bandmates, which hadn't been obvious behind his drum kit. And he'd ripped the sleeves off his plaid shirt, giving her a view of extremely well-muscled arms. *Why am I noticing this stuff?* She wasn't prone to ogling over muscles and butts, in general. But something about this man had her tongue-tied and drooling, from the moment she'd heard his voice.

"It's no trouble," she managed to say. She wanted to offer to help, but *I've got this* echoed in her mind and she doubted he'd take assistance from a stranger if he wouldn't from his own bandmate. So she waited with a hand on the door to stop the automatic mechanism from closing it on him. *You could do this in two trips,* she thought, though he was clearly determined not to.

At last, he was clear of the door with all his bags and turned to her with raised eyebrows. "I guess you weren't standing here just to hold the door for me?"

"Any chance you could sign my t-shirt?" Then she laughed self-consciously as it clicked that his arms were full. She was holding out her silver fabric paint marker and he didn't have a free hand to take it.

He said, "Sure," then paused and looked around with a grin as he too realized the impracticality of it. Then he set down his cases, all of them, and asked, "Where should I sign?"

He has such a sweet smile, Kimmy remembered thinking, even as something in her brain fused and she mumbled, "Whatever you like," which wasn't an answer to *where* at all. The others had signed near the collar or on her shoulders, but Dice leaned in, his hair flopping forward around the bandanna that held it – sort of – back from his face, and signed the upper curve of her left breast. She still couldn't be sure whether he'd done it on purpose to be flirty, or whether he'd just seen a blank bit of t-shirt and gone for it without thinking, but his wrist brushed over her nipple as he scrawled his name and their eyes met in an awkward blend of horror and flirtation as the pen slipped out of his fingers and bounced to the ground.

"Sorry," he muttered, and began gathering up his equipment.

As he moved away, she heard Angel say to him, "Dyl, I know you like to take care of your own kit, but you need a drum tech. This is getting ridiculous."

As they walked away, she heard – she remembered it so clearly, even so many years later – the frustrated desperation in the drummer's voice as he said, "I know, but how will I find someone who can get me set up how I like it?"

"I could do it," she called out on a wild impulse, then bit her lip as they both turned back to look at her.

"We're not looking for a runner or PA," Angel clarified kindly, and she could tell he wasn't trying to be dismissive. "We need to find him a drum tech, someone who can take care of his kit, pack it around, repair shit as needed."

She knew what they saw – a girl in a miniskirt, concert makeup, and sparkles. She'd just discovered how to spangle her high fade with tiny rhinestones using eyelash glue, and maybe she'd gone overboard a bit, but it was over-the-top fun for a concert, and she'd never thought to be pitching herself as road crew that night. "I know; I heard what you said. I do pretty much everything for my brothers' band and have since my early teens."

"Fetching beer for a garage band doesn't mean shit, Sparkles," Easy said with a smirk.

"Maybe I shouldn't have offered," Kimmy said with a shrug. "I don't really know why I did. I don't have a music degree or fancy courses in live sound. But I can drum well enough to cover for my brother Gareth if he's sick, I can tune and mike up a kit, and I've replaced a broken drumhead onstage during a concert more than once. And they've been playing shows in actual bars all over the state for four years now, so..."

"That's cool," Angel said, and she could tell he still wasn't sold on her offer, still thinking of her as just a fan outside a concert, which was fair.

But Dice asked, "What's the band called?"

"Friends With Royalty – it's mostly a cover band: Queen, Prince, and Elvis, you know? They've got a few original songs, but the bar crowd likes their classics."

When Dice grinned, appreciating the name, Kimmy felt warm all over.

She saw Angel looking at Dice with affection, then he glanced over at the other band members. "Well, I guess we can give you a try, if that's what Dice wants."

Dice nodded.

"Okay, let's get on the bus, then." Angel turned to board the tour bus behind Easy, obviously expecting her to follow with Dice. Right then and there.

Angie and Gina looked at Kimmy in dismay. "You can't just get on a tour bus in the middle of the night!" Gina said. "You don't even have a toothbrush."

"That's true. I... I can't just leave *now*. I didn't plan this..."

But even as she could see the moment slipping away in front of her, Dice said, "You could join us in Grand Rapids tomorrow. Couldn't she, Angel?"

Angel stepped back down from the bus. "Sure. That works. Here – what's your name, babe?"

"Kimmy – Kimberley Baker."

"Take my card, Kimmy. If you can get to Grand Rapids by four tomorrow, give me a call, and we'll let you try out for the job. Cool?"

"Cool," said Kimmy, tucking the card into the pocket of her skirt, feeling like heaven had opened up for her. She still had it, six years later, pasted in a scrapbook alongside the train ticket that got her as far as Kalamazoo, the bus ticket from there to Grand Rapids, and a selfie she took with Dice behind the drum kit she set up for him that day.

There was another picture in her scrapbook of them having drinks after that first show, all of them smiling, Dice's arm around her shoulder. Just after the picture had been taken, she'd asked him how old he was.

Drinks were going around and she had a beer in her hand and then someone, maybe Blade, handed her a tequila shot. She tossed it back with the others, unfazed, but it did take the edge off any last formality or discomfort she might have had with her new employers. Dice was sitting next to her, and suddenly in the shifting light reflecting from the dance floor, he looked younger than she'd noticed before. "How old are you, Dice?" she asked.

"Just turned nineteen," he said, looking slightly embarrassed. "But don't worry. The rest of the guys are legal to drink and no one ever checks my ID."

Practically a baby. Only three years younger than she was, but it seemed like an eternity from a flirting point of view. Not that age mattered in any practical sense, but... well... friendship was good. In that moment, she set aside the spark of attraction and chemistry that flickered between them, and focused her intentions on being the best drum tech and friend she could be.

She'd been rewarded with a closeness she'd never had with anyone, not even her beloved older brothers. They could tell each other anything – almost anything – and she knew deep in her bones that Dice would have her back and be at her side, her best friend on the entire planet, no matter what happened.

Once Kimmy had her immediate post-show checklist squared away, she headed for the band's dressing room for the technical debrief. Nothing had come up from her point of view, but she always checked whether Dice had any concerns for her, and she liked to see how he was doing after the show. The Smidge tour was a family. All the musical and technical crew gathered for the debrief, to support each other and so they were aware of any issues.

The remnants of Chinese takeout, the band's post-show meal, were spread out on a table. Dice gave Kimmy a wink and handed her an egg roll wrapped in a napkin – knowing how much she liked them, he'd evidently saved one of his for her. "Aww, thanks, you lovely man," she murmured before biting into it.

Everyone seemed tired. Hell of a long tour, so it wasn't a surprise, and this particular run of shows stacked up in a way that struck Kimmy as unnecessarily exhausting and honestly cruel. It wasn't Phil's fault – the road manager was doing his best, but the label and production company had worked out the schedule with the various venues and promoters and presented it as written in stone, not listening to objections.

The guitar and bass techs talked about strings and tuning, getting a quick listen and nod from a distracted Angel, whose attention was divided between them and the sound team. He'd apparently had an issue with his in-ear monitor during the second half of the show, and the sound team was trying to figure out what had happened.

Blade appeared somber and distracted, glancing over often at his extremely pregnant wife Crys, who sat tiredly on a couch in the corner with a cushion wedged behind her back. She was due in two and a half weeks, but with Blade barely eight months clean after an eight-year dance with heroin, she soldiered on with the tour, keeping him calm, keeping him focused. It was nice to see Blade doing so well – he'd gained some much-needed weight and looked properly fed and rested, and his skin had a healthy glow.

Easy listened attentively to his bass tech, Gary, who wanted to restring his blue Warwick, then good-naturedly teased Erva that he'd been out of the light during part of one song, implying that was somehow her fault, and gently punched her arm when she sassed back that he should know to stay in the light because it wouldn't follow him if he wandered out of it. Once he'd dropped the arrogant act, he was fun to have around. Falling in love had been good for him. His partner Nell, who was also his bodyguard, stood out of the way by the door, keeping an eye on everything, and the other bodyguards were just a shout away in the hall.

Jed, in charge of backstage public relations and first aid, stuck his head in to remind the band that they had a meet-and-greet group to see before the end of the night. "Just one, which is a mercy."

Just then, Crys let out a meep of embarrassed distress and crossed her hands over her lap in an instinctive effort to hide herself as something dripped off the couch onto the floor and a wet patch spread out around her.

Jed turned at once to look at her and said, "Looks to me like your water just broke, Crys. Are you in labor?"

Blade's face paled as he moved to his wife's side, saying, "But she's not due for another seventeen days, and they say first-time moms are always late." *He's more scared than she is,* Kimmy thought.

"Well, unless she peed herself, dude..." Angel said, trying for humor, though he too looked concerned.

"Crys, are you in labor?" Jed repeated. "Are you having contractions?"

Crys looked painfully embarrassed as she murmured, "I thought it was just Braxton Hicks. I've been crampy and uncomfortable for weeks, and it didn't seem much worse than the usual, and... now I'm sitting in a puddle."

"Oh, honey," Sally said, and dug a couple of hand towels out of one of her makeup boxes to mop up the wetness and try to make Crys more comfortable.

"Okay," Jed said, taking charge. The former ER nurse had a tone to his voice that compelled everyone to cooperate. "Angel, Easy, Dice, you go do the meet-and-greet. They'll just have to do without Blade. Who can go with them to be me and supervise?"

Sally got up as if to volunteer, but Kimmy saw how Crys clutched at her hand, then Sally gave Erva a look.

"I'm on it," the lighting assistant and rigger said. "You want to come help out, Kimmy?"

Kimmy shot a quick look at Crys, who was holding her husband's hand and looking decidedly not ready for any of this. "Sure."

As the room cleared out, she could hear Jed asking, "Are you comfortable with me checking your cervix, Crys? Or would you rather wait until we get you to a hospital? We should know how much dilation is happening at this point. But I think your baby's going to be born in L.A."

She shut the door behind her and quickened her steps to catch up with Erva and Dice and the others. Dice dropped back, slowing his pace so her shorter legs could catch up, reaching out as she closed the distance to ruffle her hair and destroy what was left of the gelled shape she'd given her three inches of hair on top. He often did that, but only at the end of the night when it didn't matter – he'd never wreck her hair when she was trying to look presentable. It felt good, and she had to stop herself from leaning into his touch. "You think Crys is okay?" he asked.

Erva overheard and turned back for a moment to look at him, laughing at him but not unkindly. "She's having a baby. Her first baby. She's probably pretty damn scared, dude."

At the room designated the meet-and-greet lounge, the band members peeled off and went in, the bodyguards settled themselves against the wall opposite the door, and with a quick smile and tiny wave for Dice, Kimmy followed Erva along to the holding room where the guests would be waiting, with an ice bucket full of sodas and a basket of packaged snacks. "You want to scan the barcodes or do the waivers?" Erva asked.

"Barcodes, please – if you don't hate doing the waivers," Kimmy said. Zapping the barcodes on the backs of the VIP passes was an easy job. All she had to do was check the guest's ID and make sure it matched the barcode's purchaser information on the scanner. Doing the waivers meant explaining that they couldn't take their phones into the meet-and-greet, which didn't always go so well.

Erva nodded. "Sure. We'll split them up into smaller groups to go in. Take turns walking them over?"

"Seems good."

An average group of guests waited, excited to be meeting Smidge.

An older couple said hi to them and asked where Jed was, so it was plain they were die-hard fans who'd seen the band and done meet-and-greets often enough to be familiar with some of the crew. A cluster of younger guys in Smidge shirts from the *Human Lollipop* tour greeted the older couple and were clearly regulars too. And one of the youngest women had a Smidge tattoo on her arm and carried a painting she'd done of Angel as a gift for him. "I'm doing one of each of the guys," she told Kimmy seriously as she was having her barcode scanned. "This is just the first one I've finished. I'm seeing them again in Phoenix, so I'll bring the next one then."

But quite a few of the women were young and pretty and single, and some of them looked like would-be groupies or at least willing to have a night with the unattached members of the band – Angel and Dice. Kimmy suppressed a prickle of discomfort at that, as she always did. Angel could look after himself, of course, and in any case, she had a suspicion that he was already taken care of in that regard. But Dice? He deserved the best that the entire planet had to offer. Maybe the young artist was looking for a date. She looked kinder than some of the others. *Better to be busy in some other part of the arena.* She didn't usually have to look the girls in the face, and could pretend not to see them, not to know anything.

Oh, she knew the boys had indulged in wild parties and women were involved. Not so much now that Blade and Easy had permanent partners, but that had to focus more of the women's attention on Dice. She tried not to think about what might be happening in the meet-and-greet lounge or back in the dressing room, or out on one of the buses, or wherever the party migrated to. She'd walked in more than a few times on things she'd rather not have seen – half-naked people, blow jobs in progress, sex – and no one wanted that sort of brainworm featuring one's employers, so it was always *oops* and an about turn and she'd come back later.

I just want Dice to be happy, she reminded herself. *And it's not like I'm a nun.*

After she walked the last group of guests to the meet-and-greet lounge, she waved to the group of waiting bodyguards before heading off to catch a ride back to the hotel. They were a friendly lot once you knew them, even if they looked rightfully intimidating to outsiders. Nell was more than halfway to becoming a real Smidgette, as the longstanding women of the crew called themselves, no matter that she'd only been with the tour and Easy for a matter of weeks.

Kimmy had gone on a few dates with Blade's bodyguard Ryan – a genuinely decent guy, cute and fit, and good in bed. He wasn't with the others since Blade wasn't with them, but earlier that day he'd texted her to ask whether she wanted to get coffee after the show if Blade didn't need him for anything, and she'd said sure. He called just before midnight to say that he was at the hospital with Blade and Crys and didn't know when he'd be able to take a break, given the circumstances – probably only when one of the others covered for him so he could sleep and shower.

"Oh, too bad," she told him, trying to sound disappointed. But she was tired, and not honestly in the mood for bunk gymnastics, or even company. Qingshan and Gary were in the van with her heading back to the hotel, and they invited her to join them for a drink at the hotel bar, but she declined that too. When she got to the room she was sharing with Trish the tour accountant and Lulu who ran the merch table, her roommates were already asleep. She brushed her teeth and got into bed as quietly as she could. Snug in her bed, she put earbuds in and listened to the playlist she'd named *dreamtime* until she fell asleep.

With her last waking thought, she wondered whether Crys and Blade's baby would be born by morning. How long did it take to have a baby?

♥

The next morning, Ryan texted Kimmy to say that he was still at the hospital but that one of the others would be coming by to cover for him so he could take a break, if she still wanted to get coffee or lunch or something.

"I was just heading out to get a haircut," she told him. "Lunch after that would be great."

Most of the time, on the road as a drum tech for a rock band, she kept her hair neat herself with the trimmer kit she carried with her. She found barbershops comforting, though, and when she felt stressed or blue or at loose ends, she'd look for a red-and-blue-striped pole twirling in a shop window. She could nearly always find one. This time, it was almost too easy, across the street from the hotel and down half a block.

"Are you sure?" the barber asked, when she walked in and told him she wanted her high fade freshened up, on the softer side, starting with a half-guard and blended into the top, and it would be great if he could trim that to about two inches. "There's a salon in the next block, unisex, they do all kinds of things. Pixie cuts and all that." He seemed taken aback at first, but that didn't surprise her. Her short hair and facial piercings weren't most people's cup of tea, not to mention her ripped-up jeans, leather choker, and the fact that she'd cut the sleeves off her current Smidge t-shirt. Once she left home, she'd learned that a lot of older male barbers were reluctant to cut a woman's hair at all, especially in more conservative places. But she'd found over time that if she smiled and asked nicely, most would agree to do the job.

She'd waved his suggestion away with hopeful eyes. "I don't want anything feminine. Just... do my hair like you would a guy's. When I was six, I insisted on going to the barber with my brothers, and it was so great, I've never wanted anything else. I don't feel comfortable in fancy salons. Please?"

It was the pure truth. There were photographs of her with braids and pigtails as a small child, but she'd adored her four older brothers and begged endlessly to get her hair cut just like theirs. She had few firm memories of being six, but the vivid delight of being granted her wish still stuck with her.

The place was empty and her money was as good as anyone else's, so the barber shrugged and gestured her into the chair. She settled into place and let him cover her in a voluminous black nylon cape that draped around her like she was some kind of historical romance queen, and she relaxed at last, eyes half-closed as she focused on the comforting buzz of the trimmer skimming over the back of her scalp.

At the barbershop, Kimmy Baker was secretly a queen on her throne – sometimes a warrior queen, sometimes a diplomat queen, sometimes a captive queen or a wealthy and powerful queen or a long-reigning gracious monarch. At the same time, she was entirely present in the moment, enjoying the Barbicide smell, the sensation of the hot towel on the nape of her neck and then the chill as it was replaced by the gentle scrape of the razor.

The door swung open with a jingle of chimes, and although she didn't dare turn her head while the barber shaved the back of her neck with his old-fashioned straight razor, she could see in the mirror that it was Dice entering the shop, followed by Angel and Easy.

"Ryan told us you might be here," Dice said. "The baby came. It's a boy. No one's allowed in to visit until Blade and Crys have had some, you know, bonding time with him? So we're getting something to eat that isn't hospital cafeteria food, if you want to join us."

"Sure." She looked at the shadowy figures standing on the other side of the barbershop's frosted window. "Who's with you?"

"Just bodyguards," Dice said. "You know. Not supposed to go off without them, and all that."

The barber held up an admonishing finger – he clearly didn't know, or didn't care, that three-quarters of Smidge had just entered his shop. "Your friend is almost done here," he said soothingly. "Have patience for another few minutes."

The three rock stars waited in silence as he finished up and whisked the cape away. "Thanks," Kimmy told him, getting cash out of her pocket. "It looks great."

As they left the barbershop, Kimmy saw that only three people waited for the band. "Hi, Will. Hi, Aidan. Hi, Nell," she said. Will, an Army veteran, was Angel's long-time bodyguard. Aidan had been promoted from a regular concert security position to watch over Dice after his old bodyguard left to get married. And it was nice to have Nell as part of the bodyguard crew now, too. Ryan wasn't there, presumably stationed outside the hospital room where Blade and Crys were getting to know their newborn son, and Kimmy wasn't sure whether to be disappointed or relieved. Casual dating was far too much work, much of the time.

"The restaurant across the street looks okay," Will said. "I checked it out while you were in the barbershop. Not crowded, seems clean. Usual suspects in terms of food, burgers, sandwiches."

They nodded.

"I told Ryan I would have lunch with him," Kimmy said, feeling guilty.

Aidan waved that concern away. "Don't worry about him. He was having a sandwich from the hospital cafeteria and chatting up one of the nurses when we left."

Oh. Well.

As they crossed the street to the restaurant, Dice reached up and rubbed his fingers across the freshly buzzed back of Kimmy's scalp. "Mmm, velcro," he said, laughing.

♥

Kimmy had no expectation of being invited to meet the new baby right away. She considered Crys a friend, but assumed that priority would go to the band and Sally and maybe whoever they considered family. Blade's family was no-contact, and no one from Crys's family had come to their wedding, but Angel's father called Blade "son" and his mother sent care packages to both Angel and Blade, so maybe they would travel for this moment? It would be nice for the baby to have grandparents.

After lunch, when they got back to the hotel, big notes were taped to the door of each band member's suite, with *Shower and change your shirt if you want to hold the baby!* in Sally's round bubble handwriting.

Kimmy gave everyone a nod and a wave before heading to her room to relax and maybe nap a bit before showtime. As she passed Erva and Sally's room, the door was open, so she stopped for a moment to say hello. Erva was sitting on the bed listening to music, freshly showered and wearing a hoodie with that laundry-fresh look, her braids wrapped into a high bun that sat like a crown. "Oh, hi, Erva!" Kimmy said. "I just wanted to ask Sally how it went at the hospital overnight. I bet she's exhausted?"

"Sure is! Dudette hasn't slept at all, I don't think, unless she dozed in a chair at some point. She's just showering now." Erva grinned, and gestured toward the bathroom door, where Kimmy realized she could hear the shower running. "Well, Crys needed her, and being there for people is what Sally does best. She'll be out in a minute."

True enough, the water sounds came to an end, and shortly Sally stepped out in a towel. "Hey, you're back! Better hop in the shower quick if you want to come with us, honey."

"Me?" Kimmy asked.

"Yes, you. Come on, you're Smidge family – you were with us for Blade's bad times, you should be here to see his best times. Unless you don't want to?"

"I'll shower really quick," Kimmy promised. *Smidge family.* It was true, she'd been around longer than a lot of the crew. Longer than Erva, who'd joined the tour as a rigger when Smidge moved up from bars to bigger venues and had since cross-trained to the lighting crew as well. Longer than Jed, though not by much, since they'd hired the ER nurse after Blade's first bad overdose, which wasn't long after Kimmy joined the tour... *Smidge family.* Hearing Sally say those words felt good. With a big smile, she held up a finger to show she'd be quick, and bolted to her room to get that shower.

HE TOUR'S RUNABOUT VAN PULLED UP AT THE HOSPITAL just behind the limo carrying the band. Will got to ride shotgun in the limo and Nell of course was in the back with the boys – a privilege of being both bodyguard and partner. But Aidan had been sent back to ride in the van with Erva and Sally and Kimmy and Trish. He laughed about it to the Smidgettes, saying, "Dice and me, we're always Team Little Brother. The youngest band member and the least-trained bodyguard." Everyone chuckled along with him, but Kimmy wondered if Dice felt that too, and if he minded.

When they arrived at the hospital, the van pulled into a side parking lot while the limo continued on to the main entrance. "It's kind of a public appearance," Sally explained. "Scott came over earlier to get some photographs of the baby and new parents, and he'll be at the front doors now to make sure we have some official pictures of the rest of them arriving. But I'm told that the label has dropped the word to the vultures, so we can expect paparazzi all over the place."

"That's rotten," said Trish, her British accent intensifying with indignation, but none of them were surprised. Publicity – *good* publicity – was everything to the powers-that-be at Arleigh Hayward Music.

Sally led them around to a clinic entrance, saying, "They'll let us in here and we can meet up with the others inside." And true enough, the receptionist at the desk in the clinic nodded to Sally and waved them through, to follow a green stripe along an interior corridor to the lobby and an elevator bank. A directory next to the elevators listed maternity as being on level 2, pink stripe. Up they went.

The nurse filling out paperwork at the station smiled at Sally, who of course had been there all night, and pointed down the hall, saying, "You know the way." It would have been impossible to miss the room anyway, even if Sally hadn't been there only an hour before, because of the bodyguards clustered outside the door. The boys must already be inside.

"We shouldn't all crowd in," said Trish in her polite British accent, so Kimmy hung back with her, still not certain that she belonged, not certain that she felt comfortable in this setting. Maybe it would be better just to hang out in the hall with the bodyguards – with Ryan, waving at her and giving her a wink, letting her know he wanted another date, another chance. And Will and Aidan were nice, comforting and kind.

Looking around, Kimmy wondered why she felt so out of place. Maybe it was her general sense that working for a touring rock band as a career was just generally incompatible with maternity wards and all the happy-families energy that seemed to carry.

But Sally had realized that Trish and Kimmy hadn't followed her into the hospital room, and she stuck her head out, calling, "Come on in, we'll squish and make room!" Faced with that, it would be rude to refuse. Smidge family, after all.

So they shuffled inside.

It was crowded, with the hospital bed and the clear plastic bassinet on wheels and four band members – who were not small men by any means, all of them tall, broad-shouldered and fit – plus Scott the photographer, and Sally and Erva, so there wasn't much room for two more. Kimmy, half a head shorter than Trish, ended up in a corner by the door.

Crys looked exhausted, circles under her eyes, and her normally perfect hair was up in a messy struggle bun. But she glowed, elated, the happiest woman in the world as she cradled the small, blue-swaddled bundle in her arms. And Blade, sitting on the edge of the bed beside her – he looked radiant like never before. "We're parents," he said in wonder. "Can you believe it?"

"We're calling him Luke Andrew," Crys said. "You want to hold him, Uncle Andy?"

Andy? Oh, right, Angel's real name. Kimmy couldn't help smiling as Blade tenderly took the baby from his wife and passed the little fellow to his best friend.

Angel looked a bit choked up as he held the baby for the first time. "Hi there, Lukey," he murmured. "This is going to be such an adventure for all of us."

"I grew up on tour buses," Easy reminded them. "It'll be great."

"Cool name," Dice said, which drew agreement from everyone.

"Like Luke Skywalker," Kimmy added, not to anyone in particular and she hadn't intended it to be heard distinctly beyond the general chiming in of approval for the name, but Blade heard her, and their eyes met.

He grinned. "I was thinking Luke Spiller, but that works too."

Scott's camera flash reminded everyone that he was taking pictures. "Don't worry, guys, you know I'll get you to approve anything I send to the label or make available to the media. Private stays private. Just figured you might want some real first-moment shots as well as posed ones."

"Fuck Arleigh Hayward," Blade muttered, but he moved to stand with Angel so Scott could get a picture of the two of them together with the baby.

"Get in there too, Easy. And you, Dice," Scott said. "Let's have a picture of the whole band with the little guy." More flashes. "Good. Do you and Nell want to hold him together, Easy?"

"No way." Nell rejected that idea at once. "He's really cute, but it might give people ideas." And Easy just chuckled and nodded, unfazed. Kimmy was pretty sure he liked babies, in general, but he and Nell seemed to have a thing that didn't involve anyone but the two of them, which was fair. *I don't really get it, but fair.* She couldn't imagine not wanting babies someday, with the right person, if she ever got a chance to settle down. *But... settle down and leave the band? Leave Dice?* Not that she'd ever get half a chance to meet anyone from outside the rock world, even, living on the road as she did.

Then Sally said, "Crys, I brought my kit. Are you up to letting me fix your face and hair for some portraits? We're going to have to give something to the label and the media, you know."

Crys sighed, but nodded. "More than anything, I want a shower, but I feel so tired and wobbly when I get out of bed."

"I can help you shower, sweetheart," Blade offered, and the loving look he gave Crys made Kimmy feel a tiny bit envious – not in the sense of wanting Blade, but it would be nice to have someone look at her like that.

"Nope," Sally told him briskly. "*You* are going to let your band brothers take you down to the coffee shop in the lobby for a cup of coffee. *We*," and her gesture included Kimmy along with Erva and Trish, "will take care of Crys and the baby."

Angel nodded his approval of the plan and gave Blade a friendly punch on the arm as a prompt to agree. "We'll leave one of the bodyguards up here. Will can stay, unless Nell wants to...?"

Nell grimaced at the other women. "I could use some tea, honestly. And I'm better at protecting Eamonn than watching over babies, cute as this one is," she added with a wry laugh.

The room emptied out as Sally plugged in a set of hot rollers, then produced a couple of fluffy towels from her bag. "See? I've thought of everything. And I've got your shower gel and shampoo so you can feel as normal as possible."

"That's sweet of you." Then, glancing over at the baby Erva was holding, Crys asked, "Is it time for him to nurse? Should I do that before I shower?"

Sally looked at a notebook on the bedside table. "Close enough. See if he wants to?"

So Crys took her baby back from Erva and unsnapped the shoulder of her hospital gown, draping a flannelette blanket over herself and Luke's head so she wasn't exposing a breast to the whole room. Even so, Trish got up and excused herself, awkwardly offering to bring tea or coffee up for any of the women who wanted it.

"Oh," Crys said, looking worriedly at Trish's back vanishing through the door.

"Don't mind her," said Erva. "Full back tat, travels with a rock tour, doesn't flinch when the boys walk around naked, but she's still somehow uncomfortable with toilet functions and bare boobs."

"Do you want me to give you some space too, Crys?" Kimmy offered, wondering if she was intruding on the new mother's privacy. "I mean, nursing doesn't bother me, two of my brothers have had kids and Marisa and Ella – my sisters-in-law – were *not* shy about it. Marisa says babies don't want their heads covered up while they're eating. But I can go out if..."

"No," Crys shot her a look of gratitude before pushing the cloth out of the way and looking down at Luke with adoring exasperation as she tried to get him to latch properly. "Please stay if you like, and thank you. I'm not very good at this yet, and it's easier if I can see what we're doing. Oh! There..."

Kimmy didn't mean to stare, she really didn't, but there was something compelling and fierce in the way the newborn baby nursed, utterly committed to the moment, and the scattered, bemused joy written all over Crys was mesmerizing.

"You want babies, Kimmy?" Erva asked casually, her voice a little too dry.

"Me? Well, who would I have babies with, working on a rock tour? I don't see myself meeting Prince Charming anytime soon out here." Kimmy tried to match Erva's nonchalant tone.

Sally let out a bit of a laugh at that. "True enough, honey."

"You never know," said Crys, making heart-eyes at her baby as she switched him to the other side. "I did."

The other women shared a look. "I'm glad your fairytale worked out," Sally said to her. "It's nice to see Blade happy like this." And that was something they could all agree on.

Gradually, Luke's nursing slowed and he relaxed into sleep, his tiny jaw falling slack as he dozed. "I think he's done," Crys murmured.

"Great." Sally leaned over and took the baby from her. "Let's get you into that shower." She went to put him down in the bassinette, and Kimmy sucked in a breath, inadvertently loud enough that Sally glanced over at her. "What?"

"Doesn't he need burping? My sisters-in-law always..." Kimmy's voice trailed off. She hadn't meant to criticize, and was by no means an expert on infants, but she had a clear memory of Marissa saying *never, ever put him down without burping him or he'll be up screaming all night,* and another of Ella saying *got to get the bubbles out* as she bounced her little girl.

"Okay, sure," and Sally turned around and held Luke out to Kimmy. "You burp him while Crys showers, huh?"

And that was how Kimmy found herself holding the small, warm bundle against her shoulder, patting and rubbing his back as she remembered her family doing with their babies. "You're a precious darling, aren't you?" she found herself whispering to him. She wasn't sure how one knew when the burping process was complete, but he seemed fast asleep. Still, she didn't put him down in his little plastic bed, but cuddled him all the time Sally and Erva helped Crys with her shower.

A nurse popped in briefly and tutted at Kimmy's uncovered shoulder before tucking a cloth over it, then said she was glad Crys was showering and that she'd come back later.

Soon Crys was out of the shower and dressed in a gorgeous powder blue eyelet nightgown and matching robe – not practical at all but perfect for photo portraits – with her hair wrapped around hot rollers while Sally applied some barely there makeup. "Not that you need it in the slightest," the makeup artist muttered, "but why give the world anything to pick at?"

"Seems silly to have to be perfect after giving birth," Erva grumbled, but she got the matching powder blue eyelet baby blanket out of Sally's bag.

The men returned, and Sally immediately pounced on Blade to fix his hair and touch up his eyeliner.

"You look like you know what you're doing," Dice said to Kimmy, who was still holding Luke.

She cuddled the baby close, hoping he'd stay asleep with all the increased noise in the room. Not for the first time over the past couple of years, she was surprised at the pleasure she found in holding an infant, warm and tiny and trusting. "Yeah, well, I've got two nieces and a nephew, so I get a lot of practice whenever I'm home for a holiday or whatever." Dice's eyebrows rose at that, so she added, "I have four brothers, remember. Big family."

"Right. Well, I brought you a brownie."

"Aww, thanks! Do you want to hold him so I don't wake him up trying to eat it?" she asked.

Dice gave her a doubtful look. "What if I drop him? I haven't held babies much, myself. At all, really."

"You wouldn't," Kimmy said encouragingly. "You're strong. Drummers have great coordination. And sleeping babies are lovely to cuddle, like little hot water bottles with heartbeats."

He put the paper bag he held down on the windowsill and reached out tentatively, letting her place Luke into his arms, smiling as she guided his hands into a secure hold. "He's a sweet little fellow, isn't he?" Dice whispered in wonder.

But Sally looked over with kind concern, as though she'd forgotten he was twenty-five years old now and not in the habit of dropping his drumsticks or breaking things. "You should sit down to hold him, Dice! And make sure you're supporting his head."

"Here, I can take him," Blade said, getting up and coming over to take his son. "I think Scott's about ready to snap some family portraits." No one could mistake the proud emphasis on *family* in his voice. Kimmy didn't think he meant to imply that he didn't trust Dice to hold the baby, but the timing – coming right after Sally's words – was unfortunate.

"Congratulations, man," Dice said, handing the baby over. He didn't seem bothered, so Kimmy decided it wasn't her place to mind for him.

A minute later, as they watched the photo session, she nudged him with her elbow and said, "You want some of this brownie?"

"What, you can't eat it all?" he teased.

She grinned. "Well, I *could,* but I'm willing to share." She held it out and he broke off a corner. "Thanks for getting it for me," she added.

"Got to keep my drum tech happy."

"Got to keep my drummer happy." She broke off another corner and passed it to him, and a warm feeling filled her as his fingers brushed hers in taking it. Happiness.

Later, during soundcheck at the venue – because concerts didn't stop for a little thing like a baby, as the label put it, and they had a responsibility to the fans who'd bought tickets, especially the ones who'd bought VIP Soundcheck Experience packages, which meant doing an extended soundcheck and fan Q&A on every show night – Dice told Kimmy that the band had decided to buy Blade and Crys a nursery bus as a baby gift. Not just a rented tour bus, but a proper custom job with a soundproofed nursery room so Luke could sleep and be changed and fed in comfort no matter where they were or how loud things got. "Not that it'll help if we have to go to Europe again in the fall," he muttered with displeasure. They had a bit of privacy, him up on the drum riser with her standing behind it, and he didn't have a vocals mic, so talking between them was confidential enough if they took their monitors out of their ears and didn't shout. "I'm all in favor of a chance to eat baguettes and gelato again, but this tour was supposed to be over. The contract was for three albums. We've done that. We've toured and toured almost non-stop. I don't understand how they keep on extending things, saying we're not out of contract."

"Europe again?" It was the first she'd heard of them going overseas again so soon, though it didn't surprise her.

"That's what Angel said. He was *told* it's because the European special edition CD for *My Tainted Baby* hasn't sold as well as they'd anticipated and we need to tour there again to push it – when really the issue is their total lack of awareness that vinyl's been seeing mega growth, especially in the UK and France, streaming is on an exponential rise, and CDs just aren't hot. Special edition vinyl would have made more sense, but no."

"Angel's pretty smart," Kimmy agreed.

Dice snorted. "He is, but he only said Mofford was bitching about disappointing sales and wants us over there to push the Euro *Tainted* CD. I figured the rest out myself." Edison Mofford was the new A&R manager they'd been stuck with after Blade flat-out refused to go onstage again until Magus Horton was removed from all contact with the band.

"Oooh, you're a bright one... for a drummer," Kimmy said with a giggle. It was one of their jokes, based on things people said about drummers. "Bet you can even count above four." All kidding aside, though, he *was* bright. She'd always thought he had a fast brain, even though he tended to play into the jester role he'd been stuck with at a younger age. *Look at him paying attention to global music sales trends,* she thought proudly. Her drummer wasn't only a pretty face.

"D'you think they'll like a nursery bus as a gift? The only thing I know about parenting is that everyone thinks the preacher's kid is going to knock some girl up in high school and get married young – especially if he's a drummer in a rock band." He spoke with a bit of resentment, and Kimmy patted him soothingly on the arm.

"It's a perfect idea," she assured him. "And I'm sure you'd never... be irresponsible like that." It was the closest they'd ever come to talking about sex – some things were better left off the table to keep their friendship within safe bounds – but Dice was so thoughtful and kind-hearted, he'd never risk leaving a woman with unwanted consequences. Still, she was surprised when he blushed a deep scarlet and couldn't meet her eyes. Had he had a scare? Then she realized he might think she was referring to Luke's arrival a scant week after Crys and Blade's wedding. "I'm not judging anyone, I swear! Things happen, condoms break. But they're happy, so it wasn't even bad luck! I wasn't calling them irresponsible."

"I know that. You're the least judgy person out of this whole crew, Kimmy. A person could tell you almost anything."

Almost?

Dice looked like he was going to say something more, but Mack broke into the moment with an edge to his voice, "Dice! We need a drum solo! Are you fucking asleep back there?"

"Sorry, man." Dice waved an apology, and Kimmy realized that Mack must have called him at least twice. The man didn't usually resort to profanity when fans were in the house, so the edginess was likely at least half embarrassment. A distracted drummer wasn't a good look for the band, and as their stage manager, Mack tended to feel personally responsible for smooth soundchecks and shows.

Quickly, Kimmy moved away from the drum riser and shoved her in-ear monitors into her ears to protect her hearing from the amplified thunder. *A person could tell you almost anything.* So, what *couldn't* he tell her? Or was she reading too much into a casual compliment?

❤

It was a travel night, so after load-out, after the band and their bodyguards and travel entourage had headed back to the hotel – they'd fly to Milwaukee the next day, well rested – Kimmy boarded her bus and crawled into her bunk, settling herself for the first of two nights on the road. Some of the guys were playing cards in the front lounge. She could have joined them, but somehow it didn't appeal to her.

Am I getting too old for this life? The thought worried her. She had no other skills, hadn't known any other career through her twenties, and most of all, she loved her nomadic, music-filled life. But holding Luke had been... something. She couldn't think of the right word for the complicated feelings inside her.

Of course, Crys wouldn't be at the hotel. Kimmy was pretty sure they didn't let new moms out of the hospital for at least twenty-four hours after a birth. Had Blade gone back to the hospital to be with her? And what would happen the next day? He'd have to be in Milwaukee for the concert.

Usually, she would put her earbuds in and listen to her *dreamtime* playlist or another one she'd called *bunk tunes* to mask the bus noises until she dropped off. This time, she lay in the semi-dark of her bunk, listening to the sounds of traffic and the bus engine and the low voices of the card players up front. Nice. Comforting.

She slept.

♥

Blade didn't get on the plane. "He just refused," Sally told them when she arrived before soundcheck – the makeup artist and wardrobe mistress had traveled by air with the band, so she'd had a front row seat for the drama. "Said, 'I'm not leaving my wife on her own in the hospital with our baby and flying out of reach if she needs me. I told Mofford we'd need to schedule a break when the baby came and he just fucking ignored it, and I'm done.' And that was that. He told everyone they'd have to carry him onto the plane and tie him down to keep him there, and wouldn't that be bad press?" Sally chuckled rather grimly, and Erva put a comforting arm around her shoulders.

"Wouldn't have thought that man had such a romantic streak in him."

"So, what are our boys going to do?" Kimmy asked. "If he's there and we're here, and there's a show tonight..."

"Angel says he's got it handled," Sally said. "I don't know how, he's just grinning and being secretive and pleased, but he seems sure."

When the band arrived, Kimmy asked Dice if he knew what the plan was.

"No, but Angel says it's all good, and Easy is looking smug too, so there's a plan. I just don't know it. I feel like there's more going on here than just tonight." Dice paused, then added, "Something Angel said makes me wonder if he encouraged Blade to throw a tantrum and refuse to get on the plane. Like, was it planned? Blade's such a pro, he'd never leave us truly stuck. I think he must know something too."

Kimmy thought about that. "I bet you're right. But they should have told you."

Dice shrugged. "Doesn't really matter. As long as we can do the show and not disappoint people, it's all good. I trust them." But he looked a bit hurt all the same.

"Soundcheck in ten," Mack called, walking up and down to make sure everyone heard. "Fans are in the house, so best behavior – no daydreaming today, Dice!" In a slightly less projected but still audible tone, he grumbled, "Does *anyone* know what the plan is?"

"I guess they didn't tell him either," Kimmy said.

And just as everyone took their places to start soundcheck, Joel Bonamour walked onto the stage with a gig bag slung over his shoulder and said, "I hear you lot are short a guitarist for tonight."

The Bad Luck Opals' guitarist was instantly, universally recognized. A lean older man in black leather pants and a studded vest, he had short dark hair with some slight streaks of silver – he'd famously worn it waist-length in the '90s but had opted for a variety of shorter styles in recent years, and right now it just skimmed his cheekbones. Angel walked over and shook his hand, completely unsurprised, and Easy got a hug from the man, who was like an uncle to him.

"Welcome, Mr. Bonamour," said Mack in a tone of awed respect, and the legendary guitarist laughed.

"Call me Joel, man. Everybody here, call me Joel. Can I get a set list?"

As Mack hurried to grab a set list for him, and Cal the guitar tech sprang forward to offer help with amps and cables, and Trick approached to get him set up with in-ear monitors and a wireless pack, a feeling of relief settled over the stage.

With a big smile, Angel stepped up to his mic and announced to the cluster of fans who'd paid for the soundcheck experience, "As you probably know, Blade is a new father as of yesterday, so today he's with his wife and baby. We're honored to have Joel Bonamour stepping in to cover for him at tonight's concert. Cool?"

It was definitely cool. The claps and whistles of encouragement and excitement were powerfully appreciative of the senior guitarist, who accepted the praise as his due with a raised hand of thanks.

Dice was already up on the drum riser, caged in by his gear, which didn't make it easy for him to greet the new arrival. It was always a problem for drummers. Unlike the others in any band who could move freely around the stage and interact with each other and the crowd, a drummer couldn't go up to the edge of the stage and high-five someone, except for one brief chance at the end of the show before going offstage. Kimmy, in her spot behind the drum riser, wondered if Dice would get up and go down to greet the Opals' guitarist, and for a moment he looked like he might, but then he settled back down on his throne and contented himself with a wave.

She saw the determined set of her drummer's shoulders, though, and the way he paid extra sharp attention through the soundcheck, attentive to anything Mack asked for, giving concert-level energy to a drum solo. Channeling his feelings into professionalism and music, as always.

It paid off toward the end, when Joel approached the drum riser and reached up to offer a fist bump. "You remind me of Rudy's younger days, Dice," the legend said – Rudy Matchett was the Opals' powerhouse drummer. "Keep doing what you're doing, and by the time you're our age, you'll be an absolute icon. I'm looking forward to performing with you tonight."

♥

Late that night, or early the next morning, depending on how one looked at it, Kimmy had collapsed into her hotel room bed and was almost asleep when her phone buzzed on the nightstand. When she reached out sleepily to grab it, the lock screen showed a text message from Dice: *Hey Kimber.*

She took the phone into bed with her and pulled the covers over her head so the lighted screen wouldn't bother her roommates. Typed a response: *What's up?*

Were you sleeping?

Not yet, she told him.

There was a pause before he replied. The ellipsis of a text being typed appeared, then disappeared – he'd stopped typing, or deleted what he'd typed – then appeared and vanished twice more again. Finally: *I can't stop thinking about what Joel said.*

That he compared you to Rudy Matchett? That he said you had icon potential? He's right, you know.

Another long pause. Then: *I know he was probably just being nice. But I'm kinda feeling feelings.*

Kimmy smiled in the dark, under her blankets. *Good feelings, I hope. Or do you need me to come find you, get a hot drink or something?*

I'm okay, he texted back. *I know you need your sleep. Big show tomorrow. I just needed to be sure I didn't imagine it. Goodnight, Kimber.*

You didn't imagine it. Sleep well, she sent back, with an emoji of a moon.

♥

In due course, the nursery bus was delivered, and became a fixture alongside the rest of the tour buses outside Smidge's concert venues. Smidge went to Europe in the fall, as Dice had predicted, and Kimmy ate fabulous gelato in Italy and beignets in the south of France. She rode the London Eye and ate fish and chips in England, and Smidge performed at the O2 Arena.

Baby Luke laughed out loud for the first time in Paris and rolled over in Amsterdam, and at each of these milestones she felt a strange tugging in her heart.

And they were back in the US in time for Thanksgiving.

chapter

3

KIMMY LOOKED OUT THE TOUR BUS WINDOW AT THE snow starting to fall on a familiar stretch of freeway as they rolled into Detroit. The sky was still dark in the early morning, but everyone on the bus was up and dressed for load-in; she had thermals on under her jeans and hoodie, and a beanie to keep her head warm. Catering would make sure they got coffee at some point, but they'd be out in the cold and hauling gear into the arena as soon as the bus parked, and the weather app on her phone agreed with what she could see out the window. Cold. Still, she felt her mood lift. Snow in early December shouldn't have been a surprise, here or anywhere, but the first snowfall of the year for her – wherever she happened to see it – was always something magical.

They had two shows in the city, the first at Little Caesar's Arena and then a smaller one on the Sound Board stage at the Motor City Casino, with a lucky night off between them, no doubt because Arleigh Hayward couldn't resist squeezing an extra date in to fill up the gap before the tour headed across the border to Windsor and then over to Toronto. Neither show would be much like the time she'd seen them at the Royal Oak Music Theater, but shows close to home made her smile all the same. And this time, oh, this time her brothers were opening for Smidge at the casino. It was the smaller of the two shows, and Friends With Royalty only had a quick set ahead of the main opening band, but it would be by far the biggest stage the Baker

34

brothers had ever played. Still, that was two nights away, and they had a busy day ahead.

♥

Her only roommate on this stop was Lulu, given that the hotel they were in didn't have triple rooms, and Angel wasn't the sort of boss who'd ask crew to share a bed with another adult they weren't voluntarily sleeping with. Sometimes it was a cot or a pull-out couch, but everyone who wanted it always got their own space. Trish had drawn the lucky card and got a room to herself this time. But Lulu was a good sort of person to share a room with – tidy enough, low on drama, and willing to share toiletries or necessities in a jam.

Kimmy was stretched out on her bed in a onesie printed with prancing reindeer and holiday lights, reading a paperback romance novel Ruby had lent her, while Lulu finished up her post-concert pre-sleep routine. *It's not what it says on the tin,* Ruby had said when passing it to her on the bus. And it wasn't. The pastel-candy illustrated cover hinted at a fluffy romantic comedy; it even had cupcakes and an engagement ring on it, leading to natural assumptions about a lot of bakery humor and a tame to nonexistent heat level, but wow, was that ever incorrect. Technically, there was a cupcake-bakery-owning heroine, but *nothing* about the cover prepared the reader for a dragon shifter hero with a near-uncontrollable mating urge and a filthy mouth. Not even halfway through the first chapter, there was already banging – from behind, up against a wall in an alley where anyone could walk by, with the hero's dirty talk implying things might get kinky further on. *I want to talk about this,* Kimmy thought, but Lulu wasn't a reading sort.

When she heard a knock on the door, she kept reading and let Lulu go see who it was. Probably another crew member who'd run short of toothpaste or something. But then she heard Lulu say, "Hello, Dice, you here to see Kimmy?"

Oh. A goofy rush of warmth came over her as she turned to see her friend there in the doorway.

"Yeah. I mean, both of you? I was wondering if Kimmy – well, if both of you want to go out with us, I mean with the band, tomorrow night?" he asked, hands in his pockets, leaning against the doorframe.

"Got a date," Lulu said, with an apologetic glance around at Kimmy, "at least I do if he's not called to work. But I guess Kimmy's free."

"Oh?" Kimmy asked, sitting up and stuffing the book under her pillow. "I mean, I am, but why do you say that? Who's your date?"

Lulu shrugged. "Ryan asked me to go to a movie. He was hoping he'd have a free night, you know? If he doesn't have to go do the bodyguard thing for Blade, that is. He said you and he were done, Kimmy."

Not a conversation Kimmy wanted to have in front of Dice, honestly. "That was a while ago, yeah."

Dice nodded. "I think we were only planning on taking two bodyguards anyway. Limited seating, so... I know Nell's going, and the rest of them were going to draw cards for the other spot, so I'm thinking Ryan won't have a problem getting the night off."

"Thanks," Lulu said, with another apologetic look at Kimmy. If she kept it up, she was going to give Dice the impression that Kimmy was heartbroken over Ryan or something, when they simply hadn't suited each other after a few dates.

"It's cool. There is *nothing* going on with Ryan and me, Lu." The words came out a bit more forcefully than Kimmy had intended, and Lulu widened her eyes in surprise. *Easygoing Kimmy doesn't usually snap, right? I'm going to beg Trish to be roomies on the next stop, whatever.* Kimmy took a deep breath. "Sorry. You go to bed. Dice and I can talk in the hall."

She grabbed her key card and slipped on her shoes, then followed Dice out the door, letting it close behind her.

The hallway wasn't a particularly comfortable place to chat. "They have an all-night café downstairs," he offered, "if you want to get a bedtime drink or something?"

She looked down at herself, at the festive print of her onesie, and laughed. "Like this?"

"It's cute," he said. "I don't mind if you don't." Then, as she opened her mouth, he waved away her remaining objection. "And yes, I know you don't have your wallet on you. My treat."

"Well, I could do with something warm to drink, sure. Please." She kept her voice casual, not letting on that she was spinning inside. *Cute*, he'd said, and now she *felt* cute in her reindeer-printed sleepwear, almost like she was going on a date.

The café was almost empty – a family with suitcases were presumably fortifying themselves for a red-eye flight in one of the booths, and a handful of Smidge crew winding down the night had pulled a couple of tables together, playing cards and eating pie.

"You want your sweet milk?" Dice asked. Some of the other crew thought it funny that Kimmy's preferred late-night drink was steamed milk with flavored syrup, especially if they were having something boozy or caffeinated, but he never teased her. "They might have some fun holiday flavors here. Let's take one of the booths, yeah?" In other words, *let's not get drawn into that card game or we'll be here until morning.* And she agreed.

"That would be perfect. Are you having hot chocolate?" She knew his likes and habits as well as he knew hers, and his eager smile warmed her. She slid into the farthest booth from the red-eye family, and he took the opposite side, his shoes bumping against hers under the table. She hadn't particularly noticed his feet earlier, but she guessed he was wearing his Vans, same as she was. Boots for shows, but Vans for kicking back on the bus and off the clock.

She liked seeing the offstage side of him. Not all the guys had one – Blade wore eyeliner all the time and tended toward black and punk no matter where he was or what he was doing. Angel? Well, he wore reading glasses when he wasn't in public, and she knew he read science fiction and had a Picard-like preference for Earl Grey tea, which wasn't part of his public persona. Easy had a definite public face, but it was more about putting on the flirt and attitude of a rock star and less about dressing the part. Dice, though... *He plays dress-up for the fans. Maybe even for the crew.* The cut-off sleeves, the ripped jeans... even the bandanna was part of the act, and she'd noticed that when he wasn't working, he'd take the ever-present hair tie from his wrist and pull his hair back out of the way into a neat ponytail.

Tonight he wore an old waffle-knit Henley in a washed-out mossy green, and he had his hair tied back. Definitely off the clock. She knew his father was an Episcopal priest, and somewhere in the back of her mind, she thought, *Preacher's kid.* Tidy and modest, but with a spark of something not so restrained inside him.

The server came over to their booth, and when asked about flavored syrups for steamed milk, suggested Winter Spiced Nut. Kimmy's eyes met Dice's and she choked on a giggle as she nodded. Trying to keep a straight face, Dice said that he would have his hot chocolate with a shot of Winter Spiced Nut as well.

"I wonder if the marketing department told them North Pole Jizz would be too much," he said in a dry undertone as the server walked away, making Kimmy collapse with laughter.

"Let's hope it tastes all right. It'd be a shame to waste good milk." They looked at each other, suddenly not laughing so hard, and she thought maybe the expression on her face matched the suddenly wry one on his. She wondered if his family was sternly against wasting food and drink too, if he'd grown up with the same rules she had – expected to finish anything he'd taken or ordered or asked for, like it or not.

Fortunately, the Winter Spiced Nut flavor turned out to be an agreeable blend of almond and hazelnut with nutmeg and cardamom and a hint of burnt sugar. Plenty of whipped cream and festive red and green sprinkles made the bedtime drink feel more than a bit special. Or was that from being with Dice? *If only...* But that was a silly thought. *Employer. Best friend. Who in her right mind would rock that boat, even if he were interested? Even though he's perfect...*

"So, what's this thing tomorrow night?" she asked.

He grinned. "Right. Well, you remember the drag queen at Crys and Blade's wedding?"

"Sure. Ripped Creme? We watched her win season four of *Drag Dolls* on TV this summer. I saw her – him? them? – arriving with the dress before the wedding." No one could forget the athletic and beautiful fashion designer who'd showed up with Crys's wedding dress for a final fitting looking intensely masculine in shorts and a t-shirt, then re-emerged for the ceremony in gorgeous full drag.

"Right. Crys and Nell's friend. Call him Johnny when he's a guy, but always Rip and she/her when she's in drag."

"That makes sense to me. I grew up in Ferndale," she clarified. "Up the road, huge Pride energy. But you're sure he/him pronouns are right when he's Johnny? I'd never want to inadvertently hurt someone."

"You're good. Rip's website bio is clear on that. Anyway, there's this touring holiday drag show and cabaret thing, and she's one of the headliners. It turns out we're in Detroit at the same time as they are, and since we've got no show tomorrow night and they do have one, we're invited. Band and guests, but there are only twelve seats for us, so honestly it's just as well Lulu had other plans." Dice turned a bit pink at that.

Kimmy knew his impulsive good nature would have prompted him to extend the invitation almost automatically, before thinking about whether there were enough tickets. Which raised another thought. "Are you sure there's room for me? Surely someone else–"

"No. I want you to come," Dice said firmly, interrupting her. "Anyway, Crys specifically said I should ask you."

But Kimmy's brain had fused into mush. *I want you to come.* In the book she'd been reading when he showed up at the door, the hero had said those words in an entirely different context, and now she was hearing it in her mind in Dice's voice. Did he talk like that to women in bed? Logically, he was too sweet a person to have dominant tendencies between the sheets, but the thought of it made her breathless.

"Kimmy?" Dice's voice broke into her thoughts, and she realized that he was looking at her with concern, and she hadn't responded to his invitation and he probably thought something was wrong. "You don't have to join us if you'd rather not," he said, his face a mixture of disappointment and concern. "Drag shows aren't everyone's jam, I guess. Or is something else bothering you?"

"Oh, no – I'd love to! So sorry, I was... I was reading when you showed up just now, and something you said made me think of – never mind. I got distracted. If there's a ticket for me, I'm totally in." She gave him a big smile, hoping to erase the crestfallen look from his eyes. "Is it in the city?"

He blinked at her, and she could see he wasn't sure what she meant.

"Like Detroit proper? Not the suburbs?"

Understanding dawned. "I'd think so. It's not far from here, apparently. The National something-or-other?"

"I think that's the place they restored from an old vaudeville theater. Cool! I'd love to go."

"Good, that's great!" He smiled back at her, sunshine restored. "What were you reading?"

Orp. Um. She could feel her face getting hot. "You know, a romance novel. Like I always do." There was nothing embarrassing about romance novels. She could even show him the cover of this one with no reason to blush.

He cocked his head to one side, looking at her across the table as he took a sip of his hot chocolate, then licked a stray bit of whipped cream from his upper lip. "Why're you blushing, Kimmy? I know you like romance novels. Is this one, like, extra dirty or something?"

Yes. "Romance novels aren't dirty," she reminded him. But why lie? "This one comes close, though. Closer to dirty than anything I've ever read. It's more than just steamy or spicy – I don't know."

He chuckled. "Interesting. Does it make you *feel* dirty? Will you lend it to me when you're done?"

"It's Ruby's. I'll have to ask her." Kimmy took a big gulp of her steamed milk to avoid answering his first question. *That's silly, though. He's my best friend.* So she shrugged and said, "I don't think I'm particularly sensitive or shockable after six years with a touring rock band – I've heard every dirty term for anatomy and, well, I've walked in on you guys doing enough things that not a lot surprises me. But this is... a lot. Raunchy sex with a bit of plot, instead of the other way around. Kinky, to the point of being uncomfortable even if you're into kink. Blurred consent so you feel weird about finding it hot. Maybe it's more shocking because the cover looks so innocent."

"Do you think people are like that sometimes? Not what it says on the cover?" Dice asked thoughtfully.

"Like all sex and kink underneath but walking along looking like cotton candy?"

"Or the other way around. Looking like a sex bomb but secretly uptight."

"Maybe." Kimmy thought about that. After all, her short hair and practical work clothes hid a taste for pretty lingerie and pedicures. Lots of people hid things – weird food preferences, crushes, secret longings... "Maybe no one is exactly what their exterior advertises, I don't know."

It was snowing again as they got out of the stretch limousine outside the National Cocktail Palace, which had been converted from an old theater into a renowned cocktail lounge and live performance venue. Passers-by stopped and turned at the sight of the fancy car and a few raised their phone cameras once they realized it was Smidge arriving – not to perform, for a change, but to join the audience on a rare night off.

Kimmy emerged last, feeling a tiny bit intimidated. She was accustomed to tour buses or the back of the runabout van, and sure, sometimes crew members took cabs or ride services together for a night out. She very rarely got the chance to ride in a limousine, and here they had two of them. She was glad Dice waited for her, reaching out a hand to help her to the sidewalk.

The marquee was hung with swags of festive garland and glittering balls, and under the words *Rip & Etta's Holiday Drag Show and Gender Affirming Cabaret*, the performers' names were featured, including Ripped Creme and Etta Aubergine in the biggest letters.

"This is going to be great," Sally said, her arms linked with Angel on one side and Erva on the other.

Crys and Blade were gazing at each other under the marquee lights, grinning like fools. "It's nice to be out on a break night without Luke," Crys confessed. "I love him so much, but this is... really nice. I know we should do it more often, but I feel guilty asking Camillo to work extra nights when he already does so much for us. I'm so happy Ruby offered to babysit."

Kimmy felt an uncomfortable surge of mixed emotions at that. She adored Luke and would have loved to be asked to babysit on the nanny's night off. But she hadn't thought – or dared – to offer. And anyway, Dice had asked her to join what was clearly not an all-crew outing, and she was glad to be there with him. Almost like a date.

Well, we're friends, she reminded herself. *Sometimes we do friend stuff.* But she remembered him saying *I want you to come,* and her being part of the occasion seemed important to him. What was the difference, anyway, between a date and an outing as friends? Once a kiss goodnight was ruled out, there didn't seem to be much difference.

"Come on," Nell said, "we want good seats." But that wasn't an issue.

As they gathered around the will-call ticket window of the club, the man behind the counter smiled adoringly at them all as he handed them their tickets. "Aren't we honored to have Smidge in the house tonight! We have tables reserved for you at the front. One of our hostesses will take you in."

The two hostesses were drag artists themselves, in glittering holiday-themed outfits for the event and season. There seemed to be a moment's debate between them as to who would escort the Smidge group, then the one with the fabulous green wig and matching eye makeup stepped forward with a big smile. She had a peppermint-candy nametag that read *Minty.* "Right this way, if you'll follow me."

There was a staircase with a *Balcony* sign, but their hostess led them past it to the main floor of what had once been the movie theater itself, and they stepped into an over-the-top wonderland. Everything glittered, from the stage set to the chandeliers and disco balls on the ceiling to the centerpieces on the tables – bedazzled candy canes and glitter-dipped holly with gemstone berries. Small half-circle tables sat four each around the curved side, so no one would be facing away from the stage; three of the tables right at the front had *Reserved for Smidge* signs.

Kimmy assumed that Angel and Blade would sit together, as they'd been best friends from before the time she'd known them, but Nell and Crys sat down together in the middle of one of the tables, leaving Easy and Blade to take the seats on either side of them, and Angel moved along to the next table with Sally and Erva and Jed. That put Kimmy next to Dice at the last table with Trish and Aidan.

"Awesome," their hostess enthused as they sorted themselves out. "We're so glad to have you with us tonight! I know Rip will want to come out and say hello, so I'll let her know you're here. Oh, and we have some audience-participation bits, so does anyone in the group have any objection to being called up on stage? Anyone uncomfortable with sitting on a lap, talking into a microphone, or getting a hug or high five or anything like that? Band members, would you be willing to sing with us?"

"I can't sing," Dice muttered, but Minty didn't hear him over the others expressing their agreement.

Kimmy glanced at him but assumed that he'd spoken quietly because he didn't want to be heard. *Can't sing?* She thought about it, and realized that she couldn't recall a single instance where he'd sung along with the others at any point, on stage or in rehearsal. Nor had he ever taken a turn at karaoke night, and he'd never joined in singalongs on the road, back when the crew was smaller and they'd all shared one or two buses.

Since no one spoke up or raised a hand in protest or anything, Minty told them a server would be over to get their drink orders, blew them kisses, and hustled away, graceful on tall platform shoes that Kimmy knew she'd never be able to walk in.

Smidge's group had obviously been tagged as a priority for the National, because a server was at their tables almost immediately, then despite the busy bar and the rapidly filling house, he returned with their drinks faster than should have been possible. Kimmy reached for her wallet, but Dice stopped her. "This is going on the band's tab. Angel said crew doesn't pay for anything tonight."

Sally's voice rose from the middle table, calling to Blade on the other side. "What d'you think of our server's lipstick?" Their masculine-presenting server wore shimmery metallic lipstick. "Something to try for your next stage look? Maybe all of you in different shades?"

Easy laughed as Blade called back, "Fine, as long as mine isn't pink."

"It's bad enough having to wear triangles of glitter on my face for shows," Dice grumbled so only Kimmy and Aidan and Trish could hear. He'd been wearing jester makeup since the early days, in various iterations from stylized wedges to tearful emo streaks, and Kimmy was startled to realize that she'd never known he minded.

"You don't like it?" she asked softly.

"I don't mind, really. Sally started it as a way to hide that I was younger than the others, which kind of showed when I was still in my teens, and now it's just part of my stage makeup – the jester behind the drum kit."

"At least she didn't stick you with full KISS face makeup, though," Aidan pointed out. Trish laughed appreciatively at that, and Kimmy noticed that she and Aidan were holding hands under the table. *Sweet.* It'd be nice to have someone to hold hands with, but there were only so many dating possibilities on the tour, and trying to date someone who *wasn't* with the tour would be impossible. Anyway, they mostly ended up comparing unfavorably to Dice, and after ending things with Ryan, Kimmy had decided to put dating on hold for a while.

Maybe the determining factor had been the conversation where Ryan indicated that he wasn't interested in having children in the foreseeable future. *It's not like road crew are any good at settling down,* he'd said, and Kimmy wasn't sure whether he'd meant himself or her.

A commotion around a side door drew her attention, and there was Ripped Creme, wrapped in a fluffy hot pink robe, greeting fans as she made her way slowly across to the Smidge tables. "Apologies for the robe," she told them. "I've got part of my first outfit on already and I don't want to give anything away, but when Minty told me you'd arrived, I had to come out and say hello. I should warn you that Etta is a massive Smidge fan, and I know she's hoping to get you all up on stage, so don't be shy."

"I'm never shy," Easy said with a laugh. Angel flashed everyone a devilish grin, his green eyes saying *bring it on*.

"I might need a drink first," Blade cracked – a private reference to his sometimes-devastating stage fright, which was only known to the band and crew – and everyone laughed.

Then Rip swept away, calling, "I'll see you from the stage. Enjoy the show!"

Before long, the house lights went down, and the first number was under way – four queens in sexy reindeer outfits shaking their fluffy tails to the cabaret band's version of "Run Rudolph Run" – with a crowd response ranging from chuckles at the adorable costumes to appreciative cheers for the choreography.

Ripped Creme came out in a long white Victorian nightgown as Florin Street Band's "My Favorite Time of Year" played softly on the sound system in the background.

"I love this song," Kimmy whispered.

"Me too," Dice whispered back.

From behind her back, she produced an oversized bunch of glittery mistletoe which she hooked onto a convenient cord dangling over the front of the stage. "I'm just going to leave this here," she said with an exaggerated wink. "So anyone who comes up on stage with us... don't stand under it if you don't want a kiss!"

This comment was punctuated by a drum roll from the cabaret band, and the music on the sound system shifted to RuPaul's "Hey Sis, It's Christmas" as Rip then proceeded to strip off the nightgown to reveal a red-and-green elf costume. "Is it even the holidays if you don't sit on someone's knee and ask for gifts?" she called out. "It gives me great pleasure to introduce my friend and co-host Etta Aubergine as tonight's Mrs. Claus – because why should Santa have all the knee-sitting fun?"

Two of the reindeer wheeled out a big Santa Claus throne, and then from behind it, a beautiful queen in a powerful silver wig and sweeping red velvet gown emerged in a burst of glittering fake snow, waving greetings. "Beautiful people, it's such a pleasure to be here in Detroit tonight," she proclaimed, brushing a few snowflakes off the fluffy white faux-fur trim around her shoulders. "I can't wait to find out what your Christmas wishes are – or Yule wishes, or whatever you celebrate at this time of year." She sashayed around the stage before dramatically removing the full outer skirt of her gown to reveal a much, much shorter skirt and fantastic legs. "How about *this* lap for sitting on, mmm?"

The crowd gave her an enthusiastic response, clapping and cheering. She took a seat on the throne and nodded to Ripped Creme, who pointed to the audience and asked, "Okay, who's first?"

People from several tables in the audience waved and stood up to attract attention. One table, apparently a stag party, was particularly noisy with their enthusiasm, and shortly an awkward-looking young man wearing a *Bride-To-Be* sash was drawn up onto the stage.

"Well, ho ho ho," said Etta Aubergine, patting her knee. "What's your name? Sit down and tell me when the wedding is."

The man perched tentatively on her lap. "I'm Paul," he said into the microphone, "and we're getting married Christmas Day." A sigh of appreciation swept the audience.

"Great to hear. Give your man a kiss from me, honey. Now, tell me what Santa should bring you. Looks like a lifetime of happiness might be on your list?"

"Oh, Mike has already given me that. That's my fiancé–" His table let out some whoops of encouragement. "And we were thinking of getting a new Xbox as a sort of combined wedding and Christmas gift to each other. Two controllers, you know?"

The stage band's drummer punctuated that with a sting – *ba-dum-tshhh* – and the audience laughed. Kimmy wasn't entirely sure what was funny about it, but she laughed along anyway since Paul looked like he was having the time of his life.

"Well, then," Etta Aubergine said slowly, drawling out the words, "I think Santa had better bring you... a lot... of... *batteries*." The sheer silly fun of the innuendo had the whole room laughing. "Where's my elf? Elf!" She snapped her fingers.

"Right here, dear." Rip produced an oversized gift box with a big bow and presented it to Paul. "Okay, Paul, you take this home and put it under your tree... and there's a lovely bunch of mistletoe right there, if *someone* in the house wants to give you a kiss."

"Sweet," Paul said, arms around his gift box, and shuffled over to the mistletoe ball. After some clapping and shoving from the stag party table, a man in a *Kiss the Bride* t-shirt was thrust toward the stage, where he joined Paul under the mistletoe and planted a big loving kiss on him.

"Let's all wish Paul and Mike a lifetime of love," Etta called out. "Not that they need our help." The cabaret band launched into "All I Want for Christmas Is You" as the couple got a standing ovation from the crowd.

A few more people were drawn up onto the stage.

A pre-med student celebrating the end of exam week wished for world peace. A small press publisher said she wanted a bestselling title, then changed her mind and admitted that she really just wanted her old car to keep running through the winter. A newbie drag queen confessed she was out in public in drag for the first time and wished for fame, so Etta asked her what kind of queen she was – when the newbie said she was a singer, Etta handed over her microphone and said, "Go for it. Tell the band what song. No time like right now!"

"Has to be a plant," Trish whispered. "No one sings that well unprepared." But Kimmy wanted to believe it was unplanned and all for real, just holiday magic and someone with big dreams given a serendipitous chance.

They all got huge glittery gift boxes in holiday colors, and the publisher's husband gave her a kiss under the mistletoe.

"One more," Rip said, "then we'll go on with the show. Who wants to make a wish with us? You never know, maybe we really do have a bit of holiday magic right here and that thing you're dreaming of will come true..."

Wouldn't that be nice? All around her, the audience stood and waved and called out, trying to attract attention, so many people wanting to be the last one called up. Kimmy smiled, thinking how easy and wonderful it would be if some fairy-Santa-mother drag queen could wave a tinsel-covered wand and make all the impossible contradictory wishes in her life coalesce into something possible and attainable. But nothing about her dreams was within reach. She couldn't keep her road crew life and have anything approaching a stable home and family life, and every time she went on a date, she felt like she was cheating on her friendship with Dice. "It's not like I even want a *house* or anything," she muttered to herself, just as Etta's eyes met hers.

Etta Aubergine held up a hand for silence, then pointed directly at Kimmy. "Right there, with the cute butch haircut and sparkles. Come sit on my knee and make a wish, glitterfriend."

What? Oh! The queen must have seen her lips moving and thought she was asking to be chosen. *Shit.* Everyone was clapping, and Rip came down the steps from the stage to escort her up.

"You don't have to do it," Trish said kindly, misunderstanding her hesitation. "Rip won't make you. One of us can go instead."

But Dice gave her thigh an encouraging pat under the table. "You're always backstage or off to the side, Kimber. Go enjoy the spotlight for once – you know you want to."

He knew her so well.

I want to be touched by the magic of the evening. I want to be part of it.

The problem was not knowing what to wish for.

She got up and let Ripped Creme lead her onto the stage.

"Welcome," said Etta as Kimmy approached the throne. Close up, she was even more spectacular than she'd looked from the audience, and her legs were impossibly toned, white fishnet stockings standing out like frost against her skin, bedazzled ruby ankle boots flashing in the spotlights. She patted her lap. "Sit!" Then more softly, with her thumb over the mute button of the mic, "Unless you'd rather kneel before me, or perch on the arm of the throne. All about comfort, here."

Kimmy smiled hesitantly – her mind filled with a panicked litany of wishes, both possible and impossible, but *nothing* she could say aloud – and choked out, "It's fine," as she settled herself gingerly onto Etta's firm thighs.

Then Etta spoke into the mic. "What's your name?"

"Kimmy."

Etta nodded appreciatively. "I love your hair, Kimmy. Thank you for coming to our show tonight. So, have you been good this year?"

The mic tilted toward Kimmy. "Yes – I mean, I think so?"

Clapping rose from the audience, punctuated with some shouts from the Smidge tables, a warming jumble of "we know so" and "you're awesome" and "we love you, Kimmy!" That made her feel nice, appreciated.

"Ooh, it looks like you're on *their* nice list, for sure. You're with the Smidge tour?"

Kimmy nodded. "I've been Dice's drum tech for six years now."

"Think if we asked nicely, they'd come up on stage with us?" Etta asked.

Since both Minty and Rip had already confirmed this, Kimmy knew the question was just for the audience to hear, so she had no problem answering, "I think they would, sure."

"Holiday wishes coming true all around, then," Etta said. "Isn't that right, everyone?" That got a roar of approval from the audience; evidently there were Smidge fans in the house. "But first, tell Mrs. Claus... what do you want for Christmas?"

The question she'd been dreading.

"I..." *Peace of mind, somehow?* A vision of Dice popped into her mind, wearing nothing but giftwrap and a Santa hat. *Can't say that! Shouldn't want that!* Others had already wished for the low-hanging fruit, fame and world peace, and Kimmy's mind was blank. She looked frantically at the audience, and spotted Crys smiling happily, content in her marriage and motherhood. "I... want to have a baby," she blurted out, then realized with crushing embarrassment what she'd said.

"Aww, how sweet," Etta said. "And is your special someone in the house tonight? Maybe a kiss under our mistletoe could bring you some luck."

So embarrassing. "Oh, no, I... I'm single, just... that biological clock is ticking, and all."

"Then maybe a pinch of magic is all you need. You don't have to wait for a partner if you don't want to, you know? I hope you get your wish, Kimmy. Good luck!" For one moment, it wasn't Etta's silky stage voice talking, but a different tone, giving an entirely genuine blessing.

Then Kimmy was on her feet, letting Rip present her with an oversized glitter-covered gift box – red like Etta's shoes, with an extravagant green bow that made it hard to see over the top. She thanked them in an awkward mumble and rushed down the steps to the audience and back to her seat, feeling entirely discombobulated but also touched by the experience. Her friends cheered her like she'd done something worth cheering for, more than just sitting on a lap like any toddler could do and managing to say coherent words into a microphone. She wasn't sure what to do with the giant gift box, so she wedged it half-under the table beside her and tried to position her legs comfortably next to it without bumping her knees against Dice's, acutely aware of his proximity.

The show went on. Rip and Etta performed a lip-synched duet. An aerial burlesque artist gyrated to music suspended mid-air on a hoop and some silks. A gender non-conforming ukulelist and vocalist debuted an original song that would later go on to win awards.

And then Etta reminded everyone that Smidge was in the house, and invited the boys up on stage to sing "a holiday song or two" with her. That drew a huge round of applause, and Angel and Easy got up at once, going around to drag Blade to his feet, all of them laughing. Dice gave Kimmy a panicked look.

"I really can't sing," he said, or at least that's what she was able to read from his lips since the noise in the theater made it impossible to hear clearly. He half-rose from his seat, looking unsure, and she reached out to take his hand and give it a squeeze of encouragement, though she didn't know whether she was encouraging him to go on anyway or telling him he didn't need to do anything he didn't want to do.

Halfway up the steps to the stage, Angel and Blade and Easy turned back to beckon Dice along, and half laughing, half panicked, he pushed back his chair and left the table to join them. Rip brought out a couple of mics on tall stands, decorated with big red and green bows. "Can you boys share? Two to a mic."

Dice shrugged, stepped up to one of the mics, tapped it to see that it was live, and said firmly into it, "I'd love to, but I seriously can't sing." The crowd laughed at this, seeming to think it was the beginning of a skit or joke or something. Eyebrows lifted as if to say *you asked for it*, he launched into the first verse of "Jingle Bells" – flat. Well off pitch and wincing at himself. Not the sort of thing anyone could fake. "See? Can't sing," he repeated.

Kimmy could feel her face heating, embarrassed for him although he seemed to be rolling with the situation just fine. Objectively she could see the charm of it, the famous drummer admitting such an ordinary human shortcoming, but again she felt like the others must have known. Had they set him up for this, knowing he'd be most appealing as his adorably unprepared, unscripted self? Maybe it was best for the band, maybe he didn't mind, but it didn't seem fair.

"That's all right, darling," Etta assured Dice in the spotlight. "Lots of *us* can't sing either. Lip-synching is just fine."

Rip shimmied over and handed him a tambourine. "Here. We *know* you've got rhythm."

"No one bangs like a drummer, right?" Etta said. *Ba-dum-tshhh!*

The audience whooped and clapped as Dice gave the tambourine a jingle with one hand and blew them a kiss with the other. It was hard to tell under the stage lighting, but Kimmy thought he was blushing a little, despite the polished reaction.

"It looks like our Dice has found his confidence," Trish commented, leaning over to Kimmy to be heard, and then turned to Aidan, who hadn't been with Smidge as long as the others. Kimmy couldn't quite hear what Trish was saying to him, but she caught fragments of the accountant's words. "Dice used to ... so flustered whenever he ... out from behind ... drum kit on stage."

Sure, when he was nineteen, Kimmy thought. But to be fair, she herself had only recently noticed her friend's increased self-assurance and maturity.

"Do you ladies know Matt Peach's 'Rock n Roll Xmas'?" Angel asked into his microphone. "Because that's our kind of holiday song."

Kimmy was more certain than ever that Angel had orchestrated the whole scene in advance with the drag queens, because it wasn't a broadly known song, and yet Etta nodded regally, without a hint of hesitation, and gestured to the cabaret band to play.

♥

Snow was falling again as they left the National Cocktail Palace.

Kimmy's gift box was an awkward size – nothing like a drum case, but it didn't have handles or wheels or a shoulder strap to make it more manageable. She'd wrapped her arms around the box and made it work, leaving the theater, the way they always did with the odd-sized things during load-in and load-out. As they waved goodnight to the hostesses at the front door, Dice noticed the trouble she was having and took the box from her, saying, "My arms are longer, I've got this."

When they piled into the limo for the trip back to the hotel. Kimmy expected to find a spot with Aidan and Trish, somewhere at the back or front, but she felt a tug on her arm and found herself pulled into a seat next to Crys, right in the middle of the long limousine, with Dice on her other side and Angel and Easy across from her.

Dice put the gift box down in front of her. "There's your present, Kimmy. A little bit snowed-on, but all good."

"Going to open it, Sparkles?" Easy asked with an amused grin.

They were all looking at the box. She didn't have a tree to put it under, after all.

"Okay." She untied the ribbon and lifted off the lid, and the limo was filled with laughter as they at last had an explanation for the size of the box. Taking up by far the majority of the space was an eggplant-shaped pillow in purple velvet, complete with a green satin stem and embroidered with Etta's signature in gold. Other small swag took up the corners of the box, but the keychain and travel mug and pack of drag queen playing cards paled in comparison to the aubergine cushion. She lifted it out of the box and gave it a hug, to more laughter because it was, after all, an eggplant.

Crys laughed too, but she seemed thoughtful. And having Kimmy sit next to her in the limo was apparently not an accident, because once the general attention had moved on from Kimmy, Crys turned to her and said quietly, "You know, if... if you meant it about having a baby... there's lots of room in the nursery bus for a second crib, and I'd be totally thrilled about sharing our nanny so you could keep working with Dice. It'd be good for Luke to have someone to grow up with on the tour."

Oh. Kimmy forced a laugh. "Thanks, but I'm not even dating anyone right now."

Crys turned a bit pink, pressed her lips together for a second, then said, "The relationship part isn't strictly required. Unless you want it to be."

Blade, overhearing, raised an eyebrow at the two of them. "A broken condom'll do the job okay, but the relationship part is nice."

Angel laughed at that. "Kind of hard to guarantee a broken condom, though. Sperm bank and a turkey baster is probably more reliable. Or just find a guy you like the look of and offer him a bareback ride, no strings attached."

Easy chuckled along with the rest of them, but Kimmy had the impression his amusement was a bit forced. And she didn't dare look at Dice.

Find a guy you like the look of.

chapter

4

Kimmy was back in Ferndale for one joyful week leading up to Christmas. She'd seen her family briefly when the tour had come through Detroit a few weeks before, but a quick cup of coffee during a break in the day and hugs after the show hardly counted as a visit. A full week of vacation put her back around Woodward and Nine for a marvelous and much-needed respite.

To her, early December felt like a century ago, and yet all anyone could talk about was how the Baker boys had performed at the casino. The whole family was duly appreciative of Kimmy for introducing them to Smidge and getting them that chance.

"You should have been singing backup with us," Bryan said on Christmas Eve, as the whole extended family sat in the living room watching old holiday movies and drinking hot chocolate, a tradition since their childhood. This year it was *Babes in Toyland*, with a very young Keanu Reeves. Kimmy shook her head.

"I can't be two things at once, Bry. How can they trust me to be the best possible drum tech if half my mind is still coming down from performing?"

He leaned over for a quick bro hug. "I get it, Kim. We just wanted you to share our day."

She gave him a fake punch on the arm. "It's okay. I love that I had a chance to get onstage with you guys at the Magic Bag this week, that's all I need now and then."

"That was awesome," he agreed. "I wish you could come home more often."

"Yeah," Trevor said. "Auntie Kimmy should come home more often." His four-year-old daughter Polly, currently on Kimmy's lap, adored her. All the cousins loved their Auntie Kimmy, but she and Polly had a special closeness.

"I know. I want to. I miss you all terribly when I'm on the road," Kimmy assured them. It wasn't a lie, although she didn't spend time pining for her family or anything – a person could love her home and love being on the road all at once, and she did miss them when she thought about them.

"Shush, I *watching* it," ordered Bryan and Marisa's three-year-old son Tim, pointing at the television screen. Everyone laughed, though Marisa gave her son a quelling look and a reminder to say please. "Pwease," he added obediently.

As they settled back to watching the movie, Kimmy's phone blerped, and a text from Dice appeared on the screen. *Happy Christmas Eve, Kimber. See you in two days.*

She texted him back: *Can't wait! Happy Christmas Eve to you too.*

Sipping her hot chocolate – which always made her think of him anyway – she smiled.

♥

No one wanted to do a show on the day after Christmas. Not all members of the crew celebrated Christmas, but it was a family occasion for enough of them that cutting the holiday short hurt. Worse, it was the first time in years that the band had planned to spend Christmas at home, not to mention baby Luke's first festive season ever. But along came the powers-that-be at Arleigh Hayward to spoil things, dropping a post-Christmas gig on them in St. Louis – where none of them lived or had family – and that didn't feel good.

Angel gathered them all together for a meeting before soundcheck, where he had a stack of envelopes with holiday bonus checks tucked into cards. "Sorry, everyone. I wanted to have these for you before the break we just had, such as it was–" He paused to allow for the grumbles over the shortened break. "Unfortunately, they weren't cut until after you'd all dispersed. It isn't as much as I'd hoped, but they tell me they can't justify anything better."

"At least we got to go home for Christmas this year," Phil called out, referencing the time they'd been surprised with a Christmas Eve show at short notice.

"At least we get a bonus at all," Ruby added. It wasn't a nice gesture from the production company – everyone knew they were owned by Arleigh Heyward, no matter how much they pretended to be a separate entity. They withheld money from the band to fund bonuses for the crew, of course they did, and probably skimmed a service fee off it – but extra money always helped, especially in December.

"And we *did* get to see our families for a week," Angel agreed with heartfelt satisfaction. For almost a decade, Smidge had been hiding their real identities behind band names only, encouraged by their previous manager to believe that it was the only way to keep Blade's poisonous family from *causing trouble and damaging their rise to the top,* as they'd been told so many times. Magus Horton had orchestrated a complex web of difficult-to-arrange clandestine family visits, certainly never at holidays or in their hometowns, and increasingly infrequent. It had taken them all far too long to recognize that for the manipulative tactic it was.

"You should all be off again after today until the New Year's Eve party for the Arleigh Hayward execs and their guests," Phil the road manager said, tapping his clipboard, "unless they drop another surprise on us."

"Thanks, Dad!" someone called out, maybe Ramón, who'd recently been promoted to head of concert security. Phil acted as the tour's road parent, making sure everyone ate properly and got on the buses in time, and Ramón and some of the others had nicknamed him Dad.

"Four days is enough time to go to Vegas," another voice suggested – Gary the bass tech, Kimmy thought. He was one of the perpetual card players.

"Well, let's get started," Angel said.

They quickly slipped into the usual routine, a soundcheck packed with VIP guests and a solid concert. Maybe it wasn't one of their best, no extra electric energy, but they kept it professional, band and crew alike, and the fans seemed happy.

During the debrief after the show, a phone chimed an incoming message alert. Sally, who always had custody of the band's phones during the show, held Angel's out to him – and that was a bit unusual, since he usually didn't like anything to disrupt their debrief. He held up a hand for quiet from the room while he answered it. Listened for a moment.

"Now?!" he asked, followed by a long, listening silence. Everyone in the room was staring at him. "Done. I'll call her when we're clear here. Thank you, Mr. Stirling."

Huh. Kimmy looked at Dice to see if he knew what was going on, but he looked as curious as everyone else. Valancy Records, the label that had lifted the Bad Luck Opals and Mad Gilbert to fame in the 1990s, was owned at least in part by an enigmatic silver fox named Torquil Stirling – was *that* the Mr. Stirling who'd phoned Angel just now?

It didn't seem likely that Arleigh Hayward would ever let Smidge out of their control, but it was nice to have another label taking an interest, anyway.

The band moved from debriefing to relaxing, eating and getting their makeup off before they moved on to showers and street clothes. Kimmy gave Dice a gentle punch on the arm and headed off to do her part of load-out.

She expected to pack up and lug gear out to the trucks for several hours before, as usual, crashing in her tour bus bunk for a few hours, since it wasn't a hotel stop. They'd be given breakfast before being released on another break the next day. But once the drum equipment was all safely stowed, while she was trudging back for another load in the process of helping the rest of the crew with the rest of the gear, she felt a tap on her arm and there was Dice, silently getting her attention and jerking his head for her to follow him.

He was clearly looking around for a place where they could have privacy, and finally – after trying a few locked doors – he found a men's room and opened the door. It was dark, evidently empty, and he felt around by the door to locate a light switch. When the lights came up, he gestured her inside with a crooked grin.

"What's going on?" she asked, assuming that it was safe to break the silence once the outer door swung closed. "Why are we in a bathroom?"

"Are you doing anything much for the next few days?" he asked her, leaning against one of the sinks in an effort at casualness, though she could sense the tension in him.

She shook her head. "Not really. I'm not going to Vegas with that lot, or anything. I hadn't honestly decided, but I'll have something figured out by breakfast tomorrow." The crew were always given breakfast the morning after load-out before being cut loose on a break. Which gave her maybe eight hours to decide what she wanted to do and where she was planning to sleep on her four free days before New Year's Eve. Not Vegas, but there was a group going to Hunter Mountain to ski, others were moving straight on to New York early for the concerts and nightlife... or she could always head back home.

"You want to go somewhere warm?" Dice asked.

"What, with you?"

He played with the hair tie on his wrist, not looking at her. "With the band. Which includes me. So yeah."

No, of course he's not asking me out. Instead of thinking about that, she shifted the subject to the next big question in her mind. "What warm place are we talking about?"

"I can't say. Nothing until we're on the plane. And if there's anyone who might ask questions about where you are over the break, like your family, tell them... say you're going to Vegas, or if they wouldn't believe that, maybe... Disneyland or something?"

"You asking me to lie for you, Dice?" She knew the preacher's kid in him didn't *like* lying, even if he could do it with a pretty good poker face.

"No, I – okay, say you're going off on a getaway weekend with me," he suggested, then a rush of pink stained his cheeks as he realized what he'd implied. "I didn't say a *dirty* weekend," he added in a hurry, looking flustered. "You're my best friend, Kimmy, and I... I respect you. I'd never..." He paused. "I wouldn't risk that."

But in the privacy of that deserted bathroom, he was looking at her mouth like he'd at least thought about kissing her. Had he? Her stomach flipped at the thought of such a fundamental shift in their relationship. She shouldn't want to risk it any more than he did. "I know," she said. "Don't worry."

Dice pulled his hair into a ponytail, using the hair tie from his wrist, almost as though he was putting on armor against temptation. "You deserve a nice holiday, right?" he said. "Let the band take you with us. It'll be nice. And I want to have a friend there, since we don't know how long..." His words trailed off and he swallowed, looking as though he'd said too much.

Kimmy smiled. "Sure. I'll go with you. Going somewhere warm sounds nice."

"Okay. Go back and finish up with load-out. Don't say anything to anyone. Get into the van with Sally and Erva when you're done – don't get on your bus or go off with anyone else."

"Do they know I'm going with them?"

He took out his phone and typed a quick message. "They do now."

It was almost three in the morning before load-out was done, and Kimmy went in search of the van. She couldn't find it at first and had to ask where it was parked, saying she'd left her overnight bag in it, which was almost plausible.

When she finally found it at the end of the parking area, the van was warm and running, and she heard the click of the doors unlocking as she approached. The side door slid open and she scrambled in, surprised to find all her bags there in the back of the van, and a warm smell of breakfast.

"Hi, Kimmy, grab a seat," Erva said from the driver's seat, nodding her head toward the jump seat behind the front two.

"Hope you don't mind we got your things from your bus," Sally added, riding shotgun. "And we thought you might be hungry." She passed back a paper bag.

With a grateful murmur of thanks, Kimmy opened the bag and found a breakfast sandwich and hashbrown biscuit. *Heaven.* She was always hungry after load-out.

Then Sally passed back a coffee as well. "This should help keep you awake, unless you want to nap on the drive. We're flying out of Columbia Regional, not Lambert International – it's about two hours away. Oh, and turn off your phone's location services."

Kimmy took the coffee. "Somehow I'm not feeling too sleepy," she said.

Erva laughed. "You're probably dying to know what's going on."

"A little," Kimmy agreed drily. "Dice didn't tell me much."

"Here's the thing." Sally twisted herself around in her seat so she could look at Kimmy as she talked. "The band's been talking about how to get out from under Arleigh Hayward, and we're all pretty much sure they've got no intention of letting Smidge go. Angel said Mofford's been pushing him to agree to re-sign for a fourth and fifth album deal, and practically said right out that they'll keep us in an endless circle of touring and promotion for *My Tainted Baby* unless and until the band signs on the dotted line. There's ways they can do it, accounting tricks and legal loopholes."

Erva nodded seriously as she took the van onto the freeway, her eyes on the road. "Don't know if you know this, but the Bad Luck Opals have been kind of mentoring Smidge, since it came out that Zam is Easy's father, and... well, they introduced the guys to their label guys. Valancy Records."

Sally took up the story again. "These guys are from a different era of record labels. They do things their way. Barely legal, some might say. But they're loyal *to* their bands, and they've decided they want Smidge. Mr. Stirling says possession is nine-tenths of the law, so Arleigh Hayward needs to *not* be in possession of Smidge for negotiating to go our way."

Kimmy blinked and took a big sip of her coffee, wondering if she was falling asleep and dreaming things. "You can't be in possession or not in possession of a band," she pointed out. "It's people."

"If you can't *find* the band..." Sally said.

"We're disappearing," Erva added.

I'm definitely too tired for this, Kimmy thought.

Despite the coffee and Kimmy's intention of staying awake, she was half asleep and borderline hallucinating from tiredness by the time they reached the FBO at Columbia Regional Airport. It was dark and deserted, just a U-Haul van sitting next to the small building that served as a terminal and guest lounge for private flights, and a sleek black jet parked on the tarmac leading to the runway. There were no lights except the logo and position lights required of a plane parked in a night flight operations area of an airport after sunset, no indication that anything was happening with the plane or the van. *Move along, nothing happening here.*

But as the Smidge tour's runabout van pulled up beside the U-Haul, the door to the building opened and Jed's familiar tall form and bandanna-covered head leaned out. He waved for them to hurry inside, although the parking area seemed deserted, with no one to observe their arrival.

The frosty air was an effective way of waking up after the cozy warmth of the van. Kimmy hitched her big duffle bag onto her shoulder and followed Sally and Erva as they careful-ran to get inside, their hurry to get out of the cold tempered by the icy footing.

Inside, in the darkened lounge, barely visible by the light of a couple of vending machines and safety lighting over the exit doors, Blade paced with his infant son cuddled against his shoulder while

Crys slept hunched over in one of the chairs. Nell, always watchful, stood by one of the windows where she'd been looking out, and Easy sat nearby, chatting with a man Kimmy took a moment to recognize in the dark as baby Luke's nanny. Angel was reading a book with the aid of his phone's flashlight. Dice's long form was stretched out on a table, fast asleep.

Jed hugged the newcomers, and he and Erva traded keys. "Wish I could go with you," he said, pulling on his jacket. "Bye, guys! Be good, Lukey, don't give your parents or Camillo any trouble." Then he was off, taking the Smidge van this time, red taillights fading into the snowy night.

Kimmy looked at the group around her, and it occurred to her that there were no bodyguards. And Jed had left – Jed, who was always with the band, backstage, on flights, everywhere. The ex-nurse, nominally in charge of backstage public relations, was much more of a team medic and adviser and above all a friend. "Where's he going?" she asked Sally, as they lugged their bags over to stack them with everyone else's bags on a cart.

"Covering for us, honey. Someone had to take the van back, and he's making sure it looks like the boys' hotel rooms were occupied overnight, doing whatever he can to see that they aren't missed until well after we're gone. He volunteered."

"Oh. I see. That makes sense." It struck Kimmy as sad and sort of unfair that Jed should miss out on a holiday with the band, especially somewhere warm. "I could have taken the van back and done that," she said apologetically. "Then Jed could be here."

Erva put a hand on Kimmy's shoulder to get her attention. "Don't worry about Jed. Trust me, he's got plenty going on. And Dice invited *you*, so you're here."

Angel looked up from his book. "Welcome, Smidgettes. Glad you could make it," he said quietly. "You might as well grab a seat and relax." There was plenty of empty seating, all of it business-class comfortable for the private jet market. "It shouldn't be too long before we can board."

Sally broke into a smile and trudged over to flop down next to him, Erva following to sit on her other side.

Kimmy could have joined them, but she went over to the table where Dice was sleeping and hitched a hip onto the edge of it next to his head. He looked fully fast asleep, and didn't respond when she gently tugged his ponytail. *Should I wake him?* It seemed a shame to spoil such a peaceful deep sleep, but she knew from experience that he'd be groggy on first waking, and Angel had said they'd be boarding the plane soon.

Putting a hand on Dice's shoulder, Kimmy gave it a squeeze, then shook him gently. "Wake up, Dice! Come on..." She gave him another gentle shake, and this time succeeded in getting a groan and a muttered curse from him. "I don't want to wake you, but you've got to get up, things are happening."

He opened one eye, then smiled and murmured, "Kimmy! You got here."

"I did."

♥

A shuttle bus from the main airport pulled into the parking area, disgorging a pair of pilots and a flight attendant. The bus wheeled away to its next destination as the flight crew approached the building.

The door opened. One of the pilots, on entering, waved everyone to move back against the walls. "You all must be our unofficial passengers. Lights coming on," he called softly.

Kimmy moved away from the windows with the others, squinting her eyes against the sudden brightness of the overhead lights. Dice rolled himself off the table and followed, staggering unsteadily and still half asleep.

"Catering truck's on its way," the flight attendant said. "If y'all want to go help him load stuff, that's probably the smartest way to get anyone recognizable on the plane. Just put on the hi-vis jackets," she pointed to a row of blaze orange outerwear on hooks by one of the doors, "and you'll fit right in. No one'll look twice." Sure enough, when

Kimmy looked out across the airport, she saw a small truck on its way from the direction of the main terminal.

"Sounds good," Easy said, and shrugged himself into one of the jackets. Angel nodded and followed suit, watching as Blade cautiously transferred the baby into Crys's arms before putting on one of the jackets as well. Dice, still not entirely awake, just leaned against a wall until Kimmy took a jacket and thrust it into his arms.

The first pilot went out through the door closest to the parked airplane, where the catering truck had come to a stop. It was just a short walk away and the tarmac had been de-iced. They talked for a moment, then the pilot turned back to give a thumbs-up toward the building before he activated something near the front of the plane. The door opened outward, self-contained airstairs popping into position, telescoping handrails sliding up into place.

The second pilot knew what the thumbs-up meant. "Off you go, gentlemen – one at a time, just head on over to the catering truck and they'll hand you something to carry onboard. We're already de-iced and fueled up, so we'll be able to take off as soon as our official passengers arrive."

Official passengers?

Angel nodded and headed out the door. They saw him approach the catering truck, take a box, and carry it over to the plane, up the airstairs and in. Blade gave Crys a kiss and said, "See you in a few minutes, sweetheart," before following. Easy went next, then Dice.

"I've got to go over and make sure Nick does the preflight properly," the second pilot said with a wink. "I'm Ji-tae, by the way, but most people call me Jet. Simran will bring you over once the Stirlings arrive, okay?" He indicated the flight attendant with finger guns and a cheesy grin, at which she rolled her eyes.

"We've been flying for the Stirlings a long time," Simran explained, watching affectionately as the pilot headed for the plane. "Maybe ten years now? Jet and Nick alternate pilot and co-pilot, and they do actually know what they're doing. Jet's just being a goofball."

A wave of tiredness hit Kimmy, and she yawned before she could realize it was coming to try to suppress it or even cover her mouth. "Sorry," she muttered. "Long night, haven't slept."

"We'll have coffee and breakfast as soon as we're in the air," the flight attendant assured her. "And nearly all the seats recline, except the couch."

Eventually a sleek black car pulled into the parking area and came to a stop right at the steps to the door of the building. The chauffeur got out and opened the rear passenger door, offering a hand to help an older lady disembark. The lady wore a plum velvet coat and a diaphanous black scarf dotted with silver sequins, and her silver-white hair was up in an immaculate French twist topped with victory rolls. *Fashionable and powerful.* Even at a distance, her deep crimson lipstick said *don't mess with me.* Behind her, a slender man of a similar vintage emerged, a dark wool coat open over a suit that probably cost thousands of dollars, his lean, foxy features and neat steel hair instantly recognizable within the music industry – Torquil Sterling, owner of Valancy Records. The lady had to be his wife. They both carried themselves like royalty.

The flight attendant hurried to open the door for them, and they greeted her with appreciation and kindness as they stepped inside. The chauffeur followed with their bags, which he carried through to the other door, evidently taking the luggage right out to the plane.

Kimmy happened to be standing closest to Mrs. Stirling, who turned to her with a smile and a hand extended to shake. "I don't think we've met, my dear?"

Of course not. I'm just a drum tech. But Kimmy gathered what was left of her brain together and said, "I'm Kimmy Baker, drum tech for Smidge, Mrs. Stirling."

Mrs. Stirling smiled. "Yes. Dice's friend. We're delighted to have you with us. Please, call me Cynthia." She moved on gracefully to embrace Nell and Crys, expressing her pleasure at seeing them again and cooing appreciatively over the baby.

Delighted might be an exaggeration, Kimmy thought, but the older lady seemed pleased to be taking them all on the plane with her. It wasn't long before they were leaving the terminal and heading for the plane – Crys with her baby next to Cynthia Stirling, Nell and Sally and Erva following behind.

Kimmy hung back, seeing that Camillo was struggling to carry the car seat and portable crib and diaper bag. "Can't you put some of this on the cart?" she asked him, seeing that their bags were still waiting to go out to the plane.

"I'm pretty sure everything there is going into the baggage compartment, and we'll need all Luke's things on the flight," he said. "Little dude needs a lot of this and that." So she offered to carry the baby's diaper bag for him, and he handed it over with alacrity.

With the load divided, the two of them hustled to catch up with the others. When they reached the plane, they had to wait a moment to let a baggage handler carrying an armful of blaze orange jackets go down the airstairs before they could go up. Returning the jackets the band had worn to the building, Kimmy understood, on his way to collect and load the baggage cart.

Camillo seemed surprised when they boarded, and said, "This is laid out a bit different from the Smidge plane. More like... a plane."

It wasn't like any plane Kimmy had been on, but she didn't want to admit to Camillo that this was her first time on a private flight – crew flew commercial overseas, and otherwise traveled on buses.

Two comfortable-looking cream leather armchairs faced each other on either side of the aisle at the front, and Mr. and Mrs. Stirling occupied one set with Nell and Easy in the other. Farther back, there was another grouping of four, but instead of being either side of the aisle, these were squashed together to the right, like two loveseats facing each other. Angel sat in the back window seat looking toward the front, and the back of Dice's head was visible over the top of the seat opposite him. Beyond that was a bulkhead with a curtain drawn back, revealing what looked like a couch.

Mrs. Stirling touched Camillo's arm with perfectly manicured fingertips to get his attention. "The Blakeharts are sitting in the rear compartment. They thought it would be nicer for you and Luke to have some room to spread out on the couch."

Camillo nodded. "Thank you, uh, ma'am. I'll take Luke's things back there. 'Scuse me, Sally, Erva." He edged his way past them where they stood by the second group of seats, maneuvering the cot and car seat not to hit anyone, and moved to the back of the plane.

"Dude," Erva was saying, "it doesn't matter."

"You always–" Sally began, then cut her own words off. She shrugged and sat down next to Angel. "I don't care, then. Suit yourself."

Angel and Dice both looked uncomfortable, and it struck Kimmy that there was one seat left... and Erva and herself still standing. She could see into the rear compartment, now, where Blade and Crys sat in another pair of armchairs, and Camillo had perched on one end of the three-seat couch and was currently occupied with anchoring the car seat into the middle seat to prepare for takeoff. One space was open on the end of the couch.

It was like looking at a jigsaw puzzle and seeing how the pieces had to fit to make the right picture. *If Erva sits with Sally and Angel and Dice, I'm the leftover, the staff, the helper who goes to sit in the back with the nanny and the baby. If I sit, I force Erva into that position.* In the middle of what should have been excitement and a treat, flying on a private jet with the band for the first time, Kimmy let herself feel a moment of sourness – *I should get to sit with Dice, he's my friend, I'm his guest on this flight* – and then let it go. Erva deserved a nice seat with the band and the people she cared about too. And if Kimmy felt like an afterthought sitting at the back, it would surely be worse for Erva. As Kimmy's eyes met Dice's, she knew what he was thinking.

Even as he moved to stand, opened his mouth – about to offer, she was sure of it, to go to the rear compartment himself and let the ladies have the good seats – she cut him off. "Sit here, Erva," she heard herself saying. "I'll go sit next to Luke. I love babies. It'll be fun!"

I love babies.

Could a person sound any more inane?

But the flight would be spoiled for her if she got the cushy armchair at the expense of Dice sitting at the back.

A soft chime jingled through the overhead speakers, and the seatbelt signs lit up. "Please take your seats," Simran asked them politely. "We're just waiting on clearance from the tower, and I need to secure the cabin for takeoff."

With no more time to debate the issue, Kimmy thanked her and moved past Erva to the rear compartment, where she handed over the diaper bag before sitting down on the end seat of the couch. She did up her seatbelt. Luke squirmed in his car seat, not too impressed at being strapped in, and she smiled and cooed at him. "Nice way to travel," she commented to Camillo.

"It is," he agreed. "A bit better for Luke on the Smidge jet because it has a bedroom, though. We'll see how this goes without a quiet dark place for a nap. But he's a pretty easygoing baby."

"A flying bedroom sounds nice," Kimmy said. She'd heard about the Smidge jet, how it was more like a flying apartment than a plane, but she was happy enough on the ground and had never minded sleeping on tour buses.

Crys looked over from her seat a few feet away. "I can take him if he fusses, Camillo," she offered. The love in Crys's eyes for her baby made Kimmy's heart flip over. *I want a baby to love like that.* She wondered if she could do it, have a baby on the road with the band. Crys made it look easy and tempting, but Luke's rock-baby lifestyle was backed by Blade's star status and income. How would a baby-toting crewmember fare, even with Crys's offer of sharing the nursery bus and Camillo's services? And without really meaning to, she looked over to where Dice was sitting, Erva beside him.

The chime sounded over the speakers again, followed by the first pilot's voice. "Nick here, your captain for the flight, with Jet in the co-pilot's seat beside me. We're about to start moving. Taxiing to our runway, then we'll be up and away, so please keep the tables stowed and your seatbelts on until we're at cruising altitude."

And what am I doing here, anyway? This holiday isn't for crew.

Kimmy settled into her seat and tried to relax.

♥

Three hours into the flight, Luke was asleep in his car seat, after fussing and nursing for a while, and both Crys and Blade had reclined their seats and fallen asleep too. Camillo was deeply engrossed in some kind of game on his tablet, and Kimmy kept trying to read, but her mind wandered and she couldn't keep her focus on her book. The agonizing slow burn in this one was killing her, to the point that she wanted to reach into the book and smack the main characters. *Just get together already.* Four chapters in, and they hadn't even kissed... It almost made a person think about re-reading the book she'd mentally tagged *that dirty one* – the one she'd borrowed from Ruby in Detroit. *I could use some hot sex with a dirty-talking dragon shifter right about now,* she thought ruefully. Not the dragon part, really... just... it had been a while since anyone had made her feel properly good, and somehow even a dragon seemed more realistic and likely than...

Approaching footsteps interrupted her thoughts and made her look up, and there was Dice, towering above her in the narrow airplane aisle – he had to stoop and duck his head a bit to avoid bumping the six-foot ceiling.

"Hey, what's up?" she asked.

"Just thought I'd come back and have a visit." He cleared his throat, a polite interruption, and waited until Luke's nanny looked up from his game. "Camillo, since Luke's asleep, would you be okay to swap seats with me for a bit? Just go up and sit with Angel and Sally and Erva so I can hang with Kimmy a bit?"

Camillo shrugged and got up. "Sure."

Dice flopped down into the vacated seat, then shot a cautious glance at Luke to make sure the movement hadn't woken him, but the baby slept peacefully on.

"I wanted you to sit with me," he said to Kimmy, his eyes full of apology.

"I know," she told him. "I wanted to sit with you too. But I know Erva wanted to sit with Sally, and..."

"Yeah."

They nodded at each other, knowing there'd never been a choice. If she hadn't gone to take the couch seat, he would have. *You do the right thing because it's the right thing.* He was a preacher's son, and she was the daughter of a mechanic and a baker, but in many ways, there wasn't much difference between their families.

"Has it been okay sitting back here?" he asked.

She shrugged. "Sure. Not much excitement, but Luke is sweet, and I was reading."

Dice looked at the sleeping baby, then at Kimmy. "Did you mean it, about wanting to have one?"

"My Christmas wish, you mean?"

"Mmm."

Why lie to him? He's my best friend. Surely I can talk to him about this? "I don't know, but yes? I mean, it just kind of came out of my mouth in the moment, but... I'm turning twenty-nine this year, nearly thirty, and... there are times when I feel almost an ache to have a baby. Not a physical ache, though. More like a punch in the heart when I think about what the rest of my life will be like if it doesn't happen for me." She sighed. It sounded so weird out loud.

But Dice only reached across Luke's car seat and put a hand lightly on her shoulder. "I'm sure it *will* happen for you, Kimber. You'll be a great mom." His fingers gave her a comforting squeeze.

Such strong but gentle hands her drummer had.

I shouldn't like his touch so much.

And for the first time, an awful, addictive, mind-blowing thought formed itself clearly in her mind, though it had probably been there in her subconscious all along.

Dice would make beautiful babies.

Somehow, she didn't say it, just managed to paste what must have been some weak sort of smile onto her face and said, "Thanks, Dice. You always make me feel better." And that was the truth, too.

Almost as if he'd read her mind, he leaned as close to her ear as he could over Luke in his car seat between them and said very quietly, so no one else on the plane would overhear, "I heard you and Crys talking about... doing it on your own at some point, and I was thinking..." His fingers drummed out a complex rhythm, one hand on his thigh and the other on the back of the couch next to her shoulder. "If you were going to go with donor sperm, you know, I could – I mean, maybe you'd rather have a complete stranger, no connections, but – in case you wanted a friend..."

"I couldn't ask that of you," she whispered back.

He shrugged. "If you're not looking for a father, I'm just offering some biological goop. I'd donate a whole damn organ if you needed one, and it'd be a hell of a lot easier than that."

Fortunately, Luke hiccupped in his sleep and woke himself, starting to fuss, and Camillo immediately jumped up and came back to the rear compartment, hoping to settle the baby before he woke his parents from their much-needed sleep.

"D'you want to go up and sit with Sally and Erva for a bit, Kimmy?" Dice offered, getting up to give Camillo back his seat.

She waved the offer away. "Thanks, but I've got my book. I'm fine. You go." Any distraction from the thoughts bouncing around in her brain would be good.

The plane landed briefly in Miami, where the Stirlings disembarked to board a cruise – their ostensible purpose for the flight – then went on to the island of Charlotte Amalie in the US Virgin Islands, from which a water taxi took them to Lovango Cay, where the Stirlings had a vacation home.

♥

The property was a lovely one – though Kimmy had nothing to compare it to, what wouldn't be lovely on a tropical private island, with a short walking trail down to a white sand beach? She had a bedroom in one of the three small guesthouses, with Dice's bedroom on the other side and a sitting room between them. Crys and Blade had another guesthouse, with Camillo and Luke in the other bedroom, and Sally and Erva took the third one. Nell and Easy chose one of the guest bedrooms in the main house, and Angel occupied the other one, all of them in tacit agreement that it wouldn't be appropriate for anyone to use the Stirlings' own suite.

It was odd having nothing to do. To not be on the way somewhere, or about to be on the way somewhere. To not be loading in or loading out or working a show.

Kimmy couldn't even occupy herself with unpacking, as she'd hardly brought anything appropriate to wear, going straight onto the plane from midwinter Missouri with barely any warning and no time to shop or prepare. Fortunately, she always had her swimsuit with her; anyone on the road knew that an unexpected chance at a hot tub or pool could come up at any stop, and a swimsuit didn't take much room.

The housekeeper who'd showed them to their rooms had brought in a box of spare garments suited to the climate, maybe things left behind by previous guests, possibly supplemented by additions Mrs. Stirling had chosen, Kimmy wasn't sure. There were sundresses and wraps and beach coverups in light colors and tropical prints, and she doubted she'd feel like herself in any of them.

After a bit of reflection, she cut the legs off the more worn-out of her two pairs of jeans. Cut-offs would do for anything that didn't involve swimming, and she at least had plenty of t-shirts to wash and wear, between Smidge crew work shirts and the ones she'd acquired from their various opening bands. *No hibiscus-print loungewear, thank you!* Her purple shower shoes would do as sandals.

The houses were surrounded by wide verandas and connected by stone paths, ideal for spending time outside, day or night. Propane fire pits sat ready for nighttime warmth and marshmallow toasting, when the various patio and veranda coverings were lit up with strings of white fairy lights. Hibiscus, frangipani, and ginger thomas bloomed everywhere, and coconut palms and hog plum and genip trees cast much-needed shade on the paths and blocked some of the ocean breeze. And the Stirlings had assured them, before leaving on the cruise, that the housekeeper and cook, a married couple from St. Thomas who lived there year-round, were well paid to be discreet.

Just stay out of sight for a week or two while we negotiate for you, Mr. Stirling had said. *Sam and Mariel will take care of everything, and we'll get Arleigh Hayward off your backs.*

So the next days and nights blurred together into swimming and sun and food and drink, firepits and toasted marshmallows. Dice was, as always, her best friend and a perfect gentleman as they swam and ate and lay on the beach or sat on patio lounge chairs, him with a graphic novel and her with a romance, and when her marshmallow fell off her stick into the flames, he just winked and gave her his perfectly toasted one, saying he didn't want it after all.

No one was counting the hours, never mind the calendar, until Sally woke Kimmy up one morning a few days after they'd arrived, banging on her bedroom door, saying, "Kimmy, honey. Do you realize it's New Year's Eve today? We've got to *do something.*"

chapter

5

Something evidently meant a New Year's Eve party.

Kimmy eyed herself in the bathroom mirror, not certain how she felt about the gold sequined tunic that hung from her shoulders to mid-thigh, casting reflected dots of light around the room every time she moved. One of Sally's suitcases had contained "emergency" party wear for the occasion – cocktail dresses for the Smidgettes, and something for the men too.

"Do you have it on yet?" Sally called from outside the bathroom door. "Does it fit? Do you like it, honey? You can trade with Erva for the night if you don't like that one, she won't mind and you're about the same size."

"It's very sparkly," Kimmy called back. "But I like it. Thank you."

"Come out and let me see you, then! And I've got gold glitter hairspray. Can I do your hair?"

"Sure. Might as well go all in with the shimmery look."

When Kimmy opened the door, Sally clapped enthusiastically. "You don't show it often, but I *knew* you had a sparkle mode inside you. I've seen the bling you put on your hair sometimes, and the pedicures you get."

Of course, Sally would notice something like that. Road crew didn't often wear open-toed shoes, so Kimmy's enjoyment of having her feet pampered and pretty was easily kept to herself. *Just a private thing for me.* But sharp-eyed Sally, with her eye for costumes and dramatic presentation – as one would expect with her being Smidge's wardrobe mistress and makeup artist, after all – must have spotted her changing shoes or coming out of the shower enough times over the years to realize it was consistent.

Kimmy gave a rueful snort of self-deprecating laughter. "I suppose it's that I could never forget Easy calling me 'Sparkles' the first time we met. So I always try to look like proper road crew should..." Businesslike, practical, punky, a little bit beat-up, and a lot of yes-I-can attitude. "It's not an act. I mean, that's really me. But I like pretty things too."

Sally nodded, a look of understanding in her eyes. "And we're not on the road, and this is a party. Almost like we've stepped out of time for a little bit, out of our real lives."

"True." And the gold tunic was comfortable, swingy and fun.

"And you've got pockets," Sally pointed out. "Johnny never makes a dress without pockets."

"This is a *Ripped Creme* dress?!" Kimmy looked down at herself in awed concern. The drag queen and fashion designer didn't make cheap clothes. "What if I rip it, or spill something on it?"

"You won't. Anyway, it's yours to keep. He was having a clear-out to make room for next season's things, a sort of word-of-mouth private sale that I found out about from Nell and Crys, so I got a few pieces at rock-bottom prices like you wouldn't believe, and then he put a couple of extra ones in the box with them as a bonus. But that gold's a little tight in the bust area for me and the sequins annoy Erva, so it's yours. And I didn't pay anything for it, so don't even try."

"Wow." Kimmy petted the glittering fabric, feeling the texture of the sequins, then slipped her hands into the pockets. "Thank you."

"I want the boys to have a nice party tonight," Sally said. "It's been such a hard year, and all this..." She gestured out the window at the tropical surroundings. "I know we're here to stay out of the way so Valancy can negotiate for us, but it's also a treat, a real vacation. You *know* how long it's been since the boys have had anything but a working holiday, and New Year's Eve has always been a work night. Some big show somewhere, or one of Awfully Hateful's corporate bashes."

"That's true. A *real* New Year's Eve party..."

"Yes. Here, let me put some glitter in your hair, and we can break out the party hats."

♥

Formalwear would have been too hot for the men in the Caribbean climate, so they had LED light-up ties to wear over tropical-print linen shirts. If it didn't exactly make sense with the women in cocktail dresses, that didn't matter. The playlist on the sound system was a mix Easy had that didn't include any Smidge songs, since none of them wanted to feel like they were at work. Cardboard top hats and tiaras rounded off the celebratory atmosphere – Nell took a top hat, and when everyone else had taken theirs, Dice was left with a tiara.

"You don't mind, do you?" Nell asked him, already with the glittery hat on her head.

Dice looked at the flimsy cardboard-and-foil tiara in his hands and laughed. "No, but Kimmy's going to have to put it on for me. I'm not sure how to wear one of these." He held it out to her.

She fitted the little crown onto his head, tucking the ends of the foil band into his hair so that the tightness of his ponytail would hold them in place. Stray glitter got onto her fingers and sprinkled his hair.

The cook had provided a buffet with a mountain of food for them, along with an enormous bowl of rum punch and a cooler full of beer and champagne bottles on ice, before he and his wife headed off to take a boat to St. Thomas for the night, leaving the Smidge group with complete privacy for their celebration. And privacy was a rare commodity for a band.

As it got closer to midnight, they danced.

Kimmy expected to mostly watch from the sidelines, dancing on the edge of the group when faster music allowed it. But to her surprise, first Angel danced a slow song with her, then Easy twirled her about like a ballroom dancer at half-speed on the next slow one, and Erva came over and asked her to dance the one after that while Sally danced with Angel. Blade danced all the slow ones with Crys, but he crossed the floor and danced half a faster song with Kimmy. Even Camillo, who had joined them to eat, danced with her once before the baby monitor squawked and he had to go up to settle Luke. All of them made a point of including her.

But Dice still hadn't danced with her. He smiled encouragingly at her, and brought her drinks when he saw her glass was empty, and danced *near* her when they were all in a group. But not *with* her, not a slow dance.

Just before midnight, though – what had to be the last song before midnight – Otis Redding's classic "These Arms of Mine" began to play, a song Kimmy had loved since she first heard it as part of the *Dirty Dancing* soundtrack. And she looked for Dice, thought about maybe asking him to dance, just as friends, but he was already walking toward her with a slightly hesitant grin.

"Dance with me, Kimber?" he asked, as though she might ever say no. And at her answering smile, he pulled her close and held her against him. They swayed to the music, rocking comfortably together to the rhythm, and she laid her head against his chest, hearing his 6'3" heartbeat thumping under her 5'2" ear, totally at ease and yet she'd never felt so attuned to his body, so physically aware of him. He stroked the sequined fabric down her back, and commented, "Pretty dress."

"Thanks. Sally gave it to me. To be festive." *Why are we talking about my dress?* She wanted to arch like a cat under his hand, but that would be all kinds of wrong... and maybe start something they couldn't undo. But she couldn't stop herself from saying, "You haven't danced with me all night."

"I know. I've been thinking about something," he murmured against her hair, sounding rueful and uncertain.

"Don't get glitter in your mouth," she warned him. His lips were inches away from her ear. "What were you thinking about?"

He hesitated, and the song came to an end. A reminder chime pinged somewhere, and Sally announced, "One minute 'til midnight." She and Erva handed around glasses of champagne.

"I was waiting to dance with you until now," Dice said into Kimmy's ear, his voice low and full of intensity, "because I wanted to be standing next to you at midnight."

"Fifteen seconds," said Angel. "Ten... nine... eight..."

Other voices joined in the countdown.

They never got to do this, not in private, with friends. New Year's Eve was always a work night, and if the band wasn't still on stage at midnight, the crew would be somewhere in the middle of load-out. Sure, there'd be a quick round of champagne after, at two or three in the morning, but in all the years she'd known him, Kimmy had never been standing beside Dice at the moment the year changed over.

At midnight, a burst of fireworks filled the sky, and Dice looked down at Kimmy, put two fingers under her chin to tilt her head up, and bent to kiss her. It was just a momentary press of lips to lips, nothing much as kisses went, nothing a person couldn't give a friend, really. But the brief contact tingled through her like a shock of electric joy. She felt both dizzy and bereft as he pulled away and clinked his glass against hers, saying, "Happy New Year, Kimmy!"

"Auld Lang Syne" began to play on the sound system.

Above them, the fireworks display continued – the nearest ones had to be from the resort right there on the other side of Lovango Cay, but they also rose in more distant parts of the sky, some to the southeast from St. John, and more a bit farther away to the southwest over St. Thomas.

There were many things she could have said. Wished him a happy New Year too, for instance. Commented on the beauty of the fireworks, the islands, the night itself with all its stars. But she wanted what had just happened to count, and ignoring it meant it didn't count. "That wasn't much of a kiss," Kimmy said, and she could hear the daring, teasing sound in her voice. *Flirting. I'm flirting with Dice.* She'd always been so careful not to cross that line. But so had he.

"Oh?" he asked softly. "Did you want more?" Flirting back. Or... putting a potential change to their relationship on the table.

And she wanted to chase the flash of awaiting glory a mere brush of his lips had given her. Could it be that good with him? "I think I do. If you want to."

He took her hand.

"Go for a walk?" he asked, his voice a little deeper than usual, full of tension and promise.

"Sure."

♥

His hand was warm and firm around hers as he led her away from the covered patio where they'd been eating and dancing, up one of the flagstone paths that linked the various guesthouses and outbuildings with the main house. They didn't go far, though. As soon as they were out of the others' sight around a corner, Dice stopped, breathing hard, his chest rising and falling as though he'd been running.

"This won't change anything," he promised her, with a hint of desperation. "You're my best friend, Kimmy. You'll always be my best friend." Then he pinned her up against the wall of the house, and this time he *really* kissed her, his whole big body firm against her as his tongue explored her mouth. The sheer hunger of it stunned her. And then time and the world around her slipped away as she got lost in the pleasure of the moment.

Eventually, he pulled back, his eyes slightly wild at what they'd just done, his cardboard tiara askew.

"That was lovely," she assured him. So lovely, better than she could have imagined. When he didn't say anything, she moved one hand to his shoulder and gave it a comforting squeeze.

He sighed. "Oh, Kimber," he whispered. "I don't want to break what we have, but that was so damn good. And I want to keep doing it."

They pushed themselves away from the wall and walked along the path, still holding hands, and she had the sense that neither of them wanted to lose the physical connection that was grounding them, as though they'd spin off into the starry night if they weren't anchored to each other. But when they came to the porch of their guesthouse, he let go and dropped onto the end of one of the sun loungers there, twisting his tiara in his hands, staring down at it. So she perched on the railing of the porch near him, letting her legs dangle against the slats.

"Nothing's broken," she said. "Maybe kissing is... part of our thing, now."

He was quiet for a minute, then tossed the twisted tiara onto the other lounger and looked up at her. "Just kissing?" he asked, his voice oddly neutral, like he was holding something back.

The universe juddered to a halt for a moment, then time and breathing started up again. "I'm open to negotiation," she managed to say.

He gazed at her, his dark brown eyes intense. It was hard to be sure in the dimly lit night, but she thought his cheeks looked flushed. Blushing? "Something I want to tell you," he muttered, or at least she thought that was what he'd said, "but I think I'll do better if you come and sit close to me." He patted the space next to him on the lounger.

"Of course." She hopped down from the railing and settled herself next to him, nestling against him as he wrapped an arm around her shoulders. *A person could tell you almost anything,* he'd said to her the day Luke was born, and she'd wondered then what the *almost* was about. "Say whatever you like. I'm right here." She put her hand on his thigh, aiming to reassure him – but also deliberately, wickedly aware that she was only inches away from a far more intimate touch.

He cleared his throat, and laid a hand over hers, but he stared off into the sky as though he couldn't look at her. "Got a bit of a problem. Defective equipment."

"Oh?" she asked gently. "You felt pretty fine to me back there when we were kissing." And now they definitely couldn't go back to being purely platonic, not when she'd admitted that she'd noticed his erection pressing into her.

His bitter laugh broke her heart. "Sure, everything works great until I'm expected to..." He coughed, swallowing whatever he'd been going to describe. "We have the hottest, flirtiest groupies literally throwing themselves at us, offering... whatever we want, in exchange for nothing but bragging rights. But no. I can't stay hard long enough to..."

"I *know* I've walked in on you getting a blow job." That image had lived fulltime in Kimmy's brain for months afterward, and would still spring vividly to life if she let herself think about it – the girl's head bobbing up and down, and Dice with his head thrown back, back arched, eyes closed in the tense pleasure of being very, very close to orgasm. But he'd heard the door and his eyes had shot open, meeting Kimmy's gaze in horrified, red-faced embarrassment. She'd bolted away without a word, and neither of them had ever mentioned it.

"Yeah." He looked close to tears as he gazed at the brilliant stars. "I can sometimes get there if I pretend... the mouth belongs to someone... well, someone I have feelings for."

"How long has this been going on?"

"Always," he admitted, in a barely audible whisper. "I've never been able to stay hard, no matter how pretty and nice the groupie is. I just can't do it with a stranger. And I've been living this rock band life so long, I've never honestly known anything else. Christ on a stick, I'm twenty-five years old and I'm still a virgin, Kimmy!"

A virgin. Of all the things she'd imagined he might hide from her, that wasn't it.

"That's a pretty big secret to keep from your best friend," she teased, trying to coax him out of his slump of distress and shame.

He shook his head. "I mean, I've done stuff, but... I've never managed to get tab A into slot B – hell. It's too damn hard to talk about, even with you. Especially with you."

"Especially?"

"Because I feel safe with you. I trust you. I... think maybe I could..." He shifted on the sun lounger, turning to face her, taking her hands in his and finally looking into her eyes. "Would you ever want to do more than just make out? I doubt I've got much to make it tempting for you, but... I think my DNA is all right. You could get a baby the old-fashioned way, and I could finally lose my god-fucking-damned virginity already!" In an electric wave of frustration and need and self-loathing, he let go of her hands and ripped the hair tie out of his hair, letting the floppy, silky strands fall around his face.

And Kimmy sat there in shock, trying to process what he'd just said.

I doubt I've got much to make it tempting for you. That, at least, was plain wrong.

You could get a baby the old-fashioned way.

She thought about him coming inside her and had to suppress a moan.

But was she just someone he thought of as safe? The thought stung.

"Either put your hair tie on your wrist or give it to me. If you keep flipping it about like that, you'll only lose it," she pointed out, her words a bit sharper than she'd intended, but his offer had sent her spinning and she was struggling to find familiar ground.

With a huff, he snapped the hair tie onto his wrist, his shoulders slumping. "Stupid idea," he muttered. "I'm not ready to go back to the party, but you can if you want to."

"It isn't a stupid idea." But he still looked sad, defeated. *Time to go all in.* "And you're all kinds of tempting, Dice, don't ever think you're not."

"Yeah?" His shoulders straightened a little, and he looked up at her again, a flash of hope in his face.

"Yeah. The first time I saw you, I noticed your cute butt. You were backing out of the stage door in Royal Oak, butt-first, and it was instant lust, okay? And you *know* you've got ripped arms and a pretty face. But I found out you were just nineteen, and then we were co-workers, and then friends. Still, I've always liked looking at you, and I've wondered what it'd be like with you. I'm not saying no, did you notice that?"

"Oh, Kimber..." he breathed. Then he hesitated, and carefully clarified, "Do you really mean you'll let me... try?"

"It won't be *trying*," she promised him. "I can be your safe place. We can make it happen for you." After all, what did it matter if that was why he wanted it with her? Her best friend deserved to experience pleasure without frustration or shame, and if she could give him that... "We're only going to make out tonight, though," she told him – and herself – firmly. "A little anticipation will be good for the main event, I think. And we'll talk about that *and* the whole making a baby thing when we're both completely sober. No matter what happens, I don't want anything to wreck our friendship."

"Me either," he agreed. "Can I kiss you again now?"

She drew in a breath, sensing that if he did, it would make everything somehow real. They could have pretended the midnight kiss was nothing, and they could have walked away from the kiss that came after that because it was just once. But a third kiss would irrevocably change their friendship, no matter how much they said it wouldn't. Change, not wreck. *Change can be good. And anyway, I've pretty much promised to let him bang me, so...* She nodded.

"Say it out loud, Kimmy. I need to hear it," he told her, almost on a growl, almost an order, with an instinctive deepening of his voice that had her helpless and suddenly wet.

"Kiss me," she said. "Please kiss me."

He rolled her onto the sun lounger and covered her mouth with his, one hand on the back of her neck and his weight on that elbow. It was fierce and needful and tender all at once, and there was nothing wrong with what she could feel against her thigh, nothing at all. Her knees automatically spread wider for him, prompting his free hand to drift down and slide up her thigh. "Lacy panties?" he murmured in surprise.

"I like pretty underwear."

With a pleased groan, he dropped his head to lick and kiss the tender skin of her neck as his fingers played with the lacy trim of her panties, inching closer and closer to where she urgently needed attention but never quite getting there, until she was squirming and panting. "Fuck, Dice," she gasped in frustration.

"You want to come, Pretty Girl?" he asked, in a wickedly calm and sensual tone that she'd never known he possessed.

"I... yeah. But you don't need to call me pretty, just because..."

He paused and raised his head, a faint blush staining his cheekbones. "I won't call you that if you don't like it. But you *are* pretty."

His fingers brushed lightly across the gusset of her underwear, sending a ripple of sensation through her, and she moaned, her mind reeling. *He's too sweet a person to have dominant tendencies, isn't he?* Yet with the way he called her Pretty Girl and asked her if she wanted to come, she wondered if she was wrong about that.

"You can call me whatever you like... Boss," she offered, testing for his reaction. The deepening blush and the almost-ashamed flare of excitement and desire in his eyes were interesting, to say the least.

He pushed her gently back against the lounger and moved down between her legs, with one knee nudging hers farther apart. Her skirt was already rucked up, but now he flipped the gold fabric all the way up to totally expose her lower half and the lacy pale gold panties with silver ribbons that she wore. "Very pretty," he commented, touching the lace just above where it would matter, then slowly traced his finger downward in a teasing figure eight, grinning when she raised her hips to get more of the delicate touch. "You've absolutely soaked your panties. Should we take them off, or do you want me to work around them?" He illustrated his meaning by slipping a finger underneath the thin scrap of wet fabric, tugging it to one side.

"Whatever you like," she managed to say. "Just don't rip them, please, I like these ones."

"Off, then," he decided, standing up for a moment to help her remove the panties. Then he positioned himself between her legs again and settled into creating a blissful rhythm with his fingers, both hands working her into a puddle of need. "Not yet," he warned, as she felt herself getting close, and that hint of control nearly pushed her over the edge, but she held on, biting her lip. He paused, locking eyes with her. "You want to come on my tongue, Pretty Girl?"

"How the fuck are you so good at this? Yes, please!" she gasped.

He gave her a wry smile. "Oh, Kimmy, I've had a lot of practice distracting women from the fact that what they wanted didn't work. And you *know* I can count to four."

"Drummer jokes at a time like this?" she managed to ask, borderline exasperated at being just out of reach of her orgasm.

He chuckled. "Come on my tongue, then." And he bent down and did something utterly magic with fingers and tongue and she was gone in seconds, shredded into tiny stars and coalescing back into her body limp and moaning with delight.

"Well, hidden talents, who knew..." she muttered when she could speak again.

"That was good for you, Kimber?" he asked gently.

She smiled. "Oh, yeah... Thank you." Her eyes rested on the unmistakable tent in his shorts. "What can I do for you in return? Want me to blow you?" she offered.

He shook his head. "Another time. I'm already so close, and there's something... I've never asked anyone... but maybe you won't laugh..."

"Go on..."

"Could I... come on your stomach? Like, just make a mess on you with my cum? God, that sounds awful." He put a hand over his face like he couldn't believe he'd just said that out loud.

Someone absolutely, definitely has a kinky side. She fought to keep her expression serious, and by the time he lowered his hand and looked at her again, the urge to giggle had passed. "You like that idea, huh?" she asked. "You want to jerk yourself off while I watch and shoot your load all over me?" It was adorable to see him light up and blush and get flustered when she put it into blunt words like that, and she felt a secret thrill at how quickly he got over the embarrassment and leaned into the moment.

"Pull your dress up higher, Pretty Girl, I want more of a canvas for my art."

"Art." She laughed and wriggled the dress up under her armpits to show him her breasts, cupped in the sheer lacy bra that matched her panties – easy to be generous and let him have his fun once she'd already got hers. But then he stood and unzipped his pants and freed himself, and her mouth fell open in surprise. "That's quite the baseball bat you have there, Boss," she joked, not quite able to square away the revelation that the dear friend she'd worked with and lusted after for years had an unexpectedly enormous cock, easily the biggest she'd ever seen.

"Do you like it?" he asked, with a moment of hesitation, and she understood that he was asking if the way he was made was acceptable to her.

"Absolutely," she assured him. "I'm going to need a bunch of foreplay to take all of that, but you're perfect. Now, show me how you make love to yourself. Show me what you've got for me..."

With a startled blink at her, he looked down at himself. For a moment she thought he was going to spit in his hand as lube, then he held the hand out under her chin and asked, "Spit for me?" So she licked her lips and summoned up as much spit as she could, and let it dribble out over her lower lip onto his palm. It was a weirdly intimate thing to do, spitting into someone's hand. It even felt sort of dirty, though that made no sense since he'd get her spit on him anyway if she went down on him and she wouldn't think twice about that.

He took himself in hand, eyes locked on hers. Slicked his big cock with the wetness in his hand and started pumping. And it was clear from his face that he was already close to the edge.

"God, Kimmy," he choked out. "Are you sure...?"

"Yes. Yes! Paint that cum all over me," she encouraged him, arching her back and spreading her arms and legs wide.

"Christ, this is so dirty, I don't even know... I'm sorry..." He groaned and let loose, shooting his load across her stomach. He squinched his eyes closed, as though he couldn't quite believe what he'd just watched himself do.

"Don't be sorry," she told him gently. "I liked it. I guess I've always been a bit of a sub at heart, though I don't mind vanilla sex at all."

Oops, might have scared him there, she thought to herself, as he muttered about getting a cloth to clean her up and bolted.

He came back with a warm, damp hand towel, and carefully cleaned up every bit of the mess he'd made, swiping the towel tenderly over her skin. At first, he seemed unable to meet her eyes, but then he sat down next to her on the sun lounger and helped her pull her gold tunic dress down into place. "You looked so sexy with my cum on you like that," he said, finally gazing at her with contentment and appreciation. "Thank you for letting me try it. I've had so many fantasies..."

She held her arms out, inviting him to lie down and snuggle with her on the lounger, and he complied. "I'm up for trying anything you're curious about," she said, loving the feel of his big body cuddled against hers. She'd always loved being near him, touching him, being with him. Without the weight of having to pretend it was all platonic, she felt free and exultant and capable of flight – for however long this thing between them would last.

"We should go back to the party," he offered after a while, sleepily.

"True," she agreed, feeling wide awake. "At least to say goodnight."

It seemed that no one had even noticed they'd been gone.

The group had moved inside to the sitting room of the big house. Notwithstanding the late hour, Angel and Blade and Easy had got their instruments and were in the middle of a songwriting session, playing bits of melody and trying out lines of lyrics, scribbling this and that into a notebook as they went. Tea and coffee had taken the place of punch and champagne. Crys was fast asleep on the couch, while Nell rolled on the carpet with Erva, apparently teaching her some sort of self-defense move, and Sally played solitaire on the coffee table.

"*Midnight in a strange town / And it's another year...*" Angel sang softly.

"*Champagne out of plastic cups...*" Easy added in.

"No. *Champagne on the tour bus / Something something into gear,*" Blade suggested.

"*Driver puts it into gear,*" Easy agreed.

"*Band on the road / It's a workday, far from home,*" Dice said, walking over to them. All three of them looked at him, surprised. He shrugged. "Just because I can't sing doesn't mean I can't help with lyrics. You all give me a writing credit anyway, so...?"

Kimmy felt a surge of pride for him. Speaking up, joining in the songwriting, getting them to see that he was more than a pair of drumsticks and a pretty face.

"True enough, Dice." Angel nodded, considering the suggestion. *"Band on the road / It's a workday...* I like it. *Home* isn't great to rhyme with, though."

"What about *Band on the road / Far from home, just a workday...?*" Blade offered.

Dice grinned. "Band calling home / Reaching out, waiting to hear her say..."

Nell snorted with amusement from where she was on the floor. "It's the new year, you should be here, you haven't been home in a month." She mimicked the voice of a displeased girlfriend, and all the guys laughed.

"That's it, though," Angel said. "We can use spoken 'girlfriend' voices, record them with static for a bad connection."

Crys flopped over on the couch, far gone in sleep, and muttered, "It's your turn to change the diaper."

"Is she talking to you or to Camillo?" Angel asked Blade, as they all laughed again.

"Me, for sure," Blade said, smiling fondly at his sleeping wife. "She'd say please if she were asking him."

"Midnight in a strange town / And it's another year / Champagne on the tour bus / Driver puts it into gear," Angel sang, trying out the new song.

The others joined in. *"Band on the road / Far from home, just a workday / Band calling home / Reaching out, waiting to hear her say..."* Their voices trailed off.

Work began on the next verse.

"Kimmy, I need to show Erva how to do this thing, and she can't see properly when I'm doing it on her. Would you be okay letting me demonstrate with you?" Nell asked, rolling up off the floor to her feet in a smooth motion.

Oh, great. What Nell meant was that Kimmy should learn the thing too. But it was nice to be included, part of the Smidgettes, part of the family, and she could see Nell's point that self-defense was smart for road crew. She put on a smile. *It's got to be at least two in the morning.* "Sure, okay. What do I do?"

"Hug me from behind, like you're a big drunk guy getting friendly." When Kimmy complied, Nell's leg swept hers out from under her, and whomp, she was on her butt on the ground – but not too hard, because Nell was gentle on beginners like that. *Fun.* "See, Erva? Twist to the side, your knee goes behind, sweep the leg forward and straighten your back. Now you try it on me. Then it's Kimmy's turn. Sally?"

Sally shook her head at them, utterly uninterested.

Eventually Kimmy just lay on the floor, tired out, listening to the songwriters. Snippets of music started and stopped, the different voices trying out lyrics and melody, punctuated with Dice's spoken suggestions and his hands drumming a rhythm on the table and his thighs.

"You know, the Stirlings have a fully equipped recording studio here," Easy commented casually. "We could record this as soon as we've got it right. The Smidgettes can do the phone voices for us."

"Let's have Crys tell me I'm changing all the diapers for a week when I get home," Blade agreed, sleepily amused. He rubbed his eyes.

Angel chuckled. "Perfect. Okay, we'll finish writing it tomorrow and see where we are, polish it up the next day, and get into the studio by Thursday if everything's good. But it's almost three and we're all wrecked. Time to crash."

"Luke will be up with the sun," Blade said on a groan. "Goodnight, all." He hauled Crys up from the couch and steadied her with an arm around her waist.

"Goodnight, happy New Year!" she said, dozy and unfocused, prompting a chorus of the same as they headed out the door.

Dice came over and reached down a hand to pull Kimmy to her feet, then he did the same for Erva. Nell showed off, even at three in the morning, doing a shoulder roll and bouncing to a standing position. Then she and Easy waved goodnight and disappeared into their bedroom, and Kimmy followed Dice out the door.

"You wrote a song with the guys," she said to him as they walked back to their guesthouse. He didn't take her hand or anything, though they walked with a companionable closeness. The earlier sexy mood was gone, and she wondered if he'd still want to sleep with her the next day, sober and without the New Year's midnight magic.

"I did," he agreed, pleased. "It's been a good night."

I wouldn't trade a single moment of it, Kimmy thought, remembering the ecstasy of the orgasm he'd given her, and the rest of it. She hoped he felt the same.

When they got to the guesthouse, she took a last look at the starry sky before going inside, and made a wish. *Please let it happen. Please let us have each other, at least once.*

"You were wishing on a star, weren't you?" Dice asked.

She nodded, smiling. "And you're going to ask me what I wished for, and you *know* telling wishes means they won't come true."

His mouth curved into a half-smile, acknowledging the response she made every time he caught her wishing – on stars, on pennies in fountains. "Superstitious."

"Sometimes." She wouldn't wish him luck before he went onstage, either. *Good show, have fun, break a leg, rock out,* but never *good luck.* "Can I use the bathroom first?"

"Go ahead."

"Goodnight, Dice," Kimmy said, trying to keep things as normal as possible. He hesitated for a moment, then pulled her into his arms for a goodnight hug as he usually would. But feeling his body against hers hit differently now, and she sucked in a heavy breath.

"I know," he said, so softly she could hardly hear him, "I can't wait for tomorrow, Pretty Girl." With a muttered curse, he let her go, adding, "We're going to do this right, though." Then he headed into his room, turning back for a moment to give her a wry grin. "Sleep well."

A SOFT KNOCK ON THE DOOR WOKE KIMMY. SHE COULDN'T have been too deeply asleep for such a light sound to wake her, and given the way sunlight was streaming in between the slats of the blinds, painting glowing stripes of light on the floor and the end of the bed, she'd slept late and was probably halfway to waking already.

Dice's voice called, "Are you decent, Kimmy? I brought coffee for you."

"Yeah, come in," she called back, hitching herself up into a sitting position, with a quick check to make sure the spaghetti-strap cami she'd slept in hadn't skewed itself around and was, in fact, decently covering both her nipples. Her sleep shorts didn't hide much, but she wasn't bare below the waist, and in any case, she twitched the bedsheet over her legs for additional discretion. *Does it matter?* She'd never thought much about covering up around him before. She'd never thought he'd be looking. She changed her mind and flipped the sheet off again, just as he opened the door and edged his way in, balancing a tray with two steaming mugs and a cloth-covered basket which she guessed held some of Sam's johnny cakes – once the cook realized how much his guests enjoyed the sweet fried dough bites, a batch of them showed up with breakfast every morning.

"Hi," Dice said, lowering the tray to the bed by her knees. He sat down on the other side of it, near the end of the bed. He looked good, dressed for sun and the beach in a tank top and board shorts, his hair tied back in a ponytail.

"Hi," she said back, wondering if he liked what he saw too.

He took one of the coffee mugs from the tray and handed it to her. "I put your cream and sugar in for you."

"Thanks."

He took his coffee from the tray as well, and they sipped in silence for a minute.

"I don't want us to be awkward," he muttered under his breath after a while. He looked at her, his eyes serious. "Kimber, are we – what we talked about last night, I mean – do you still want to...? I mean, we should talk about it. Instead of just sitting here being weird."

"Wouldn't you think a bit of weird is normal in a situation like this?" she asked, and that made him crack a smile. "And yes, I still want to."

"Good." The relief in him was visible in his shoulders and the way his reluctant smile blossomed into a genuine one.

She shook her head at him, feeling the same relief inside herself. "You didn't think I'd take that away from you, after I promised?" she asked. "I only wanted to make sure it was a real decision for you, not a champagne decision."

"Which part?" he asked, his expression quizzical. "I mean, I'm up for all of it. But there were two parts to the arrangement. Are you still wanting me to... try to give you a baby?"

"I was *thinking* about your first time doing this, if you want it to be with me. But yes." She pulled her knees up and leaned forward to wrap her arms around them. "I want a baby. Dating as part of a road crew hasn't worked out for me, and I don't want to give up..." *My job. My life. You.* "...everything. But I also can't imagine living the rest of my life without being a parent, and if I'm going to do it on my own, then why not now, while the baby would be close in age to Luke and they could grow up together? There's a nanny on the tour, a nursery bus, catering has baby food. Maybe it's a dim idea, but..."

Dice nodded slowly, thoughtfully. "It'd be nice for Luke to have a sort of band cousin, yeah. If you're going to do it... now would be good."

"I couldn't ask for better DNA, if you're still offering. No strings, I promise. But you don't have to." She took a big gulp of coffee to quell the wobble she heard in her voice.

Dice reached out, waiting with an open palm until she put her hand into his. "Kimmy, you're my best friend. I would literally put my life on the line for you. If you're sure you want a baby, it would be an honor to participate in that, and I'll be whatever the baby needs me to be down the line – a father, an uncle, a friend. We can figure it out as we go." It sounded like a promise, a vow, and all at once everything felt just a tiny bit too big and real for her to handle.

"Thanks," she whispered, and his big warm hand gave her fingers a reassuring squeeze before letting go. She wondered if he was expecting to proceed to the devirginizing process right then and there, in full daylight, but he just laughed, almost as if he'd read her mind.

"Drink your coffee," he said. "Eat a johnny cake. I'm not going to jump on you right this second." Someone thumped on the front door of their guesthouse, and he added with a grimace, "No privacy in the middle of the day anyway." He hauled himself to his feet and grabbed a couple of johnny cakes out of the basket, to eat on the fly as he left her room to answer the knock.

Kimmy took a johnny cake too and ate it meditatively, listening to the voices in the main room. The band were going down to the beach to work on their new song and wanted Dice to come along with them. *Good.*

Within minutes, he stuck his head back into her room. "Are you coming to the beach? The others will be there too, I think."

She waved for him to go. "I'll walk down when I've finished my coffee and got my swimsuit on."

"No hurry. See you down there." And he was gone.

She had no intention of hurrying. She wanted to shave and moisturize her legs – who knew if there'd be time later.

♥

She noticed at dinner that he seemed tense, despite the relaxed day of songwriting and swimming and casual rounds of beach volleyball. Well, it wasn't surprising. She also spotted that he wasn't drinking, though she didn't think anyone else had noticed his glass held only fruit juice or sparkling water all evening. So she did the same, respecting his choice for them to be fully present and unaltered in the moment, even if a beer or a glass of wine might have eased the tension a bit.

Everyone was tired after staying up so late to greet the new year the night before. It was barely past nine when Crys started fading and said she'd rather sleep while she could, and Blade agreed. Camillo, who hadn't stayed up late and was off duty for the night, wanted to go down to the beach to see if there was any bioluminescence on their beach, given the famous bioluminescent bays in the Virgin Islands, and Easy and Nell said they'd go with him. Sally and Erva were in the middle of a game of poker with Angel and waved for the others to go without them.

Dice wrapped a friendly arm around Kimmy's shoulders as they walked back to their guesthouse, both of them hyperaware of Crys and Blade on the path ahead of them and the rest of the group heading down to the beach. *Don't mind us, just negotiating some friendly sex,* Kimmy thought, and a burble of laughter escaped her, making Dice jump. But he didn't say anything.

It wasn't until the Blakeharts' guesthouse door thumped shut and the footsteps of the rest of the party faded that Dice let out a long breath. "I'm so goddamn nervous, Kimmy," he whispered.

"No pressure," she whispered back. "It's only me."

She could almost hear him thinking *what if I can't?*

"We can just make out for a bit and go from there," she suggested. "Wanna kiss?"

"Yeah." Too gently, too carefully, he gathered her into his arms and lowered his mouth to hers in the tropical darkness. But it didn't take long before the hesitant kiss blossomed into something much more intense, his tongue parting her lips and thrusting deep with urgency and need. He sucked on and nipped her lower lip, then his mouth traveled to her earlobe, her neck, his hands rising to cup her breasts and thumb her nipples until she moaned and squirmed. "Oh, Kimber," he groaned. "I need..."

"I know," she gasped. "I feel it too. I want you so bad."

"Hold tight," he muttered, and hoisted her up over his shoulder like she weighed nothing. He'd lifted her like that plenty of times goofing around backstage, along with fireman's lifts and princess lifts, and she'd always laughed and had fun with it. Now, as he carried her up the steps to their guesthouse door, she was acutely aware of her position – her head hanging down his back and her butt vulnerably up on display, with his arm locked around her knees to hold her in place. An involuntary squirm of arousal got her a pat on the rear with his free hand, not quite a spank but enough to fuel her imagination and wet her panties. Had he meant to do that?

Call me Pretty Girl again, Boss, and tie me to the bed. But it wasn't the moment for that sort of thing.

He paused for a moment inside the door, then asked, "My bed okay?" in a way that wasn't really a question.

"Sure." It didn't matter to her which bed they used, and if he'd feel more comfortable in his space, she was all in favor of that.

A few powerful strides brought them into his bedroom, and he tossed her onto the bed without turning on any lights. She wondered for a moment if he was feeling shy and wanted darkness, then the hiss of a match was followed by a flame, and she saw that he was lighting candles. Many candles. He'd gathered at least a dozen and had them grouped on the bedside tables and windowsill, and the warm, flickering light as he lit them all showed an extremely tidy room and a neatly made bed. She could smell fresh linen and realized that he must have asked Mariel for clean sheets and changed his bed for this.

"This is pretty," she said, gesturing at the candles. "You wanted a romantic setting for your first time, huh?"

"I wanted to make it nice for *you*, Kimmy. You're such a gift in my life, I can hardly believe it."

And then he began to strip off his clothes.

One couldn't belong to a rock tour and be self-conscious about nudity. But she'd always tried not to look at him specifically, not fully nude anyway, because it seemed better not to seek out temptation. Now, on this island, in this place that seemed almost unreal, like it was set apart out of time, she could look, and the thing that she'd so carefully not thought about for years was happening. She watched as his shirt fell to the floor, and then his shorts and underwear. And there was nothing wrong with him at all.

Naked, he got onto the bed and lay down beside her, settling a hand onto her bare abdomen where her t-shirt rode up. His fingers stroked her skin lazily, then he started to work the t-shirt upward. She lifted her shoulders from the bed and raised her arms so he could slide it off.

"You have such nice underwear," he said, tracing the edge of her bra down the slope of one breast in appreciation. "And an even nicer body."

She'd chosen a sheer set with tiny pink rosebuds embroidered all over, the cream silk so translucent that it hid nothing. Visibly entranced, he bent his head to kiss her there, gently at first, then teasing her nipples through the silk with his lips and tongue. As she gasped and squirmed, she could feel his arousal growing even firmer against her inner thigh, which reminded her of how very big he was. "I'm going to need some pretty good foreplay to fit you," she mumbled, her body tingling all over as he unsnapped her shorts and tugged them and her panties down.

"How about I get you good and wet, then?" he asked with a grin, moving down to settle himself between her thighs and apply his tongue for that purpose with dizzying effectiveness.

"Dice," she panted. "Dice." Then his fingers were involved too, probing and stretching, turning her into a mass of sensation. Time lost all meaning. "Please..." She tried to hold off her climax, wanting him inside her. Blessedly, he was climbing over her, positioning himself, and she reached down to guide him in. "Oooh..." *Fuck, he's big.*

His eyes got really wide and he paused, breathing hard. "You good?"

"Yeah. Just... slow."

"I can do slow," he gritted out, even though his tense face suggested he was holding on to an impossibility.

She breathed and told her body to relax, to adjust. Inch by inch, with gravity and small movements, he pushed in until she'd taken all of him.

"Christ, Kimber, you're absolute heaven," he groaned, overcome with sensation. His hips jerked, inexorably needing to thrust, though he held himself as still as possible. "Can I move yet? I don't want to hurt you."

"Go ahead, I'm fine," she told him, but he gave her a doubtful look, and she knew he could tell she'd lost the urgency of before. "Helps if you touch me," she explained.

"Ahh, got it. Sorry." Bracing himself on one arm, he reached down with the other hand, his fingertips exploring, feeling himself embedded in her, caressing and seeking until he found the spot that made her twitch and moan. At the involuntary movement of her hips, his hips flexed too, and he started to move, pumping into her faster and faster. The overwhelming fullness and friction mixed with the stimulation from his hand and Kimmy once again found herself on the edge of orgasm. Somewhere, she heard Dice's voice saying, "Come for me, Pretty Girl," and she let herself be carried away on a wave of bliss. "Holy fuck," she heard him say. "Oh, Kimber..." and his full weight collapsed over her in a moment of mindless satiation before he rolled them to their sides so he wouldn't be crushing her. "Thank you," he whispered.

"Drummers do it better than anyone else," she murmured against his chest. "That was lovely."

They lay there together in the afterglow, skin to skin, bodies still joined. It wasn't until they slipped apart and she felt his semen oozing out of her that reality hit, dissipating the hazy pleasant feelings. "Got tissues?" she asked wryly. He wouldn't have a clue about this part, and she had no practical experience with it since she'd always used condoms, but what went in had to come out. *It's no worse than letting him come on my stomach*, she reminded herself, *and I liked that.*

"Oh," Dice said, with a hint of a blush creeping across his face as he figured out why she was asking. "Hadn't thought about that. Sorry! I'll go get you some." He came back with a whole box of tissues, and a wet washcloth too, which cleaned things up enough that she could scoot to the bathroom with a wad of tissues clutched between her legs.

"There's just no way to make this no-condom cleanup sexy," she grumbled as she emerged from the bathroom afterward. From where she stood, she could see through his bedroom door to where he lay on the bed, grinning at her.

"Oh, I don't know," he said. "We could skip the tissues and I could watch you walk across the room with my cum dripping down your thighs?"

"That's pretty kinky of you," she commented without inflection, and her heart beat a little faster at the thought of him ordering her to do just that. *Yes, Boss.*

He looked horrified. "I was kidding!"

"Were you?" She laughed, and ducked into her room to put on her sleep shorts and cami.

"You'll stay with me tonight, won't you?" he called out, so she headed back to his room, where he'd put on his boxers and turned down the blankets – everything had happened on top of the quilt. "I mean, you don't have to. I just... lying here alone seems so..."

"I know. A sleepover is fine," she said. But he didn't move to get into bed and seemed wide awake – maybe feeling a bit discombobulated by the whole thing – so she asked, "Do you want to go look at the stars for a bit, first?"

♥

The night was quiet, with very little breeze to rustle the palms or stir up big waves, so only the gentle slopping sound of the sea meeting the shore echoed as Kimmy and Dice walked down to the beach, each with a flashlight because the moon wouldn't be up until nearly dawn.

She wore one of his hoodies, big enough to engulf her and thoroughly cover her sleep shorts and more, and he'd pulled on the same shorts he'd been wearing before and a tropical-print shirt that he hadn't bothered to button.

They switched off their flashlights once they reached the open beach.

The magnificent sky stretched overhead, filled with stars, and Kimmy looked up at them in appreciation. "Got my wish," she said to Dice with a grin. *Thank you, stars!*

"Yeah?" he asked thoughtfully. It was too dark to see much of his expression, even in the starlight.

"You okay, friend?" She knew he might not answer, but it couldn't hurt to ask, give him a chance to talk if he wanted it. She put a slight emphasis on the word *friend,* hoping to assure him that she was his friend before anything else and that she wouldn't turn into a stranger or let emotional drama come between them.

He sat down on the sand without answering, so she sat beside him, and he automatically put an arm around her and pulled her close. "I don't feel different," he said after a while. "I thought I'd feel different. I spent so long feeling like... like I wasn't a real man... because I couldn't..."

"You never needed sex to make you a man," she told him, putting every possible bit of kindness and affection into her voice. "Think about it. It doesn't even take *having* a dick, much less using it. Trans men are men, yeah?"

"Of course."

"And if a man is in a wheelchair and doesn't have functioning equipment down there – still a man? Or someone who *chooses* to not participate in sex, because he doesn't feel the urge or for any reason that seems good to him – also still a man?"

She could feel his groan as her point hit him. "Yes. Christ, yes, Kimmy. I'm a goof."

"No, you're not. I totally get why you'd look at your band brothers as the standards of masculinity and doubt yourself when that wasn't your experience. I'm just saying you *know* manhood isn't about sex, really. But I understand expecting to feel different, when you'd waited so long to have this one particular experience." She leaned her head against his shoulder and waited for him to think it through.

"I don't know what I expected," he said after a while. "But you made it perfect."

"Good," she said. "A good time was had by all." Which then struck her as funny, so she laughed, and because laughter is contagious he laughed too, and the fact that they were laughing about it struck them as funnier still until they were hugging each other for support and wheezing.

Sometime after the laughter had died away, he asked in a diffident voice, "This baby-making thing... it's going to take more than one shot, right?"

And Kimmy felt something warm and happy begin to glow inside her. *He wants more of me.* "Oh, for sure. I think there's only something like a one-in-four chance of us getting me pregnant each month we try, so... assuming you want to keep going with it..." She hoped her voice sounded steady and nonchalant.

"Yes! As often as you want." His enthusiasm was unmistakable. Hardly surprising, of course, and she tried to remember that it didn't make *her* special. Still...

They stayed on the beach talking until the waning crescent moon rose over the horizon and they realized how late it was.

"You'll still sleep over in my bed tonight?" Dice asked as they walked back up the path, flashlight beams swinging ahead of them.

"I'd like that," Kimmy said.

♥

She woke in the morning to a sensation of unusual warmth, and only slowly remembered that she was in Dice's bed, with his big body sprawled beside her, radiating heat. Unfortunately, the urge to use the bathroom outweighed the pleasure of wallowing in comfort, so she rolled herself to a sitting position and got up.

"Come back to bed," he mumbled, half asleep.

"I'm just going pee; I'll be right back."

When she returned, feeling relieved and with fresh breath, he'd flopped over onto his back and had his eyes open. His hair, loose for once and not held back by a hair tie or bandanna, fanned out over the pillow in silky disarray. "Waking up next to you was nice," he said. "You can sleep in my bed anytime."

She got onto the bed and sat cross-legged next to him. "It was nice," she agreed. "Really nice. But I don't want to give anyone on the tour ideas. I mean, it's not like we're *dating*. I don't want anyone thinking I'm putting out to get special privileges or anything."

He bit his lip, thinking about that. "Everyone knows we're friends, first and last and above anything else. I've never thought of myself as your employer... you're like a part of me. I couldn't fire you any more than I could fire my own hands. But I don't want to make things hard for you with the rest of the crew, yeah."

It's easy to think like that when you're the employer. But he meant well, and she believed *he* believed the band would never let her go. If Angel thought she was being unprofessional, though... "You're like a part of me too. It's just better to keep things professional while we're working and around people we work with, okay?"

"No problem."

And there was another issue she needed to explain to him. "Speaking of keeping things professional, um, my kink is bedroom-only, so... well, Boss and Pretty Girl don't come out to play while we're working. That's a hard boundary for me."

He looked at her with wide eyes, and she realized that she'd just given voice to something that had been unspoken and pretty much unexplored between them. Suddenly, the room seemed hotter and there wasn't enough oxygen in the air. "Tell me about Pretty Girl, then," Dice said, after the silence had stretched on for too long.

"I..." She'd long ago discarded any shame or shyness about what got her going, but she'd never expected to be talking to Dice about it, never figured her sweet cinnamon roll of a drummer would be sitting there looking at her with an intriguingly unreadable expression on his face as he waited for her to describe her sexual self. *Tell me about Pretty Girl.* Maybe talking in third person would make it easier? "She... likes... dirty talk and being told what to do."

"I can do that. What else?"

"She likes to wait for permission to come."

He grinned at that and gestured for her to go on.

"She loves being tied up. She has the best orgasms after being spanked–" Her words and brain screeched to an emergency stop as his eyebrows rose. Had that last bit been too much for him? "None of it is *necessary* for me, though," she added quickly. "Vanilla is a very good flavor too. But something in you – Boss – brings out the side of me you've named Pretty Girl, and I'm up for exploring it with you, if you want that. Since we've got a bit of babymaking to do anyway."

"You, ah, want me to tie you up and *spank* you?" he asked, unable to meet her eyes, but she could hear an edge of curiosity in his voice, and despite the blush and hesitation on his face, his body was unmistakably responding to the thought of it.

She shrugged, laughing gently at his dismay, hoping he could see that it wasn't a big deal either way. "Only if it turns you on. What do *you* want to do with me, Boss?"

"It might take me a minute to get my mind around all this," he said. "But damn." He reached out for her, encouraging her to lie down and cuddle with him, stroking down her back so gently. But his hand paused and lingered for a moment on her butt cheek, and she wondered what he was thinking.

A bang on the outside door, which they hadn't locked, gave them a moment's notice, but there wasn't time to even move before Easy pushed Dice's door open with another token knock. Given that Kimmy was in bed with Dice and not wearing very much, it wasn't likely that *just friends* was going to cover the situation.

"Shit, oops, sorry," Easy said in surprise. "Let's pretend I knocked and waited. Uh, hello, Kimmy. Dice, we're wanting to start work on 'Band on the Road', if you're ready to get up?"

"Smooth, Ease. Really smooth," Dice said, laughing as he rolled out of bed and grabbed clothes to put on. "Give me a few seconds."

Kimmy got up too. Her sleep shorts and cami *did* sort of cover her, and Easy wasn't a prudish sort. He'd just have to deal with it. "Okay, see you later, guys," she said as casually as she could, heading for the door.

♥

Once she'd showered and dressed, Kimmy walked down to the main house in search of something to eat. She brought the romance novel she was currently reading – thankfully she'd finished the slow-burn one that had so annoyed her on the airplane, and was now enjoying a marriage-of-convenience Regency romance with lots of clandestine finger-banging under empire-waist gowns in drawing rooms and carriages.

Sam was in the kitchen and asked her if she wanted a cooked breakfast, but she could see he'd already washed the frying pan and it would probably be lunchtime soon, so she told him she'd be just fine with some toast. He laughed at her in a *that's not breakfast* way and she ended up with decadent avocado toast topped with chopped cashews and a squeeze of lime juice, which he put together for her in what seemed like seconds. She thanked him profusely and took it and a huge mug of coffee out to the patio, where she settled herself to eat and read.

Sally and Erva were already on the patio – Erva dozing on her sun lounger, and Sally watching or reading something on her phone and chuckling to herself every so often. Nell was in the small gym in the main house, visible through a plate glass window, lifting weights with focused power, evidently not planning to stop for a while.

"Where's Crys?" Kimmy asked, not seeing the guitarist's wife.

"She went back to bed after breakfast," Sally said with a grimace. "Apparently Luke was a little monster last night, up every hour. Camillo's taken him on a walk now."

Am I making a terrible mistake? Kimmy knew she could still – probably – change her mind. There was barely a chance she'd conceived in just one night. That was the stuff of romance novels, but improbable on a statistical basis. Maybe a twenty percent chance? Okay, that wasn't tiny, but... *Little monster. What am I doing?*

Somehow she ate the avocado toast and drank her coffee.

Angel came out to the patio and asked Sally if she'd record a phone call snippet for the song they were working on. "Something like, 'You're always on the road! It's never going to end. And what about me? You promised we'd go on a getaway soon, but you can't even get home for a weekend.' Make up whatever shit you like."

"Okay, why not?" Sally got up and put her phone in her pocket.

"I'll get you next, Erva. Kimmy, you want to record one too?"

"Sure."

Sally followed Angel inside, and from her sun lounger on the patio, Kimmy could see them stopping into the gym to presumably ask Nell the same thing. It would be fun to be part of a Smidge song.

♥

It wasn't until the afternoon that she got her turn. She'd read nearly a third of the Regency romance and everyone had taken a break for lunch before Angel called her and said it was time to do hers. She'd briefly seen the studio setup when they'd had a tour of the place on arrival – the space was split in two, with a control room that you had to pass through to reach the door to the soundproofed recording chamber, visible from the recording desk through a big window.

As she arrived in the control room, which was like the bridge of a ship with all the soundboards and equipment and captain's chairs, she saw that the red recording light over the door was on. Crys was in the recording room ahead of her, with a headset on, standing in front of a microphone with a pop filter, listening as Angel talked to her through the headset from the control room. "Again, babe, and try to sound a little pissed off this time. Imagine you haven't seen Blade in weeks, and you don't have Camillo to help with Luke. You've been changing *all* the diapers and doing *all* the night feedings. Go!"

Through the speakers, everyone in the control room could hear Crys saying, in a sweet but frustrated voice, "I love you, but when you get home, you are changing every single diaper for a month, I swear!"

"That's the one," Angel said, as the other band members clapped.

Blade covered his face with a hand and muttered, "I'm never leaving her at home; I don't want to hear that voice for real." But he was grinning.

"Your turn, Sparkles," Easy said to Kimmy, as the red light went out and Crys took off the headset. Was he smirking at her, or was she imagining it out of conflicted feelings and embarrassment at being caught in Dice's bed?

"You know I'm always professional when we're working," she reminded him tartly.

Angel overheard her and said, "Of course you are, Kimmy. Don't worry, you'll be paid for the recording session."

Which wasn't what she'd meant at all. "I wasn't thinking about that, honestly," she said. "I just want to do my best. What am I supposed to say for it?" Behind Angel, Easy's grin got wider, and Dice gave her a chagrined and sympathetic look. Blade, talking to Crys, was thankfully oblivious.

After a bit of discussion, Kimmy found herself in the recording room, with the headset on, saying, "The tour's been extended for another three weeks? What about my cousin's wedding? You promised you'd be home for that." The fictitious cousin had been Dice's idea.

With the phone voices done, they all listened to the playback. The band hadn't recorded any of the chorus yet, but they sang it there in the control room – *"Band on the road / Far from home, just a workday / Band calling home / Reaching out, waiting to hear her say..."* and then played the recorded voices, overlapped slightly with a hiss and pop of added static that believably sounded like bad phone connections coming through to a tour bus or the underbelly of an arena. It sounded phenomenal, a hit waiting to happen.

"I'd love to have a soprano voice doing harmony above the second part of the chorus, though – adding *When will you be home?* on top of the drawn-out *Band on the road* following the phone voices, and then *I feel so alone* on top of *Band calling home*. What do you guys think? We could leave space and add it in later..."

"I like it," Blade agreed, nodding as he considered the concept. "We've never been a backup-singers kind of band, and I don't want to change that, but I can see how it would work for this song. Who would we ask, though? Feature a big name or just get some random talent to record it?"

"Kimmy could do it," Dice said.

They all looked at her.

"Me?" she asked in what came out as a very small and squeaky voice.

"You know you can," Dice assured her. "She sings backup for her brothers' band in bars around Michigan any time she can get home for it," he explained to the others. "No earthly clue why you're so modest about it, Kimmy, you're good."

"Yeah?" Angel said drily, and in answer Dice held out his phone with an online video queued up ready to play.

And with a tap on the screen, there was Friends With Royalty doing their thing at the Magic Bag, and Kimmy right on stage singing backup, for once not keeping a lid on the power and range of her voice.

The end of the song was met with a moment of impressed silence.

"Why've you been hiding this from us, Sparkles?" Easy asked in astonishment. "You're really talented."

Kimmy shook her head. "I only want to be a drum tech. I'm not – I mean, I like singing, I like being onstage, but I don't want to give up my crew position for it. I don't want to *be* a backup singer, except once in a while for fun, if that makes sense."

"Do you get stage fright?" Blade asked sympathetically.

"No, I just... like my life as it is," she explained.

Angel nodded. "Okay, no worries, no pressure. We just want you to rehearse and record a little bit of harmony for this one song. Today and tomorrow. We'll figure out how to handle it during shows another time – if you don't want to sing onstage, we can get touring backup singers or use the recording – but let's get this song finished before we have to leave paradise, all right?"

"I'll do it," she agreed. Couldn't say no, with Dice putting her forward and cheering her on. She'd shown him, and all of them, FWR videos before – that was how the Baker brothers had got the chance to open for Smidge in December – so why had she never thought Dice might stumble across one with her singing in it?

"Good. Thanks," Angel said. "I want to have something new and complete to offer the Valancy people, if they're able to get us away from–"

"Awfully Hateful," Easy muttered, pretending to disguise it with a cough, and they all chuckled, even Angel, though he didn't usually descend to calling their label that.

♥

When they rehearsed, Kimmy discovered that the few bits of vocal harmony in "Band on the Road" were perfect for her, a soaring lonely soprano rising over the men's voices at the end of each chorus. And Dice looked so proud of her, as though she were doing something difficult or valuable. He always cheered her on and stood up for her – the perfect best friend.

So no one thought anything of it when he suggested she go up to bed early to rest her voice for the next day's recording session. "I'll bring you some lemon-ginger tea," he offered.

Angel nodded with approval, as lemon-ginger tea with honey was his own habitual throat soother, a preference well known to anyone close to the band. "Good thought. I'll put the kettle on and we can make a pot of it. The rest of us can have some too, and we should all get an early night as well."

"Yes, please, some tea would be nice," Kimmy said. "Goodnight, everyone."

"I'll walk with you," Crys said. "Chris, my love, could you bring me some tea too? Not that I'm singing or anything, I just like it," she added.

"I always forget Blade's name is actually Christopher," Kimmy commented as they walked up to the guesthouses.

Crys laughed. "It's so silly, us being Crys and Chris. I could just call him by his band name like everyone else does, but... I think it helps to remind him that he's more than just a rock star to me." They reached the point where the path split, and Crys sighed. "Wish me luck! I hope Luke doesn't wake up too many times tonight."

"You're not... sorry you had a baby, are you?" Kimmy blurted out, unable to keep from asking.

That made Crys laugh again, and an adoring look flooded her face as she thought about her little one. "Not at all. He's the sweetest. I can deal with being tired when he's not sleeping well, and gritching to my friends about it helps on the difficult days. But I wouldn't trade my little Lukey for anything in the world."

"That's sweet," Kimmy said. "I'm so glad."

Crys cocked her head to one side, looking at Kimmy thoughtfully. "I'm not saying it isn't hard, you know. Just... worth it."

"I get that. I– Yeah. Anyway, goodnight!"

"Goodnight!"

They headed off along their separate paths.

As she walked the rest of the way to her guesthouse, Kimmy thought about Dice sending her off to bed. Was that what she thought it might be? A very gentle order, the beginning of playtime for Boss and Pretty Girl? Or just a thoughtful friend wanting an early night for someone who'd be recording a very real backup track for what could be a huge hit the next day?

She'd intended to just put on her usual sleep shorts and cami for bed, but when she got to her room, she looked through her lingerie bag instead and chose a sheer lilac babydoll set to wear. *Might as well give him a clear sign that I'm up for it.*

She looped some long black satin ribbons around her wrists, leaving the ends trailing loose – a mere suggestion of bondage, aesthetic ties, but usable for the purpose if he felt so inclined. Then she lay down to read her book quietly, like a good girl, waiting for him.

chapter

7

"KIMMY?" DICE'S VOICE CALLED FROM THE MAIN ROOM of the guesthouse. "Come get your tea."

"Coming," she replied, and got up to join him, trailing ribbons from her wrists to the floor and knowing that the sheer chiffon of her babydoll sleepwear was a blatant invitation. *Why am I doing this?* she asked herself in the moment before she stepped out from her room. And although she wanted to deny it, she all at once recognized in the most guarded part of herself that she wanted him to see her as sexy, a lover, not just a friend who was willing to provide him with physical experiences in exchange for a baby. *Oh, shit.* That was a dangerous slope to go down if they wanted to keep their friendship intact. But it was too late to go back and change now. One step, two steps, and she was in his line of sight. "Hi, Dice."

He blinked at her, and she could feel herself blushing as he looked her up and down with a stunned expression on his face. "Christ on a stick, Kimber," he muttered.

Too much. Too far. "Sorry," she said. It was a good thing – and maybe a near thing – that he hadn't dropped either of the two mugs he carried. "I can go change. I'm sorry."

"No! Please don't. I–" He paused, looking at her and biting his lip. "You're my best friend and I respect you so much, but... when you look like *that*, it makes me want to do bad things to you. Those ribbons..."

A flood of warmth, of relief, washed over her as understanding hit her. "Oh?" She held up her hands to give him a better look at the ribbons. "These? That's kind of what they're for, right? Nothing's *bad* if you've got consent."

He gave a small huff of doubt, but held out one of the mugs to her. "Come sit and drink your tea. It's good for your throat, I'm told."

So they sat on the couch in the main room, sipping lemon-ginger tea and watching each other in mostly silence.

"Are you excited to have your voice on a Smidge song?" he asked.

"I guess so," she said. "I mean, I already feel like part of your music because I'm there, helping you. But it's cool to have a chance to sing. Thanks for suggesting me."

After a while, he asked her if the tea was good, and she agreed that it was. There was only a little left in her mug. Their eyes met.

"Finish it, Pretty Girl," he said, his voice deepening.

"Yes, Boss." She drank down the last few sips and placed the mug on an end table with a soft clunk. Slowly, thoughtfully, he reached out and took hold of the silky ribbons hanging from her wrists, one in each hand, and with a light tug he brought her hands out in front of her. Under his control, like a puppet.

"You got a safeword or something?" he asked tensely. "Limits? Stuff you won't do?"

"Marshmallow. And I don't like cum near my eyes, though anywhere else is fine."

"That's fair, don't think I'd want it in my eyes either."

When he stood, still holding onto the ribbons a few inches above her hands, she was drawn to her feet too. "These damn ribbons are a huge fucking turn-on," he gritted out, in a voice close to a growl. "You're making it very difficult to keep thinking of you in friend terms; all I can think about is absolutely railing you."

"Yes, please? I mean, I was hoping you would."

He grinned and pulled her close, not letting go of the ribbons so her arms were trapped between them as one of his hands cupped the back of her neck and the other gripped her upper arm – not hurting, but firm, the touch of a man who was beginning to accept and relish his taste for dominance. His lips were only a breath away from hers when he asked softly, "Is your mouth mine, Pretty Girl?"

"Yes, Boss."

"Good." He closed that last bit of distance and kissed her, hard and intense, his tongue driving into her mouth with ownership and need, making her melt. Then his kisses moved on, to her ear, to her neck, to her shoulder, licking and sucking and lightly nipping, a restrained threat of teeth. When she shivered at the thought of being marked by him, he laughed against her skin. "Don't worry, I won't leave a mark where anyone might see it." And he knelt down and brought his mouth to the sensitive skin of one inner thigh, pushing the fabric of her babydoll shorts out of the way and sucking a love bite into existence with a sting of pressure-pain, then soothing it with kisses. "There. Mine. Marked at the gate to heaven."

Mine. Yes, for as long as this lasted, her body would be his.

"Got an idea. Put your hands behind your head," he told her, and when she did so, he tied the ribbons at her wrists into a bow, effectively keeping them there. Then his hands were free to roam over her body, stroking and caressing but not quite getting to anywhere that mattered until she was squirming with frustration and need.

At last, he turned her around and bent her over the thick, padded back of the couch, lifting her feet off the ground. Pulled down her shorts, leaving her desperately exposed and vulnerable, still with her hands tied behind her head and her face pressed into the cushions. "Can you breathe like that?" he asked, and gave her shoulder an encouraging squeeze at her muffled affirmative. "Good girl." His hand stroked over her bare butt and gave her a firm pat – not a slap, not even a tap, but the mere hint of it sent her to the edge. "Some things I've got to work up to," he admitted with a rueful chuckle. "But damn, you look adorable like that. Don't come yet," he warned her as his fingers slipped between her legs.

"Dice!" she protested, squashing her face deeper into the cushions, trying to resist the temptation to let his touch carry her away. "I can't–"

"Tell me," he commanded, his fingers tormenting her with pleasure. "Tell me you want me inside you. Tell me you need me."

"Yes," she gasped. "I need you inside me."

This time, the pressure of him filling her was easier to take, and he was able to thrust all the way in with little adjustment and more confidence. He began to move, a slow and sensual thrusting – natural rhythm which should not have been surprising from a drummer. The angle of it was perfection and she could feel herself coming to the edge again when she felt his hand at the base of her spine and then his wet thumb stroked her rear opening, gently probing but not yet entering. "Dice!"

"You have a safeword," he reminded her, with a thrilling combination of curiosity and authority. "Do you want to use it?"

"No, just... surprised." She somehow made herself form words to answer, since he'd asked her a direct question, but her brain was fused with pleasure. "I want... everything. Please. I need to come." Begging now, shameless, trembling on the edge of a powerful orgasm that waited like a tsunami to rush over her. The slippery pressure of his thumb penetrating the tight sphincter combined with the fullness she was already feeling from his cock to create an overwhelming sensation.

He picked up pace and force until he was driving into her hard and fast, his hips slapping against her backside. And just when she thought she couldn't possibly hold out any longer, he reached around with his other hand to add his fingers to the mix, groaning, "You can come now, Pretty Girl," as he pushed her past her breaking point – and his too, because somewhere in the utter disintegration that followed, she could feel him slumped over her, gasping for breath as though he'd run a marathon.

♥

She felt herself being lifted, but only realized that he'd carried her to the bathroom when he laid her down in the empty tub. "You all right, Kimmy?" he asked gently, removing the ribbons from her wrists and pulling the babydoll top over her head. She still felt incoherent but must have answered in some way because he stroked her cheek and said, "It was amazing for me too. Thank you."

He turned on the water and tested the temperature against his hand before using the handheld sprayer to clean her up, chuckling softly when the jet of water stimulated too-sensitive places and made her moan. Then he stepped into the tub as well, giving himself a rinse-off before putting the plug in. He dumped a capful of bubble bath under the faucet and shifted her around so that he sat behind her with his knees on either side of her and her head leaning back against his chest. It was a bit of a tight fit, but soothing and cozy with the warm water rising and the scented bubbles everywhere.

Blissed out and safe, she floated in a place between sleep and waking, and gradually became aware of Dice talking – maybe to her, or maybe to himself.

"I still feel kind of dirty for some of what I was thinking and even what I did, but Christ, what a rush to be assertive and in charge, taking care of things, calling the shots, being the one to give you what you needed." He hummed with satisfaction, a deep vibration she could feel against his chest. "Didn't know sex could be like that. Would you really have liked it if I'd smacked your butt, Kimmy?"

"Light smacks, sure," she murmured, feeling sleepy and lazy. "Harder, I don't know if *like* is the right word, but it sends me into orbit after. Endorphins or something. Tonight was a good one, though. You did me good."

"Not bad for a second time out, hey?" Both laughter and contentment were evident in his voice. "We should get out of this tub and dry off at some point. Get some sleep."

"We should." She couldn't put much enthusiasm into that, because moving didn't seem like much fun, but eventually he hauled her upright and they rinsed the bubbles off before getting out.

This time, Dice locked his bedroom door.

♥

Recording a song lent a semblance of normalcy to the tropical vacation.

Kimmy was so busy trying to get the drum kit set up to suit Dice, she didn't have time to worry about singing. The others had their easily portable instruments with them, of course, but even if they'd known they'd have access to a recording studio and the inspiration for a song, it wouldn't have been feasible to bring Dice's drum kit on their getaway. Fortunately, the studio had an enviable drum kit in situ, and with a concentrated bit of effort, Kimmy and Dice got it adjusted to mimic his usual setup.

Maybe she was thoroughly relaxed from the night before, or maybe her drum tech role kept her in the right headspace, or maybe it was just such a gloriously engaging song that the backup vocals were a pleasure, but when it came time to record her part, Kimmy flew through it without hesitation. They ran through a few variations, until she nailed the exact sound that Angel had wanted. He hugged her afterward, telling her it was the perfect touch for the song. "We can use the recording if you don't want to sing onstage," he said, "but if you like the idea, we can set up a mic for you at the back, and you'll never be far from the drum riser."

She'd never wanted anything to distract her from complete efficiency and focus as a drum tech. *I can't be two things at once,* she'd told her brothers over and over. How could the band trust her to be the best possible drum tech if she was also riding the rush of singing for an audience? But it was hard to argue with Angel's encouraging, approving smile.

Dice came up behind her and put a friendly arm around her shoulders, saying, "You can do both," as though he'd read her mind. Maybe he *did* know what she was thinking; over the years of their friendship, they'd had a few conversations about the rush of performing and others about her concern that taking on more backstage tasks might divert her focus from the drum riser. He'd always reminded her she was capable of multitasking. "No pressure, but trust yourself."

"Anything for the band," she said lightly. "I'll give it a shot."

"Good." Angel gave her a friendly fist bump, pleased, before he turned back to the sound desk. "Go relax now, Kimmy. You did great."

The others added their appreciation with a round of applause, and Blade gave her one of his rare genuine smiles. *Friendship.* She'd always thought of Dice as her friend, but they were all her friends too, far more than employers or workmates or even friends of her friend. Raising a child around the Smidge family would be good. It would be enough.

♥

They listened to the finished track at dinner. Got up from the table and danced to it, knowing beyond a doubt that they'd recorded a hit, something that would be played at New Year's parties for decades to come. *Midnight in a strange town / And it's another year...* Angel opened a bottle of champagne and poured a round, saying they needed to toast the song and wish success for it.

Kimmy listened to her voice rising over the second half of the chorus, like a train whistle in the night – *When will you be home? I feel so alone.* When Angel handed her a glass of champagne, she looked at the bubbles rising and tried to wish for the song's success, but the wish wouldn't form in her mind. She could only think of Dice.

"Funny how it's both true and not true," Dice was saying to the others. "I mean, we are on the road a lot, more than any of us want, and most holidays are workdays and we do end up drinking our New Year's champagne out of plastic cups at three in the morning on our way to the next city, but... not this year. And the song makes it sound like there's conflict, but no one's actually separated and alone."

Angel nodded. "And yet, that lonely vibe is what's going to give it the potential to go platinum. No one really cares if we're tired and worn down from too much touring. The relationship tension is what's going to feel real to people, the idea of being far from someone you love, and that love getting strained. The fake bit."

"People are weird," Blade said.

"Cheers," Easy said, holding up his champagne, so they all ended up toasting the idea that people are weird along with the song's future success.

Someone's phone chimed an incoming message alert. *Not mine,* Kimmy thought, having kept hers in airplane mode as instructed.

"YES!" Angel shouted, startling them all as he pumped a fist in the air, his phone clutched in his other hand. "Valancy fucking did it! Arleigh Hayward's going to let us go. I can hardly believe it, but Torquil Stirling just texted me, *Success, you're ours, a bit of litigation around concert no-shows to sort out but we've got it handled.* I guess that was their New Year's Eve bash we blew off?"

"The Stirlings are pretty badass," Sally agreed. "I want to be Cynthia Stirling when I grow up."

Easy smiled. "They've taken very good care of the Opals and Gil. I think it'll be a good move for us."

"For sure," Angel said. "This is the beginning of our best era yet, I can feel it." He looked down at his phone again. "He wants an online conference tomorrow morning. I've told him we recorded a song today; they're excited and want to hear it. I hope you've all had enough vacation, though, because this probably means we're going home soon."

"There's no such thing as enough vacation," Erva pointed out, "but we've got shows waiting – or do we?"

"We'll find out tomorrow," Angel said, "and it'll depend on the lawyers, but I expect we'll be able to honor anything we've already committed to."

Crys smiled as she stood by the table bouncing and cuddling a fussy Luke. "Even if we fly home tomorrow, it's been so lovely to have this escape week in paradise, though I feel like I've slept through most of it. We all needed it."

♥

In the middle of the night, Kimmy woke to find Dice lying awake next to her. "What's wrong?" she asked him.

"Nothing," he said, then sighed. "I don't want this to be over, Kimber. Not the vacation – I mean, Crys wasn't wrong when she said we'd all needed one, but I'm rested and ready to get back to work. It's being here with you that I'll miss. Coming up to our guesthouse together at night. Lying in bed with you at night, waking up together. Discovering... things."

"You don't think I'm a freak, then?" she asked, too sleepy to censor herself.

"Christ, no!" He rolled up onto one elbow to look down at her. "Pretty sure I'm the freak, thank you. Might take me awhile to admit to all the things I fantasize about..."

That made her smile. "Nothing's over," she reassured him. "It'll be a bit different, but not over. We'll find a way. I still want that baby you promised me," she added, just in case he might think she was expecting something awkward from him, a romantic declaration of some sort. Above all, she wasn't going to break their promise to each other not to let their friendship be affected. "And you deserve to try everything, find out what really gets you going. Why settle for a vanilla life?"

He flopped onto his back, looking up at the ceiling. "It won't be the same."

"I know." She stroked his hair away from his face, savoring the moment. He was right. It wouldn't be the same.

♥

Kimmy, naturally, wasn't included in the online meeting with the Valancy board the next morning, but they were done before noon. "They loved 'Band on the Road' and want to release it as a single before our next album," Angel said over lunch. "We'll go home and sign things officially, but we've got a verbal commitment and these old-school guys are the sort to honor that stuff. No hateful shenanigans." It was the closest he'd ever come to using the nickname for Arleigh Hayward that the others had gleefully embraced. "But we've got to get home tonight. Tomorrow's a show day."

It was a Friday – they'd all lost track of the days – and Smidge was booked for a Saturday night concert in Chicago, a commitment that Valancy was keen for them to live up to. Phil and Mack would be rounding up the crew and getting the buses and trucks on the road already.

Accustomed to road life, none of them needed long to pack up their things.

Kimmy decided to take a last walk down to the beach, just to remember sitting there in the middle of the night sharing thoughts with Dice after he'd given her his first time and she'd let him come inside her unprotected. *Two firsts, I guess.* One didn't do either of those things lightly.

She thought she'd be alone, but before long, Dice was crossing the sand toward her carrying two ice cream cones. "Soursop ice cream," he explained. "Sam said we all have to try it before we leave." He held one of the cones out to her. "I had to lick yours on the way down; it was dripping."

That made her laugh. "No worries, drummer boy, I've already got any cooties you're carrying." She took the cone and gave the ice cream a cautious taste. The name soursop wasn't reassuring, but the flavor was a pleasant surprise, definitely tropical, somewhere between pineapple and papaya with a bite of citrus in the cold and creamy treat. "Oh, wow, this is good!"

"Yeah."

They ate their ice cream in silent accord, both looking out across the blue water and not at each other, soaking in the beauty of it all and the deliciousness of the treat, and the fact that they were together. *Nothing can take this moment from me,* Kimmy thought, *no matter what happens going forward.* "I guess we should head back up to the house," she said, looking at the last bit of her cone before popping it into her mouth.

"I know, but... I want to see if you taste like ice cream."

His sweet smile tempted her, even though *just kissing* seemed like it might fall outside of their arrangement – neither sexual experimentation nor babymaking. *Dangerous.* But he reached out to trace one fingertip down her arm, and the gentle touch stripped all caution from her mind. "Okay. One kiss."

She stepped into his embrace, then squeaked as he lifted her to eliminate their height difference, so she had to wrap her arms and legs around him and hold tight. "I'm not going to drop you, Kimber," he assured her with a soft laugh, one arm securely under her backside as his other hand cupped the back of her head. Then he brought his lips to hers, and the world stopped. His tongue was cool and tasted of soursop and cream, not thrusting or demanding but tenderly exploring her mouth as though he had infinite time to know her on a molecular level. The comfort and affection she felt almost brought her to tears. *How will I ever date again? Nothing can compare to this.*

He broke the kiss and set her gently on her feet. "That was nice," he said, with a smile that was like sunshine. "Thanks. Should we go up now?"

Nice? She nodded and set out for the path, taking one more glance back at the blue water and white sand, wondering if she'd ever be back again. It wasn't impossible. The Stirlings owned the house, after all, and Smidge was signing with their label. But the random chance that had brought her, a drum tech, along on the holiday... that seemed unlikely to repeat itself.

Dice's long legs easily caught him up to her, and he adjusted his stride to keep pace with her up the path. "Has it been a good holiday for you?" he asked casually.

"Can't complain," she replied equally lightly. "Thanks for bringing me along."

She thought he might say something more. She wondered if *she* should say anything more. They'd been friends long enough, though, that maybe nothing more needed to be said. He reached out and grabbed her hand, gave it a quick squeeze – appreciation, thanks, caring, friendship – and let go before they reached the house.

♥

Kimmy boarded the Stirlings' private jet that night with the assumption she'd sit at the back as before. She'd been picturing the same full plane with all seats occupied but two, and it hadn't occurred to her that the Stirlings weren't flying with them this time. When she followed Dice to the top of the airstairs and entered the cabin, she saw Easy and Nell settling themselves where they'd been before, but the other pair of seats at the front, which had been occupied by Mr. and Mrs. Stirling, now had Sally and Erva ensconced.

Angel stood near the four-seat arrangement, looking slightly disconcerted, but he pulled himself together as Dice approached, with Kimmy behind him in the aisle. "Dice, Kimmy, sit with me?" he asked, as though there were other choices in the small plane. Always courteous, he gestured toward the two window seats. "Kimmy, would you like the forward-facing window seat? Unless you prefer the aisle side."

"Thanks, Angel, I–" she began, not even sure what she was going to say, because she hadn't expected to be sitting with him or Dice at all.

"Yes, she would," Dice interrupted, setting his hand on the small of her back and giving her a gentle push toward the mentioned seat. He sat beside her on the aisle, leaving the rear-facing window seat for Angel.

"Thank you," she said, feeling awkward. Angel was a wonderful man but very much the front man and leader and decision-maker of Smidge – in other words, her employer. She never felt that as an obstacle with Dice, who was always a friend first.

She was also aware that she'd seen Angel in his worst years, the heroin and hard-drinking years, before he'd gotten a grip on his life, and he would know she'd remember. None of that should have mattered on a plane going home from a vacation, but she couldn't help feeling the weight of it.

"Did you have a good time on Lovango Cay, Kimmy?" Angel asked her kindly.

That at least was an easy one. "Oh, yes, I loved every moment of it. Thank you so much for including me," she said, meaning it. She could feel Dice's leg casually pressed against hers, easily mistaken for an accidental touch – with his height and long legs, keeping to himself would be a nearly-impossible feat anyway – but she could tell that the pressure was deliberate.

Once those pleasantries were out of the way, she settled into her seat and took out her book, ready to read, though her attention was fixed on the two men as they talked about their new song, the album taking shape that it would eventually go on, and their hopes for their new association with Valancy Records.

The flight attendant, Simran, whom they'd met on the flight out, came around with drinks and snacks after takeoff, and eventually Angel got a novel out of his bag and opened it. Kimmy was interested to see that he was reading *Kushiel's Dart*.

"I can't find my puzzle book," Dice said to the plane at large, slightly grumpily. He liked to do puzzles on flights, word search and sudoku and logic puzzles and that sort of thing, and usually had a book of them to occupy himself.

"I have it," Sally told him, getting up from her seat and coming over to give it to him. "You left it on the patio. It's a good thing I saw it."

"Thanks, Sally!"

He was never the sort to hold onto a bad mood for long, and appeared to cheer up after that. But Kimmy touched his arm and gave him a sympathetic smile, because she too was feeling the loss of their blissful island time and knew it wasn't about the puzzle book.

♥

The icy gusts of wind were a bit of a shock when they arrived at O'Hare in Chicago, but the media greeting them was more of a shock, along with the giant black limousine bus that awaited them as they descended the airstairs from the plane.

With only seconds to adjust, Kimmy shrank to the back of the group and asked Camillo if she could carry the diaper bag for him, hoping to blend into a general impression of entourage. She didn't want any questions or gossip about why the drum tech was on holiday with the band, if anyone noticed her. She could see Erva doing the same, but Sally was unbothered, a frequent enough flier with the band that disembarking from a plane with them was nothing unusual for her.

The night was clear – no snow to contend with in the air, at least, though there was plenty of it on the ground – but the wind chill reminded them all to be grateful that Sally had mentioned long pants and long sleeves toward the end of the flight home, and they'd taken turns changing in the small airplane bathroom. The walk across the tarmac to the bus would not have been fun in shorts. Kimmy zipped her jacket tight and felt the wind scudding up the legs of her jeans, and thought it was a pity that the camera flashes didn't at least provide some heat.

"This has got to be Valancy's next move in their chess game with Awfully Hateful," Dice said as the door of the party bus closed behind them. The driver had the thermostat cranked up, and the toasty warmth inside was a welcome relief.

"How's that?" Blade asked, flinging himself down on the leather bench seating, looking skeptical. "Siccing the media on us is something Horton or Mofford would do. I don't get the sense that Torquil Stirling and his people are that sort."

"No, but they'll want the gossip rags to see us getting off the Valancy jet. I'm guessing they're obligated not to say anything about signing us until all the paperwork is finalized and any court stuff is sorted out, but if we're *seen* like this..." Dice gestured in a *you get where I'm going with this* way as he took a seat. He made eye contact with Kimmy and patted the seat next to him, encouraging her to join him, so she did. They were friends, after all. They'd often sat together in the past.

Angel nodded, surprised but agreeing with the argument. "Good point. The more time Arleigh Hayward has to spin this their way, the greater the chance that they'll find ways to make us look bad, so I can see why Valancy would want to get a jump on that in the media."

"We'll be at the hotel in about half an hour," the driver told them as the big vehicle began to move. His announcement was met with general satisfaction.

Blade held out his arms to Crys. "I'll take Luke, sweetheart. You can sleep until we get there."

"I can take him," Camillo offered, but Blade shook his head.

"You've worked hard enough, man. I've got this."

Nell and Sally looked at each other and made gagging faces, obviously fond of the Blakehart family but not at all into procreation.

Crys handed Luke to her husband but then glanced around in concern. "Should he be in his car seat?" she asked.

Sally waved away her doubts. "No one uses car seats on buses. Right, Camillo? Right, driver? This is a bus. Luke is perfectly safe having cuddles with his daddy. So lie down on some of these comfy seats and get a bit of sleep."

Camillo nodded and the driver called out his reassurance too.

Maybe I'm not pregnant yet, Kimmy thought. It all seemed like a lot of worry and work. But then she looked at Blade with Luke snuggled against his shoulder, radiating more happiness than she'd ever imagined he could show.

♥

Kimmy had assumed that they'd be meeting up with the rest of the crew, that she'd either be dropped at the buses to find her bunk or assigned to a hotel room with Lulu or Trish or both of them and would have to sneak in without waking anyone, if they were already asleep. But the bus pulled up to a very nice hotel indeed, and no other crew were anywhere to be seen.

Angel was handed a note at the front desk, and he read it with raised eyebrows. "This is the hotel where the Stirlings prefer to stay," he explained to the others. "They booked us in here so they could have brunch with us before we go to soundcheck."

And Kimmy had a room to herself. The front desk agent didn't just hand over a jumble of key cards but passed them each one in a cardstock folder with their name written on it. *Ms. Kimberley Baker,* she read. As though she were someone important.

When she got to her room – next door to Dice, she noticed, which was very kind of Mrs. Stirling for remembering that she was Dice's friend and also a graceful touch not assuming that she and Dice were shacking up – she found a basket of snacks, an arrangement of flowers, and a note card with the Valancy logo on the front and the inside filled with elegant calligraphic handwriting in the sort of ink that had to come from a fountain pen.

> *Dear Kimmy,*
>
> *Thank you for keeping your friend Dice company on this unexpected vacation. We recognize that, while it was a vacation, it wasn't something you planned or chose, and as such, we would like to compensate you for your time spent supporting Smidge and Valancy Records during the delicate negotiations we just concluded.*
>
> *Best wishes,*
>
> *Torquil & Cynthia*

Enclosed was a check for a week's wages.

As she sat there looking at the check in her hand, completely unexpected and generous, there was a soft knock on her hotel room door. When she got up to open it, there was Dice, grinning at her. "Invite me in?"

"Always," she said automatically, moving aside to let him into the room. "Look at what the Stirlings gave me..."

"Generous," he commented, seeing the amount on the check. "I mean, it's the right thing for them to have done. That's your full week's wages. I think I've just gotten used to Awfully Hateful and their ways of seeming to give with one hand while taking more away with the other."

Kimmy nodded, knowing he was right. She suspected that as crew she didn't know half of how the Arleigh Hayward people treated the band, and she wondered if Dice, always the protected little brother, even saw everything that went on. Maybe he did, though. They tried to protect him, but he had his eyes open all the time. "Things will be better now," she told him.

"Yeah. Well, I just wanted to come say goodnight. Sleep well, Kimmy." He turned to go.

"Hey. You... don't want to stay?" She spoke without thinking. *Maybe he doesn't want to stay,* she told herself. *The novelty has probably worn off. We're just friends.*

He smiled – a wide, sweet, genuine smile that brought an answering beam to her face. "I didn't want to assume."

"Assume all you want, Dice. For you, the answer will always be yes." And where did that come from? It sounded far too much like a declaration of... something that might compromise their friendship. So she shifted gear and shimmied her rear end in his direction. "Come on, I dare you to give my bum a smack tonight."

He hadn't yet crossed that line, despite all signs pointing to curiosity and arousal whenever it came up. She wondered if he would take the dare.

He did.

THE NEXT DAY, KIMMY COULDN'T STOP SMILING.

At sound check, Angel came over to her and asked if she'd sing for their debut of "Band on the Road" that night. They had a mic set up for her at the back on a raised platform next to the drum riser – all she'd have to do is take two steps up and she'd be in position. She could make sure there were plenty of spare drumsticks ready in the holder clamped to the hi-hat stand and more in the stick bag Dice liked to have on one of his floor toms, and Gary and Cal, the other backline techs, said they could cover for her during that song if Dice needed anything while she was singing.

Maybe they couldn't change a drumhead fast under pressure, but anything apart from that, sure.

"You don't have to wear anything special," Sally said. "Your crew shirt is fine. Maybe put some statement earrings in – your lowest earlobe piercings, that is," she added, acknowledging that she wasn't recommending changes to the industrial in Kimmy's left ear or the barbell in her eyebrow, or the daith piercing in her right ear or... well, there were quite a few. And Kimmy was feeling the itch to get another, though she was running out of real estate for them. "I'd like to put a bit of stage makeup on you, if that's okay. The lights will wash you out, otherwise. But it's your call."

Kimmy shrugged. "Sure. The point is to sing, but I don't mind if you want to put makeup on me; that's fine."

When no one was looking, Dice gave her butt a squeeze and whispered, "You were right. Last night was so hot."

He'd only smacked her bare cheeks a few times, barely hard enough to sting, but combined with his voice dropping into that deliciously commanding tone he sometimes had and how he obviously found it wildly arousing and also forbidden was a delight. His conflicted face and the dirty talk and the sting of those little slaps were so erotic... and so much fun.

But he respected her wish to keep their intimate arrangements private. She felt confident of that, and even when he murmured things in her ear or gave her a secret caress, she never worried that he'd do it in view of anyone else. She was never afraid that he'd make her work life difficult or cross any boundaries without negotiation. Maybe there was something to be said for best friends with benefits.

"Are you nervous, Kimmy?" Qingshan asked, crossing behind the drum riser to where a truss with an array of small black cylinders was suspended from the rigging, currently in a lowered position but with a pulley to raise it. He began attaching small wires. "Will you like singing for so many people?"

"Maybe a little? It can't really be much different from singing in a crowded bar or whatever. Stage lights get in your eyes just the same." But the truth was that singing in front of people had never made her nervous. Any anxiety she had was for letting people down, and the fear that to be a good singer she couldn't be a good drum tech, or vice versa.

"She'll be fine," Dice said, overhearing the conversation. "Kimmy's an excellent multitasker. Everything will be great." His reassurance warmed her. He knew what her real worries were and had faith that she could manage both roles.

"That is good," Qingshan said, raising the truss overhead. "Please be careful not to step into the hot zone near the drum riser. These waterfall gerbs are new and I'm afraid someone will walk under them."

"Of course," Kimmy agreed, and Dice chimed in with confirmation even though he rarely left his throne during a show. Pyrotechnics were no joke if safety precautions weren't observed, and any change to the setup needed a bit of caution until all crew were accustomed to the change.

And when the time came, "Band on the Road" was an instant hit with the audience. Dice pointed to the riser where the mic was set up when Blade played the opening chords, and Kimmy scrambled up the two steps to her mic with a panicked nod. But everything went smoothly. She brought her focus to the song, trusting suddenly that Dice would manage and that Gary or Cal could get him anything he needed. The lights were bigger than she was used to, out from behind the drum riser, and the crowd was much more vast than any she'd sung to before. But that was okay. In the chorus moment, her voice soared, and when the song came to an end, Angel clapped for her, telling the audience, "Our backing vocalist, drum tech Kimmy Baker, everyone." And the roar of applause was warm and lovely and she gave a grateful bow before retreating down the steps to her usual place behind the drum riser.

"You were so good," Dice said. Not that she could hear him with her ear monitors in and all the ambient sound, but between lip reading and the proud expression on his face, it was clear enough.

The show went on. *I did it,* she told herself, momentarily weak with relief now that everything had gone smoothly. *I can do it.* Maybe it was okay to do both, to be both a drum tech and a backup singer. Being more than one thing *was* possible. *Like being both a friend and a lover,* a small voice in her mind pointed out. But could any of it last?

♥

Valancy seized the moment, releasing "Band on the Road" as a single the next day, a surprise drop that capitalized on the video clips all over social media. If fans were excited about a song, the label said, why wait? They should be able to buy or stream it right then while the moment was hot. It made a nice change from Arleigh Hayward's infuriating preference for always making fans wait, and even then restricting streaming until several weeks after the track was for sale to try to push those who preferred streaming into having to buy it.

They would keep it on the set list until February 1st, then bring it out again for the following year's holiday season with a music video. Kimmy figured she would enjoy the experience of singing with Smidge for the rest of the month, and anything beyond that could be left up to whatever the future held.

She also bought a bottle of prenatal vitamins.

♥

Around the middle of January, Kimmy noticed that her breasts felt slightly tender, and she had more cramping than usual in the few days before her period was due. *I'm probably not.* Statistically, the odds of getting pregnant in the first month of trying were only something like one in four, as she'd told herself many times. But that didn't stop her from surreptitiously getting a pregnancy test out of the case where Jed kept that kind of thing for the crew. When Crys had first suspected she might be pregnant, the year before, she'd waited several weeks in secret anxiety before finally asking him if he could get her a pregnancy test, well after nausea and other fun changes had set in. Kimmy vividly remembered Sally asking at the time, "D'you think she's preggers? Her boobs have tripled in size, I swear." Since then, Jed kept a stock of pregnancy tests and the morning-after pill in the case with the condoms and dental dams and lube for easy access, no questions asked.

A tour bus toilet cubicle wasn't the most ideal place to pee on a stick, but it had to be done. And since she couldn't very well spend eternity in there waiting for it to show a result, she hid it in a rolled-up magazine and took it to her bunk. Fortunately, Jed bought them the good kind with a cap to cover up the stick part, so it wasn't gross.

Is that a line? She used the flashlight on her phone to get a better look. The control line was dark pink, nice and sharp, so the test was working... but was there a second line, or just a shadow, or a faint indentation where the line would have shown up if there'd been one? Impossible to say.

Hope was an odd thing. She'd wondered occasionally if going for the single-mom thing was a mistake, but faced with actually looking for a second line on the test, she felt oddly desperate for it to come up positive.

Later, when the bus pulled into a rest stop, she smuggled the stick outside to look at it in daylight, despite knowing that it was well past the window where pregnancy tests should be read and that drying out could cause false positives to show. *Still impossible to say.* It might have been a faint line, or just an artifact of drying, or...

Kimmy threw the test in a trash can at the rest stop. No sense in staring at it. No sense in having anyone catch her with it.

♥

Her period started the next day.

It was a show day, of course. She dosed herself with Aleve and got her work done as any professional must – extra important now that she had a song to sing backup for, because if she messed up as a drum tech, unless things went terribly wrong, only Dice would know, but if she messed up her backing vocals, everyone in the arena would know. Of course it had to be an extra bad month: twice the cramps, demonically heavy flow, fatigue to the point of exhaustion, and to add to the fun of it all, she was hit with hormonal moodiness, something that didn't normally affect her much but could throw her for a loop once or twice a year.

It shouldn't have surprised her that he could tell something was wrong. He pulled her aside during load-out, saying, "Hey, what's up, Kimmy? I can see you're not quite... your usual self tonight."

"It's nothing, I'm fine. A little tired, but I can hit my bunk as soon as load-out is done."

"Right," he said, and she could tell by his tone that he didn't entirely believe her but wasn't going to contradict her. Which was wise of him.

She pushed on through the rest of the load-out and then headed for the crew buses and her bunk. They still had an hour and a half before the buses would roll, and some of the crew were off to get a late-night breakfast before boarding, but it was a cold January night and her cramps were getting stronger. She only wanted another Aleve and a hot water bottle.

When she saw Dice leaning against the door of her bus, she couldn't have been more surprised. He'd borrowed someone's crew jacket and had a beanie pulled low on his forehead and down over his ears, rendering him relatively unremarkable except for his height, which even a thorough slouch couldn't do much to disguise.

"Don't go on the bus tonight," he said as soon as she was close enough to hear him. "Stay at the hotel with me and fly to Fort Wayne with us tomorrow."

She shook her head, feeling so incredibly weary of everything. "That's not fair, Dice. I don't want everyone to know we're friends *with benefits* now. I don't want my professional life tainted with that." *Girl roadies are just groupies who get paid for it.* She'd heard variations on that line often enough, even from crew lifers who'd never call *themselves* roadies but were happy to fling it around as a term for women crew. They didn't tend to last with Smidge, not once Sally or Nell caught any of their attitude, but still...

"I know. And I'm the one who hasn't been fair." He gave her a wry smile, reacting to what must have been a *what the fuck* look on her face. "We *are* friends, and it was shitty of me to never bring you along on our flights and stuff," he explained. "I never thought about it, but I should have done that for you. As a friend. Long ago. Jed flies with us, and Scott does too. *They* aren't sleeping with the band. And this isn't about sex. I can see you're having a rough night and I want to take care of you."

"Oh." That made her feel foolish, that she'd assumed it was about sex, when he'd meant friendship. "Well, I never expected anything like that."

That brought a grin to his face. "I know. But maybe you should have. Come on, let your best friend take care of you. We'll watch a movie and get room service to bring us steamed milk and chocolate chip cookies, and you can sleep on the plane tomorrow morning. We'll be there in plenty of time for load-in, I promise."

Hot milk. Cookies. A comfortable bed. "You're making it hard to say no."

He just looked at her, amused. *Obviously,* his expression said. *That's the idea.*

"You'd do this even if we weren't...?"

"Of course. Come on, then. I'll text Phil to let him know you're with me so they won't be looking for you."

It struck Kimmy that they were standing by the buses in a relatively empty arena parking lot at two in the morning. "How are you even here?" she asked, puzzled. "I thought the band went back to the hotel ages ago. Weren't there fans waving and trying to get photos and stuff as you all got into a limo?"

Dice shrugged. "I asked Jed to get me the keys to the van. He did. Grab whatever you need for the night, and let's go!"

She didn't see the tour's runabout van anywhere, but as soon as she'd snagged her overnight bag from her bunk, he led her down the line of vehicles and around a sort of alley along the side of the arena, and there it was. With typical courtesy, he opened the passenger door for her first, then went around to get in the driver's side.

As she put a foot up on the running board to boost herself in – and the high van seats took a bit of an effort at her height – a bad cramp hit her and she hunched over, hoping it would pass quickly.

"Kimmy?" Dice asked, leaning over from the driver's seat, holding out a hand to help her up. He looked concerned.

"It's just my period," she said with a sigh. "Started this morning. I'm clearly not pregnant. Also not remotely interested in having anything except a hot water bottle near my pelvic area right now. And not much fun to be around. But I'm *fine.*"

"Aww, Kimber." He hauled her into her seat and leaned across her to pull the door closed and help her with her seatbelt. "I'm sorry. I mean, maybe I'm selfishly glad we can keep trying for another month? But I'm sorry you're disappointed."

She shrugged. "I can deal with it. I knew the odds of winning this little lottery in the first month weren't great. I just – most of the time, that time of the month isn't so bad for me, but every now and then I have a bad one. This is a bad one."

"Must suck to be a girl," he said, but he didn't seem grossed out, which was nice. She wondered why, through six years of friendship and working together, she'd pretended her monthly cycle didn't exist instead of telling him when she needed a painkiller and a bit of a rest and why.

The drive to the hotel only took a few minutes. Jed was waiting in the lobby with one of the drivers and Dice's bodyguard.

"When I got you the van keys, I wasn't expecting you to go off without your bodyguard," Jed said with a bit of concern. "That's the kind of stunt I expect from Blade, but not you."

Out of the corner of her eye, Kimmy saw Aidan the bodyguard retreating several paces – distancing himself from the scolding?

"Mmm, well, there was something I had to do." Dice tossed the keys to the driver, then handed him a twenty-dollar bill. "Thanks, Mario. Drive safe." The young man would be heading out shortly, driving the van in convoy along with the rest of Smidge's vehicles, all the big rigs with the equipment and the tour buses full of crew. "Jed, Kimmy's feeling kind of rough so she's crashing with me tonight and coming on the plane with us tomorrow."

"Just cramps," she explained quickly, faced with Jed's assessing-nurse look. She didn't want him thinking she needed to be quarantined or anything. "I'll take an Aleve as soon as I can find some liquid to swallow it with."

Jed nodded. "Ask for a hot water bottle at the front desk," he suggested. "I'll see you both in the morning."

♥

In the elevator, Dice turned to Aidan with an apologetic grimace. "Sorry I took off without you. It's only... I'm never without a guardian one way or another, and I needed to do *something* by myself for a change. Even just going to get my friend from her bus. I hope you didn't get any grief for it."

Aidan shook his head. "It was fine. But, like, you should take me with you when you want to do shit. I know what it's like; I'll stay quiet, I won't try to boss you around. Just... take me with you next time." He looked at Kimmy for corroboration, asking for her support.

"He's not wrong, drummer boy," she told Dice. "Aidan's your bodyguard for a reason. Don't start thinking Blade is cool because he used to ditch Ryan any chance he got – have you noticed he hasn't tried that stunt since Luke was born? You lot are such attention magnets, it's asking for trouble to walk around alone."

Dice gave her a disappointed frown. "Not you too, Kimmy? I don't need a goddamn babysitter." The elevator eased to a stop at their floor, and as soon as the door opened, he strode out with a slight huff, not waiting for either of them.

"Don't be pouty, Dylan Ignatius Satwyn," she called after him as she followed.

He whipped his head around to stare at her. "How d'you know my middle name?"

"Two ways, even. You told me once when you were drunk, probably about four years ago now. And I overheard your mother giving you a talking-to on the phone another time, too. It's... quite a middle name."

"Yeah. Quite." He sighed and gave himself a shake, letting go of his bad mood like a dog shaking off water. "I was born on the feast day of St. Ignatius. My dad is so Episcopal he's almost Catholic – you know, what my Canadian cousins call 'high Anglican' – smells and bells and saints and stuff..." He looked over to where Aidan hung back, trying to stay out of it. "Sorry, man. I'm tired of being protected in a metaphorical way, and I guess I got that mixed up with literal protection from unhinged stalker-bunnies or ransom artists or whatever, which I do need. I won't ditch you again. But... forget you ever heard my middle name, okay? That needs to stay between me and my parents. And you two, I guess."

"Never heard a thing," Aidan swore with an effort at a straight face.

Kimmy stuck her tongue out at Dice, laughing. She wasn't promising to forget any such thing, and reserved her right as a best friend to tease him about it.

He chuckled, good humor completely restored. "You're going to hold this over me, aren't you, Kimmy? Come on, let's get that movie on and order some room service. I'll open up the pull-out couch for you," he added for Aidan's benefit.

Aidan stopped at one of the doors and got out his key card. "I'm in here. Shout if you need me. Goodnight, guys."

Dice had his key card out too and was opening the next door even as he said goodnight to his bodyguard. "We're in here, Kimber." He pushed the door open, ushering her in. "Not a suite, but it's nice and there *is* a pull-out couch if anyone looks."

"Thanks for thinking of that."

"Oh, the couch is what made me think of going to get you. I'm just sorry I don't have a suite so you can have your own space, but our new label's management team pointed out that extra spending on luxury penthouse suites is money that doesn't go into all of our pockets. They also told us we need to buy our own plane – did you know, Awfully Hateful was leasing our old plane to us at an inflated rate? They let us think using the plane was a perk, but they were counting huge lease payments against our income as a miscellaneous expense, over and above fuel and maintenance and all that, using it as one of their schemes to make sure we never earned out our old contract. So Valancy has financed a plane for us, and we'll be making payments to buy it for ourselves rather than pouring never-ending payments into a lease. Mr. Stirling likes planes. He owns three himself, including the one we took to St. Thomas, and he says he's found us a good one, a little older but in beautiful condition."

Kimmy patted Dice's arm. "Hey, relax. I don't need a suite, and this is plenty luxury enough for me. You're saving me from a bunk and road noises all night, remember."

"That's true. Make yourself comfortable, and I'll call room service. Their all-night menu has a scoop of ice cream as an option with either the chocolate chunk or peanut butter or snickerdoodle cookie. Yes?"

"I'm good with just the cookie, thanks. Chocolate chunk, please," she told him before heading into the bathroom.

"Getting ice cream with mine. You can share it if you change your mind," he called out after her.

She'd never understand how he could eat ice cream year-round, and she was still chilled from load-out. But a hot shower would help. She stood under the steaming water for what felt like a long time, soaking away the cold and soothing the cramps gripping her abdomen.

By the time she emerged from the bathroom, cozy in her pajamas with her hair already almost dry just from a brisk toweling – another excellent reason to keep it short – the room service cart had already arrived and Dice had called up the hotel's movie streaming menu on the big screen television across from the bed.

"Hop into bed and get comfy," he told her. "Did you already take your painkiller?"

"No... I hate swallowing them dry and didn't want to drink the tap water. Figured I'd wait for hot milk." She got the little bottle out of her bag and climbed into the king-size bed, sighing in pleasure at the plushness of the mattress and the multitude of pillows to sit back against. Even when the crew got hotel stopovers, it was two or three to a standard room and not on a premium floor. "It's like having a cloud to sleep on."

That made him smile. "I feel so bad that I never thought about us having a sleepover like this before," he said. He brought over a tall mug with a little paper cover on it, and when she lifted the cover away, the milk was still hot enough that a wisp of steam escaped. And then he went back to the cart and produced a hot water bottle in a flannel cover with the hotel's logo. "Look, I remembered what Jed said about them having hot water bottles if we asked the front desk, so..."

She settled it on her abdomen gratefully. "Thank you, it's just what I needed until the Aleve kicks in." Then, when he brought her cookie over, she broke out in astonished giggles. "That thing is the size of my face!"

"You don't have to eat it all." He'd chosen a snickerdoodle cookie topped with an enormous scoop of vanilla ice cream. "You want to try a taste of mine?" He broke off a bit of cinnamon-sugar-coated goodness and held it out to her. So she broke off a bit of hers for him to try, and they agreed that both were delicious.

My best friend, she thought fondly as he started the movie and they settled in to watch.

It was a relief beyond measure that their friendship was still intact, same as it had ever been. He didn't try to make everything about sex – in fact, he seemed super attuned to her need for friendship and comfort, and leaned into that like the dear person he was. Even when the movie got a bit steamy and the main characters were gripping bedsheets and making o-faces for the camera, Dice didn't do anything but adjust the way he was sitting and rearrange the blanket over his lap.

"I'm sorry," she mumbled, replete with hot milk and slightly too much cookie. "I feel too gross to do anything remotely sexual tonight."

He shook his head. "Honestly, Kimmy, I went six and a half years without once even saying anything dirty or touching you anywhere off limits. I can manage a night or two of abstinence when you feel under the weather, trust me. Let's just watch the movie."

"Wait. Like, you were thinking about me that way *since we met?*"

The blush that rose up his neck and colored his cheeks was a confession in itself, but Dice had never been a coward. "I tried not to," he said softly. "I knew I shouldn't think about you that way, my best friend, my Kimmy. But Christ, all my hottest fantasies... As if it weren't enough of a curse to be unable to get it up with any of the groupies throwing themselves at me, I was also fighting dirty thoughts about someone I knew I couldn't touch." He hid his face in his hands and choked out the next bit. "And once in a while when I felt desperate to fit in with the groupies and the other guys, I let myself use fantasies of you to stay hard while..."

Kimmy laid a comforting hand on his shoulder, remembering that time she'd walked in on him. *The girl's head bobbing up and down. Dice with his head thrown back, back arched, eyes closed in the tense pleasure of being very, very close to orgasm.* He'd been thinking of *her* in that moment?

"It felt so wrong to use thoughts of you like that," he said, his voice quiet and small, muffled by his hands. "I'm sorry."

"Don't be." She rubbed his shoulder encouragingly. "Private thoughts don't hurt anyone. It's not like you told anyone, or made me feel uncomfortable, or creeped on me. I'm flattered to have been your fantasy pin-up. You have my permission to imagine whatever you like, anytime."

He looked up at her, and she saw that he was feeling a little raw from the confession. "Thanks," he said shyly. "I... think I'm a bit kinkier than I ever let myself really consider. I have some pretty messed up dreams sometimes."

"I like kinky," she assured him. "In a few days, when I'm feeling more... into it, you can tell them to me as bedtime stories, okay?"

"Maybe." He got up and took their empty plates to the room service trolley, then came back and snuggled up next to her. "How're you feeling now, Kimmy?"

"As good as it's going to get, thanks. The Aleve is working, I'm full of cookie and the milk is making me sleepy, and this bed is heaven."

"That's all right, then. I think there's about an hour left in the movie; are you going to make it? We can just turn it off and sleep, if you'd like."

Movie? She'd half forgotten that they were theoretically watching a movie, distracted as she was by his revelation. "Oh, no, we can keep watching it. Unless you don't want to."

"I do. As long as you're happy."

"Oh, I am."

♥

In the morning, Kimmy discovered that no one raised an eyebrow about her coming on the plane. She was just one of the entourage who trundled off to the airport's FBO for private flights in a rented van – Sally with her box of makeup tricks, Scott the photographer, Jed who'd stayed close to the band since the days when the guys were often dope-sick and needed a nurse on hand and still flew with them because he always did, and Camillo with Luke and all the baby gear.

Two of the bodyguards were with them in the van as well. Will got to ride shotgun in the limo transporting the band, and Nell was of course sitting in the back of the limo with the boys and Crys. Aidan seemed to accept being relegated to entourage status without a worry, but Ryan seemed a little put out and grumbled about how Will always got to go with the limo.

"How come *you're* flying with us?" he asked Kimmy when he saw her.

"Oh, I..." she began, then trailed off. What had she been planning to say? *I have really bad cramps? I slept in Dice's room last night?*

"Kimmy is having some physical discomfort, so she's traveling with us, a courtesy I would hope we'd extend to any crew member who needed it," Jed called from his seat in the back row of the bus, hearing this.

Ryan, who wasn't a bad guy, read between the lines and nodded sympathetically. "Rough time of the month?" he guessed.

"Yeah. I'll be fine by tomorrow."

Kimmy, who'd never flown with the band, had no particular expectations of the plane, but the others oohed and aahed when they arrived, looking up at the Smidge logo splashed onto the exterior skin of the jet, with a stream of trailing music notes onto the wings and tail. "What's the big deal?" she asked Sally quietly.

"New plane," Sally said. "This one is really ours. The band's, I mean. But... ours."

Smidge was family. The crew tended to feel ownership in that. It made sense.

When they boarded, Kimmy looked on in astonishment as Sally hugged the flight attendants. "Dizzy! Cindy! How are you here?!"

The flight attendant with pink hair laughed. "Oh, your new bosses hired us away from Arleigh Hayward. Said our boys would do better with their familiar crew. Matt and Danno are up front."

"This is Cindy," Sally said to Kimmy. "And the blonde there is Dizzy. They've been taking care of us in the air since we graduated to jet status. Four years ago?"

Maybe more like five, Kimmy thought. It hadn't been very long after she'd joined them that the label had started flying the band around, at first just for longer distances and then more and more of their travel.

On the inside, it looked quite a lot like the Stirlings' plane, but a bit different. "This one is a Gulfstream G650 and theirs is an Embraer Legacy 650," Camillo explained. "I like planes. I'm taking pilot lessons in my free time, as often as I can."

"Cool," Kimmy said.

At the front of the plane, on either side of the aisle, a pair of comfortable-looking seats faced each other, and each pair had a table stowed flat against the wall that Kimmy guessed could be raised into position for a meal or to work. In the midsection of the plane, a pair of three-seat couches faced each other across the aisle, like a sort of lounge area, and then farther toward the back of the plane there was a group of four armchairs around a larger table, much like the one where there hadn't been a seat for Kimmy on the Charlotte Amalie flight. Beyond that, there was a bulkhead with a curtain pulled across. "Camillo, why don't you and Luke take the rear section, through the curtain," Jed said. "It's really the crew's rest area back there, but Dizzy and Cindy don't mind sharing their space with you and the baby."

"Hi, Camillo, I'll help you get settled," Dizzy offered, holding out a hand to take the diaper bag from him.

"Make yourselves at home, everyone," Jed continued, raising his voice a bit to be heard. "Angel asked me to tell you all that we're going to be flexible about seating on this plane. You might notice the conference table, and those of us who play cards are probably eyeing it, but if the band needs to write music or we have someone from Valancy onboard to talk business, we'll need to let them have it on occasion."

Kimmy stood in the entrance, letting the others move past her. Sally headed for the conference table, and Jed was plainly moving in that direction too, along with Scott. The card players? There was a fourth seat at the table. Was she supposed to join them? She wondered if she should go to the back and sit with Camillo and Luke – there'd be room, back there.

As she watched, undecided, Ryan took the last seat at the table, removing the option of sitting with the card players. Then, just as she was about to walk back to sit in the air crew and nursery area, Aidan called her name and waved for her to sit in the lounge section with him.

"Are you sure it's okay to sit here?" she asked. "What if the band wants to sit here."

"Then we'll move," he said easily. "They'll tell us. But I'm guessing Nell and Easy will sit in the front section – she likes a little space. Angel will very likely sit up there and read too, and if no one takes the other seat, I bet you Will sits there. So we'll end up here with Dice and probably Blade and Crys." He leaned in a bit, sharing gossip. "Crys sometimes joins the card bandits but she's not very good so they're probably glad to have Ryan."

Kimmy smiled. Aidan's friendly chatter made her feel comfortable and welcome.

An exterior commotion, audible through the open boarding door, heralded the arrival of the band. Out the windows, those already on board could see the usual media scrum, and then the sound of booted feet on the airstairs echoed and the band was on the plane.

Aidan had been right on all counts, Kimmy thought in amusement as she watched them take their seats.

After an alert glance around the plane, Nell touched Easy's arm and gestured for him to take one of the club seats up front. Angel nodded and waved for the pair of them to go ahead, and he too stayed in the club section, not sitting yet but Kimmy thought his body language suggested he was claiming one of those seats too. Not surprisingly, Will stayed near him, not moving back to the lounge area as the others did. Dice waved a greeting to Aidan and Kimmy, heading over to sit on the couch beside Kimmy, and Crys and Blade, as Aidan had guessed, sat on the other couch opposite them – or at least Blade sat. Crys dropped her purse and hurried to the back of the plane, and as she disappeared behind the curtain, they could hear her saying, "Luke, were you a good boy for Camillo? Do you like the airplane?"

Blade shook his head, watching her go. "She doesn't like sending him ahead with Camillo, she'd rather keep him with us, but I don't like him being photographed by the vultures, and that's going to happen if he's anywhere near me in public. She didn't even want a nanny at all, do you know? But we've got to have someone to guard his privacy, and I – I need her with me." He said the last bit with a deep breath, as though he struggled to admit to needing anyone.

"You're smart to protect Luke's privacy like that," Dice agreed.

Kimmy nodded. "Camillo's really nice. He takes great care of Luke," she assured Blade, not quite sure how she was daring to speak so familiarly to him since he'd never been one to make small talk with the crew, and even her friendship with Dice and six years with Smidge hadn't given her any kind of closeness with the guitarist.

She was surprised when he smiled at her – a rare, small smile, a slight upturn of the corners of his mouth but definitely a smile – and said, "Yeah. I know. It's just a lot, starting a family in front of the world like this. We're lucky to have all of our tour family around us."

When Crys came back to buckle in for takeoff, she smiled at Kimmy. "It's so cool that you can sing like you do," she said in an admiring tone. "I wish I could help the band like that."

"You're perfect just as you are, sweetheart," Blade said quietly, even as Dice assured her that she did plenty for the band and Aidan nodded his reassurance.

I guess my singing does help the band, Kimmy thought. Recorded backing tracks were never quite as flexible or responsive as a real voice, and hiring a designated backup singer for one song – because she couldn't see Smidge needing specifically feminine-sounding backing vocals all that often – would be an extra body to feed and house on tour and another person moving about in the backstage area, and it was nice that she could save them that.

Before long, Kimmy settled comfortably into her dual role as drum tech and one-song backing vocalist. She added her mic setup to her pre-show list of tasks, listened for Mack to call her up at soundcheck, increased the number of spare drumsticks stowed in various places, and soon found that Dice had been right – she was excellent at multitasking and could handle it without trouble.

But that assumed her mic setup was directly to the right of the drum riser, about four paces away. After a dozen performances, she could have made the transition in the dark – one, two, three, four, up a step onto the riser with the mic, and she was in position. So when she discovered, in the middle of load-in for the first of two shows in New Orleans, that her mic platform and cables were on the other side and farther away, it threw her.

"Why is my mic over there?" she asked Mack, feeling the beginning of anxiety at the change and the distance. "It should be stage right and much closer to the drum riser."

The stage manager gave her an impatient look. "There was a power fault and they couldn't get it sorted, we had to shift your mic. You'll just have to walk a few extra steps. Only for these two shows, Kimmy."

"Right, okay," she agreed. It shouldn't make any difference. She checked out her mic setup and then headed back to the drum riser, noticing the caution tape on the ground warning of the hot zone from Qingshan's waterfall gerbs – downward-pointing fireworks that would create cascades of falling silver and gold sparks – and thinking that it would add a dozen or more steps to her crossing the stage as she'd have to go around behind the dangerous area. It would be fine.

But things don't always go as planned during concerts.

Toward the end of "Star Shot Down" – the song before "Band on the Road" on the set list for the night – Dice cracked a pie. It didn't happen all that often, but he was an intense and powerful rock drummer and tended to go through one or two cymbals on each leg of a tour. *At least it's not a drumhead,* Kimmy thought as she rushed to change it over to a new one, doing her best not to get in her drummer's way as he finished out the song without that cymbal.

She could hear Angel's between-songs banter with the audience as she finished up, and then the intro to "Band on the Road" started up.

And her mic was on the other side of the stage. She saw the caution tape around the hot zone area, knew the extra steps to go around it would delay her getting to her position and no pyrotechnics were planned to go off until the end of the song, and took a calculated risk.

She got to her mic in time for the first chorus, came in on cue. The song went smoothly. The gerbs went off in the last chorus as planned, dropping their showers of sparks into the safely empty hot zone. And when it was over, she took the long way around to get back to the drum riser, relieved that everything had turned out well.

As soon as the concert was over, though, Mack stormed up to her in a fury, right there behind the drum riser, the moment the encore came to an end and the band were taking their bows, preparing to leave the stage. He gestured wrathfully for her to take the IEMs out of her ears. "What the utter hell were you thinking, Kimmy?!" the stage manager shouted as soon as she could hear him. "I saw you cross through that hot zone. You nearly gave Qingshan a heart attack – what if something had gone off early? Pyro is dangerous shit! People can die! Do you know how responsible he'd feel if you were hurt doing that?"

"Sorry, Mack. I'm sorry. I'll tell Qingshan I'm sorry. I won't do it again."

Now that the pressure was off, she could see how foolish she'd been to risk it.

He just shook his head in disgust. "That was a real dumbfuck move. Somebody ought to give you a good hard spanking; pity it won't be me." With a final hard glare and lips compressed in displeasure, he turned and stomped away, leaving her shaken.

Feeling ashamed of her choice to cross the hot zone fought with regret that she'd ever dated Mack – they had some similar tastes, but he was too hardcore for her and didn't know how to keep it in the bedroom. She knew exactly what she'd earned, what he'd do to her if they were still dating, and...

She turned to start breaking down the drum kit, and there was Dice, standing by the riser with raised eyebrows, crossed arms, and an unreadable look on his face. There was no doubt in Kimmy's mind that he'd heard every word of Mack's tirade, including the last bit. *Somebody ought to give you a good hard spanking...* She could feel her face burning and hoped the blush wasn't too noticeable. "Dice! Great show! I'm just going to start–"

"So – you and Mack, huh?"

"It was years ago, and we only dated for a couple of months." Was Dice jealous?

"He said someone ought to..."

"Oh, that. Yeah." She could see Dice looking a bit perturbed. "It's okay. It's just talk. He's annoyed at me and he'd feel better if we could act it out in a scene and let it go, but he knows he can't. I guess he knows I'd feel better too, but whatever."

"Annoyed seems like a pretty mild word. I saw you cut across the hot zone too," Dice said. He didn't raise his voice or scowl, but his suddenly set face and the edge in his voice were enough. "Please, please don't ever pull such a goddamn dangerous move ever again."

His disappointment was worse than anything Mack could dish out, verbal or otherwise. "I'm sorry," she mumbled, her voice small and guilty. "Never again, I promise."

"You don't have to be sorry," he said more gently, then tried to smile, but the smile looked wrong and lopsided and troubled. "I thought my heart would stop, watching you. I couldn't breathe until you were safely across. You could've been–" He broke off, sighed, and gestured toward the drum riser. "Just pack up the kit, okay?"

"Right. Quick as I can," she agreed. And she did, but nothing felt right.

chapter

9

T WAS NOT A GOOD NIGHT.

Kimmy finished her load-out chores as quickly as possible, feeling all the weight of her bad choice. And the worst of it was that she wanted to go to Dice for comfort, for reassurance that a split-second decision to run across ten feet of taped-off floor didn't mean she was an utter screwup forever, but she kept thinking of his face when he said he couldn't breathe until she was safely across. She didn't think he was angry, exactly, but she also – for the first time since she'd met him – felt something uncomfortable between them. She skipped the debrief, with a further twinge of guilt, and stayed away from the green room until she was reasonably sure the band had left the building.

They were playing two dates in New Orleans so everyone had a hotel stop that night and wouldn't be back on the road until after the following night's show. As it sometimes happened, the hotel was some distance from the arena, so the crew had to wait their turns to be shuttled over in a rented passenger van that took twelve at a time.

Waiting, she decided after all to text Dice. *Hey,* she typed, *are you still awake?*

He would be, of course. But asking gave her something to say... and gave him an excuse if he didn't want to answer. There was barely a minute's wait before he texted back: *Of course I am. Are you still at the arena?*

Just waiting for the shuttle to get back and pick us up, she told him. Then, *I'm sorry about earlier. That was dangerous. Never again.* She wanted him to tell her it was okay. It was just one bad choice, wasn't it? And nothing happened.

There was a long pause, and then: *What did you mean, you'd feel better too?*

You mean if – she hesitated, then continued typing – *someone gave me a hard punishment spanking?* Like Mack said? She hit send.

There was another long pause before he answered. *Yeah, that. How would it make you feel better?*

She could imagine his face as he waited for her answer, the same way he looked when learning something or problem-solving – focused, curious, trying to understand. And she wanted him to understand, to not think her a freak. How could she get him to see that it was a direct path to relief for her, faster and more cathartic than days of stewing over what happened? *It's like a ritual,* she explained. *I made a bad choice. I feel down about it. If I get to play out my feelings around that, take punishment and be forgiven, I can let the feelings go and put the mistake behind me.*

That makes sense. Then she could see that he was typing for what seemed like an eternity before his next words popped up on her screen. *Is it something you'd want from me?*

A shiver of want, need, and trepidation rippled over her. Would he really? Was he offering? Her fingers fumbled as she tried to type. *If it's something you can do for me. If it's something you want too.*

I think we need to be in person for this conversation, he texted, and this time she couldn't picture the expression on his face.

He was right. *Honest truth is I'm feeling a bit upside-down right now,* she told him. If sex had altered their friendship, even talking about something like this had the potential to reshape it altogether. But she couldn't take back what she'd already said.

I'll find us someplace to talk, he replied.

♥

When she got to the hotel, there was a note at the front desk for her in Dice's handwriting on a piece of folded hotel notepaper. *I'm in the Domino Room if you want to come find me.*

"Where's the Domino Room?" she asked the night clerk, as though it weren't at all odd to be asking for a meeting room in the middle of the night.

The woman smiled. "Oh, for sure! That's the one your band wanted for something. Songwriting, maybe? Can we expect a new album soon?" An expectant pause told Kimmy that the clerk was hoping for an inside scoop about what Smidge was working on.

"Sorry. We're not supposed to talk about what the band is doing." And that was the truth, at least. The whole crew knew not to talk about band business.

"I get it, no worries, I wouldn't want to get you in trouble. Your meeting room is right at the end of the hall there. Please remind them to keep the door closed. The soundproofing is excellent but doesn't do much with an open door, and I'm sure no one wants to bother the other guests."

Kimmy nodded and thanked the clerk before heading down the hallway, her overnight bag on her shoulder. She was too wound up to waste time finding her room and risk getting stuck chatting with her roommates, so she shoved the key card in her pocket for afterward.

She found the meeting room and knocked lightly on the closed door. For a moment, nothing happened, and she stood waiting, feeling nervous in a way that reminded her of being called to the principal's office at school. Then it opened, and Dice was there, gesturing for her to come in.

The room looked like some interior designer's idea of an old-fashioned library or a gentlemen's club room from a historical romance novel: a masculine room, smelling subtly of leather and beeswax furniture polish. It could also pass as the headmaster's office in a kinky boarding school story, she thought with a flicker of amusement. Shelves of leather-bound books lined the walls – maybe real books, or maybe insulation and soundproofing crafted to look like books, she couldn't be sure. A large and solid wooden table stood in the middle of the floor, surrounded by leather conference chairs. A couple of armchairs on either side of a fireplace offered a more intimate setting to talk at the far end of the room, and a small desk near the door displayed a selection of pens and notepaper that guests doing business might need. "Nice room," she said.

"Yeah," Dice agreed. "I told someone at the front desk we needed a meeting room. I think she assumed I meant the band – I probably should have corrected her, but I didn't – because she just handed over the key and assured me the hotel invested in first-class soundproofing for business privacy so we can make all the music we like." He closed the door and turned the lock. It clicked into place with a metallic plunk. "There. No one will bother us."

Kimmy stood where she was, by the door, not sure what to do next.

This was Dice, after all, her friend and companion and defender. Some sexy bondage and playful light swats were one thing, but the shaming and vulnerability and raw feelings of a real spanking would cross into something else entirely. It wasn't a thing they'd be able to pretend hadn't happened.

"We don't have to do this," he said kindly, and she knew he could see her hesitation.

"You don't want to?" she asked, unsure what she hoped his answer would be.

He bit his lip. "I only want to do this if *you* want to. The idea is hot as hell, but causing pain to someone I care about goes against all my social conditioning, so I need to be absolutely sure you're into it."

That prompted a nervous giggle from her. "Being scared and conflicted is part of the... experience for me, I guess. But I want it. I'm... mostly worried you might not like this truly kinky side of me, though. I might cry; it's not always pretty. If you can handle that, I'm in."

"Okay. Promise me you'll safeword if you need to?"

"Yes."

He nodded and crossed his arms, taking on a powerful stance. His face grew serious, and she could see him gathering the energy to commit to the scene. *We're really doing this,* she thought, anxious butterflies doing flips in her stomach, as she adjusted her own stance to a more submissive posture, hands clasped and head bowed, waiting.

Even before he spoke, she knew his voice would come out deep and authoritative. "Look at me." He waited until she looked up, and his dark brown gaze held hers like a lifeline. "Pretty Girl, I'm going to need you to tell me why you're being punished and ask me for your punishment."

Oh. "Yes, Boss. I chose to run across the hot zone today and it was dangerous and foolish. I'm lucky nothing bad happened. Please give me a hard spanking."

"How many swats?" he asked, stern-faced. Taking it seriously.

"Twenty?" A lot, but she could handle it.

"Twenty if you take it like a good girl," he agreed. "Twenty-five if you squirm and beg. Understood?"

"Yes, Boss." *Oof, that would be tough.*

He walked over to one of the armchairs and grabbed a thin velvet cushion, slapped it down onto the edge of the big table. "Okay. Pull down your jeans and underwear and bend over the table."

"Yes, Boss," she said again, approaching the table. At least he'd given her something to protect her hips from the hard wood. She unbuttoned and unzipped her jeans slowly. The anticipation was both awful and delicious. He tapped the table, indicating that she should hurry up, and with a long anxious breath she pushed both jeans and panties down to mid-thigh in one motion and bent over the table as directed, adjusting the cushion over the edge of the wood to preserve her hip bones from hard contact before resting her head on her folded arms. The shameful feeling of getting into position and waiting for her punishment to start made her tremble.

"Legs apart."

Obediently, she spread her legs as far as the panties and jeans around her thighs would allow. Exposed, vulnerable. The air was cool on her bare skin, reminding her that she was on display for him. She wondered if he could see how wet she was getting.

She flinched when his hand touched her hip. "Breathe, Pretty Girl," he murmured, as he began to rub and caress her backside, stroking and then kneading her buttocks. Just as she was beginning to relax a little, he landed a light swat on one cheek, then rubbed the sting away. Moments later, he did the same on the other side.

"I can take it harder than that, Boss," she told him with reluctant honesty.

He laughed, and it sounded teasing and dark and full of promise. "I have no doubt that you can, and you will. This is just a warmup." A shower of small slaps made her gasp, but he quickly took the bite away with more massage.

"How did you know to–" she started to ask, and a slightly harder smack reminded her that a good submissive didn't ask questions during a scene.

"You didn't think I'd be researching the fuck out of this since I found out you were into it? Since I realized I might be into it?" He aimed a couple of swats at the crease where butt became thigh, sending mind-melting vibrations through her most sensitive parts. "It's important to me to make this good for you, Pretty Girl."

It already is. She could feel increasing heat and stinging tenderness spreading over her bottom as he delivered a thorough warmup spanking, keeping her on a knife-edge between discomfort and kinky pleasure, pausing after every few swats to caress and massage her. When she found herself fighting the urge to squirm and moan, he stopped.

"I think you're ready. Still want to do this?"

"Yes, Boss."

The first punishment stroke landed harder than she'd expected, with a heavy sting-thud that made her let out an unintentional whuff of startled pain. *Shit. Oh, shit.*

He paused and leaned over, touching her shoulder to focus her attention on his face. "Check in for me, Kimmy. Is it too much?"

"I can take it," she gasped, breathing hard.

"Good girl." Another hard stroke raised searing heat where it landed, bringing tears to her eyes. A third and fourth followed, fierce and firm with mind-erasing pain.

I can take this, she reminded herself desperately, pushing away the initial panic she always felt at the onset of a disciplinary scene. She buried her face in her arms. *I won't squirm or beg.*

The strokes kept coming, and the panic melted into hazy endurance, the pain morphing into stinging fire. She lost count of the strokes in a flood of endorphins and tears, lost all sense of anything but the hard table under her and the sting of each impact on her throbbing bottom.

And then it was over.

She didn't move from her position – couldn't have moved if she'd wanted to. The table was the only thing holding her up. She could hear his footsteps moving away, then returning, and suddenly the sharp stinging pressure of a felt-tipped marker made her flinch as Dice wrote something across her spanked cheeks, then gave her one final light swat.

"All done, Pretty Girl," he said in a thick voice. He laid a hand on her shoulder, rubbing gently. "I... Christ on a stick, I feel so dirty for thinking it, but you're so sexy with your bare ass all red and written on, and I did that to you, and – fuck, you're so wet it's dripping down your thighs!"

Without lifting her head from where it was hidden in her arms, Kimmy mumbled, "What did you write, Boss?"

His laugh in response was appreciative and full of sensual promise and need. "Punished. But it's over now. Come here," he said, helping her up from the table.

Almost automatically, she began to lower herself to a kneeling position at his feet, wanting to show him how much she'd needed and appreciated the catharsis. But he caught her elbows with his hands, keeping her in a standing position. "Thank you for my punishment," she said, gazing up at him, feeling light as a feather and flooded with adoration and sincerity and desire.

"You took it well," he said, his voice warm with approval and admiration. "You're so brave and sexy and amazing, Kimber." He pulled a tissue from his pocket and wiped her eyes and nose, dropping feather-light kisses all over her face as he dried it, then wrapped his arms around her. She snuggled against him, comforted and safe. Then – gently, carefully – he rubbed a hand over her sore backside, his fingers drifting closer to the cleft between her legs as he soothed her.

As the immediate sting of the spanking started to fade, a different sensation was building in its place, tingling and buzzing all over the spanked area, spreading to between her legs, making her squirm in his arms and press her thighs together. "I need you."

"Thank God for that," he muttered, taking her mouth with his in a deep, sweet kiss and finally sliding his hand between her legs, fingering her until she moaned out loud. "I bet you can't sit or lie on anything easily right now. If I sit in one of the armchairs, can you ride me without too much discomfort?"

Barely able to talk, she nodded against his chest, wriggling desperately against his wicked fingers, not even caring when his forearm pressed against her buttock and triggered a flare of hot discomfort. When he withdrew his hand, she let out a little mewl of disappointment.

"Patience, Pretty Girl. I got you." He knelt to take off her shoes, then got rid of the jeans and panties that were still bunched around her lower legs. Mindful of where she'd be tender, he lifted and carried her over to the nearest armchair and set her down for just a moment while he undid his pants and freed his cock. Then he sat down and leaned back, giving his already-stiff member a stroke to show her how ready he was for her, a bead of pearly fluid already leaking from the top. "Climb on and take what you need," he told her. "I'll hold out as long as I can."

Gingerly, she moved onto his lap and positioned herself over him before easing downward, so wet and needful that she took all of his thick length at once, faster than she ever had before. With a hungry grunt of satisfaction, she braced herself with hands on his shoulders and began to move, and he caught her rhythm and joined her, thrusting up to meet her downstrokes. There was deep, deep intimacy in the erotic motion and the way his eyes held hers, looking right into her soul. The same hands that had delivered such harsh punishment caressed her hips and thighs, encouraging, adding power to her ride, and with every slick impalement his pubic bone sent a cascade of sensation rippling through her on contact, accentuated by the jiggling of her sore backside, building and building until she trembled on the edge of orgasm.

"Never forget, drummers bang harder – in every way. Come for me now," he commanded, gripping her tender buttocks as he ground up into her to create an intense combination of hurt and pleasure that shot her over the edge. All the fireworks in the world had nothing on the explosive release that tore through her – a rollercoaster rush, an out-of-body experience, the burst of sweet flavor at the center of a hard candy – dissolving her into star stuff, carrying her away.

♥

She was never sure afterward how long they lay there together, snuggled in the armchair, partially dressed, their bodies still joined. It might have been two minutes or five, or an hour or more. She maybe dozed, and he maybe did too.

I've never felt so perfect, she thought peacefully, blissfully. There was something wonderful about letting him into her world so completely, not only as a best friend but also as a lover and a partner in kink. *He's seen every bit of me now and hasn't run screaming.*

Eventually she groaned and started to peel herself off him and upright. "Ooh," she gasped, feeling all the twinges and throbbing and heat reawaken with movement.

"You okay, Kimmy?" Dice held out a hand to steady her, with an immediate look of concern.

"Better than okay," she assured him, still feeling floaty and relaxed. "That was maybe the best orgasm of my life."

"Mine too." He blushed, and she caught a pleased smile hovering at the corners of his mouth, but he still looked concerned. "Apart from that, though, I meant... you're still pretty red back there."

"You've got a firm hand, drummer boy. It's an excellent quality. And don't worry; my butt's just sore, not damaged or anything. Some arnica cream will take care of it. Maybe not by morning exactly, but soon enough – oops!" She looked down and giggled, too relaxed and happy to mind or be embarrassed at the post-coital mess that was making itself known.

Dice grinned too, digging some more tissues out of his pants pocket for her. "I came prepared." Pushing himself upright with a sigh, he packed himself away and zipped up. "Let me help you," he said, fetching her pants and underwear and helping her step into them. When she winced at the fabric brushing across her reddened backside, they both laughed ruefully. "Can I at least walk you to your room?" he asked.

"Sure." She looked at the key card for the room number. "Room 246," she told him.

"Okay. Let me carry this for you," he offered, picking up her bag. "Don't want it bumping anywhere uncomfortable."

"Thank you," she said gratefully.

But when they got to her room, a man's sock over the doorknob signaled that whoever was in there – probably Lulu, Kimmy thought, since Trish would never – didn't want to be disturbed. "Why can't she go to Ryan's room?" Kimmy muttered, tired now and wanting her bed.

Dice ruffled her hair sympathetically. "He probably has to share with Will or someone. Come and share my room, then. No one will mind or care, and you need your sleep. Unless you want to waltz in and interrupt them, or sit out here waiting all night..."

"Thanks." She didn't even bother with a token protest.

"Poor tired Kimmy," he said, and put an arm around her shoulders as they walked to the elevators, since the band and bodyguards were on the next floor up.

Aidan was sitting on a chair in the hall. He waved a greeting when Kimmy and Dice stepped out of the elevator, and when they got close enough that he didn't have to shout, he said softly, "Hey, guys, have you seen Ryan anywhere? I'm supposed to be off shift to sleep, and I don't want to wake Will up and get Ryan in trouble."

Dice grinned. "We haven't seen Ryan, exactly, but... Kimmy found a sock on the doorknob of the room she was supposed to share with Lulu, so..."

"Aww, man," Aidan groaned. "At least you can come and crash up here, Kimmy. I can't go to sleep until I'm relieved from my shift."

"Just wake Will up," Dice said. "You can't always be covering for other people so they can do what they want."

"When did you get so mature?" Aidan asked, laughing silently. "You know I'd cover for you anytime if you needed it."

"What would we need cover for?" Dice asked with a wide-eyed innocent look.

We, Kimmy thought. *He said we. Self-incrimination at its finest.*

But Aidan just laughed again. "Sleep well, guys."

Kimmy stepped out of Dice's shower, feeling fresh and somewhat restored, though still filled with the usual lassitude that overcame her after an intense scene. The cool water had done a lot to soothe her skin, in addition to washing away sweat and other remnants of the discipline session and the ecstatic intimacy that had followed it.

As she was drying herself, she caught a glimpse of her rear view in the mirror. Some of the redness was already starting to fade from her buttocks, although they'd probably stay a bit pink and tender at least through the morning. But she still looked obviously spanked, and Dice had evidently used a permanent marker because even after her shower, the word *punished* stood out in vivid black letters across her butt. *Sexy.* She'd carry that private reminder for a few days before it wore away.

She put on one of the hotel bathrobes hanging on the back of the bathroom door.

He wasn't in the room when she stepped out of the bathroom, but before she'd even gotten clean pajamas out of her bag, he was back. "You said you'd want some arnica cream..." he told her, holding out a brand-new tube of it. "Is this the right stuff? I asked the concierge downstairs, and this is what he gave me."

"That's really nice of you, but it's not so bad. I probably don't really need–"

"Let me take care of you," he coaxed, the corners of his mouth quaking. Was he holding back a smile? "Isn't that part of this whole... experience? I was the one who gave you a sore ass, and I want to be the one to make it feel better."

"You already did that," she muttered, remembering the bliss he'd given her afterward. But when he patted the bed encouragingly, she lay down on her front and let him flip up the bathrobe to gain access to her sore spots. She tensed momentarily at the first touch of his fingers on her punished buttocks, but soon tolerated the gentle massage and the feeling of the slick cream as he rubbed it into her sensitive flesh.

"You're so hot, Kimmy. Is it terrible that I want to make love to you again?" His voice was heavy with arousal, even in a near whisper. "I know we just did, but damn, I'm hard as a rock again."

"It's not terrible at all," she whispered. "That's enough massage. I'd rather have you." She shifted onto her side and put her arms around his neck, expecting him to roll her over and plunge in, but he pulled her close and devoured her mouth, slowly and with aching tenderness, caressing her tongue with his and gently biting her lower lip.

If their earlier joining had been a storm, a cataclysm, this one was a slow melting – she felt like butter sizzling in a frying pan as his leisurely kisses intensified, and she felt cherished, treasured in his arms as he eased her leg over his hip, keeping her on her side and angling himself to fit her as gently as possible. The slow rocking lasted for a beautiful eternity, and the release that followed was a gentle extended ecstasy.

♥

The next day, when Kimmy arrived at the venue for the second concert in New Orleans, she found that the hot zone under the gerbs had been cordoned off with a couple of metal security barricades and some lengths of chain.

She found Qingshan and said, "Look, I'm sorry I ran through the hot zone yesterday. I know it wasn't smart, and I shouldn't have done it."

"You are okay," he said kindly. "Nothing bad happened, and I got my barriers. I had asked for them but no one listened. Now I have them. I do not think I would if you had not run through it."

"I'm sorry no one listened to you at first, Qingshan," she told him.

Second concerts in the same venue were always a bit easier on the crew. They had a short soundcheck to work out a couple of minor issues from the previous night's show and tweaked a few lighting cues as well.

Unlike Arleigh Hayward, Valancy didn't expect them to put on a mini-show for paying VIPs at every soundcheck, negotiating no more than six a month at the band's choice of venues as a special opportunity to premier new songs, try out different arrangements, and do fun covers. Kurt Daygood, their new A&R manager, had also suggested they move the regular meet-and-greets to before the show, so they wouldn't have to entertain fans afterward. However, Blade's stage fright was bad enough right before shows that he wouldn't be able to cope with strangers and small talk until after he was done performing, so they kept those sessions after the concert the way they'd always been.

There was good, smooth energy at this second show, and everything unfolded just as it should. There were no drum kit issues, and Kimmy had plenty of time to stroll around behind the hot zone barriers and across to her mic during Angel's patter between the end of "Star Shot Down" and the beginning of "Band on the Road" – she didn't even have to jog.

It would be her last performance for a while, since the band was pulling the song from their setlists until the next year's holiday season. All the complex energy of the past day flowed through her, and she sang beyond her best ability. Not that anyone would notice nuances in a backup singer's voice, she thought, but she gave it her all and felt good.

♥

At the end of the night, after load-out was done, Kimmy stumbled onto the tour bus where her bunk was, ready for sleep. Everyone on the bus was in the front lounge area having a beer, and to be sociable she joined them, not feeling much interested in beer but knowing there'd be some sodas and juice in the cooler as well.

She grabbed a grapefruit juice, the first thing to hand, and without thinking flopped onto a nearby seat a shade harder than she'd meant to. *Ouch.* With a wince she tried to hide, she shifted to find a more comfortable position, trying not to blush, trying not to think about the word *punished* in Dice's handwriting where she sat. She busied herself opening her drink, took a big sip, and glanced around. All seemed good – someone had started a video game on the big screen and a handful of the crew were arguing about who should have first go at the two controllers.

And then she saw Mack watching her with eyes narrowed in speculation, and a grin beginning to spread broadly over his face. *Shit.*

He was standing at the back of the lounge area, by the kitchenette section, right where she'd have to pass to go to the bunks, and he didn't look like he was planning on moving. The gamers were settling into their evening's entertainment, and it was late. Finished with her juice, Kimmy got up and put the bottle into the recycling compartment in the kitchenette, steeling herself to walk by Mack, knowing what he'd seen.

"So, someone gave you what you needed, huh?" he said for her ears only as she moved to pass him.

"Fuck you, Mack," she shot back, just as quietly but with a deadly look. It wasn't any of his business.

He laughed silently. "Hey, I just want you to be happy. I know what makes you happy. Was it your drummer? I've seen how he looks at you, but I never figured him for a kinky sort."

"Not everyone is what they look like on the outside," she snapped, then realized how much that sounded like a confession, even as her mind was reeling. *I've seen how he looks at you.* What did that mean?

"I know, Kim," Mack said. "I just wasn't expecting it. You've got that look you always had after a satisfying scene, and maybe I'm a teensy bit jealous of anyone else who can give you that. But it's all good."

"Goodnight, Mack," she told him firmly. "I'm hitting my bunk. And... I'd appreciate no speculation, okay?"

He nodded briefly, just a quick dip of the chin but enough to assure her that he'd drop the subject. "Sleep well."

She nodded too and moved on down the passageway, making a quick stop in the bathroom cubicle before stretching out in her bunk, earbuds in to mute the road sounds and the other onboard noises. *I've seen how he looks at you.* Mack's words echoed in her mind. How *did* Dice look at her when she wasn't looking at him? And if Mack could figure out that something was going on between them, how long until the whole crew knew, and the rest of the band?

How bad would it be, she wondered sleepily, if everyone knew, if it just became accepted fact that the drummer was banging his drum tech as a recreational no-strings benefit?

When it was just a private idea between her and Dice, at the outset, it had all seemed so possible – to explore his sexual initiation and self-discovery, and to start a baby for her, two separate and self-contained goals that no one else needed to know about. But she couldn't shake from her mind Aidan saying *you know I'd cover for you anytime,* and then Mack *asking was it your drummer?* They knew, or at least guessed. And Easy had already walked in on them. That was three.

Nothing I can do about it right now, she told herself, trying to settle into sleep. She imagined Dice stretched out on his king-sized hotel bed, all alone, his silky hair sliding over his pillow. Would he have the blankets pulled up over him, or just a thin sheet? She wasn't sure if he ran cold or hot when sleeping alone. He'd be boarding the Smidge jet in the morning when she'd already have rolled through the night on the road, and maybe they'd find a chance to be alone together in the next city or maybe they wouldn't.

Waiting for the bus to rock her to sleep, she let herself wonder what it would be like to be his girlfriend – his hotel room hers too, a seat for her on every flight, a shared bed every night. But that wasn't the deal she'd offered him, and anyway, letting their thing become a real relationship carried with it the risk of a breakup, and then what?

Her phone buzzed under her pillow, and she felt around to grab it. On the lock screen, there was a text message from Dice. *Sleeping yet?*

No, she texted back. *Almost.*

Wish you were here, he told her.

More comfy than my bunk, she agreed. She wondered if she should tell him that she thought Aidan and Mack might have guessed something was up between them, but decided it wasn't a conversation to have over text, if at all. Instead, she asked: *Silly question, but do you have all the blankets pulled up or just a sheet?*

Blankets, he replied. *It's cold without you here.*

She adjusted her mental picture of him to add blankets bundled around him. Wondered what color the bedding was. *Send me a selfie?*

After a pause, a photo popped up on her screen. There he was, shirtless, his hair loose and flopping forward, snuggled up in bed under a royal blue quilt with white linens. Adorable.

Selfie of you? he asked, so she sent him the best picture she could manage – wedged into her dark bunk, in her sleeping bag, with her earbuds in to block out bus noises, wearing a cat-patterned onesie. It wasn't particularly glamorous, especially as the flash washed her out and the angle wasn't flattering, but he sent back a heart emoji. *Sleep well, Kimmy,* he texted. *I'll see you at our next stop.*

You sleep well too, Dylan Ignatius, she told him, because it wouldn't do to get all mushy and his middle name would put a stop to that. But she sent a heart emoji too because she didn't want him to feel unloved. Then she looked at the selfie of him in his hotel bed for a long time before she fell asleep.

chapter

10

"WE'VE GOT BACK-TO-BACK CONCERTS IN DES MOINES next week," Dice said to Kimmy casually as they were waiting for soundcheck to start. It had been a week since the concerts in New Orleans and no one had said anything – not Mack, not Aidan, nor did there seem to be any rumors floating about as far as Kimmy could tell. And Dice, wonderfully, mercifully, hadn't let anything change him either. He'd seen her at her messiest and most vulnerable... and at the next concert he was totally himself, no innuendo or treating her differently, talking to her comfortably about ordering more drumsticks and whether one of the toms needed its drumhead changed, and now the schedule.

"I'm looking forward to it," she agreed, busy with the drum kit. "At the very least, we get to sleep in." Back-to-back shows meant hotel rooms for the crew and not rolling through the night or having to be up at the crack of dawn. "I haven't heard anything about a party night yet, but I wouldn't be surprised. I'll let you know if there's something happening." Even after six years, she still wasn't entirely sure how a party night got started, but somehow word would spread through the crew that they were going out together after the show, and the band would often join them, the whole group hitting a nightclub together from the end of their show until last call.

"Oh," he said. "Yes." He sounded disappointed.

She stopped what she was doing and turned to look at him. "What is it?"

"It'll be Valentine's Day. I know we aren't – I mean, not really, but – I... would you let me take you out somewhere? Just the two of us?"

"On a date?" she asked quietly, clarifying.

He didn't answer, instead looking out over the empty arena as if it were extremely interesting.

"You know we'd get photographed," she pointed out. "People would talk. There'd be assumptions."

"Would that be so terrible?" he asked.

She shook her head. "I'm trying to protect you," she pointed out, keeping her voice reasonable, practical. "Hanging out as friends doesn't tell anyone anything, but if I turn up pregnant after we've been seen on an obvious date together, you won't be able to walk away from it."

He nodded slowly. "I guess I appreciate that. I just... there's always such a fuss about Valentine's Day, I wanted to see what – to do something special. But partying with the crew will be fine. Or whatever you want to do."

What harm could playing at romance for one night do? The temptation to let herself pretend it could be real felt dangerous, but... "If you can think of something where we won't be photographed or gossiped about, I'm up for it," she offered.

"I don't want to take you away from a party night," he said.

"There'll always be more party nights."

He grinned. "I'll think of something nice."

Doing a bit of quick math, she squinched up her eyes and said, "Just one thing. I might be getting my period around then. So maybe don't count on..."

"Or you might not. I've been doing my best." He stuck his tongue out, making fun of what would otherwise be maybe a bit of a heavy conversation. "But seriously, I don't hang out with you for the sex, even though it's amazing. I just want to do a Valentine thing for you, and if it has to involve painkillers and a hot water bottle, that's okay."

His earnest reassurance made her smile. "Thanks. I guess we'll see. No signs so far."

♥

Kimmy's guess about the party night had been accurate – word spread over the few days leading up to Valentine's Day that there was an afterparty planned at a popular club within walking distance of the arena they were playing at. And it wasn't so much that she had no signs of pregnancy but the fact that early pregnancy signs were virtually identical to premenstrual signs. Tender boobs? As the week went on, check. But were they *more* tender? Bigger than usual for day 26, day 27, day 28 of her cycle? Hard to say. Was she crampy and bloated? Sure. But again... And after her last effort at taking a pregnancy test and agonizing over whether it was a line, she'd promised herself that she wouldn't test again before her period was overdue.

The morning of Valentine's Day, she woke up on the bus feeling mildly unsettled and desperate to pee. She rolled out of her bunk, felt around at the foot of her bunk for her bathroom kit, and stumbled to the toilet cubicle, grateful that no one else was awake and it was unoccupied. Part of her expected to see spotting on her just-in-case panty liner, a signal that her period was coming, but there was nothing. She looked at the pregnancy test in her bathroom kit, bursting to go and needing to decide. Technically it was day 29, but her cycle varied from 27 to 30 days. *Do I take it now?*

She did.

Same as before, after she snuck it back to her bunk and waited the required amount of time, the test was inconclusive in the dimly lit sleeping space. Trusting that everyone else was still asleep, she got up again and walked casually out to the lounge area. Gary the bass tech was passed out on the couch, but otherwise the space was empty, so she held the test up to the window to get a look at it in the natural early morning light.

Maybe?

She definitely sort of thought she saw a faint line this time.

I really think I see it. The month before, the line she thought she might have seen was greyish, more of a shadow in the test window. *It's pink this time, isn't it?* But that could also be wishful thinking. It was probably wishful thinking. *Too early to be up, anyway.*

She dragged herself back to her bunk and tried to go back to sleep until it was time to get dressed. Dice hadn't said anything further about his plans for them, but she put on scarlet lingerie anyway to match her pedicure – at their last stop, she'd found a nail spa to get a special pedicure for the occasion with ruby heart-shaped glitter. No matter what else happened, at least her feet would look pretty.

She'd never been the sort to dress up for a party night – if she ended up going to the club with everyone else, her work jeans would be fine, though she'd change her t-shirt if she felt sweaty after the show. Doing anything different for this occasion would be like waving a flag.

♥

After the concert, she didn't want to worry anyone, so she told Sally she didn't feel like going out and was heading back to the hotel. One of the drivers, who was conveniently waiting nearby, offered to run her there right away if she was ready to go. Kimmy wasn't sure where Dice was, since he'd been swept away in the band limo after the concert as usual, and she was fairly confident they'd all been going to the club. Mario gave Kimmy the slightest secret wink when he said to Sally that it would be no trouble to run the drum tech back to the hotel before he went on to the club himself. It was so slight and imperceptible that she wondered if she'd imagined it. But she put her jacket on and declared herself ready to go, if it wouldn't be too much trouble.

Once they were in the runabout van, he gave her a bigger grin and said, "Don't worry. Your plans for the evening are still good."

He refused to say anything more, just turned up the radio and drove for about two minutes before heading down a heavily graffitied alley, pulling to a stop where a back door bore the logo of the club everyone was going to. He got out his phone and texted something, and barely a minute later, Aidan popped his head out the back door, scanned the area, then approached the van and opened the side door. Dice shot out of the back door and scrambled into the van, lying flat instead of taking the jump seat. Aidan followed him into the van, pulling the door closed, and the van pulled out immediately, taking them smoothly back to the hotel.

"Thanks, man," Dice said when Mario dropped them at the hotel. She saw her drummer pass something to the driver, and figured it was a wad of cash in appreciation of his effort and discretion.

"Anytime. G'night, then," and Mario was back in the driver's seat and off to the rest of his evening.

Aidan walked with them to the elevator bank. "Pretty safe around here, I should think," he muttered, almost to himself. "I might go work out in the gym for a bit, if you're cool with that."

"You probably wanted to be doing something else for Valentine's Day," Kimmy said, feeling guilty for their bodyguard friend. Hadn't he been with Trish at Christmas?

Aidan shook his head. "I got no special girl or anything. So it'd just be spending twice the money for pink heart decorations at the club. I might go chat up the babe on the front desk overnight when I'm done working out, though. You never know. Text me if you need me, my dudes." With a cheerful grin, he spun on his heel and strode toward the gym and pool signage, leaving Kimmy and Dice to themselves.

"Come on," Dice said, taking her hand. "I've got the coolest thing to show you."

She thought they were going up to his room, but he pressed the button for the penthouse floor, unlocking it by tapping the card reader with a black key card unlike the regular room ones. "Where are we going?" she asked, curious now. It didn't make sense for him to rent one of the ridiculously expensive penthouse suites when he had a perfectly nice room on the floor below, but...

"Here." Ignoring the entrance doors to the suites, he followed the hallway to the end, where a door bore a sign saying *Sky Garden*. Tapping the black key card again, he opened it and gestured for her to go ahead of him into a stairwell that housed an elegant wrought-iron spiral staircase, the metalwork cleverly crafted to represent vines and flowers. The night sky was visible at the top through what looked like a glass roof. "They have this cool place for private parties," he said, as she started up the spiral staircase with him close behind her. "And tonight, we have it all to ourselves."

At the top of the stairs, she discovered that she was indeed in a sky garden. The staircase opened into a greenhouse-like structure of glass panes, from which multiple sliding glass doors allowed access to the roof garden itself, forming an indoor-outdoor conservatory-and-garden space. Sofas and armchairs were clustered around coffee tables, offering visitors comfortable places to sit, and fairy lights strung up in the roof of the structure cast a magical light over everything. It was warm enough inside the structure for orange trees and orchids and jasmine to grow, infusing the air with their scents.

Spread over one of the elegant sofas, there was a luxurious red faux fur snuggle blanket and a pink teddy bear holding a red satin heart that said *Be My Valentine*. Next to the sofa was an enormous bunch of heart-shaped helium balloons, and the coffee table held a picnic basket and a champagne bucket with a couple of bottles in a mound of ice.

Dice looked at Kimmy, his expression full of hope and the pleasure of giving her something. "I *think* this is what Valentine's Day is supposed to look like... Do you like it?"

Weirdly, she felt like crying. "No one ever did anything like this for me," she muttered, choking back the emotion. Growing up, her gifts had been the same as her brothers' – they all got hockey skates and Lego and bikes and science kits and baseball gloves, and the pretty things she had now, the lingerie and the pedicures, were things she did for herself and kept mostly hidden. Slowly, she walked over to the sofa and picked up the teddy, gave the plush toy a cuddle. "It's so soft and cute, I love it! Thank you."

He scuffed the toe of his boot along the elegant tile floor, his eyes intent on his phone as he typed something. "I, uh, value all the different sides of you, Kimber. I like your sweet and cute and sparkly bits as much as your tough and pierced and kinky bits. I want you to know that." Then he looked up and smiled at her so sweetly, as soft music began to play from hidden speakers, one of her favorite songs. He must have been connecting his phone to the Sky Garden's sound system.

She grinned at him, a bit wobbly but recovering fast. "Hey, well, I like the kind and funny and thoughtful side of you as much as the dominant and sexy and metal side of you."

"Metal? Nobody calls me metal," he said, laughing.

"You haven't seen yourself behind that drum kit, I guess. You play hard rock because your band does, but I think you lean more to the metal side. Tell me I'm wrong?"

"Can't. Okay. I'm as metal as fuck. Does that make you happy?"

His good-natured acceptance of her assessment made her feel warm somehow. "I'm so full of happiness you'll have to scrape me off the ceiling. What's in the picnic basket?"

"I asked for a bunch of things," he said. "Make yourself comfortable and let's see what we actually got." He helped her off with her jacket, then gestured for her to open the basket. "Go ahead, it's yours."

So she sat down on the sofa and opened the lid of the basket. There was a box of little sandwiches with different fillings inside miniature croissants, and a tray of chocolate-dipped strawberries, and a pair of enormous heart-shaped chocolate chip cookies. And in the corner of the basket, she noticed a bottle of Aleve. "Oh?" She lifted it out and looked at Dice quizzically.

He shrugged, busying himself with removing his jacket. "You mentioned you might be... not feeling awesome. I thought we should have something on hand, just in case." Then he paused. "You, ah – how *are* you feeling?"

Such a typical Dice way of asking, giving her room to answer in a way that gave no answer if she wanted to. *Always so sweet.* "No period yet." Then she caught the way he was looking at her, tense and concerned, and she wondered what he was thinking. It was only fair to be honest with him, her best friend, the father-to-be if there was a baby.

"I took a test this morning. Inconclusive. There might have been a faint line, or it could have been wishful thinking; I couldn't honestly tell. I don't...*feel* pregnant or anything."

"Well..." He nodded toward the ice bucket, and she saw that one of the bottles contained champagne but the other was sparkling apple juice. "We can drink as though you are, or drink as though you're not. Up to you."

"I don't know," she said. "I don't know. I think... I don't want to think about it tonight."

"Have a strawberry," he said, taking one from the platter and holding it out for her to bite. She let him feed her, savoring the juicy sweetness of the fruit combined with the smoothly bittersweet chocolate, and wondered how she'd gotten to this point of mixing romantic inclinations and sexual explorations with the most important and precious friendship she'd ever had. Eating romanticized food from his fingers like the main character in a rom-com...

He sat next to her on the sofa and offered her the box of sandwiches, so she picked one at random and ate it in three bites, tasting chicken and mango chutney.

When they'd eaten several of the small sandwiches and strawberries each, and broken off a bit of cookie to try, he leaned over to the ice bucket and lifted out the champagne bottle. "Want a little bit of this? I can't imagine it'll hurt if it's too early to even know."

"You're right. Sure, please. Half a glass, maybe."

So he poured them each half a glass of champagne, and when they clinked their glasses in a toast it reminded her of New Year's Eve and their dance and how all of this had gotten started. But when she took her first sip, it tasted off to her, and she put the glass down. She reached for another strawberry, wanting to erase the nauseating taste.

Dice asked, "It's, you know, February, but do you want to go out and walk around the Sky Garden itself?"

Kimmy nodded. Since they had a whole Sky Garden all to themselves for a night, it seemed a shame to let it go to waste, even though the northern states were in the grip of a cold snap. So, they put their jackets back on and left the glassed-in conservatory area for the chilly outside rooftop garden.

It was a proper garden, with maze-like flagstone-and-gravel paths leading around bushes and trees and raised planter boxes. More strands of white fairy lights provided enough illumination for walking, and high glass barriers around the perimeter of the roof kept garden visitors safe without obscuring the view of the city around them. The air was breathtakingly cold, with frost on the trees and bushes reminding them that February was still very much part of winter. The paths were slippery in spots and Dice put his arm around Kimmy as her foot skidded on a patch of black ice. "I got you," he said, and kept his arm around her.

She tucked her arm around his waist and leaned into his warmth.

"Look, Kimmy, the stars are out," he said, pointing upward with his free hand. "You should make a wish." The sky had been grey during the day, but sometime while Smidge and the crew were busy with the show, some of the clouds had blown away, leaving ragged patches of clear sky. The stars weren't as vivid as they'd been in the Caribbean, but they were there.

"Oh, good, yes. *Star light, star bright, all the stars I see tonight...*" She'd never been able to wish on just one star – how could you tell which one you'd seen first, when there were so many? – so she always wished on all of them. "*Wish I may, wish I might, have the wish I wish tonight.*"

Looking up at the stars, she took a breath.

Please, I want to keep him.

She'd meant to wish for a positive pregnancy test. She'd meant to wish for a healthy baby. But the thought that filled her mind was of Dice. *Forever.* And she knew her wish hadn't meant anything platonic. *Oh, shit.*

"What's the matter?" he asked, looking down at her face.

She made herself smile. "Nothing, just... concentrating hard."

"I love how you take your wishes seriously." His voice was full of such affection, it melted her.

"They're just wishes," she said. "I know they don't really change anything. But I like wishing on stars."

"Do I know what you just wished for?"

"I hope not," she said, feeling a chill trickle down her spine. "Please don't try to guess, it ruins the wish." *He mustn't know, ever.* If they were just fooling around having fun sex, she could tell him she was having romantic feelings. But she'd asked him for a baby and promised there'd be no strings.

Maybe if her period came, if there was no baby, she could tell him that she wanted something more. Maybe they could date a bit instead, and see what might grow from that, and a baby could come later – if they stayed together, if they formalized their relationship the way their families would expect. Maybe a baby would follow an engagement and a wedding, in the traditional order of things... if she wasn't already pregnant.

"Let's go inside," he suggested. "You've made your wish, and it's cold out here."

"Okay," she agreed.

"I love you so much, Kimmy," he said casually, dropping an affectionate kiss on her forehead, and she thought her heart would stop. "Don't ever change."

Of course he loved her, and she loved him too. They'd been best friends for years. That was normal. She'd heard him say it before, but it hit differently now. "People always change," she reminded him. *If I'm not pregnant, I'll tell him I'm crushing on him,* she promised herself.

He held the door for her, ushered her inside. Helped her off with her jacket.

They ate the last of the strawberries.

The music from his playlist continued in the background. "Want to dance?" he asked lightly, as though it didn't matter.

She wanted to ask him why, but it seemed rude when he'd gone to such trouble to make a fairytale of an evening for them. *There's always such a fuss about Valentine's Day,* he'd said. *I wanted to see what* – then he'd broken off and instead talked about doing something special. She supposed what he wanted was to feel the romance of the day, even if it was slightly pretend, with his best friend who happened to provide some sexy, kinky benefits. Her suddenly fragile heart wasn't his fault. And why not dance? He was lovely to dance with. "Sure."

For someone so big and strong, he could be surprisingly gentle. He drew her into his arms and she settled herself against him, her head on his chest, listening to his heart, letting him move her around the floor. They hadn't danced together since New Year's Eve, right before he'd kissed her for the first time. It was only a month and a half before, but it seemed much longer than that. *A perfect night, a fairytale night,* Kimmy thought as they danced.

The bunch of heart-shaped balloons bobbed in the corner of her vision, filled with helium and straining at their ribbon tethers, as perfect and buoyant as the night. She knew she couldn't keep them, but it would break her heart to pop the lovely things. Maybe they could be left at the front desk of the hotel. Maybe someone would take them...

♥

Three days later, her period still hadn't started, and the smell of bacon in the biscuit breakfast sandwiches catering handed out after load-in made her gag. Averting her eyes and breathing through her mouth, she managed to eat half a plain biscuit between sips of coffee –she didn't feel like throwing up or anything, unless she looked at or smelled or thought about bacon, at which point her stomach felt distinctly uneasy.

The band arrived while most of the crew were still eating, and headed straight for the food. They'd have plenty of snacks later – this type of concert always had a rider specifying what would be wanted backstage, but for Smidge it had to be low-odor, non-obtrusive items like pretzels and candy and fruit that wouldn't trigger Blade's stage-fright nausea. At this point, before soundcheck, that hadn't kicked in yet so they all tended to eat like fiends earlier in the day since they wouldn't eat substantial food again until after the show. Dice saw Kimmy and waved, striding joyfully over to join her, already biting into his sandwich, and a waft of bacon smell made her stomach churn as he sat down next to her. He looked at her, surprised and concerned, and she realized her reaction must have shown on her face. "You okay, Kimmy?"

Her first instinct was to pretend, to say she was fine, but... "I don't know. Bacon is one of my favorite things, but today even the smell of it is making me want to puke."

His face blanked, then he gave her a small smile, as if asking whether he should be happy for her. "So, are you...?"

"I guess that's something I need to find out." She remembered how the champagne on Valentine's Day had tasted off to her, and decided it was time to acquire another pregnancy test from Jed's supply.

"Is there anything I can do?" he asked.

She had to know. She didn't want to wait until she was on the bus again, and really, shouldn't he be there to find out with her? Not that it was his responsibility, but she wanted his company. "Not really, but... come with me?"

"Of course."

With everyone busy eating and talking and relaxing before the next burst of activity, no one noticed as they slipped away. Kimmy got to Jed's box of supplies and scooped up a test, noticing that he'd replenished them since she'd last taken one. He must have spotted that a few had been used, then. *Oof.*

Dice waited outside the bathroom, a utilitarian multi-stall affair deep in the bowels of the arena. "Be right back," Kimmy told him as cheerfully as she could. *If I'm not pregnant, I'll tell him I'm crushing on him,* she'd promised herself on Valentine's Day, and she could feel that slipping away as she let herself into one of the toilet stalls, even before she peed on the stick.

This time, the second pink line showed up right away, unmistakably clear. She didn't need natural daylight to see it, didn't even have to wait one minute. *Pregnant.*

For a moment, she felt dizzy, glad she was sitting so she couldn't stumble, glad she was hidden away alone but also wanting someone to hold her.

What the fuck have I done? I can't do this.

She took a deep breath and jammed the test into the waste container on the wall, wadded up in toilet paper so no one would see what it was. Then she got up and left the stall, washed her hands, and headed out into the hallway to tell Dice.

She couldn't make herself smile. Wasn't sure what to say. Opened her mouth, but no words came out.

He took one look at her and opened his arms. Gratefully, she stumbled into his embrace and leaned against him, letting him wrap her in his arms and strength and the safe feeling he'd always given her. He didn't try to talk, just waited, holding her and rubbing her back.

"I'm pregnant," she mumbled against his shirt. It was supposed to be a joyful announcement, but she only felt numb.

"No," he said, "you're Kimmy." The terribleness of the dad joke made her snort with bizarre reluctant laughter that was somehow close to tears. "Look," he continued, "if you *want* to be pregnant, yay, we're having a baby! If you don't want to be pregnant, we get you an appointment to deal with it. I can go with you, or I know Sally would if you'd rather–"

She pulled her head away from his chest to look up at him, surprised. "*We're* having a baby?"

"It's your body, Kimber. But I'm the one who came inside you; I'm at least partly responsible for helping with... whatever choices you make." He seemed puzzled, worried, maybe even a bit sad, and above all, so gentle and encouraging. "I thought you *wanted* me to give you a baby, but it's okay if you've changed your mind. Just tell me what you need."

"I did. I think I still do. I'm just a little overwhelmed right now and I don't know what I need." She shook her head. "I know I didn't want there to be any strings for you."

He grinned. "You're my best friend. Practically family. I'd be here for you even if I hadn't contributed DNA to you being a party of two, okay? *No strings* is something you say to, like, a one-night stand or something."

She choked back her feelings and tried a grin on in return. "Yeah." *Now I can never tell him I was falling in love with him. Besties forever.* "Don't... please don't say anything to anyone just yet. I thought I knew I wanted this, but now it seems I need time to adjust."

"It's a big thing," he agreed. "And no one's business but yours." He gave her shoulder an encouraging pat. "Are you ready to head back up there?" he asked. "They'll be wanting to start soundcheck any time now."

By the time they'd rejoined the rest of the group, she'd regained her grip on herself, and was able to wave a cheerful greeting to Crys and smile at the rest of the band and interact with the crew in her normal way. Practical, positive, confident Kimmy with the boyish haircut and the most piercings of anyone in the crew, always ready for anything – she'd made a point of portraying that image over the years and now everyone just accepted it. At least having everyone assume she wasn't the emotional type let her hide things when she needed to, she thought with wry satisfaction. Growing up with four brothers had given her a lot of practice at that, when hurt feelings and a wobbly lower lip might have meant the difference between being included in their games or left behind. She stuffed her wobbly-lip feelings into a mental box and pushed on with what she needed to do, surface smile in position.

♥

"What d'you want to do this week?" Dice asked, turning around on his drum throne to chat with her as they waited for soundcheck to start, taking out his IEMs so she took hers out too, risking Mack's annoyance if he caught them.

They had a week off after this concert – one of the benefits of Valancy Records having a more rational approach to touring and work-life balance. Torquil Stirling believed that bands performed better if given a full week off every two months, and Smidge being a generation younger than the rest of his artists didn't factor into it.

Before seeing the positive pregnancy test that morning, Kimmy had assumed she'd go home for the week. The more affordable flights from Nashville to Detroit had lengthy layovers, though, and the thought of dealing with connections and delays and airport security didn't hold much appeal. She wasn't used to having a week off mid-tour, in any case, and even without feeling like she was carrying a strange passenger around in her uterus, she hadn't been firmly set on heading home as an option.

"I don't have much of a plan," she told him. "Go home, maybe?"

"You don't sound enthused. Want to do something with me instead? Easy and Nell are going to Paris; we could go too. Or Dublin, or Monte Carlo?"

"Are those places you want to go?" she asked, surprised. He'd never expressed an interest in traveling outside of the band's touring schedule.

He dipped his head, embarrassed. "We already fly around so much, it seems goofy to want to go more places. But I want to drink a Guinness at the real place it's brewed, and even when we've played Dublin, we've never had time – well, I never asked the guys if we could. And I want to gamble in Monte Carlo like James Bond someday. I'm fancy like that," he added with a self-deprecating shake of his head.

"It's cool. You should. I don't think I'm up to traveling the world right at the moment, though. Got a little too much on my mind and I don't think I'd be good company."

"You're always good company," he assured her. "What would you like to do, though, if you could do anything?"

She sighed. "Find somewhere to hide from everyone for a week? I don't know."

"Hiding sounds good," he agreed. "I can go play James Bond another time. How about we find an apartment to rent for the week and just hang out."

"Could it really be that easy?"

"DICE!" Mack bellowed. "Put your monitors in!"

Oops! Soundcheck had started. Kimmy fumbled to put her IEMs back in, listening as they tested the talkback mic system.

♥

After load-out, some of the crew left right away to start their week of vacation – which felt like a luxury so soon after the break they'd had over the holidays, but no one was complaining – while others took advantage of the hotel rooms and breakfast that the tour provided before heading out the next morning.

"I've got us an apartment," Dice whispered to Kimmy during the post-show debrief. "Want to wait until morning or should we go right over after the show?"

Maybe it *was* that easy. "Let's go have a look, if you can get the key this late. If it's a disaster or something, we can always head back to the hotel and sort things out in the morning."

He nodded, seeming pleased that she wanted to go right away. "There's no key to worry about; it's got one of those electronic locks with a code, so we can go anytime."

"Sounds good to me. I'll ditch out of here and finish my load-out stuff as quick as possible," she told him. Catching Mack's attention, she told the stage manager that she had nothing to report with regard to the show and that with his permission she'd like to go and wrap up her tasks for the night. He nodded and dismissed her.

Not too long after that, her phone buzzed. Dice texted: *I've got a car booked to pick us up in an hour. Is that enough time?*

Sure, she texted back, and doubled her working speed to get everything done.

It barely seemed any time at all until she grabbed her bags and met Dice in the loading bay, where a black car waited, with a uniformed driver from the car service the band used across most of the Southern states.

"What about Aidan?" she asked as they got into the car. "I thought you're not supposed to go off without him."

"Yeah. I talked to him, told him where we're going. He agreed that we won't get into much trouble in an apartment by ourselves overnight, so he's sleeping at the hotel and he'll come by and check on us tomorrow. Good enough?"

It seemed like a fair compromise. Much as she wanted to run away from everyone at the moment, someone had to know where they were. "He'd better not show up too early. I want to sleep in," she said, half-joking but also looking forward to not getting up before sunrise and lugging gear around in the cold before she'd even had coffee. It would be nice to doze in bed until she was ready to get up. "Hopefully the place is decent and has clean sheets and stuff so we can stay there tonight."

"It has good ratings, should be okay," Dice assured her, then added, "Looks like we're about to find out," as the car came to a stop with a soft rocking motion in front of the entrance to an apartment complex. The driver got out to open the door for them.

"Thank you so much," Kimmy said to the driver, passing him a tip before Dice could do it. Dice chuckled, seeing it, but didn't protest. She knew he was aware of the difference in their incomes and he tried to cover small costs when they were together as much as he could. Most of the time, she let him. But he had the sense to know that when she insisted, he should respect that. The driver got their bags from the trunk and wished them a good evening, and Dice led her up to the entranceway and punched a code into the lock panel to let them in.

Their apartment was on the top floor of three, at the back, which Dice told her he'd chosen for security – it was less likely that an intruder would somehow scale a way up to a third-floor balcony, and passers-by weren't realistically going to spot his famous face at that height around the back of the building over an alley. *Smart man.* It wasn't a super posh or prestigious address, just a nondescript but pleasant apartment complex in a reasonable neighborhood in a place that neither of them had family or friends. No one would be looking. No one would expect Dice to be there. He punched another code into the apartment's door lock.

"You first," he said, swinging the door open and gesturing for her to enter.

It smelled clean and pleasant, with a hint of Pledge and lavender air freshener, and the carpet of the entrance hall and main room had the faint lines of a recent vacuum's passage. In the small kitchen area, everything from the tiled floor to the sink drain was sparkling clean, and Kimmy was glad to see a coffee maker with a basket of everything needed to make their morning coffee. A note stuck to the basket read: *Coffee creamer is in the fridge, please enjoy.*

"This is nice," she said.

He nodded his agreement. "It only has one bedroom. I hope that's okay. There weren't a lot of choices for a whole week at short notice and this was the nicest one, but I would have liked to get you your own room."

Oh. She tried not to feel hurt. "Don't you want to share a bed? Because honestly, it'll be nice for once just to cuddle and fall asleep and not always be having to sneak back to my room or make up some story about sleeping on a couch or cot."

He looked a bit bewildered at that. "Of course! I only meant... I want you to be comfortable. If it works for you, it works for me."

"It does," she confirmed, relieved, and crossed the main room to the door that had to lead to the bedroom. It was nice in there, too – she felt relieved to see that the bed looked neat and freshly made, and when she sniffed the pillow nearest to her, it smelled only of clean linen and dryer sheet fragrance, evidently freshly laundered for their arrival. The duvet cover was pale grey with tiny white-petaled and gold-centered daisies, and it too looked and smelled like it had come right out of the dryer. Short-term rentals weren't always so nice...

There was a big television on the wall in the bedroom as well as one in the main room. "You want to go to sleep right away or watch something to wind down?" Dice asked, and Kimmy realized she must have yawned without noticing it.

"I'm pretty sleepy, but if you want to watch something in here, it won't bother me."

He got her wash kit out of her bag for her, and she popped into the bathroom to brush her teeth and get ready for bed while he flipped through the various streaming and television options. With his warmth in the bed, she wouldn't need a flannelette onesie to stay cozy, so she opted for a t-shirt and sleep shorts. Then she got into the very comfortable bed – it had an incredible mattress and such a fluffy duvet – and by the time Dice had emerged from his turn in the bathroom, she was almost asleep.

"You sure you don't mind if I watch TV for a bit, Kimmy?" he asked, getting into bed beside her and arranging his pillows so he could sit up and lean back against the headboard.

She wiggled closer to him, getting comfortable. "As long as you like," she mumbled. "Don't know why I'm so tired." There were plenty of nights where she'd be out at a club or in a café after a show, staying up much later than this with no effort.

He draped an affectionate arm over her, his hand resting on her hip. "You've had a lot to think about, I guess," he said, his voice tender and kind. "It makes sense that you need sleep. So sleep well. I'll be right here."

chapter

II

KIMMY WOKE UP TO THE SCENT OF COFFEE. SHE WAS alone in the bed, but Dice's body heat still lingered under the covers, and before she could get out of bed, he appeared in the bedroom doorway with a coffee mug in each hand. "Is it okay for you to have coffee?" he asked, suddenly looking uncertain. "I made it assuming you could, but..."

"I think one cup a day is considered fine," she assured him, reaching out to take the mug he offered her. The first sip told her it was good stuff, and she enjoyed her coffee in silence for a minute or two, breathing in the lovely aroma and letting the taste and warmth wake her up as she savored it. But it wasn't long before the pressure in her bladder became too much to ignore. She set her mug on the bedside table and excused herself to pee.

When she came back, Dice was doing something on his phone. His head whipped around at her footsteps, and his cheeks wore a hint of a blush. "I was going to go to the grocery store," he said, "but I... I haven't been anywhere public by myself in years – there are always bodyguards and crew around me, and my bandmates. That one time I snuck away with the van to get you, I didn't see or talk to anyone. I don't even know what would happen, if I'd be asking for trouble walking around in a store on my own or if no one would pay any attention to me. So I did an online grocery order just now and it'll be delivered this afternoon between two and five, but that doesn't give us anything to eat this morning, and I'm guessing you're hungry. Sorry."

"I didn't think about that either. It's not a big deal. We'll think of something." She *was* hungry, but the coffee had taken the edge off for the moment. "I can go out and see if I can find a café or corner store nearby. Or... Aidan's coming to check on us at some point, isn't he? Maybe he could bring us snacks."

Dice nodded. "Yeah. I'll ask him. Then I want to grab a shower. Unless you want to go first."

That seemed like too much effort compared to lounging in bed. "You go ahead. I'm going to lie back down and finish my coffee and enjoy being on vacation."

He smiled and came over to ruffle her hair and drop an affectionate kiss on her forehead before heading off for his shower, and she thought what a perfect morning it was.

She grabbed her current read out of the top of her duffle bag and got back into bed, listening to the faint sound of the shower running and briefly letting herself imagine him in the shower before she dove into her book. She didn't often read rock star romance because the inaccuracies and impossibilities tended to be so ridiculous, but Ruby had promised her that this was a good one, with a sweet, likable heroine and a fairly genuine representation of a troubled bad boy guitarist. *We've got one of those,* Kimmy thought, though Blade wasn't nearly so angry these days now that he had Crys and Luke around him. He still had the occasional bad day, especially when the media tried to provoke him, but it was orders of magnitude better, and without the messy and destructive influence of drugs and dealers and the desperate highs and lows of those years. *Bad boys are better left to fiction.* Sure, Kimmy liked a bit of kink in the bedroom, but she knew she wouldn't be interested if it didn't come with a solid helping of respect and responsibility. *Give me a real-life cinnamon roll any day.* In books, though? She was an equal-opportunity reader and enjoyed the cinnamon rolls and the alphaholes in equal measure.

As luck would have it, Dice emerged from his shower just as Kimmy had settled into the book's first truly spicy bit. *Damn.* But also, *hello?*

"What're you reading?" he asked with a smile, and she showed him the cover – a classic hot rocker dude with a guitar.

"It's good, if you suspend a bit of professional disbelief. I like the characters, and it's well written. Sexier than I thought it was going to be at first..." She hoped he'd take that bait and join her for a snuggle, and was disappointed when he just nodded, dropping his towel but only to pull on clean boxers and then a t-shirt and jeans from his bag.

"Nice. Aidan's downstairs and I haven't figured out how to do the door-buzzing-in thing yet, so I'm going to go down and let him in. You might want to get dressed..."

That had her jumping out of bed in a hurry. "I'll shower later," she muttered, rummaging around to find something to wear.

♥

Aidan had stopped by a bakery and brought them an enormous box of assorted pastries: muffins, croissants, strudels, eclairs, and coffee cake slices.

By now quite hungry, Kimmy bit eagerly into a cherry strudel and sighed with satisfaction. Dice brewed another pot of coffee for himself and Aidan, and put the kettle on to make a cup of tea for Kimmy. She wanted a second cup of coffee but wasn't quite sure what "moderation" meant in terms of caffeine and had grudgingly decided not to risk it, at least until she could find out more about what was safe.

They talked and ate and watched television, and later Aidan checked out the apartment and the building and said he thought it was a safe enough place for them that they didn't need him hanging around, getting in their way.

"You never get in our way, Aidan!" Kimmy said at once.

"You're our friend," Dice added. "Hang out with us anytime."

Aidan raised his eyebrows at them, laughing. "Unless you two are inviting me to be a third in something I don't think you intended me to know about, I'll give that a pass."

"Aidan! We're friends. Best friends," Kimmy said, trying not to blush.

"In a one-bedroom apartment, with no pull-out couch and one very nice king-size bed. Suuure, my dudes."

Dice shrugged. "Yeah, well, Kimmy and I are... exploring some possibilities, okay? She's not lying; we *are* still best friends. Just..."

"It's cool." Aidan gestured with his hands as if to wave away any worries they might have. "You're the two nicest people I know, it's totally logical that you'd fall for each other. So, like, carry on, none of my business."

"Thanks, man." In typical fashion, Dice didn't get emotional or overly expressive, and nor did Aidan, but the two of them shared a half-ironic fist bump that said more than a whole lot of words could.

Surprisingly, Kimmy didn't feel disturbed at the idea that Aidan knew about at least part of her private arrangement with Dice.

"I've got a room at the Comfort Inn because it has a pool and fitness center," Aidan was saying, "so I'm only a phone call away if you have any security problems or need me to run errands or anything. I'm just taking it easy this week, working out and swimming. Might catch a local concert on Friday, if you wanted to come along. There're some cool bands here."

That sounded like fun. "I love seeing local bands in small venues," Kimmy said. "You never know... maybe we'll see the next big thing before it happens."

"I'd be up for that," Dice agreed, and they left it open as a possibility.

The grocery delivery arrived just as Aidan was leaving. Dice said goodbye quickly and ducked into the bedroom – the whole point of anonymity didn't include a grocery delivery driver knowing that Smidge drummer Dice was one of the occupants of this particular apartment. Once both Aidan and the delivery driver were gone, Dice emerged from the bedroom and he and Kimmy began unpacking the groceries for their week.

"Kraft Macaroni and Cheese?" Kimmy asked, unable to suppress her amusement. There were eight boxes of it. "Hot dog wieners but no buns?"

"You put the chopped-up wieners *in* the mac and cheese," Dice explained. "Haven't you ever had that? It's delicious. I also got eggs – I can make pretty decent scrambled eggs – and bread for toast, and I got peanut butter and jelly and pasta and sauce."

When Kimmy thought about it, she realized that she shouldn't have been surprised. Dice's idea of groceries and cooking revolved around bachelor foods, things he knew how to cook, things he and his bandmates would have eaten before stardom had catapulted them into a world of fine dining and catering services. *Let me guess... yes, there they are. Cup Noodles. A full dozen of them.*

He saw her looking and gestured a wordless *what's wrong with that?* "I like Cup Noodles, okay?"

"I didn't say anything," she pointed out. "There's nothing wrong with Cup Noodles."

"Want one for lunch, then?" It was almost a challenge.

So she nodded. "Sounds good."

He'd made a gesture toward good nutrition with a bag of apples and a bunch of carrots, a cucumber, and a couple of avocados. "I know you like them," he said when he saw her eyes light up. "I can make you avocado toast for breakfast tomorrow."

"Thank you." She took an apple from the bag and ate it while he made the Cup Noodles, feeling in harmony with him, the world, and even the clump of rapidly dividing cells inside her. And it turned out that the salty, noodle-y goodness was exactly what she wanted.

♥

Later, when they got into bed, Kimmy snuggled up to Dice after he turned out the light... and was dismayed to find that he only cuddled her into a spooning position and settled down as if to sleep. They hadn't had sex since her positive pregnancy test. "Hey," she whispered in the dark, feeling both hurt and cross. "Am I a turn-off now that I'm pregnant or something?"

That had him sitting up in the bed, reaching to turn the bedside lamp back on. "Christ on a stick, Kimmy! Why would you say something like that?"

She flopped onto her back in a huff. "Only because you haven't touched me since we found out. Like I'm ruined now."

"I thought you wouldn't need me for that anymore, now you got what you wanted," he mumbled. "I didn't want to be rejected."

How could the man be so clueless? But he looked so adorably embarrassed. She wanted to tell him that she loved him, that he'd been her first and best choice forever, that he gave her more pleasure than anyone else ever had, but she only managed to express an inarticulate invitation that came out as, "Always want you."

He gratefully gave her the most tender lovemaking she'd ever experienced. He was such a man of contrasts, sometimes entirely given over to a dominant role and other times the sweetest, most intuitive and affectionate lover she'd ever known. This time, it was nearly all sweet, though he did give her a *very* light slap on the rump at one point. "I just can't be rough with you knowing you're pregnant, Pretty Girl," he murmured in her ear. "Going to have to figure out some other way to give you what you need."

Then he proceeded to make her wait for her orgasm, teasing and edging her until she was begging before he gave her everything she was hoping for and more.

♥

Before long, the vacation week was over and the interminable *My Tainted Baby* tour was back on the road. Not interminable anymore, though – only another three months, and then Smidge would take a break from touring and go into the studio to record *Reaching for Starlight*. It was good timing, since the crew could pick up lots of festival work over the summer and then come back when touring started for the new album. They'd likely lose a few people, of course, and pick up a few new ones – that was the nature of the business. But the core crew that kept Smidge going had stayed together over the years.

I probably won't be showing much before the tour ends, Kimmy thought, rubbing a hand over her still-flat abdomen in the shower. Would it be easier not to say anything, and then deal with the crew's surprise in the fall when she showed up with a third-trimester baby bump? Either way, the next year or so was going to be chaotic. *I'll figure it out.* She tried not to add a desperate *somehow* to that thought, even in her mind.

A few people would have to know sooner, anyway. "Have you been to a doctor yet?" Dice had asked her earlier that day. When she reluctantly admitted that she hadn't, he asked her if she'd at least be willing to let Jed know what was going on. "He'll know what you need to do when, and he'll arrange for a doctor who can do your prenatal checkups and all that, just like he did for Crys. You won't have to go to a clinic or anything."

Kimmy had intended – at some point – to find a Planned Parenthood and get herself checked out, but doing that had the potential to offend Jed, so she agreed to talk to him. Soon.

Someone banged on the shower cubicle door to hurry her up, so Kimmy finished rinsing and got out of the shower, drying off and getting dressed as quickly as possible so that someone else could have a turn. This wasn't a hotel stop, so everyone in the crew was taking advantage of the arena's showers to get a wash after the show before boarding the buses.

She was on her way out to board her bus when she spotted Jed walking the other way. *No time like right now.* "So, Jed..."

He stopped and looked at her with raised eyebrows, waiting.

Just say it, she told herself. "I'm about seven weeks pregnant, so, um..." Her voice trailed off as she braced herself for his reaction.

"Okay, Kimmy. Do you need help with an abortion, or prenatal care?" He seemed totally matter-of-fact about it, and only his habit of sticking a finger under the edge of his bandanna to scratch his scalp when he had to process unexpected information let on that he was surprised.

"Prenatal care," she managed to say.

He nodded. "All right. Have you started taking prenatal vitamins yet?"

"Yes, right away." She didn't want to tell him she'd been taking them since the band got back from Lovango Cay, which would lead to the inevitable conclusion that the conception was intentional, and right at the moment she didn't feel up to having that conversation.

"Good. Got any questions or concerns right now?" When she shook her head no, he patted her on the shoulder. "Then go board your bus and get some sleep. I'll check in with Dr. Robinson and let her know we have another patient for her."

"Thanks," Kimmy said, feeling rather in awe. Dr. Robinson was Crys's obstetrician, and Kimmy had occasionally seen the doctor coming and going for appointments, flying into whatever city the tour was currently stopped at. As a drum tech, not a band member's girlfriend, Kimmy had never expected to have the same arrangement offered to her. *But wait...* She'd only factored Planned Parenthood clinic visits into her budget. "I mean, will I be able to afford...?"

Jed cracked a grin at that. "Can I assume Dice is the father?" he asked, his voice very dry.

Shit. Shit. How does he know? She couldn't imagine what kind of expression she had on her face, as she felt all the thought wheels in her brain grind to a halt at once. "That's..." She couldn't lie about it, couldn't say it was none of Jed's business. "I'm the one choosing to have this baby," she said, settling for the simplest answer. "It's no one else's responsibility."

"I understand that, Kimmy. No one's trying to get in the way of that." Jed spoke calmly, soothingly. "But Dice will want the best care for you, and... just trust me. It'll be better for everyone to have Dr. Robinson come to you, for continuity of care as well as privacy and confidentiality. Let the band cover any medical costs. Consider it a top-up of the health insurance you already get as a crew member. Leave it in my hands, okay?"

"How did you know?" she muttered numbly.

Jed shook his head, laughing at her, but kindly. "The two of you've been watching each other with hungry eyes for years. It was only a matter of time."

Kimmy thanked him and headed out to her bus, gladly seeking her bunk, her mind full of whirling thoughts. Easy, Mac, Aidan, and now Jed knew, and according to what Jed had said about the way she and Dice looked at each other, everyone else would have no trouble guessing paternity once she started to show. *This was not what I'd planned,* she grumbled to herself. She thought about texting Dice but didn't know what to say.

She put her earbuds in to listen to her *dreamtime* playlist, and fortunately she was tired enough that it didn't take long for her to fall asleep.

♥

Apparently, bacon would be entirely off the menu for the duration of the pregnancy, Kimmy realized when once again, a couple of days later at an all-crew brunch meeting with the band, the mere smell of it had her queasy and contemplating running for the bathroom. She wasn't having any other nausea, so far, and hoped she wouldn't at all, but for some reason, bacon was her kryptonite. Sad. Couldn't it have been anything else but bacon?

This time, Crys noticed her gagging, and with a curious and thoughtful glance, took a wrapped candy from her purse and held it out.

"What's this?' Kimmy asked.

"Ginger chew," Crys said. "Settles your stomach. Trust me."

"Thanks." Kimmy took the candy, unwrapped it, and popped it into her mouth, concentrating on the ginger taste as she tried to both chew discreetly and breathe through her mouth at the same time so she wouldn't smell bacon.

Crys gave her a kind smile, with the kind of benign expression people wear when they badly want to ask about something and are restraining themselves.

She knows. Or guesses. Kimmy smiled back, unsure what to say. *I'll have to tell my friends sometime, but it's too soon.* She wanted to talk to Dice first, anyway. Was he expecting her to acknowledge him as the baby's father? Did he want to tell his bandmates before she told their other friends? Fortunately, no one else seemed to be paying attention to them, so Kimmy mouthed, "Too soon to say anything," with barely a whisper of sound, in the hope that Crys would be able to make sense of that and leave it alone for now.

A sympathetic nod indicated that Crys had understood, then the younger woman passed over a whole handful of the chewy ginger candies without saying another word.

♥

The tour went on.

Toward the end of March, when Kimmy was ten weeks pregnant, Dr. Robinson flew in to meet the tour in Austin. With utmost tact, the doctor met with Crys first, the public purpose of the visit to see how little Luke was doing and talk about postpartum health and family planning. Jed brought Kimmy along to the doctor's hotel room just as that conversation was being wrapped up.

"Come in," Dr. Robinson called in response to his knock. When Kimmy followed Jed into the room, she saw that the doctor was holding Luke and grinning at him as his little hands grabbed at her earrings and a few corkscrew curls that had escaped from her updo. "Who's my little doll? You be a good boy for mama, now."

Crys held out her arms to take her son and thanked the doctor. She gave Kimmy a small wave as she was leaving.

"Just let me put a fresh sheet on my 'examining table' and we'll get started," Dr. Robinson said, folding away the blue cotton sheet that covered one of the two beds in the room. She then stepped into the bathroom and washed her hands before ripping open a sealed plastic bag and taking out a new blue cotton sheet to spread over the bed. "All nice and sterile," she said cheerfully, as she put on a fresh pair of examination gloves. "You'll need your pants and underthings off. Do you want a gown, or just a modesty drape for your lower half?"

"Whatever's easiest. I'm not pressed about getting naked; it's probably all the locker-room showers." Though to be honest, she'd felt a bit odd about it recently, worrying that someone would notice changes to her abdominal area before she was ready to say anything.

"Just lay this over your lap, then." The doctor handed her a pastel pink sheet of some kind of disposable paper-cloth. "I'll just step into the hall while you get yourself settled."

To Kimmy's astonishment, the doctor had a portable ultrasound machine with her. "The fetus is about the size of a kumquat at this point. Shall we have a look? You're far enough along that we should see a heartbeat today," Dr. Robinson said after the internal exam and blood draws were done.

"Oh, yes, please!" Kimmy said. *An ultrasound!* Maybe seeing a picture would make it all feel more real. Except for the bacon thing, and needing to pee more often, she didn't honestly feel any different, and could hardly believe she was actually growing a baby. Then she hesitated. "But... I think Dice should be here, if that's possible?"

The doctor smiled. "Dice is the father?"

"He's my best friend," Kimmy explained. "He got me pregnant as a favor, because I want to have a baby. It wasn't a mistake. But he's not my boyfriend or anything." *Babbling, rambling, explaining too much.* "Sorry. You probably didn't need to know all that. I just think it would be nice if he got to see the ultrasound."

"Of course. Let me just see if someone can find him for us." The doctor stepped out into the hall for a moment and was back, smiling as she offered a hand to help Kimmy sit up. "Jed will find him. You can put your underwear back on while we wait. No need to be feeling bare for this part." She bent down to take a bottle of water from the mini fridge and set it on the bedside table next to Kimmy. "Now, we want a full bladder for this, so let's just have you drink a bit of water – and you probably need to hydrate anyway."

While they waited, Kimmy consumed the whole bottle of water and was already feeling a mild need to pee when Dr. Robinson suggested she lie down and get into position for the ultrasound. The doctor arranged a fresh modesty drape over Kimmy's lower body, tucking the upper edge into her underwear to keep it from getting splodged by the ultrasound gel.

Dice burst into the room ahead of Jed, his brow furrowed with anxiety. His hair was loose and his green Henley was unbuttoned. "Kimmy, what's going on? Jed said you needed me right away. He–" He broke off, caught his breath, and looked around, taking in the calm doctor and the fact that Kimmy was smiling.

"I'm having an ultrasound, Dice! I... well, I thought you might want to be here."

A sweet, heart-melting smile blossomed across Dice's face and he rushed over to sit on the edge of the bed next to her and take her hand. "Really?" Then he gave Jed a slightly grumpy look and grumbled, "You couldn't have told me, man? I thought something was wrong."

Jed wasn't one for rolling his eyes, but he had a *you didn't listen to the nurse and now look where we are* expression that was equally pointed. "And who rushed out of the room without waiting for more information?"

Dice hung his head. "Fair. Sorry, Jed. Hi, Dr. Robinson, sorry for the interruption."

The doctor, who was probably used to all kinds of celebrity dramatics, just chuckled and squeezed a big glop of cold gel onto Kimmy's abdomen, which wasn't quite as flat as it used to be, although she thought she looked more pudgy than pregnant.

After a few passes of the transducer, Dr. Robinson pointed to the screen and said, "Look, there's the heartbeat, my dears. Nice and strong." And true enough, there was a pulsing flicker on the screen and a shape that might vaguely be a baby, a blob of a head and a curled body like a little shrimp.

"Wow!" Dice said in awe, his voice all choked up. "It's really a baby."

"Technically a fetus," the doctor corrected him, in a kindly tone. "But yes, your baby-to-be is very real. Congratulations! Good cardiac activity there... I'm just going to take a few measurements, but I'm seeing what I want to see."

Kimmy looked at the flickering greyscale blob on the screen, struggling to get her mind around something that hadn't seemed quite possible or believable until this moment. *It's happening. My baby. I'm going to be a mother.* The desperation she'd felt before, fearing that she'd never have a child of her own, was soothed away, along with her brief fear that it had been a mistake, that she couldn't do it. *Of course I can. I've wanted this for a long time.*

She glanced at Dice and was surprised to see his eyes shining with excess moisture. He reached down and gripped her hand, then clasped his other hand over it like a sort of three-handed prayer. "Kimber," he said softly, "do you think... could we date a bit while you're pregnant? Officially, I mean? I want to be with you for every step of this."

That was not what she'd been expecting at all. Emotion, yes. Excitement about the baby, sure. He was always very sweet with Luke and evidently adored children, so his enthusiasm for this one didn't surprise her. But the idea that he'd want to date her blindsided her. And the thought that he'd do it *officially* just to be close to the baby...

"All done," Dr. Robinson said cheerfully, putting down the transducer and wiping the ultrasound gel off Kimmy's abdomen. "I'll email you some images from the ultrasound, Kimmy. You might want them for your baby book."

"Yes, please, and thank you, Doctor," Kimmy said.

The doctor smiled. "You can call me Bev, or Dr. Bev if you wish. We'll be getting to know each other pretty well before this is all over."

"Dr. Bev sounds cool," Kimmy said, glad that she liked the woman so much.

"Then I'll call you Ms. Kim since we're both professional ladies. I liked your voice on that 'Band on the Road' single your boys released in January. I'll see you in a month, all right?" And with that, the doctor stepped into the bathroom to wash her hands, and Dice helped Kimmy up from the bed so she could get her pants on.

"Thanks, Dr. Bev," Kimmy called out, and Dice echoed her, then a few strides brought them out of the doctor's room and into the hallway, where they were – for a moment – alone.

She would have walked on, heading to her room, or somewhere, but he put a hand on her shoulder and asked, "What d'you think, Kimmy? Could we date a little? Or would you hate that?"

Shit. He has no idea, does he? She pasted a smile onto her face. "Just for show? Or like, for real?" she asked, trying to sound as unperturbed and open to it as she could.

"Whatever you want," he said, sounding helpless in the face of everything. "I'll do whatever you want, you know that. You're my bestie, my whole heart, my Pretty Girl, and now my baby mama. You get to tell me what you want this to be."

It was going to be chaos either way, wasn't it? No matter what she chose, there was nothing simple about *just having a baby* when the other half of the DNA came from someone who mattered so much to her. And they were already sleeping together – maybe doing dating-type things publicly would create even more of a mess in her heart, but... maybe it was okay to accept that risk. *Careful what you wish for,* she told herself mockingly. If she hadn't been pregnant, she'd planned to tell him she wanted to try dating for real. Here they were, and she couldn't be sure if it was just because of the baby.

I want to be with you for every step of this, he'd said. But he'd also called her his whole heart. He was looking at her, his hand still on her shoulder, waiting for an answer.

"What would dating involve?" she asked cautiously.

"You could share my room, travel with me on flights. We wouldn't have to sneak around for privacy. Maybe go on an actual date the odd time or two? But mostly I could take care of you. Would you like that?" He looked so hopeful, she didn't have the heart to refuse.

"I won't lie, it sounds pretty nice," she agreed. "And then you can be there for my appointments with Dr. Bev and no one will think it's weird."

"Starting now?" he asked. "Are we a thing?"

When Kimmy nodded, feeling a sudden sense of well-being and hope as she let herself embrace the idea, he swept her up into his arms and had her back against the nearest wall in seconds flat. "Thank Christ," he muttered, and kissed her.

It wasn't a tame kiss; it was deep and passionate and demanding and grateful all at once. She wrapped her legs around his waist and kissed him back just as fiercely. And there was no one in the hallway to see it, but that didn't matter – the fact that they could kiss out in the open mattered, almost like a first kiss, although it was far from that. *First official kiss,* she thought with amusement when she was back on her feet and capable of coherent thought.

"I love kissing you," Dice said, with a huge smile on his face. "We can do it lots more now. Let's go tell Phil, because he'll need to adjust the hotel and travel plans going forward. You'll be with *me.*"

Kimmy laughed. "Okay. I don't want our road manager to be the literal first person to know, though. I'm texting Crys." For keeping quiet about Kimmy's bacon-induced nausea and giving her ginger candies without asking any questions, Crys deserved to be the first to hear their news. Officially.

♥

Nothing changed, but also everything changed.

From that moment when Kimmy texted Crys, saying *Got some news, Dice and I are a couple now, also I'm ten weeks pregnant,* the guitarist's wife started treating her like a sister.

So happy for you! You can borrow my pregnancy book if you don't already have one, Crys had texted back right away. *And I know we don't dress the same style, but if you want to wear any of my maternity clothes, I'd love to share.* This was followed by a whole string of heart emojis.

Kimmy couldn't imagine herself in most of Crys's things, since the younger woman tended toward a more feminine look and most of her maternity things had been softer colors and pale greys in floaty fabrics. She did accept a grey denim top and a charcoal fleece hoodie, and let Crys take her shopping for a pair of underbelly maternity jeans on one of their tour stops. Her old pants were getting snug, and she'd need the stretchy waistband soon.

And being a rock star's girlfriend was lovely.

No more tour bus bunks, rushed locker-room showers in drafty arenas, or long hours on freeways between cities. The upgrade shocked Kimmy a bit, even though she'd always known there was a difference in lifestyle from the crew to the band. Someone else took her duffel bag to and from the hotel rooms – and Dice had offered to get her a nice luggage set for her things instead, but she'd refused, saying the duffel bag was fine. She traveled with the band by limousine and airplane, and occasionally for short hauls in the lounge area of the nicest Star Sleeper bus. And she was officially part of Aidan's job.

It was all a bit complicated, because she still had to be at the venue in time to do her part of load-in – that is, to get the drum kit set up for Dice. Suddenly, she was no longer expected to do a share of hauling the rest of the equipment in, and even the drum cases were brought in and set next to the already built-up drum riser for her.

When she protested to Phil, the road manager shook his head. "Consider it a maternity adjustment, Kimmy. You wouldn't be able to haul heavy things much longer anyway."

"But..." she began to protest, then fell silent as Phil looked at her patiently.

"Try to see it this way," he said. "Dice is a rock icon to a lot of fans, and there's always the potential that some sour, twisted person out there won't take well to the thought of him dating or becoming a father. So you can't just go about your business. We have to make sure there's security coverage for you, in the same way that we protect Crys."

Neither of them mentioned Nell. She *was* security coverage – for herself, for Easy, and for anyone else around her – and she was damn good at what she did.

The way I'm good at what I do, the best drum tech I can be. "I don't want to let anyone down or do less than my share," Kimmy said.

Phil sighed. "We'll make it work. The big thing is that you're still doing the drum kit setup, soundcheck, and support during shows. Your drummer needs *you* for that. He doesn't like anyone else messing with his kit. Anyone can lug boxes around, and they'll all understand that you have both security and health limitations right now. You'll arrive with the band before soundcheck, and just... get the kit set up as fast as you can."

Everyone was being very nice to Kimmy. Even Nell and Sally, who weren't the biggest baby-having cheerleaders, congratulated her. Easy seemed amused.

♥

About a week after everyone found out, Dice came storming into their hotel room one night, wrenched the rolled bandanna off his head, and threw it across the room. Kimmy, reading in bed, blinked at it as it hit the far wall and slid down onto the floor.

"Fucking Angel," he snarled, in a far angrier tone than she'd ever heard from him.

"What happened?" she asked, keeping her voice soft and calm. Dice wasn't one to lose his temper, and he adored the front man, had looked up to him from the time they'd formed the band – was it ten years ago? Certainly from the time Kimmy had met and joined them, she'd never heard a cross word from Dice about Angel, so this was a surprise.

"Sorry," Dice muttered, going over to pick the bandanna up. He untied and unrolled it with a sort of methodical annoyance that was just as indicative of turmoil as the throwing part. "Everything's fine," he said to Kimmy. "D'you know where the laundry bag is?"

"It's on a hook on the back of the bathroom door. And everything is obviously not fine."

He huffed and went into the bathroom to find the laundry bag, coming out a moment later without the bandanna. "Well, it's not important."

"Come on, drummer boy, it's time for bed. We've got an early flight tomorrow."

He kicked off his socks and shoes and flopped down crosswise along the foot of the bed, not even bothering yet to take off his jeans. "He's such a dick sometimes. Angel, I mean."

Kimmy nodded, trying to look understanding, trying to suppress a grin. "Okay, sure. Everything's fine and it's not important, but he's a dick sometimes. Got it."

Dice gave a wry laugh from where he lay on the bed, his head near her feet. "You know you're important to me, right, Kimmy? I'm here for you and I'm not going to let you down."

Something about that sent a flicker of concern down her spine and she sat up straight. "Um, was this about me?"

He closed his eyes. "Sort of. Angel thinks I'm too young to be a father, apparently."

"That's... not super helpful of him," Kimmy said. "I mean, unless something happens to this little jellybean I've got on board, it's a bit late for comments like that."

"Christ on a stick, Kimmy. He was talking about whether we should go through with it at all, whether you were considering giving it up for adoption, that kind of talk. I... he just thinks I'm still a teenager. He thinks I didn't think this through. But it's none of his business, and I am all the goddamn way in for this baby."

Our baby. "I didn't want this to happen." She reached out to smooth the hair back off his forehead, trying to comfort him. "I never wanted to cause a ruckus with your bandmates. I should have realized it wouldn't be as simple as just a little help getting pregnant."

He looked up at her, shaking his head, still angry. "This isn't on you, Kimmy. Angel – and all of them – need to realize that I'm not still fifteen."

She wanted to reassure him, but he was right. It was past time his bandmates started treating him as a full equal member of the group, not a little brother to be protected. "They do. I'm sure they mean well, though. Having a baby is a big decision, and I feel like I maybe dragged you into it."

"Nope. I knew what I was doing when I offered. Remember how you made us wait? I would have jumped on you the moment you told me it was on, but you wanted us to just make out and think through our decision overnight. I thought about it good and clear. I could have decided to use a condom. But you wanted a baby, and I *chose* to be the one to help you with that. No regrets, okay?"

Kimmy smiled. "No regrets. And you don't mind that it's kind of pushed us into being a couple for now?"

Just as Dice opened his mouth to answer, there was a knock on the hotel room door, followed by Angel's voice calling, "Dyl, buddy, can I talk to you?"

Dice looked at Kimmy inquiringly, and she nodded her agreement – permission? – for him to let Angel into their room. He hauled himself off the bed and went to the door, opening it partway. "What's up?" he asked, his face noncommittal.

"You were pretty mad when you walked out on me a bit ago," Angel said, his voice calm and reasonable. "I want to check in, smooth that over, make sure we're good. Can we talk? Maybe take a walk?"

Dice stepped back from the doorway, gesturing for Angel to enter. "Come in. Anything you want to say to me, you can say in front of Kimmy. Okay?"

"If that's what you want," Angel said, coming in. He looked so normal and non-rockstar-like in a sweater and jeans, no makeup, wearing glasses. There was a writing desk with a chair against one wall of the room, and he picked up the chair and moved it over to sit opposite the bed, likely assuming that Dice would sit on the edge of the bed next to Kimmy.

Dice stayed standing, waiting.

"You don't need to be upset, Dylan," Angel began. "I'm your friend. I'm just looking out for you, helping you talk through big issues. I'd do the same for the other guys."

"Would you, though? Did you ask Blade if Crys had considered an abortion, or whether he was ready to see his life changed like that? Do you call him by his real name instead of his band name when you're trying to sound serious, like a parent using a kid's full name when they're in trouble?" The drummer's voice had a bitter, furious edge to it, and his hands curled into fists at his side.

"Okay. Dice. Sorry, you're right." Angel raised his hands in a calming gesture. "No, I didn't ask him that, but they were engaged before they found out they were having Luke."

"And that matters how?" Kimmy asked, unable to stay quiet.

Angel shifted uncomfortably in his chair. "Well... it doesn't, of course."

Dice waited, still not sitting, looking down at Angel from his full, imposing height. He crossed his arms and cocked his head to one side. His silence felt louder than anything he could have said.

"I'm sorry," Angel said at last. "Sit the fuck down, Dice. I shouldn't have said anything. You're a grown man and I'll stay out of it."

Dice nodded acceptance of that. Like a deflating balloon, he sank down onto the edge of the bed, looking satisfied but a bit lost, and Kimmy reached out to hold his hand. She knew her drummer didn't like conflict and adored his lead singer. Being at odds had to hurt.

"This wasn't a mistake, Angel," she said, deciding to level with him so he could properly see where Dice was coming from. "I've wanted to have a baby for a while now, and my best friend agreed to give me one. I set out to do this as a single mother, and I'm not afraid. Deciding to date... that was the surprise." She smiled at Dice and was glad to see his answering smile, his back straightening as his contentment and peace of mind flowed back. "So there's no pressure, honestly; no one was tricked, no one is trapped. You can trust him when he says he's here because he wants to be, for as long as it works for both of us."

She'd surprised Angel. He took his glasses off and rubbed two fingers between his eyebrows as though soothing a headache.

"You *are* like my big brother, Andy," Dice said seriously, no longer sounding angry but just tired and wanting his friend to understand. "I've looked up to you and Chris forever, from when we were kids playing street hockey and riding bikes and dicking around with our first instruments in your parents' garage, long before we became Dice and Angel and Blade. When Mark was still our bassist. When he thought I was too young to be in a band and you stuck up for me. And I don't want to fight with you about this."

Angel sighed. "I get it, buddy. And I'm too used to trying to protect you. I remember when we first started performing as a band – you'd just turned fifteen that summer, and we were seventeen and that gap seemed like a huge difference. I didn't want to somehow *break* the nice preacher's kid from our street; I felt responsible for you."

"I remember my parents telling me I had to listen to you, when you bought that van and the four of us were going to be away overnight, playing at some all-ages hall in Ashland, and we took sleeping bags and slept in the back of the van for the first time. They trusted you."

"Yeah. You've grown up since then. I just... Fuck. My best friend is a dad, and now my – basically my little brother is going to be a dad, and I... I feel responsible for everyone and my own relationship shit isn't what I ever imagined and I just don't know where I'm going. Not that I'm making this about me."

Dice chuckled sympathetically. "You're not so keen on being Uncle Andy?"

Angel grimaced. "It's not that. I love Luke. I'm sure I'll love your... what did you call it, jellybean? It's just such a shift to see Blade as a father, and now I get to watch you doing it too. I'll get used to the idea, though. And I'll try not to overprotect you."

"Thanks for taking care of me when I was younger," Dice said. "I needed it then, and you did a great job."

"And you can take it from here. I get the message." Angel stood up and slapped an affectionate hand onto Dice's shoulder. "Have a good night, buddy. I'll see you in the morning. Night, Kimmy." With that, the lead singer left the room, pulling the door softly closed behind him.

"Well," said Dice after a while. He shrugged, plainly trying to be casual about it all. "That was quite a conversation."

"Are you glad you went there?" Kimmy asked. "You know it needed to be said."

"Yeah." He hauled himself up off the bed again. "Forgot to brush my teeth. Be right back." He vanished into the bathroom, and when he came back, she held out her arms for him to come to bed. He turned off the lights and obliged.

"Just remember that Joel Bonamour said you're on your way to becoming a rock icon," she told him in the soft darkness. "Lots of people believe in you."

"And you, Pretty Girl?" he asked, his voice deepening. "Do you believe you're in bed with a future rock icon?" His hands worked their way inside her sleep shirt, caressing the increased fullness of her breasts and the curve of her lower abdomen.

"I know it, Boss," she whispered breathlessly. "I've always known it."

"Your sweet talk is going to my head, and I like it."

She couldn't resist. "Which head?"

His burst of amused laughter made her feel all warm inside. "Both," he said. "Absolutely both. Come here and ride me, and if you're very good, I'll maybe give you some light spanks as a treat."

chapter

12

"FACE IT, MAN, YOU'VE GOT TO ASK HER TO MARRY you." It sounded like Easy's voice talking, and his tone was serious, not something that could be interpreted as a joke or teasing or even affection.

Kimmy, walking by a half-open door in the warren underneath yet another arena, was about to ignore the statement and the conversation, until she heard Dice's voice answer, "Are you sure that's–"

She froze, not catching the rest of his question. *You've got to ask her to marry you.* Was Easy saying that *to* Dice, or were they both talking to a third person?

Easy's voice rose again. "Every baby deserves a father. I love my mom, she did what she thought best, but sometimes I wish–" A loud crash from the stadium floor drowned out the rest of whatever he was saying.

Shit. Shit. Kimmy craned her neck, trying to see around the door without opening it further. No, there were only two people in the room. Easy and Dice. *Walk away,* she told herself. *Walk away, it's just guy talk. Won't come to anything.*

Surely Dice couldn't, wouldn't be foolish enough to do something like offer to marry her only so their baby wouldn't have an unwed mother. His father was a priest – surely he would take wedding vows seriously, and not see them as something you could make with the intention of breaking later.

Kimmy wasn't sure exactly where she stood on matters of faith, if it came to that. She didn't think about religion or spirituality much at all, though if pushed, she'd admit that she didn't think there was *nothing* guiding the universe. She *wanted* to believe in some kind of higher power. It'd be nice to feel confident that everything wasn't random molecules, to have Crys's sweet certainty that a benevolent God had them all cradled in the palm of a vast metaphorical hand. And if there *was* a God, or any kind of guiding intelligence or energy out there, promising on the strength of that to love and cherish another human forever was something it would be unwise to take lightly.

Walking quietly, she hustled away from the area, not wanting either of the men to come out and realize that she'd heard them talking.

Since she now wasn't allowed to lift anything heavier than a drumstick – or at least it felt that way since her travel arrangements had changed, with other crew taking all her heavy-lifting jobs and unpacking everything before she arrived – she had less to do than she liked and sometimes felt superfluous backstage. Still, she could double-check the drum kit setup she'd long since finished and add an extra stick or two to the various containers of them.

When Dice caught up to her outside the green room, he didn't say anything about the odd conversation. She kept waiting for him to bring it up, to laugh, to say *Easy thinks we should get married,* but he didn't – not then, and not during or after the show, nor later in their hotel or on the plane.

Maybe I imagined it, Kimmy told herself, *or maybe I misunderstood,* although she was fairly certain she'd heard exactly what she recalled. *You've got to ask her to marry you.*

It was just guy talk. It had to be just guy talk, the sort of big words that got said without it meaning anything. When he didn't say anything, as time passed, she stopped expecting Dice to drop some kind of a conversational bomb every minute that they were alone. The unresolved thread of it worried her sometimes – if it meant nothing, why hadn't he said something, even as a joke? – but overall she relaxed and mostly stopped thinking about it.

She was short enough that she started to show early, not so long after that at around fourteen weeks. Dice noticed first, even before she did. One morning when they were showering together, he stopped what he was doing and knelt in front of her to admire her midsection, saying, "Never thought I'd develop a pregnancy kink, of all things, but damn, you look super cute with our baby growing in you." He couldn't resist stroking the new roundness of her belly starting to emerge over her hip bones. Maybe it was his admiration that drew her to enjoy her pregnant body as much as she was discovering that she did – the roundness, the extra sensitivity, the glowing feeling that she had nearly all the time.

"The second trimester is a good time, enjoy it while you can," said Dr. Bev when she visited for a checkup.

This was around the time Kimmy's pregnancy got into the media, and Aidan had to stick even closer to her whenever she was outside. She had to shop for more maternity clothes, including bras since her boobs seemed to be puffing up like muffins in the oven, so she splurged for some gorgeous matching sets of maternity underwear. She was so happy, and it was a wonderful time really. She started to feel deeply optimistic about everything.

"You're bananas, wanting to have a baby on a rock tour," Sally said to Kimmy one day, kindly but meaning it.

They were on the Smidge jet, en route from Salt Lake City to San Francisco. The Smidgettes on the flight had ousted the usual card players from the table seating and were playing a game of Spoons because Kimmy had said she'd rather not play poker. The truth was she didn't mind poker, but she remembered Aidan saying *Crys sometimes joins the card bandits but she's not very good,* and she wanted to spare her friend any stress. A silly children's game that involved grabbing spoons from the center seemed like better fun.

"She's not, though," Crys said. "Babies are nice. We have a whole nursery bus with plenty of room, and Jellybean will be a friend for Lukey." All of the Smidgettes were calling the baby-to-be Jellybean by now, just as Luke had been Pickle before he was born.

Sally didn't quite roll her eyes, but she looked like she wanted to. "Don't ask me to babysit," she said grumpily.

"Oh, Sally..." Crys said. They all knew perfectly well that Sally would be the first to offer help if anyone needed it. "The childcare situation isn't a problem. Isn't that right, Camillo?" This last bit was louder, directed at Luke's nanny, who sat with his charge in the rear section of the plane.

The crew section, Kimmy thought. The flight attendants had their seats back there. The nanny sat back there with the baby. She sometimes felt she belonged in the back too, a temporary girlfriend so that Dice could be part of his baby's prenatal appointments and birth.

"Of course," Camillo called back at once. "Lots of room for a second little one back here. I could even handle a third if Easy and Nell wanted to add to the Smidge family."

"Hell, no," Nell said at once, with feeling. "I'm in the middle of a shot at this year's World Champion title for my taekwondo division. No way would I let anything jeopardize that."

"Fair," Kimmy said. The table fell quiet, and something that Kimmy had been thinking about for a bit came to the surface of her mind. She took a breath and plunged in before she could overthink whether or not to say anything or what to say, as she had on a dozen earlier occasions. "Honestly, ladies, I *really* want this baby. Like, I was getting to the point where I was starting to have nightmares about it not happening."

She paused, and the women around her were quick to make sympathy noises and reach over to pat her hand or arm. "Are you worried about Jellybean?" Crys asked gently. "You're past twelve weeks now, and you said your ultrasound and bloodwork all looked good. There's no reason to think anything will go sideways at this point..." Her voice trailed off. They all knew there were no sure things with pregnancy. But Crys was younger than the rest of them, and incurably optimistic, and the encouragement was kindly meant.

"I'm not fishing for sympathy," Kimmy clarified at once, waving away the concern. "Yeah, any mom-to-be has occasional fears, I'm not exempt from that. But I'm good right now. What I wanted to say is, I totally get that not everyone wants to reproduce or have that in their airspace, so... I'll do my level best to not let Jellybean – before or after birth – impose on anyone's kid-free lifestyle on the tour, I promise. Crys does a great job of that, and I'm committed to doing the same. That's all."

"You know I'll always love and cherish any crotch goblins you pop out, that's what aunties are for," Sally said with a laugh, but she was also nodding her appreciation of the sentiment, and Kimmy knew she'd said the right thing.

♥

When they landed in San Francisco, Kimmy noticed bunnies and chocolate everywhere. Their hotel room had a plush bunny with a ribbon bow around its neck and a little basket of chocolate eggs nestled between the pillows of the bed. *Must be Easter weekend,* she realized. Fertility symbols and sweets notwithstanding, she didn't expect it to make much difference to the tour's routine – they had two concerts on the Friday and Saturday, and then a rest day on what must be Easter Sunday before moving on to a new stop on the tour, with just over a month more to go.

"Can I ask you something, Kimmy?" Dice said as they ate a late dinner backstage after the Friday show, Chinese food out of cardboard cartons. She ate with the band now, not the crew, which still felt sort of weird and like a betrayal of her crew friends, even though she knew they were well fed and had nothing to complain of. When she nodded encouragement to go ahead and ask, he said, "It's Easter weekend."

She waited. He said nothing more. "Yes, Easter is this Sunday," she prompted him, at which point, he put a huge bite of Mongolian beef into his mouth and busied himself with chewing it. "We have a rest day, which is nice," she added. "If you were thinking of something you wanted to do, or anything."

"Would you mind if – I mean, we have the day off, so I'd like to, well, go to church, because Easter – I'm inviting you to come with me if you want to, but don't feel like you have to. Fuck, I'm awkward. Is that weird?" He turned a bit red, trying to get his thoughts out in a rush.

She froze with her chopsticks halfway to her mouth and looked at him to see if he was serious. "Like a date?" she asked. "Or do I need an exorcism or something?"

"Dunno, About the date part, I mean. It could be a date if you wanted it to be, or just... come with me because you're my best friend and I thought I might share this part of my life with you? It's not a big deal, but I like to go at Easter if I can, if it's not a travel day and I can find an Episcopal church nearby. It's... comforting, I guess. Part of my upbringing. And the dean of the cathedral here is one of Dad's friends, so..."

The way he said *it's not a big deal* made her think that it was in fact an extremely personal thing for him. "You've never said, before."

"It never came up," he said with a shrug.

She knew his father was an Episcopal priest, and he went to church with his family when he was at home, but she'd never thought about it being part of his life separate from his parents. *How have I known him for six years and never realized this?* "Do you mind that I'm not particularly church-going?" she asked. "Given that we'll be co-parenting a newborn in about six months... Will you expect me to, you know, take the baby to church and stuff?"

Dice blinked at her. "Kimmy, you're perfect just as you are. Any God worth believing in has to see people through their hearts and actions, not the buildings they frequent. And no, I don't have any expectations of you – I might at some point ask you if *I* can take Jellybean to a church service on occasion, since I loved the organ music and choir singing and the smell of incense when I was little. Still do, to be honest. I know the church as an institution has done some problematic things, but there are good people where I go. Still, I'd never expect you to come with us if you didn't want to."

"Well, I'll come to your Easter service this weekend, if you'd like," she offered. "I won't know what to do, though."

The glowing smile he gave her told her that she was being allowed into an extremely private and precious part of his life. "You must think I'm such a weirdo," he muttered. "Easter church is so extremely not a rock star thing."

"If it's something you like to do, I'm glad you're sharing it with me," she told him.

"Thanks, Kimber," he said, and reached across the table to touch her arm, a gentle caress of appreciation and caring.

It wouldn't do to get too mushy at dinner with the others all around them, fortunately spread out enough that no one could easily listen to their conversation, but an obviously tender scene would draw attention. "Anytime, drummer boy," she said cheerfully, then couldn't resist adding, "Anything that makes you happy."

"You make me happy," he replied, with another of his sweet smiles.

Later, after dinner was over, Kimmy pulled Crys aside and asked, with a bit of trepidation, "Have you got anything I could wear to church?"

"Oh, are you going to an Easter service with Dice? How lovely!" Crys lit up with happiness at the thought. "I've got a cute dress I can lend you. I wore it at about five months but you're showing earlier than I did so it should work."

"A dress?" Kimmy asked, with a bit of dismay. She realized she'd been hoping for maternity dress pants or a skirt and sweater. Dresses were for fancy occasions. Did Easter church qualify as a fancy occasion?

"You don't have to," Crys said with a sympathetic grimace. "I mean, it depends on the church, but... there might be photographs, because you're with Dice. You'll want to look proper."

Proper. "With my hair and piercings? I don't think I can."

Crys contemplated this for a minute. "Maybe proper wasn't the right word. And you're right, my floral dress might make too much of a silly contrast with your style, instead of blending together. You want something a little more punk but in a conservative-dressy cut."

The younger woman's seriousness made Kimmy giggle. "What would you know about punk?" she teased.

"I know, I know. If I were a musician, I'd be a pop princess, wouldn't I?" Crys grinned back. "Even my edgiest outfits are punk *lite*. Still, I think if we can find you something in a very dark plaid, it could look smart and put-together. Sally might have some ideas. Do you happen to have a pair of Mary Jane shoes, or...? Let's go shopping before the show tomorrow. We'll invite Sally and Erva, have a girls' shopping morning. And maybe Nell if she wants to come, but..."

Kimmy nodded. Nell was great company, but she didn't do shopping as a leisure activity.

♥

There were indeed some photographers lurking about on Sunday as Dice helped Kimmy out of the limo and escorted her up the steps of a lovely old stone cathedral. She felt suitably proper in a deep, almost blackish blue plaid dress with an empire waist and a hem that fell just below the knee, like the Queen of England. Her hair was shaped and sprayed into an elegant wave on top instead of spiked up. "See, you can totally do the church girl look," Sally had said after putting the finishing touches on the hairstyle beforehand. Kimmy wasn't sure that a high fade and an industrial piercing quite fit the bill, but she agreed that she looked cute and had achieved a sort of semiformal punk look that suited her. Plus, the dress was comfortable and warm.

"Thanks for coming with me," Dice said softly as they passed through the doorway into the church. Rich, vibrant colors streamed in through the stained-glass windows, and organ music rose and fell around them as they found a pew with space available and sat down. A heady scent of incense lingered in the air, mixing with the fragrance from the Easter lilies in pots clustered around the altar, and he whispered, "There will have been an Easter Vigil service here last night, that's why you can already smell the incense."

The church was about half-filled when they arrived, and shortly it was packed. The people around them were largely respectful of the space and didn't do much pointing fingers or snapping obvious photos, but there were whispers as younger members of the congregation recognized Dice, especially once the dean of the cathedral came over to greet him and be introduced to Kimmy.

Dice seemed genuinely happy to shake hands with his father's friend, and evidently felt completely at home in the holy building. Ignoring the discreet attention and curiosity, he handed Kimmy a paper booklet with the order of service printed in it, including all the responses written out so she'd know what she was supposed to say and when.

The organ music was glorious, and when the service started and the choir added their voices, even more so.

When they got to the part where the priest said, "Peace be with you," and everyone replied, "And also with you," Kimmy looked over at Dice and saw how happy and at peace he was in this space. And when everyone started shaking hands and saying, "Peace," to each other, he drew her into his arms and hugged her.

There was an infant baptism as part of the service, and Kimmy watched as the parents and godparents went through the ritual and responses up at the front, the baby shrieking as the water and holy oil were applied to its forehead. The parents looked like a happy couple. A *married* happy couple. *Shit.*

After the service, Kimmy thought they'd leave right away, but Dice took her down to the church hall and got her a cup of tea so black and strong she thought a spoon might stand up in it. "Church tea," he explained with a grin. "You just need to add a lot of milk and sugar." He then spent half an hour shaking hands and signing autographs for anyone who was hopefully hovering around, which surprisingly included a few of the older generation as well as the congregation's youth group and younger adults.

That night when they cuddled in bed, he said, "I'm so glad you came with me today. I wanted to share that part of myself with you, but I wasn't sure..."

"The music was lovely," she agreed. "And your father's friend was very nice." They fell silent for a moment, then she couldn't resist asking, "Is church something you do often?"

He flopped over in bed and looked at her with his eyebrows raised, laughing silently. "You don't think you'd have noticed by now if it was? I don't often get the chance and I'm not bothered when I can't. It's just nice now and then when I can, especially for something like Easter. And my dad will appreciate that I made the effort."

♥

It was after their Easter church "date" that she started to notice a tension in him. Not all the time, but coming and going. A few times, she almost asked him if something was bothering him, but each time she was tempted, she held back, not sure if she wanted to know the answer. Sometimes she caught him looking at her with the most worried expression on his face, and she wasn't sure what to make of that at all.

There were only five weeks left until the interminable *My Tainted Baby* tour would finally come to an end. Change was in the air. The crew who wouldn't be needed for the recording studio – the riggers, the drivers, the lighting crew and special effects – had already started looking for summer gigs. Qingshan was ecstatic to be doing pyro for a short summer tour for the great Mad Gilbert, and Phil would be going with him as road manager after the older band's long-time road manager fell and fractured his hip. Erva talked about the summer festivals she was hoping to work at, and Trish was planning a vacation in Belize before committing to anything else.

♥

In the final week of the tour, after the third-to-last show, Dice puked before the show, which was something he never did. He'd never had stage fright, as far as Kimmy knew, and he didn't have a fever or seem unwell, so she assumed he'd eaten something that had gone off.

After the show, though, his tension seemed higher than ever, and he barely ate anything when the band had dinner, nor did he talk much in the limo back to the hotel. "Is everything okay?" she asked him quietly, as they waited with the rest of the band and spouses and bodyguards in front of the bank of elevators.

He bit his lip. "I hope so," he told her, with an almost furtive glance around at the others to see if anyone had heard her ask.

That didn't look like everything was okay at all, and she gave him a *talk to me, drummer boy* look. She got a small upturn at the corners of his mouth in response, not quite a grin, but almost. Whatever was chewing him up couldn't be too awful, then.

An elevator arrived at the main floor and its doors slid open with a chime. Everyone crowded in, but Dice hung back and caught her hand to keep her with him, as if he wanted her to wait and take the next elevator with him, and his palm was sweaty. *He's nervous,* Kimmy thought. *Why would he ever need to be nervous with me?*

Out of the blue, she remembered Easy's voice saying, *You've got to ask her to marry you.*

Because of the baby. And Dice had been edgy since they went to Easter church and saw the *married* couple with the baby being baptized. *Shit.* Surely he wasn't going to do something so monumentally clueless as suggest... She couldn't even make her brain think the words. *Just no.*

In the moment where she stood frozen with her hand trapped in Dice's, the elevator door started to close, threatening to leave the pair of them behind.

But then Aidan held it open and said, "Are you two coming?" Taking his duties seriously, the bodyguard was clearly prepared to wait for the next elevator with them if they didn't board this one with him. With a shrug and a squeeze of her hand, Dice strode forward and gestured the others to make a bit of space for them, and Kimmy got pulled along and into the elevator. A brass plate on the elevator wall read *Max 2100 lbs. or 16 people,* but the twelve of them were more than plenty to make the space feel full.

"Two more shows, ladies and gentlemen," Angel said cheerfully as the elevator lifted them upward.

Crys clapped with enthusiasm, just as Easy sarcastically said, "Woohoo." But he'd had a bit of a break while on hiatus from the band the previous summer, so maybe it didn't seem as endless to him as to the rest of them. Regardless, everyone was ready to be done with the tour, and the elevator arrived at their floor amid general sounds of approval. Goodnights followed as they disembarked.

"Goodnight, Dice, Kimmy," Aidan said. "As always, one of us will be awake in the hall all night. I'm going to crash, because my turn to go on shift will come fast."

And that was it. Ryan dragged a chair out into the hall by the elevators and sat on it, everyone else said goodnights and dispersed, and Kimmy and Dice walked around the corner to their room in taut silence.

Dice fumbled with the key card and dropped it, letting out a wry bark of laughter as he looked at his ordinarily deft hands. "I'm such a butterfingers today, don't know what's going on with that," he muttered, dropping to one knee to pick up the card. Then he froze. Looked up at her. Ignored the key card and put a hand deep into one pocket.

Now – seriously?! In the hallway outside our door, just like that? "Don't–" she said to him, hoping to forestall the inevitable.

"Don't be nervous?" He finished what he thought her sentence was going to be, took a huge breath, and plunged onward. "How could I not be nervous, Kimber? I'm kneeling here, asking you to spend your life with me." He looked down at his hand for a brief second, clutching a ring box, his knuckles white. "Want to see the ring? You can exchange it if you don't like it." He flipped open the small box and there it was, the prettiest, sparkliest ring she'd ever seen.

"Get up please," Kimmy said in a small voice, trying not to look too closely at it. "Let's go inside."

He looked uncertain for a moment, then stricken as he silently snapped the ring box closed and got to his feet. He leaned against the wall as if he didn't have the energy to do anything else.

"Come on," she coaxed, feeling horrible. "Come inside and sit down before you fall. I certainly wouldn't be able to lift you."

He made a weak attempt at a laugh and didn't object as she retrieved the key card and unlocked the door, and he followed her into their room without comment. Eventually he said, "You didn't like the ring? Or... it's something about me?"

"No!" Kimmy assured him. "You're lovely. I adore you; you know that. I just... as a reason to propose marriage, to spend the rest of our lives together..."

"You're my best friend," he said helplessly. "Christ on a stick, isn't that a good enough reason...?"

"It's the best reason. But we've been best friends for years. Which means you're asking because we're having sex, or because we're having a baby – those are the only two things that have changed between us – and that makes me feel you're trying to, I don't know, legitimize us. You've been weird since Easter, and I can't help but wonder... Did seeing that couple having their baby baptized do it to you? Or was it Easy saying every kid deserves a father?" She hadn't meant to say all that, but once she started speaking it just tumbled out of her mouth.

Dice sat down heavily on the end of the bed. "You heard that?"

"Not on purpose. I was just walking past the room you were in. But yeah."

"I'm sorry," he whispered.

She laid a hand on his shoulder, wanting to comfort him. It couldn't be pleasant to have a proposal rejected, even if it had been made for all the wrong reasons. *I could just say yes and marry him,* she thought. But on a deep level she recoiled at the idea of marrying because of the baby, or for any reason related to society or what other people might think they should do. Did he understand? "You don't need to apologize for him saying that," she told him, "or for me hearing it. I understand how it might have gotten into your head and made you think this was a good idea. The thing is, we don't need marriage for you to be the baby's father; you can be in Jellybean's life as much as you want to be. And I don't think there's any good reason to get married other than being in love and wanting a life together."

For a moment, she had a wild hope that he'd declare passionate love for her and tell her that *was* the reason. But he'd never given her any reason to think he felt that way, so she shoved the longing thought out of her mind. Friendship was good, friendship had to be enough.

"I think we could have a good life together, though," Dice grumbled, and she hoped what she was hearing in his voice was just pouting or embarrassment, not devastation. Admittedly, part of her wanted him to feel some feelings over her refusal, but she also didn't want to hurt him.

"We *do* have a good life together, drummer boy. Why rock that boat for no reason?"

When he didn't answer, she went into the bathroom to brush her teeth and get ready for bed, and when she came out again, he was still sitting there. She wanted to ask if he was okay but concluded that he probably wasn't and asking would make it all worse.

"Come to bed," she said, getting in on her side and propping up her pillows to make a backrest for reading.

"Going to have a quick shower first," he muttered, and got up at last, heading into the bathroom for his turn.

She settled back against the pillows with her current book, meaning to stay awake until he got into bed with the hope that cuddling would make everything all right, but as so often happened recently, she found herself dozing off. She read the same page twice, then three times, her head nodding forward, her eyes drifting closed.

Sleep won.

Sometime after that, she had a fuzzy memory of him adjusting her and her pillows into a lying-down position. He must have turned off her bedside lamp because when she woke to pee a few hours later, the room was dark. Grumbling to herself at having to get out of the warm bed, she made her way to the bathroom with the aid of her phone's flashlight.

Dice's clothes were in a heap on the floor along with a damp towel – evidence of his state of mind, because he usually kept his things organized and tidy. On any other day, the dirty laundry would be in a laundry bag, the towel hung over a towel rack to dry properly. *I didn't mean to make him unhappy,* Kimmy thought. Wakeful after her heavy sleep earlier, she considered tidying up the bathroom, but then started to worry that he'd notice that she'd noticed the chaos, and... Those sorts of thoughts never led anywhere good. Best to leave his mess alone. He could pick up his own clothes and towel in the morning.

And then she noticed the black leatherette ring box on the edge of the bathroom counter. It had been in his pocket, hadn't it? He must have put it on the counter when he undressed. She'd barely had a glimpse of the ring earlier; it wouldn't have done to seem too interested in what she was telling him she didn't want. And yet... Why did life have to be so complicated?

I'm going to regret this. But anyone would be curious...

She picked up the little box and opened it.

The quick glance she'd taken earlier had only shown her white gold, an unusual shape, and scintillating sparkles where light caught faceted stones. Now she saw that the ring was in the form of a coiled dragon, fierce rather than delicate, studded with sparkling diamonds along its spine – and low enough in profile not to get in the way if the wearer were drumming or working on a drum kit. *Perfect.* He knew her so well...

The temptation to try it on was strong, but instead she closed the box and put it back exactly as she'd found it.

Turning out the bathroom light, she crept back to bed, again with her phone's flashlight, and crawled in next to Dice. Half-woken by her movement, he rolled to snuggle close to her, an arm thrown possessively over her hips as he spooned her, radiating warmth and safety. She drifted back to sleep, thinking everything would somehow be okay, despite the upheaval.

But when she woke in the morning, he was already up and gone, without waking her or leaving a note.

♥

The band and their air-travel entourage were eating breakfast in the hotel dining room, of course, and none of them were surprised she'd overslept. Jed saw her come in and waved, and that drew the attention of the rest of them so they all looked over and waved or smiled greetings. Dice looked over too, but he didn't smile or wave. He just looked, and the corners of his mouth bent upward a bit, but his eyes were puzzled and hurt.

The smell of bacon from the buffet made her feel queasy, so she skipped the hot food service area altogether and grabbed a doughnut from the pastry display. After a glance over at the Smidge tables, she stopped at the beverage counter and poured herself a mug of coffee from the orange decaf carafe, which she proceeded to fix up slowly with a big slug of cream, putting off the moment of going to sit down with everyone.

There was an empty seat next to Dice, obviously waiting for her. But had *he* kept the seat for her, or did the others just assume...

Sally turned, scanning the room, and Kimmy knew that if she waited any longer to go and sit, more people would notice her hesitation, so she approached the table and took the empty seat.

"Good morning, sleepyhead," Dice said in a gently teasing voice, just as though he hadn't left her sleeping and chosen not to wake her.

"Morning," she said as pleasantly as she could, then stuffed a big bite of doughnut in her mouth so she wouldn't have to talk. Her mind was screaming, *I can't do this. I can't pretend you didn't ask me to marry you for all the wrong reasons. And then, I just want to go home.*

There were only two concerts left before the break.

What if I did just go home?

The others were already loading and unloading Dice's drum kit. He could handle building and breaking down his own kit for two shows, couldn't he? Or one of the other techs could do it.

As she slowly finished her doughnut and coffee, she dismissed it as idle wishing for an escape she wouldn't really take, but later that afternoon, she found herself checking out air fares online and counting the number of hours it would take her to get home.

No. She couldn't let Dice down, no matter that things were awkward between them.

After breakfast, though, Sally cornered her and asked, "Is everything okay with you and Dice, Kimmy? You both looked a bit off this morning." The makeup artist didn't miss much.

"We'll be fine," Kimmy said, trying not to be short with her friend, though she didn't want to answer the question. "I'm just a bit tired. Glad this tour is coming to an end. Aren't we all?"

"I'm not being nosy," Sally said, evidently reading a hint of rebuke in Kimmy's tone, "just trying to watch out for our band. I can see something's going on and I need to know if there's going to be fallout, and how to take care of everyone."

That made sense. If Dice needed support, Sally was one of the longest-serving Smidge crewmembers – maybe even the first, since she had stories about all the others and remembered the band's earliest days. She'd take care of him. "Fine. He asked me to marry him so Jellybean would have a legitimate father figure, which... just, no."

Sally's reaction was equal parts sympathy and exasperation. "Boys! They never get their words right. Are you sure that's the only reason he asked?'

"If he has a better reason, he'd need to say so. He didn't. And I'm not willing to use marriage vows, or even an engagement, to put on a show of propriety. It made things a bit awkward, but nothing we can't get over." Kimmy could hear a frustrated edge in her voice, but didn't bother to try to soften it. "I need some space, is all. A visit with my family."

That made Sally smile. "You're lucky you have that kind of family. Two more shows, honey. Then you can go visit them."

The last two shows were back-to-back nights in Anaheim. Dice was still nursing hurt feelings on the flight in, so Kimmy asked Sally if she could join the card game that nearly always went on during flights. That way, she had a solid excuse not to sit next to a grumpy, untalkative drummer, and she enjoyed playing pleasantly competitive blackjack with Sally, Jed, and Scott. By the time the plane landed, the photographer had lost on overall points and owed the other three a night out at the next opportunity.

"At least I'm a cheap night out these days," Kimmy pointed out. "No alcohol, and all."

Scott laughed and said she was an asset to the card table and better at poker than Ryan.

"You're fun to play with," Jed added. "Join us anytime."

Then there wasn't time for awkwardness once the flight had landed – they only had time for the fastest possible turnaround at the hotel to freshen up before heading over to the venue for soundcheck.

Kimmy got the drum kit fixed up exactly the way Dice liked it, pleased with her efficiency in the short window of time she had between arrival and soundcheck, and doubly satisfied when he sat down at the kit and didn't have to adjust anything. She mentally patted herself on the back for that, feeling tenuous as a band girlfriend and wanting to reassert her value as the skilled drum tech she was. *This is why I'm here. This is what I'm good at.*

Deep down, she wondered if she should try talking to Dice, maybe even lay her feelings open for him and make it absolutely clear that the thing she couldn't bear was the archaic idea that they *should* marry because of the baby. *I've fallen in love with you, drummer boy,* she thought sadly, watching him run through a drum solo during soundcheck, the beauty of him flowing through his movements and the music. And that was the trouble with being friends with benefits, if the other person just enjoyed the sex and didn't fall in love back. She tried to visualize how that awkward conversation would go and couldn't do it. *Nope.*

Then, after soundcheck was done, Angel sought her out and drew her aside. "I understand you're feeling some stress and need a break, Kimmy," he said. His expression was sympathetic, but those were not words anyone wanted to hear from an employer. Had Dice said something to him? Had Sally?

"I'm fine," she assured the front man, with what she hoped was a confident smile. "A little tired now and then, sure, but I swear it won't interfere with my work. Hoping for a quick visit home after this, though, if I can get the time off." Most of the crew would be cut loose for the summer, of course, but Smidge kept their techs on salary so they'd be available for recording support and one-off shows and wouldn't be lost to other bands. Nice to have job security, but it meant asking for a week off rather than just being free.

"Oh, everyone's taking a break before we get stuck into writing and recording," Angel said. "But you can go home right now. The kit's all set up, and Gary and Cal will cover for you during these last two shows."

"What? I–"

He took an envelope from an inside pocket of his leather jacket and pressed it into her hands. "That's a plane ticket home for you – Detroit Metro, right? Your flight leaves at two. One of the drivers will take you to the airport."

"Am I being fired?" she asked, filled with sinking dread.

Angel shook his head, smiling. "Not at all. You're on vacation for a week, that's all."

"But why, before the tour is over, suddenly like this? And a plane ticket?"

"Dice isn't being himself, and I need him to get his head on straight before we get into writing and recording. Maybe if we get you out of the way, he'll stop brooding and focus."

"Sally told you...?"

A brief half-nod, barely a dip of the chin, indicated that Angel did get his information from Sally. "She said you two were talking about marriage, which he's entirely too young for, even if he does have good intentions. And I don't think you'd want to tie yourself to him like that if his heart isn't involved."

If his heart isn't involved. That stung. But it also felt oddly familiar. Kimmy narrowed her eyes at Angel. "Hold on. Am I being cast as Mr. Bingley in this scenario? Because Dice isn't a Jane Bennett type."

"What now?" Angel asked, clearly not getting the reference, and it hit her that for all he was a big reader, he'd probably skipped *Pride and Prejudice.*

"Jane Austen. Mr. Darcy convinces his friend – oh, never mind. It's not important. Basically, Dice is a grown-ass adult who can make major life decisions for himself, and neither of us needs protecting from each other, despite what our helpful friends think."

"I didn't mean it like that," Angel protested. "I think I envy you two a bit, both for your closeness and..." He gestured toward Kimmy's rounded midsection. "But I've known Dice longer than you have, and he needs some space. Take this in the spirit it's given, an early start to your vacation and a free plane ticket home, that's all. We'll take care of Dice and his drum kit for you. You'll be back at work soon enough, and I might have some more backing vocals for you coming up, if you'd like."

"Well, thank you," Kimmy said, recognizing the bribery and knowing she was outflanked and defeated. "I *would* like that, very much. And thanks for the plane ticket and the early vacation."

Back at the hotel, packing her things, she considered calling Dice and telling him she was going home. *Should have talked to him before I left the arena,* she thought, feeling glum. But she'd need to be at the airport in an hour to make her flight, and when she'd taken a cursory look around for him before going back to the hotel, she hadn't seen him immediately. In the bathroom, she scowled at her reflection and said out loud, "You could have looked harder."

But she was annoyed with him. No one had twisted his arm and made him propose with the pathetic logic of *you're my best friend* and *we could have a good life together.* Couldn't he see that no woman would want a half-assed proposal like that, not even if she *was* his best friend and they *would* have a good life together?

She didn't want another awkward conversation. After six years of being able to talk to him about anything – well, almost anything;

she supposed they'd both discovered some limits on that – she didn't know what to say.

Kimmy finished packing in a bit of a huff, and a bit out of breath, and feeling borderline at the mercy of ridiculous, uncontrollable hormones. *I'll call him from the airport,* she thought as she locked their hotel room door and headed down the hall to the elevator. *Or text him.*

Texting would carry significantly less risk of her getting weepy, or saying something snarly and unforgiveable.

chapter

13

IN THE END, KIMMY TEXTED DICE AS SHE WAS BOARDING her flight, just before she switched her phone to airplane mode. *Was tired, Angel gave me early vacation so I could go home for a break. Gary has your kit covered tonight and tomorrow. Back in a week.* She contemplated adding something about missing him, then gave up and added *xoxo* at the end.

I'll miss his kisses and hugs while I'm home, she thought, putting her phone away and settling into her seat with a paperback she'd bought at the airport bookshop. There'd been barely any romance selection to pick from, as usual, and this one looked like it might be crossing genres into thriller, but at least those usually had happily ever after endings. The ones that looked like they might be dancing on the edge of literary fiction – the other two possibilities in the shop – were sometimes that horrible thing, not-a-romance pretending to be romance but ending in tragedy or a strong woman alone. Not wanting to risk that, right now of all times, she'd decided she'd rather have some high-speed chases and danger sex in her book, as long as the main couple ended up alive and together.

She tugged the hood of her hoodie more firmly forward to hide her hair and piercings as much as she could. Since she'd been linked romantically with Dice, there'd been a few photos of her in tabloids and on entertainment gossip websites, and she didn't exactly have a hairstyle or aesthetic that blended in easily. She hoped no one would look twice at a grumpy punk girl in an oversized hoodie, traveling economy with a grubby canvas duffle bag, a sleeping bag, and a backpack. As usual for the end of a tour, everything she owned needed washing.

The flight was uneventful, the book marginally better than expected.

She called home from the airport on arrival in Detroit, ignoring a cluster of text message notifications and missed calls from Dice. "Sorry to be calling so late. I got off the tour a couple days early," she told her father. She'd left California in the early afternoon, but the time change along with the flight had jumped her forward to almost 10 PM, her parents' bedtime. "I'll be home in about two hours."

"I'll tell your mother," he said, his voice so familiar and comforting, gruff and to the point. "We'll be up waiting. Hey. Nice to have you home, baby girl."

♥

On the bus home – the first of two buses – Kimmy looked through the texts Dice had sent her.

I'll see you at the show before you leave, though. Right?

That one must have been sent in response to her text earlier, likely right after she'd set her phone to airplane mode. It was followed by a missed call, then another text: *Kimmy, did you leave without saying goodbye?* And then another missed call.

More texts had been sent sporadically over the four and a half hours she was in the air, not all at once but spread out as he'd gone through his afternoon:

You won't see this until after you arrive but have a good flight.

Please call me when you land.

Soundcheck is done. Playing a show without you sucks.

I miss you already.

She did, now, feel rather badly about leaving him in Anaheim with nothing but a text message. Sure, he'd proposed for a silly reason, and then they'd both managed to get into their feelings about it, but he was still her best friend. She was supposed to be an adult – getting close to thirty, for what that was worth – and would soon be a parent. She could certainly have had the maturity and sense to make a proper effort, find Dice at the arena and tell him she was heading home and would see him in a week. Then she wouldn't be in this awkward position now.

Landed in Detroit. Sorry I left without seeing you! I did look for you but couldn't find you and was worried about missing my flight, she texted. It was still early evening in Anaheim. The opening act would be on stage and Smidge would be getting ready, but he might look at his phone and see her message.

Can I call you? he replied immediately. *Just want to hear your voice.*

Sorry, I'm on the bus now, I'd feel super rude having a conversation out loud, she explained. *Have fun on stage for me. I'll call you when I'm home and have privacy, I promise.*

Of course, he texted back. *Talk to you after the show.* Then he added *xox,* which he'd never done before.

So she sent *xoxo* back.

♥

Home was the same as it had ever been, in every good and comforting way. The Bakers lived in a large apartment that occupied the whole floor above the bakery rather hilariously known as Baker's Bakery, because of course Kimmy's mother was a baker. *A baker who married a Baker,* she'd always said with her musical laugh, up at the crack of dawn to go downstairs and whip together bread and muffins and her specialty doughnuts for the morning crowd, and everything in the apartment always smelled wonderful, warm and yeasty and sweet. The Baker children grew up helping, both in the bakery and at their father's garage down the street. Two of Kimmy's brothers currently lived at home, and all of them split their time between the bakery and the garage – she was the only one who had left.

Even at midnight, Woodward was a busy street, well-lit by streetlights and shop signs, with a steady stream of cars on the road and people coming and going from the Irish pub near the bus stop and of course the Magic Bag, where Friends With Royalty had played a show just before Christmas. The block-and-a-half walk to the bakery was pleasant after sitting all day on the plane and then two buses, and the extra profusion of rainbow flags ready for Ferndale Pride on Saturday made the lit-up shop windows she passed look joyful and bright.

The bakery was long since closed for the night, so she let herself in the side door and climbed the outside stairs to the apartment. There were inside stairs too, for coming and going from the bakery kitchen at the back, but the outside stairs led to what was essentially the front door of the home.

Gareth, the youngest of her brothers and only eighteen months older than she was, the one who shared her love for drumming, heard her footsteps and opened the door, bellowing, "Kimmy's home!" as he took the steps two at a time down to meet her and take the duffle bag and sleeping bag from her. He'd technically moved out of the family apartment to live with some roommates, but he still had a bedroom at home and tended to crash there at least once a week. By the time they reached the top together, their parents were there, waiting to wrap their arms around her.

I needed this, she thought, trying not to burst into no-reason tears as everyone hugged her at once. *I'm so happy to be home.*

"Your bag reeks," Gareth said. "I'm putting it in the laundry room. You want to borrow a clean t-shirt to sleep in? 'Cause you might be too big for the pajamas you left here last time."

He was laughing, clearly trying to wind her up, so she just laughed back and said, "No fear, Grotty, I sleep in the nude these days."

His childhood nickname – he'd been a bathtime avoider whenever possible as a small boy – combined with the idea of his little sister sleeping naked made him grimace. "Eww, you win, Kimmy. As always. I should know better than to try to tease you. Will you help me change and tune my drumheads while you're here? You do them better than anyone."

"You look radiant, dear one," their mother said, ignoring the interchange and asking permission with a glance before laying her hand on Kimmy's rounded belly. "You'll be a wonderful mother. And

I've kept a box of maternity things that should fit you, so you'll have some options while we do your laundry. Including nightgowns."

"Thanks, Mom. You know I wouldn't sleep naked in your house, right? I was just saying that to freak Gareth out for making comments. And yes, Gareth, I'll help you with your drumheads."

Their mother nodded tolerantly. "Did you eat dinner, Kimmy? Are you hungry?"

"I'm always hungry," Kimmy said with a small sigh. "A snack before bed would be nice."

"Did I hear snack time?" Jeremy said, emerging from his room to greet his sister. He'd moved back into the family apartment recently after a breakup with the woman he'd been living with. "Oh, hey, Kimmy. Glad you're home."

Gareth added that he was hungry too, and even their father said he wouldn't mind a snack and that it was nice to see Kimmy looking so well. Everyone ended up having toast fingers with peanut butter and jelly, and with one thing and another, it was after one in the morning before Kimmy said her goodnights.

She took a shower, meaning to be quick, but the hot water lulled her into losing track of time. She hurried to finish washing, grateful for her short hair that scrubbed up clean in seconds and dried with a brisk rub of the towel, and soon she was settled into her childhood twin bed, wearing an absurdly feminine Victorian-style white cotton nightgown from her mother's maternity collection. *Things I kept in case you wanted to wear them someday,* her mother had said, bringing the box into the bedroom along with a towel for the shower. *All fresh, I gave them a wash when I heard your news.* How could anyone refuse a nightgown, put like that?

Are you back at the hotel yet? Kimmy texted Dice. Maybe he'd be out at an afterparty with the band. He could still be at the venue, if the show had run late.

Got back a bit ago. I need to crash, but call me? I'd call you but I don't want to wake your house up.

Sure. She tapped the phone icon to initiate a voice call.

He picked up on the first ring. "Hey, Kimmy." He sounded sleepy, his voice thick and groggy though it was barely past 11 PM in California, and she pictured him in bed in the hotel room she'd left hours before – cream sheets and an oatmeal-colored blanket, a headboard upholstered in tan leather, art deco style bedside lamps.

"Thanks for staying awake for me, Dice," she began, then didn't know what more to say. Before his proposal, silence had never felt awkward between them, and she didn't like the change, but she didn't know how to fix it.

"I'll always stay awake for you," he said after a too-long pause. Then, after another awkward few seconds passed, "It's funny how quick I got used to having you in my bed. I don't like sleeping alone now."

"Same," she agreed, feeling like he'd given her a gift by saying it. "It's nice to be here with my family, though. I needed this. Oh – would you believe I'm wearing one of those Victorian nightgowns with ruffles and embroidery right now? I feel like I belong in a dollhouse or something. Mom kept this box of absolutely wild maternity stuff for me..." And just like that, the awkwardness evaporated, and she was talking to her best friend again.

"Selfie?" he asked, so she took one and sent it to him, giggling at the contrast between her hair and piercings and the crisp white ruffles and embroidered rosettes around the neckline. She could hear him chuckle appreciatively as he received it, too, and his voice dropped into a tone that she knew meant he was turned on. "You look good, Pretty Girl."

"What, ultra-feminine shit turns you on?"

"It's the contrast," he said. "Like when you wear pretty lingerie, or your toenails are painted all sparkly and cute. It goes with punk and piercings for me like... I don't know, chili-spiced chocolate or something. Sweet with a bite."

"Maybe the same way I like a bit of kink with my pleasure," she whispered, extra quiet even though the door was closed, because she couldn't imagine having to explain *that* to her parents or brothers if they were to somehow overhear.

"Always happy to oblige," he murmured into her ear, through the phone. "Wish you were here, Kimber." He hesitated, sighed if remembering something that wasn't quite so sexy or pleasant, and wavered – she could almost feel it – between slipping into some fun phone sex or acknowledging the weight that had been hovering between them. "Even if you're mad at me, I'd still rather be with you."

What? "I'm not mad at you. I was never mad at you." But was that strictly true? Yes – it wasn't anger, though maybe it had felt like anger at first, when she'd wanted to lash out and make him feel something. "Hurt feelings," she admitted. This was easier to say over the phone, after all. "Because it stung, the idea that you'd offer marriage for our baby when *I* wasn't what you wanted. Not in that way. I mean, I know our friendship is solid and we have seriously hot sex, and you were right, we *would* have a good life together. But I think I deserve someone who's in love with me. I'd like to think *you'd* want me to have someone who's in love with me."

"Christ Almighty, Kimmy, I–"

"You don't have to say something nice, drummer boy. I'm over it now."

"You – look, you *do* deserve someone who's in love with you, of course you do." He sounded weary now. "This isn't a conversation to have over the phone. I can't talk to you about this when I can't see your face."

That didn't sound good. "Are you breaking up with me?"

"No! God, no." At least his answer was immediate, his voice firm and absolutely certain in that moment. The quiet between them felt comfortable again. Then, with a bit of hesitation, he asked, "Do you, ah, want me to? Break up with you, that is?"

"Of course not." She didn't want to sound desperate, and grabbed at the most rational excuse. "We still have, like, five months of doctor appointments and stuff, not to mention Jellybean's birth. You promised you'd be there, and it'd be awkward if..."

"Oh," he said. "Yes, right. You're right." Then he gave what she thought was a hugely fake-sounding yawn, but maybe all yawns sounded fake over the phone when you couldn't see the person's face getting into it. "I'm sorry, I can't keep my eyes open. Got to crash."

"Yeah," she agreed. "Sleep well. One more show."

"One more show. Goodnight, Kimber." He ended the call.

It was late, but she knew she'd have trouble sleeping if she just turned out the light and closed her eyes. She opened up the book she hadn't finished on the plane – thankful she'd had the forethought to remove it from her duffel bag and bring it in to sit on her bedside table so she wasn't poking around in the laundry room at some dark hour trying to find it – and settled herself down to read a few pages.

In the morning, Kimmy woke to all the familiar sounds and bakery smell of her family home. For a moment, she almost reached for the alarm clock she'd had in high school, thinking groggily that she'd overslept before realizing that no one used alarm clocks anymore and a full bladder had probably woken her.

Her father was making oatmeal porridge in the family kitchen, Gareth poured glasses of orange juice in a row on the counter, and their sister-in-law Marisa – who would have arrived with Bryan when he came to start the bread at some ungodly hour of the morning – was in charge of coffee. Before too long, Kimmy's mother and eldest brother came up the inside stairs from the bakery kitchen, Bryan stomping like a freight train as he always did, their mother's lighter footsteps following. Jeremy emerged from the bathroom, and just as the porridge was ready and the coffee maker finished percolating, Trevor came clumping up the outside stairs and in at the door.

Kimmy hugged Marisa and the brothers she hadn't seen the night before, and they all took their coffee and juice and settled at the table as bowls of porridge and the jug of cream were passed around. Kimmy was glad to see that he'd put raisins in, probably because she was home and he knew she liked raisins in her oatmeal.

"Who's working where today?" her father asked, same as always. Bryan was always in the bakery and had never learned much in the way of a car mechanic's trade, though he'd met Marisa when she first came to work as a receptionist for the garage, where she still ran the office and now did the bookkeeping as well. The rest of them rotated back and forth as needed, and Gareth was usually the most likely to go down the street to the shop with their father.

"Need me in the bakery today, Mom?" Trevor offered.

Jeremy shrugged. "Guess I'll go to the shop, then."

"Where can I help?" Kimmy asked, because no Baker ever sat idle on a workday unless they were sick or injured, and after a brief token protest of *but you're on vacation*, she was invited to join the bakery crew.

"But you have to take it easy now you're expecting, Kimmy," her mother reminded her. "You can ice cookies and sit at the cash register, but I don't want you getting tired."

As if anything in the bakery could be tiring after loading in and out arena shows, Kimmy thought tolerantly. Her mother had no realistic idea of what she did for a living. Her parents had occasionally gone to see Friends With Royalty play at a local bar, but at an incident-free show on a tiny, familiar stage that required minimal setup, it probably looked like the job involved standing around with spare drumsticks.

"I'll tell Ella you're here; she'll be so pleased," Trevor said, getting up from the table. "She'll want to bring the kids over at lunchtime to say hi, I'm sure." His wife took care of Marisa and Bryan's little ones during the day along with their own daughter and another neighbor's child, and trips to the bakery were a favorite activity for the small daycare group.

All morning, Kimmy iced cookies and cupcakes, piped filling into doughnuts, and cut cake slices to put into fluted paper cases, ready for serving. True to Trevor's word, Ella visited with the children at lunchtime, and it was lovely to see them, but then Kimmy felt a bit worn out after all and was happy to sit behind the cash register for the afternoon. She didn't object when her mother sent her off work early to take a nap before dinner.

She heard nothing from Dice all day, though she'd hoped he might text her.

♥

Late that night, shortly after the time the last show of the tour would have ended, Kimmy was woken by a text from Easy: *What the fuck did you do to Dice, Sparkles? He wouldn't talk to anyone all day, and now he's drunker than I've ever seen him.*

This one's on you, she fired back, half asleep and not censoring herself. *You told him to propose to me because of the baby. All I did was tell him I deserve someone who's in love with me.*

Easy didn't respond.

Some time later, though, her phone buzzed again. She picked it up and looked at the lock screen, seeing a text message from Dice: *Misss yu.*

"Oh, drummer boy, you are going to feel so rough tomorrow," she muttered to herself, and against her better judgment she unlocked her phone and opened the messaging app. *I miss you too, but I'll see you in a few days,* she sent in reply.

After a pause long enough that she thought he'd maybe fallen asleep, he texted again: *Lovee you somcuh bwutifful ou are myy lift.*

She'd never known him to get too drunk to text clearly. But that looked like *love you,* and was he calling her beautiful? He'd often said he loved her over the years, but in the context of their friendship, and she realized now that he hadn't said it since they'd been officially a couple. Drunken texts didn't count for anything, though. *You've had a lot to drink, haven't you? Sleep well, drummer boy,* she told him. *I hope you don't have too much of a headache tomorrow.*

He didn't respond. Passed out, no doubt. She put her phone down and snuggled into her pillow. The moment her eyes closed, she too was asleep.

Saturday was Ferndale Pride, so all four of Kimmy's brothers were scheduled to work in the bakery and Marisa had the day off work and didn't join the family for breakfast.

Loaded with porridge and coffee and juice, Kimmy followed the others downstairs and settled in to make the lemon curd and whipped cream that would shortly go into a rainbow-iced batch of the bakery's popular "lemonade" doughnuts, while Trevor fried the rounds of dough that Bryan had set to rise before breakfast. Keeping herself busy was not an issue; with a huge mid-afternoon thunderstorm packing the bakery wall-to-wall, she had no time to fret about Dice's drunken texts the night before. She assumed he'd been safely in his hotel room bed at that point, but she hadn't actually asked, and he hadn't said anything about where he was.

The bakery stayed open late for Pride, so Kimmy had plenty to occupy herself with into the evening, and once they closed, she walked out with her mom to catch some of the singers on the small stage and wave greetings to old friends from school and the neighborhood.

Exhausted as she was by the long day, she read for a while in bed, hoping her phone might light up with a text message or phone call, but it stayed stubbornly dark. Well, the tour was over. He was probably sleeping off a rotten hangover, and she knew Jed would take care of him. Nothing to worry about. The bakery closed early on Sundays, so there'd be time to call him before dinner if he hadn't called or texted her by then. She hoped he hadn't lost his phone.

The next morning was busy for a Sunday with Pride brunches and post-wedding parties. Kimmy was too busy to worry about much except keeping the bakery shelves stocked and her all-too-frequent need for bathroom breaks. In the afternoon, she was working behind the cash register again when she once again had to call Bryan out from the back to cover for her while she dashed upstairs.

When she got back down again, Gareth was alone in the bakery kitchen, and he grabbed her sleeve before she could push her way through the swinging door to the shopfront. "Hey," he said, his voice oddly gentle for a sibling. "Take a peep before you go out there."

"What? Why?" she asked, but stepped up to what they'd always called the spy window as children. A fancy framed mirror behind the counter had the Baker's Bakery logo painted on it in black and gold, reflecting light and giving a glamorous upscale touch to the bakery, but what customers didn't know was that it was a half-silvered mirror, a one-way window from the kitchen into the customers' area. Mom had used it to keep an eye on her teenagers working the till, and the siblings had been able to watch each other talking with high school crushes over the counter.

Kimmy did not expect to see Dice standing there, with Trevor glowering at him from behind the counter and Bryan out from behind the cash register to face the drummer down, exuding confrontational energy. Kimmy's brothers weren't small men, and they kept themselves fit. Dice had a couple of inches on them, and drumming had given him a truly beautiful set of muscles, but he wasn't a fighter, plus they were two to his one. Not great odds, if the situation exploded. Eyes wide, she flew to the swinging door to try to hear through the crack what they were saying, knowing it was too late to stop whatever was about to happen. Leaning against it slightly to widen the gap, a technique they'd all learned at a young age, she created enough of an opening to see the men as well as hear them, though not with as good a view as she'd had through the mirror.

"You got our sister pregnant," Bryan growled.

A fair number of customers were in the bakery, gawking at the scene while they waited for their turns at the counter. Dice wasn't in rock star mode – he wore a hoodie and jeans, his hair in a ponytail, Vans on his feet – but he was too well-known not to be recognized, and a couple of the bystanders had their cameras out. *Shit. Filming this? Probably.*

Dice looked shocked, taken aback. "She's happy about the baby," he said in bewilderment. "At least... I think she is. Did she tell you she's not?"

Bryan ignored the question, taking a step forward. "You should have been more careful. You should have damn well married her first."

Dice's jaw firmed up and he didn't back away. "I asked her. But that's none of your business. She wanted a baby, and I love her – why wouldn't I give her anything she asked for?"

"Child support?" Trevor asked grimly.

Kimmy couldn't listen at the crack of the door any longer. She shoved the door open and stomped through. "You two are unbelievable," she told her brothers, glaring at them until their tense postures relaxed and Bryan returned to his place behind the cash register. "You do realize at least one person in this room probably live-streamed that? Thanks so much." A couple of bystanders sheepishly put their phones away and one ducked out the door, the little bell tinkling furiously against a rush of traffic sounds. She blew out a long breath as the door clicked shut. "Hi, Dice."

"I missed you, Kimber," he said, with an attempt at a diffident shrug, but his eyes were shining with longing and affection, and it was as if her brothers and the bakery customers didn't exist for him. "I had to come find you."

"I missed you too, you lovely man," she told him, ignoring everyone else too. They could deal with the fallout of that video footage later; she had no intention of giving them more to film. "Come through into the back. Not enough privacy out here." And she led him through the swinging door into the kitchen.

The moment the door closed behind them, he stopped, put a hand on her arm, and asked, "You *are* happy about the baby, right? Your brother Bryan–"

"Is being a clueless caveman all of a sudden. I'm so sorry," she said. "I have no idea why he took it on himself to go at you like that. But I guess I let my family assume that Jellybean was a surprise... I somehow couldn't bring myself to tell them that I'd set out to get pregnant on purpose."

A choking noise and a muttered curse made them both turn to see Gareth standing at the bakery work surface behind them, an exploded piping bag in his hands and tri-color icing all over the counter, his hands and arms, his apron – and judging by the way Kimmy's brother was looking down at himself in disgust, some had made it all the way to his shoes as well. "Sorry," he muttered. "Piping bag burst. Shit, I'm a mess."

"Gareth!" Kimmy said. "Forgot you were in here."

Her brother gave her a purely mischievous grin. "Bryan *is* a caveman sometimes." He grumbled some more curses under his breath as he tried to wipe the icing off, which mostly just smeared it more. "Give our big brother a bit of a break, though. Maybe you were too young to know about it, or you just weren't paying attention, but he and Marisa had a pregnancy scare when they were first dating, before they were really sure how they felt about each other. Bry took it as a personal failure at the time. Bit sensitive about it now, I expect."

"Still doesn't give him the right," Kimmy huffed. Neither Bryan nor Marisa had ever said anything about that to her, though to be fair, she guessed she'd have been around twelve or thirteen years old when it happened. "Go wash yourself off properly, Gr– Gareth." She almost called him Grotty in front of Dice, which he might not have appreciated. "That icing isn't going to improve as it dries. I'll deal with the counter and finish those cupcakes."

Gareth nodded his thanks and clomped off upstairs to wash, leaving Kimmy to take care of the cupcake situation. Dice pulled up a nearby stool and sat watching as she wiped the counter down and filled another piping bag with pink, purple, and blue icing.

"This one's unsalvageable," she said, offering him the cupcake that had been worst affected by the splatter. It technically had icing, but didn't look pretty. Fortunately, they always made some spare ones when filling a special order, for exactly this kind of situation. "You might as well eat it."

"Thanks." He ate the cupcake in only a few bites, like a starving man.

"You were hungry," she commented, watching him. "Haven't you eaten today?"

"Not much. Yesterday was rough," he admitted with a slightly guilty expression.

She thought instantly of his drunken texts two nights before, the mistyping too jumbled for her to be entirely confident of the sweet words he'd maybe said, and of Easy asking, *What have you done to Dice?* "Quite a party?" she asked neutrally, wondering what he'd say, knowing that nothing had meaning when alcohol was involved.

"I guess there was an end-of-tour party," he agreed. "I'm sorry you missed it. But I was... I suppose I thought it'd help me think."

That made her laugh, but gently, because he looked rueful and unsure. "Alcohol never helps anyone think, drummer boy.'"

"I know," he agreed with a rueful expression. "Still, it was there, and you weren't."

Finished icing the two dozen cupcakes, Kimmy sprinkled them with pink and blue candy confetti and stuck a purple macaron printed with the words *Gettin' Bi* on top of each one. "Custom party order," she said. "Sometime I'll show you Mom's toy for printing with edible ink, it's pretty cool." She loaded them into boxes for transport, then moved the boxes into a cooler near the door, ready for the customer who'd be picking them up shortly. Then she leaned out through the swinging door and told her brothers behind the counter, "The Robinson cupcakes are done, Grotty's upstairs washing icing off himself, I don't know where Mom is, and Dice and I are going for a walk."

"Cool," said Bryan. "Sorry I went off a bit."

"Thanks for protecting me, big brother. Even when I don't need it," she replied with a grin. No one could stay annoyed with Bryan for long. Back in the kitchen, she asked Dice, "You want to get out of here?"

"A walk sounds like a good idea," he said, and he sounded grateful for the chance to escape.

♥

The early June weather was perfect for spending time outside — warm enough for tank tops and shorts, but not hot enough yet to be unpleasant. A few blocks away from the bakery, Kimmy led Dice to the public park where she and her brothers had played as children. It had a few trees, picnic tables, a playground, baseball diamonds. "They're finishing a Tony Hawk skate park," she said, pointing out the waves of concrete. "I would have *lived* there as a kid."

"Looks awesome," he agreed. He hadn't spoken much on the walk over, either, responding with single-word answers or short, closed statements.

Kimmy, tiring a bit, heaved herself up onto a picnic table to sit. Perched on the tabletop with her feet resting on the seat below, she was still too short to look Dice in the eye, but it was better than sitting nearer to the ground. "You said you thought the alcohol last night would help you think. Which means you've got something on your mind. You want to talk about whatever's bothering you?" she asked at last, since waiting for him to say something didn't seem to be working.

He sighed, but when she patted the table next to her, inviting him to sit, he joined her. "I guess you should know, Kimmy. Don't hate me, okay?"

Oh, shit, that doesn't sound good. She looked up at the sky, trying to draw hope from the clear blue expanse. "When we started... this... we promised each other nothing would wreck our friendship. Nothing you could say–"

"This might." He bit his lip. "Because we also said no strings, and even when we said we'd date a little, make it official so I could be part of Jellybean's birth, I was – lying by omission is a bad kind of sin, right? Not telling the whole truth, knowing it'll lead to..." He looked away. "Christ, I'm so fucked," he muttered to himself.

"It's okay. It can't be that bad. Just tell me," Kimmy encouraged him, putting a hand on his thigh next to her and rubbing gently. He looked ready to vomit or pass out.

"It was never because of Jellybean. Any of it. I mean, I want to be the best dad I can be, but I could do *that* as your best friend. It never required dating. And Easy's dumb idea was just an excuse for me to propose." He sighed, looking down at the toes of his shoes, and an embarrassed flush rose up his neck and stained his cheeks. "I don't honestly know when it started, but... I've got feelings for you, Kimmy. Crushy, romantic kind of love feelings. I've got jealousy and heartache and all that shit where you're concerned, and I don't think I can do no-strings sex because I want to tie you up and spank you and love on you and keep you safe and cherish and adore you for the rest of our lives and I can't keep that a secret anymore." His words came out in a stumbling, chaotic rush. "I know that wasn't what you expected, and if you can't feel the same, I'll understand. But if there's any way you can give me a chance..."

This has got to be a dream, Kimmy thought hazily. But there they were in the picnic area of her neighborhood park. Dice's body felt warm and real next to her, and the wooden picnic table was firm under her butt. *Real.* "Same," she whispered. "I wanted to keep you, and I was taking what I could get because I never thought you'd feel more."

He looked down at her in disbelief. "Are you telling me that you might... love me back?"

She nodded. "Yeah. Not might. I do."

"But you said no when I proposed," he pointed out, sounding hesitant still, and she could understand now why he'd taken it as such a rejection, which had never made sense when she'd thought he was asking out of obligation. He hadn't just been nursing hurt feelings, and she felt a bit guilty for taking his reaction that way.

Still, surely he could see her perspective, the way she was trying to see his? "Flip it around. If I'd asked you to marry me and you thought I was asking only because Jellybean needed a father, would friendship and a good life together be enough for you?"

"No. I see. It would feel one-sided and kind of sad." Then he drew a relieved breath, and she felt his body next to her relax all over and sag into her, like a tension or weight had suddenly been let go, and his voice was suddenly hopeful as he put an arm around her and asked, "Does that mean..."

"You can ask me again sometime? Yes, it does." She smiled, feeling hope fizz through her too. "But maybe not in a hotel hallway, okay?"

He laughed, the sound rippling with elation, and hugged her closer. "No. I'll do a better job next time – I won't be nervous, now I know you'll say yes. I don't have the ring on me, or I'd ask you now."

"There's no rush," she said lightly. Then, because she needed just a tiny bit more reassurance after all the doubt, "Do you *really*... I mean, like, this isn't love-you-as-a-friend stuff?"

"No. I mean, it's that too, but... I love you. As a lover, as a partner. Maybe I need to show you."

He shifted his position for a better angle and brought one hand up to cup the back of her neck, tenderly but with a hint of strength that had her melting and helpless in his arms as he leaned down to kiss her. And it was as though any brakes or controls had come off between them. They'd kissed – a lot – but she'd never felt so adored or needed, and without the need to protect her heart any further, she gave herself up to the moment.

After an unknowable span of time, he pulled back, breathing hard, and she couldn't help a moan of frustrated need. "I don't *think* you want me to rail you right here on this picnic table in broad daylight, Pretty Girl," he growled into her ear, "so we need to stop. Find a room, maybe."

The idea of being taken in the open, right there on the picnic table, sent a liquid rush to the core of her, and she bit her lip and looked up at him with what she knew was a *try me* expression.

He gazed back at her, surprised and intrigued. "If I weren't in a band..." he muttered. "They'd kill me if someone took pictures, and it's a park, wouldn't want little kids to see anything... But damn, come on." Without letting go of her, he got up from the picnic table and lifted her to her feet. "Got an idea." With another fierce kiss, he led her to the back of the park near the fences of the houses behind. She could see him scanning the layout, searching. Farther down, two construction trailers, left locked for the weekend, formed an alley of dubious privacy.

"Here?" she asked, as he gestured for her to precede him.

He nodded, grinning, challenging her. "Put your hands against the wall," he said, his voice a mixture of dare and command.

"Yes, Boss," she managed to say. She placed her palms on the nearest trailer wall, feeling the slightly rough texture of it, all her senses heightened as he moved behind her, closing the distance between them, his breath warm on her neck as his hands began to caress and explore, stoking the fire back up to where she'd been ready on the picnic table to do anything he suggested. Slowly, tenderly, he kissed and licked her neck and shoulder, and slid his hands under her shirt to play with her ultra-sensitive breasts through and around her bra until she was squirming and panting.

"Anyone could walk by, see what we're doing," he murmured, his lips against her ear. "Does that turn you on? What if someone saw me pull your shorts down, finger you, spank you, thrust into you?"

"Yes, please," she moaned. "All of that."

He hooked his thumbs into the waistband of her shorts and shoved them down, baring her. The light breeze against her skin warned her how wickedly exposed she was. Somehow the daylight made it feel more public and depraved.

She waited, knowing the pause was deliberate; he was in control of the moment, letting the tension of anticipation build. Then his hand skimmed over her baby bump before slipping down between her legs and she sighed in relief and delight as his fingers began to work their magic, feather-light at first, teasing, spreading her natural wetness around, then stroking with more intensity and rhythm as her arousal built.

"Not yet, Pretty Girl," he warned her, as she felt her orgasm building.

"Please," she gasped. "I can't wait."

He chuckled. "If you come now, I'm going to have to spank you," he warned her, his voice loaded with sensual amusement, and the words – combined with a little extra pressure from his fingers – shot her over the edge. He steadied her, one strong arm holding her upright as she leaned into the wall, momentarily lost in space.

"You set me up for that," she muttered when she could talk again.

He didn't deny it, laughing out loud. "Is that such a bad thing? You know you want the consequences." Then, in a more serious tone, he added, "I can't bring myself to smack you as hard as you'd probably like, not while you're pregnant, but I'll try to make it sting a bit."

"Bring it on, Boss," she said, bracing herself against the wall.

Trust a drummer to be able to make it sting without hitting hard. His hand lit her buttocks on fire with sharp little slaps, soothing the burn away in between with sensual massage. "Do you like it like this?" he asked, his voice deep and thick with arousal. "In broad daylight on public property. Anyone could wander over here and see you getting your ass reddened..." And then his fingers were between her thighs again, probing into her, swirling around, finding the sweet spot and bringing her to the edge again. She heard the zip of his fly, then he turned her around and lifted her so that her back was against the wall. The tip of him nudged the sensitized and swollen flesh at her entrance. "Ready for me, Kimber?"

She made some kind of sound of acquiescence, couldn't be sure what she'd said but something like *yes* or *now* or *please* – it was all jumbled up in her mind – and he slid forward into her, his baseball bat of a cock filling her up in one smooth motion. And then everything was slippery thrusting and her back against the wall and his hands gripping her tender butt cheeks as he held her in place. He leaned in to kiss her hard, his tongue mimicking the thrust of his cock. "Come for me," he told her, and she did.

He rocked his hips, helping her ride out every last bit of that beautiful orgasm with a set jaw and shredding control. And only then did he let himself go, pumping into her a few more times in desperate abandon with mumbled words of praise and adoration under his breath and then coming to a moment of stillness before he eased himself out of her and set her gently on her feet.

"Thank you," she murmured, her thoughts still in a haze.

"The pleasure was mutual," he said with a grin, helping her pull her shorts up before he dealt with his own clothing. "Coming inside you is such heaven, and now I get to think about you with my cum making a mess in your panties as we're walking home," he added, a bit of a blush rising along his cheekbones. "Are you good? Not sore?"

"I'm perfect," she said. In truth, now that it was all over, she was tired and her legs and hips *did* hurt, but not from sex or the very mild spanking, just standing for too long while pregnant. "I wouldn't mind sitting for a minute before we walk back, though."

They walked back to the park, holding hands. The area surrounding them was still deserted, including the playground, though they could see a handful of teenagers slumped around a group of bicycles way over toward the road.

"Will the swings do for sitting, or do you want to walk back to the picnic tables?" Dice asked, looking over at the playground.

"Swings'll be fine."

They sat together in the late afternoon sunshine, swinging gently because somehow it was impossible to sit completely still when a push of a foot could create movement. "I feel like such a freak," Dice admitted softly. "I love you, I respect you... I shouldn't want to do the things I do with you, but I can't stop."

Kimmy couldn't help the grin that broke out on her face at the adorableness of his innocent shame. "I don't want you to stop. You're not a freak. There are people out there way kinkier than you. And you're thoughtful, considerate, you give me what I need, and I love you right back. You've got to stop feeling guilty, okay?"

Her words drew an answering smile from him. "Yeah. I'm a lucky man and I know it, Kimmy."

The sun was warm and pleasant, but she thought maybe the warmth she was feeling came from his words. "I'm the lucky one," she murmured in response. Then, more practically, "We should probably be walking back. My family will wonder..."

He shook his head ruefully as he got up from his swing and held out a hand to help her up. "Your family..." he said. "I've got to make things right with your brothers somehow."

As Kimmy stood up, she felt a ripple in her lower abdomen, a fluttering feeling like a trapped butterfly. "Oh," she said, and sat back down again, her hands cradling her belly as she waited to feel it again.

"What's wrong?" Dice asked, his eyes suddenly scared, though she could see he was trying to be calm for her.

She smiled at him in wonder and awe. "I felt the baby move!" The fluttering feeling came again, reassuring her that all was well, the miracle inside her making itself known.

"Really?" His eyes lit up. "That's so amazing!" He dropped to one knee and laid his cheek against her belly, his arms wrapping gently around her hips. "Hi, Jellybean," he murmured. "You be good for mom, now." Then he got up and helped Kimmy to her feet.

He didn't go of her hand, and kept his fingers entwined affectionately with hers as they set out to walk back to the bakery.

By the time Kimmy and Dice got back from their walk, everyone had gathered for dinner, including Marisa and Ella and all the children. Pre-dinner drinks were underway, and word had evidently spread through the family about Dice's arrival, because a place was set for him at the table. Kimmy's mom hugged him, and her dad shook his hand and offered him an Aperol spritz or a beer.

One of the many things Kimmy had always appreciated about her parents was that they ignored Dice's rock star status and just treated him as her friend – and now boyfriend, she supposed. *Maybe fiancé, soon?* The thought made her want to wriggle with happiness. She couldn't be sure because they were always gracious and welcoming to her friends, but she had the impression, or at least hope, that they seemed to genuinely like him.

Thankfully, no one had made any direct comments about her pregnancy, because that was not a conversation she wanted to have in front of her dad. She half thought Gareth might say something just to stir the pot, because he could be a joker that way, but she hoped his admiration for Dice as a drummer would stop him. Admiration notwithstanding, both Bryan and Trev were still being stiff and awkward, unfortunately, and she wanted them to get over it already.

Insufficient appreciation for the backline, she thought crossly. They'd never dare be even slightly, obliquely rude like that to Angel or Blade, not if Friends With Royalty wanted a single favor from Smidge ever again. Sadly, it was all too likely that her brothers, like so many other people, perceived the lead singer and guitarist as somehow *being* Smidge, as if the drummer and bassist were just add-ons, guns for hire who didn't have influence. Bryan and Trevor probably thought deep down that they themselves *were* FWR, she concluded – not for the first time, either – with considerable annoyance, regardless of their younger brothers' contributions. Jeremy would have made them shape up in the past, she knew, but these days her bass-playing brother barely touched his instrument except for shows and didn't seem to care much about anything at all.

While the two eldest Baker brothers were being monosyllabic and terse, their wives made an extra effort all through dinner to keep the conversation flowing smoothly. Unlike everyone else at the table, Marisa and Ella were slightly overcome by Dice's star power. Kimmy, though she liked them very much, thought wryly that they looked like they were about to whip out something to be autographed at any moment.

Over dessert, Marisa looked thoughtfully at Dice and asked him, "Where are you staying on this trip, Dice? Because you're very welcome to stay with us, if you haven't made arrangements."

"I came straight here to see Kimmy this afternoon," Dice admitted. "But I don't want to impose. I can easily get a room." He grinned. "Maybe up where we were staying when I first met Kimmy."

"Yeah, you're the kind of person they're never full for, even at Pride," Trevor muttered under his breath but just loud enough to be heard. Fortunately, no one paid attention because Kimmy's parents were of course saying that Dice could stay with them.

Before anyone could get into the details of what that meant – sleeping on the couch? Sharing Kimmy's twin bed? – Bryan smiled too broadly and said, "No, I insist. Marisa invited you first, Dice. You should stay with us."

"We have lots of room, I promise," Marisa chimed in at once. "And I won't let the children bother you."

"Children are never a bother," Dice said. "And thank you, if you're sure it won't be an inconvenience. I can easily go to a hotel if–"

"You don't have to stay up in Royal Oak, man," Bryan interrupted. "I want you to come stay with me."

Shit, Kimmy thought. She'd hoped her brothers would get along with Dice, and an invitation to stay seemed to fit the definition, but she wasn't sure what Bryan was up to.

Still, what could she say? After dinner, the party split up early as the little ones needed to be taken home to bed, and Bryan and Marisa took Dice away with them.

I came to see you, Dice texted Kimmy later that night. *I miss you. Why are we both sleeping alone?*

Kimmy sent back an eyeroll emoji. *I think Bryan was having maidenly vapors at the thought that this wasn't an immaculate conception. He probably thinks you corrupted me.*

Little does he know, Dice replied. She could imagine him laughing.

The next day, Kimmy slept in well past when she would ordinarily wake up, even after a late concert night. No one woke her. Being a Monday, both the bakery and the garage were closed, the only day of the week that all the Bakers rested.

When Kimmy finally peeled herself out of bed and stumbled to the kitchen to find the coffeemaker, she was surprised and pleased to find Marisa and Ella sitting at the kitchen table having coffee with her mother, and Polly, Tim, and Bethany watching cartoons quietly in front of the television. The moment Polly looked up and saw her there, she shrieked, "Auntie Kimmy!" and launched herself over for a hug.

"Let Kim get her coffee, you gremlins," Ella admonished, at the same time as Marisa spotted the expression on Tim's face and whisked him into the bathroom.

"Potty training!" she called out by way of explanation as she rushed past them.

"I'm not a gremlin," Polly told Kimmy seriously. "I'm a unicorn."

"You're a lovely unicorn," Kimmy agreed, gently disentangling herself from Polly's enthusiastic and sticky hugs. "I'm just going to get myself coffee now."

By the time Marisa was back from toilet duty and all three children were settled back in front of the cartoons, Kimmy had filled a mug with coffee and put a couple of bread slices into the four-slice toaster. Ella got up and joined her, adding more bread to the toaster and refilling her cup. "It's so nice that you're here," Ella said to Kimmy. "We sent all the boys to Marisa's house so we could relax here with you."

"But I want you to see what we've done with the house since you were last home, too," Marisa added, "so I hope you'll come to dinner at our place tonight. We've got a sitter coming to watch all the children at Ella's so we can have a nice evening and not focus on that. Donna, you're welcome to join us too."

"What a good idea," Kimmy's mom said. "Roger and I will have a quiet date night here since we both have early mornings tomorrow, so we won't join you this time. I can start the bread by myself in the morning, Marisa, so tell Bryan he can sleep in."

Polly looked over at the adults from her spot on the floor. "Auntie Kimmy, are you going to come here and live with us all the time, after you have your baby?" she asked. "Mommy said–"

"Let's not put Auntie Kimmy on the spot, okay, sugar cookie?" Ella interrupted hastily, looking faintly embarrassed. "The baby still has lots of growing to do before it's ready to be born, so we don't need to be in a rush to find out where they're going to live." Polly nodded acceptance of that and turned contentedly back to the television.

Kimmy made herself smile, though it sounded like they'd been discussing her future behind her back – and apparently might not see that future as including her actual career. "I don't really need a fixed address with my job, right? I'll probably stay here with Mom and Dad when I take my maternity leave, if that's what you're asking."

Her sisters-in-law and mother all looked concerned.

"You're going back to your job after the baby's born?" Marisa asked. "Back to the music industry, I mean." Her voice sounded neutral, even interested, but her eyes looked doubtful.

"You know we've got lots of work for you here, if you're ready for a change of pace," Kimmy's mom offered. "Ella would be able to watch your little one with the others."

Ella nodded. "Oh, yes. I'd love to add another cousin to my daycare."

Camillo already agreed to take care of Jellybean while I'm working, Kimmy thought, but how could she tell her family that? And she wondered if they were right. Maybe a rock tour was no place for a baby, though Luke seemed to be thriving and she suspected Camillo ran a tighter ship than Ella did. "I don't know how I'll feel after the baby's born," she said, keeping her voice light. There was no sense in getting into a fight with everyone about it.

"Of course," her mom said, reaching across the table to pat her hand reassuringly. "There's lots of time for you to decide what you want to do, and you can certainly stay with us during your maternity leave. We'll count on it."

"Thanks, Mom. Thanks for understanding. I'm just not ready to make any permanent decisions quite yet." *Decisions I didn't know I was expected to make, but still.* Kimmy sighed and took a big drink of her coffee. Being a drum tech was all she could imagine, and the thought of giving it up gave her a sinking feeling inside. And what about Dice? Where was he supposed to fit into all this? Kimmy wanted to see him, to get a hug and some reassurance. *Soon. I'll see him at dinner. I'll find a moment to talk to him, see what he thinks.* But what if he thought her leaving the tour would be better for Jellybean?

Around her, the women had moved on to dissecting how Jeremy was doing since Carly left him.

♥

As the three women followed the path around to the kitchen door at the back of the house and let themselves in, a mess on the counters was their first clue as to what the men had been doing with their day.

A half-empty pan of brownies sat on the center island, along with assorted open snacks – chips, crackers and a jar of peanut butter, a bag of red licorice Nibs, a jar of honey-roasted mixed nuts, a block of cheddar cheese...

"Munchies, much?" Ella said with a laugh, leaning over to sniff the pan of brownies.

"Bryan gets it prescribed for pain, and it's now legal for adult personal use, anyway," Marisa explained, with a concerned grimace, until she realized that Kimmy wasn't going to object. Automatically, she started tidying up the scattered snack debris.

Kimmy just laughed. "I work on a rock tour. Weed is... the least of what I encounter on a daily basis. If it helps Bry, that's great." The eldest of the Baker brothers had been in a car accident some years before, which had left him with ongoing pain in his knee and hip. She was glad her brother had found something to relieve it.

When they walked through into the den, there were two more bags of chips on the coffee table, plus a bag of sour gummy candies and a half-eaten sandwich. The five men were sprawled on the couches, extremely relaxed, with hockey on the television that no one was paying much attention to. Dice in particular looked dopily content, and it took him – well, all of them – a minute to focus bloodshot eyes on the women who'd walked through the door.

"How much cannabutter was in those brownies, you goofs?" Marisa asked, but there was laughter in her voice.

"We were careful–" Trevor began.

At the same time, Bryan said, "I cut them into really small pieces. I don't think any of us had more than 20mg. But Dice is pretty baked; I didn't know he hadn't got a lot of experience with this stuff. Sorry, Kimmy."

Hearing his name and hers, Dice grinned at them, slack-limbed and unperturbed. "I love you, Kimmy," he said easily. "I like your brothers. They let me try a special brownie. Angel never would."

"Oh, man," Kimmy muttered under her breath, before assuring Dice, "I love you too." Her annoying brothers thought this was extremely funny and gave her a round of applause. "And I'm glad you all aren't fighting anymore," she added, since they were clearly in harmony now.

"I'm going to start making dinner," Marisa announced, picking up the remains of the sandwich to clear it away. "Is anyone hungry?" That got a solid chorus of agreement.

In the kitchen, Marisa transferred a baking dish of lasagna from the fridge to the oven and started making a salad. Kimmy offered to help but her sisters-in-law assured her they had it covered and encouraged her to sit at the breakfast bar and rest her feet.

"How is this Dice's first magic brownie? He's a whole rock star," Ella burst out, as though she'd been holding in the question and then couldn't anymore.

Kimmy didn't want to talk out of turn about the band's business, but despite her not being home so often, these were her sisters, by marriage and of the heart. They would become Dice's sisters too, she hoped. She needed them to understand where he was coming from. "He's a few years younger than the rest of the band," she pointed out. "Like, he's only twenty-five now – well, turning twenty-six next month, but anyway – when they started the band, he was in junior high. So they've always protected him. He's probably had someone pass him a joint here and there, but that's it. I'm pretty sure Angel would fire any crew member who crossed that line."

"He's three years younger than you?!" Marisa asked, and her voice sounded more shocked at that than anything about him being Kimmy's baby daddy or the idea of a rock star getting knocked on his butt by a small quantity of edibles.

"Does it matter?" Kimmy shot back. "He's been my best friend for a long time, and the years we were born don't mean a thing. Ella's four years younger than Trev, and no one cares."

"True," Ella said. She cut herself a half-piece of brownie from the pan that still sat on the counter. "I mean, I'm pretty sure I'm more mature than he is..."

Marisa eyed the pan of brownies, then took the other half-piece that Ella had left. "Of course age gaps don't matter. I just wonder if a boy that age will want to settle down with a kid – ooh, this brownie is so good! I'm sorry you can't have any, Kimmy. We'll have to get Bryan to make you some with regular butter."

"He does make good brownies," Kimmy agreed. "I've had them before. I don't mind missing out on these ones." That was one thing about growing up in a bakery family: excellent baked goods. She ignored Marisa's comment about Dice not wanting to settle down, because what could she say to that? *I never asked him to settle down; this isn't about playing house.* Her conflicted feelings now weren't his burden to carry.

Kimmy knew what life would hold if she came home. Work in the bakery, work in the shop, family dinners – and apparently weed brownies on the weekends, because why not? Jellybean would grow up with cousins and go to the nearby school. It wasn't what she'd planned, but was it what she *ought* to plan?

The lasagna came out of the oven and garlic bread went in. Ella, who was clearly comfortable in Marisa's kitchen, got the pepper grinder and saltshaker from a cupboard and hot sauce from the fridge. Then Marisa called the men in from the den and they gathered around the kitchen table to eat.

The table was mostly silent at first, as everyone concentrated on their food, punctuated with the occasional complimentary "Delicious!" and "This is so good!" Once their initial hunger was satisfied – and Kimmy used the term loosely in her mind since they'd obviously been eating all afternoon – conversation sprang up again.

At least my brothers aren't still trying to fight Dice, Kimmy thought, not that one *could* fight someone as relaxed as all that, and she felt pretty sure they'd gotten over the issue and wouldn't try to fight each other when the brownies wore off either. Her sisters-in-law seemed to have gotten over their starstruck moments too, which was all to the good, although she kept hearing Marisa's voice in her mind saying *I just wonder if a boy that age will want to settle down with a kid.*

After they'd eaten, Kimmy began to feel extremely tired and told the others that she'd head back to her parents' place to sleep. "Why don't you just stay here for the night?" Marisa suggested. "We'll take you back to the bakery in the morning."

Feeling a bit punchy at this point, not to mention annoyingly sober, Kimmy asked, "Oh, Bryan doesn't mind me staying? I thought he invited Dice here to protect my nonexistent virtue." They all laughed at that, as though she'd said something particularly clever.

"I never said that!" Bryan protested, but without any heat. Had he forgotten how he'd called Dice out for getting her pregnant without marriage? *You should have damn well married her first,* Bryan had said in the bakery only the afternoon before. Apparently, they'd gotten along since then.

"Do stay," Marisa insisted. "I've got a brand-new toothbrush for you, and you can wear one of Bry's shirts to sleep – do *not* make a joke about your shirts not being big enough for your sister, Bryan Baker – and I bet Dice would rather have your company here."

Dice, hearing his name, grinned dopily at them.

Trevor and Ella got up and said they'd be heading along home to their place, which was only a block away, because the babysitter would turn into a pumpkin at midnight. Gareth agreed that it was time for him to head out as well, but that he'd be meeting some friends because it was much too early to end the night, even on a Monday. Jeremy didn't get up from where he was sprawled, and said that if it was all the same to everyone else, he'd just crash there on the couch.

It didn't take long for everyone to say goodnight, and soon Kimmy found herself getting into bed on a queen-sized air mattress that filled all the available floor space in Bethany's pink bedroom, the larger of the two children's bedrooms. The curtains featured pastel clouds and rainbows and unicorns and stars. The little girl was happily sleeping over at Auntie Ella's house, but Kimmy hoped she didn't mind letting guests use her bedroom. A bedroom was such a personal space. *Maybe I feel it more because I travel so much,* Kimmy thought. She still had a room over the bakery, but it belonged to teenage Kimmy, not the person she'd become.

She turned out the light and felt her way into bed in the dark. Dice sprawled beside her, sleepy and content. As soon as she lay down, he helped her pull up the comforter and draped an affectionate arm over her, and before she could even say goodnight, she heard his breathing relax into sleep.

♥

"You good, Kimmy?" Dice asked, his voice drowsy.

Her phone alarm was pinging a wakeup call. She opened her eyes slowly and felt for it to silence it, disoriented for a moment before everything clicked into place. *We're sleeping in Beth's room at Bryan and Marisa's house. It's Tuesday. A workday. They need us to get up so they can get to their jobs.*

"Yeah, I'm good," she agreed sleepily. At that moment, it was the truth, even though her back hurt abominably from sleeping on an air mattress all night and her heart was still full of questions and doubt about what the future held. "And you?"

"I'm good too," he said, then after a pause added, "Very good, now that we're together. I missed you the first night I got here, and before that when you were here and I wasn't. This is better."

"It's nice. Air mattress and all. I think my family wants me to stay here, though," she told him, knowing it wasn't the time for serious conversation but not wanting to hold it in anymore. "After Jellybean is born, I mean. Permanently."

"Christ, no," he said instantly. Maybe it was the lingering effect of the brownie, but he didn't sound perturbed, wasn't even arguing, just stating a fact. "Or did they mean between tours? We can live here when we aren't touring, if you like. My family won't mind, and I can live anywhere."

"I think they meant all the time," she said softly, wishing she could see his face properly in the early morning darkness.

"They want you to be a band widow? Or they want you to leave me?" he asked carefully.

"I don't think they understand. I don't think they thought through what it would mean for me. Just... they can't understand how I could plan to bring a baby up on tour, and it spooked me a little."

Dice shot up to a sitting position, rocking the air mattress. "Don't let it spook you," he said, his eyes intense. "Please. Damn, okay, hold on." He rolled out of bed and dug around in his bag for a moment before returning, only to go down on one knee, right there in nothing but his boxers with disheveled morning hair. The little leatherette box was in his hands, which shook as he opened it. "I meant to wait for a romantic occasion, to do this properly, but I can't. So don't give up on me, Kimberley Baker. Marry me and be my forever. My drum tech and my heart, together on the road and off it. *Please.*"

"You think I can do it?" she asked, struggling to get herself to a sitting position on the bouncy inflated surface. "Be a good drum tech *and* a good mother?"

"Christ on a stick, yes!" He didn't get up from his kneeling position but reached out the hand that wasn't holding the ring box to help her sit, and he didn't let go of her fingers, his strong grip begging her to listen and believe. "Crys does the road mom thing, and you're a million times tougher than she is. You'll have Camillo to help, and anything that's in my power to do. Say yes and give us a chance, because I don't want any of it if you're not with me."

How could she refuse him when his eyes were full of his whole soul and he was giving himself to her, and he was everything she'd ever wanted? "Yes," she whispered.

"Truly?" he asked, his voice barely above a whisper too, as though they were sharing something too momentous to say aloud.

She nodded, not trusting her voice with words.

"Thank you," he murmured, relief and gratitude clear in every line of his body and the fervent sound of the words. Cleared his throat, let go of her fingers to extract the ring from its velvet bed. "All right if I put this on your finger?" he asked more normally, getting up from his knees.

"Please," she said, her voice coming out wobbly. She let him take her left hand in both of his and he slipped the ring into place.

"I thought you'd like a dragon; it's small and fierce like you. But we can exchange it if it's not your jam."

"It's perfect." This time her voice sounded normal, more in control. Then, curious, "How did you find my size? I never wear rings."

"I wrapped a string around your finger while you were sleeping." The combination of pride in his ingenuity and embarrassment at the subterfuge made such a conflict on his face that she laughed out loud at his words.

"I love you so much, Dice. Dylan. Do I–"

He chuckled. "That'd be weird. Dice is basically my name at this point. Only my parents call me Dylan, and Angel when he's being extra big brother."

She grinned back. "I reserve the right to call you Dylan Ignatius on occasion, for reasons. But you're my Dice, and my Boss, and my everything."

"And now you'll be my Pretty Girl forever," he said happily. "I'm beyond lucky, Kimmy. And I could stand here forever adoring you, but we should probably get dressed."

"Probably. Can we be really cheesy and take a selfie first? Not to share with anyone, just to keep as a memory – just as we are, in Bethany's Pepto Bismol bedroom in front of the magic rainbow unicorn curtains. And then I need the bathroom."

Laughter rippled out of him, so full of joy. "Sure. Let's do it. A memory, to be sure."

She started to get up. "Oh, my back! No more air mattresses until after Jellybean is born, I just can't."

He helped her to her feet, rubbing her lower back until she was able to straighten and stand, then he put his arms around her in front of the curtains and she snapped a selfie with her phone, holding her left hand up so the pretty new dragon ring would be in the frame.

"Let me take one with mine," he said, and hunted around for his phone, which he couldn't find immediately. "I know I had it when we went to bed." She dialed his number to get it to ring, and he located it on the floor between the air mattress and Bethany's bed, where it must have slipped down in the night. On looking at the screen, he grimaced. "How in hell do I have two dozen texts and ten missed calls?"

Concerned, Kimmy came over to stand next to him, looking at the small screen that showed missed calls from his bandmates, Sally, the Valancy Records office, and a handful of unknown numbers.

He played the first voicemail on speaker. A cheerful, radio-smooth voice filled the room. "Hey, Dice, this is Robin Parker with *Morning Talk* on KTAB 102.5 – I'm hoping to hear your side of the altercation that's been making the social media rounds. Did your girlfriend's brothers convince you to marry her? Call me at–" Dice jammed a finger at the screen to end the playback and flipped through his unread text messages with a muttered curse, looking increasingly grim.

"It'll be all right," Kimmy assured him, putting her arm around him.

"I just don't want anyone thinking I had to be convinced to marry you," he said, his voice cracking with distress.

"Does it matter what they think?" she asked gently. "Come on, let's get dressed. Then call Angel, call Valancy. We'll get this sorted out. Don't worry. And I *really* need the bathroom now."

When she got back, he was dressed and on a phone call. "It was just a misunderstanding, Bettie." Kimmy recognized the name. He must have called the Valancy Records office and was talking to Mr. Stirling's terrifyingly glamorous personal assistant. "Unfortunately, Kimmy's brothers didn't yet know that we were already engaged. ... Yes, jumped to conclusions. ... Well, that will be up to her, but I don't have a problem with it. ... No, we have plans with her family today. I can do a phone interview this afternoon, and we can be on a flight tomorrow. ... Got it. ... Thanks, yes, you too." Dice's voice held a new confidence as he ended the call, calmly putting his phone into his pocket.

"We were already engaged?" Kimmy asked quizzically, looking at the very new engagement ring on her finger.

He nodded. "I'm not having anyone say that your brothers made me marry you. So that's our story – if you're okay with it. Bettie wants us to do an engagement photoshoot, show off your ring and... like, pretend we took the photos last week. Would that be okay with you?"

"Sure. Doesn't matter to me." Their *real* engagement picture would always be the selfie they'd taken in front of Bethany's curtains, him in his boxers and her in an old Friends With Royalty t-shirt, cuddled together and laughing as she held up her hand with the ring. Having some pictures they could actually show people wouldn't be a bad thing. "Did I hear you say we were flying back tomorrow?"

"Bettie wanted me to go today but I told her we had plans. Don't want to be rushed. And I thought I might ask your parents' blessing."

His words made Kimmy smile. "They'll appreciate that. We'll ask them together. Not permission, because you don't need anyone's permission but mine to marry me, but... yeah." *Blessing* sounded old-fashioned but sweet, and the idea of asking for her family's support of the marriage was nice. "Have you told your family yet? Should I ask them for their blessing?"

"My dad will take that literally, like a *Heavenly Father, bless this relationship with grace and rejoicing* kind of thing. But if you don't mind that, he'd be thrilled. And my mom will just want a chance to hug you."

She nodded. "Whenever we have a chance to visit them, then."

A knock on the bedroom door pulled them back to the present moment. It was followed by Marisa's voice softly asking, "Are you two up? We're going to need to head out shortly."

"Half a minute, we'll be right there," Kimmy called back, scrambling to finish getting dressed.

♥

The rest of the visit raced by in a flash.

Dice got Bryan to join him for the phone interview that afternoon, chatting with a radio host, making it clear in casual banter that they were good friends and their viral argument had only been a misunderstanding. Dice plugged Friends With Royalty heavily, mentioning that they'd opened for Smidge at Sound Board back in December and telling everyone they were worth listening to. Bryan told the world that Dice was on the way to being an iconic drummer

– unconsciously echoing Joel Bonamour, though he couldn't have known it – and there was no one nicer in the music world.

Kimmy's parents were overjoyed at the couple's news and gladly gave their blessing to the engagement when asked. "You know it's not because of the baby, Mr. and Mrs. Baker?" Dice asked, his face betraying a hint of anxiety. "My life wouldn't be complete without Kimmy."

"Call us Roger and Donna," Kimmy's dad reminded him approvingly. "You're family now."

"Don't worry, Dice," Kimmy's mom said, "we know." She moved in to give him a hug, adding quietly into his ear, although not so quietly that her daughter couldn't hear, "I think you and Kimmy chose each other a long time ago, and it just took you both a while to admit it."

"Oh, Mom..." Kimmy muttered, half-embarrassed, but they all knew truth when they heard it.

Kimmy's dad tugged at his collar, the way he always did when his family got mushy around him. "So, I understand you two are off again tomorrow. Where is Smidge going next, young man? Our girl didn't say."

"I'm sorry for taking Kimmy away again so soon. We were supposed to have a few more days' break, but... something happened, and they want us back early," Dice said ruefully, then smiled, his eyes lighting up at what was ahead. "We're going to Canada. British Columbia. They're sending us to a place on Whistler Mountain to finalize material for the new album for a couple of weeks, then there's a producer at a recording studio in Vancouver they want us to work with. Kind of exciting – I have some family up in Ontario, but I haven't spent time in B.C. outside of touring, and this mountain resort is supposed to be pretty awesome even outside of ski season."

"Down in Ontario," her mom said with a laugh. "Ontario is south of here."

"Oh, Mom! It's a Detroit thing," Kimmy explained to Dice, "Ontario is south of here. But tell me about Whistler Mountain." This was news to her.

"Yeah, Kurt and the people at Valancy have apparently been working on it for a while, but they only told us the other day – after you'd left – once they'd finalized all the details with the resort and the producer." He looked at her with raised eyebrows, as if to ask whether she was as excited as he was about it. "When we're not working, there'll be hiking trails to explore, and maybe they'll arrange a glacier skiing day for us, and a peak-to-peak gondola ride, and there's a village with shopping and art galleries and restaurants..."

"It sounds like a treat," Kimmy agreed, chuckling inwardly at the scale to which she'd become accustomed to nice things. Nothing would ever be quite like Lovango Cay, but a mountain in Canada... "I don't think I'll be skiing," she added, "but you can enjoy that for both of us."

"Do you think there will be bears?" her father asked. "I'm pretty sure Canada has bears."

♥

Because the Valancy Records office had arranged their flight, Kimmy and Dice got the full rock star treatment on arrival at the airport. Bettie had offered to book a car service for them too, but Bryan insisted on driving them.

And they had their bodyguard. Dice had, after all, brought Aidan with him on the flight, and booked him a hotel room near the airport and a rental car, ready to zoom to their rescue if needed – Aidan had never been more than a phone call and forty minutes away.

"See, I didn't go off by myself this time," Dice said to Kimmy when he asked Bryan to stop and pick up the bodyguard on the way to the airport. "I talked to Aidan and we had a plan. If we'd needed backup, he'd have been there."

"Just bring him with you next time," Bryan said, shaking his head. "We'll find a bed for him. The man doesn't need to be by himself in a hotel."

"I didn't know if I'd be welcome myself," Dice explained. "I wasn't going to show up with an extra person in tow. But I'll ask him if he wants to stay with the family on our next visit. Aidan's more of a friend than an employee."

"You blur those lines a lot, man," Bryan muttered, but he smiled, and Kimmy could tell that her adored big brother and her drummer were on their way to becoming real friends. No one could help being Dice's friend, honestly. All he ever had to do was smile.

From the moment they emerged from Bryan's car at the airport, an official was there to escort them. They were prioritized through airport security, and a golf cart carried them to the business class lounge, where they were offered glasses of champagne – or sparkling apple juice in Kimmy's case – before being ushered to their gate. Kimmy had seen plenty of attention given to the rock stars in her life, but it was still surreal to be carried along with that. Dice wasn't the sort of person to have his bodyguard seated in economy, either; Aidan came right along with them to the business class section and enjoyed all the same good things Kimmy was slowly becoming accustomed to.

Throughout the flight, she kept looking down at her hand, gazing in awe at the shiny white gold dragon with its diamond spine coiled around her finger. *Engaged. In love. Dice is really mine.* The joy of it felt almost too big to fit inside her, a goofy grin breaking out on her face anytime her eyes met Dice's, and his visible happiness echoed hers with an equally uninhibited smile.

"Knowing what it's like to be with you is so much better than wondering," he whispered in her ear at one point.

As the pilot announced that they were beginning the approach to Vancouver, it occurred to Kimmy that the last time she'd talked to Angel, he hadn't exactly been overjoyed about the baby or the idea of her and Dice getting married. She understood him being protective of his friend, but only to a point, and it wasn't like the two of them had made a drunken Vegas decision or been irresponsible with family planning. Two adults getting what they wanted deserved respect.

Now that their engagement was public and impossible to sweep under the carpet, she wondered what the Smidge front man would say.

The last thing she wanted for Dice was to have his band relationships strained. Nor did she want to lose her job, if it came to that.

THE DRIVE FROM VANCOUVER INTERNATIONAL AIRPORT to Whistler Village took about two hours, which hardly felt like any time at all to Kimmy, accustomed as she'd been to hours on the road. The car was a limousine with a privacy partition, so she could say anything to Dice in theory, but just as she hadn't brought it up on the airplane, she hesitated to introduce the subject of Angel's approval during the car ride. "Are you looking forward to being back in the studio again?" she asked instead.

"Studio's all right," he said. "The part I'm looking forward to most is working on new songs for the album. Like when we recorded 'Band on the Road' – recording it was cool, but the writing part... developing the song, working it out, sharing ideas..."

Kimmy understood that feeling, especially now when the other band members were actually letting him help. They'd always split the writing credit evenly between the four band members, regardless of who had done what, but they'd used some of his lyrics on their most recent song, and Angel had flat-out told him the band would appreciate his help during the upcoming writing sessions.

The route, called the Sea to Sky Highway, swooped along the edge of the coast for most of the trip, with rocky cliffs on one side, broken by the occasional waterfall, and the Pacific Ocean on the other. At first, every waterfall and view of the ocean drew admiration, but after a bit they stopped paying much attention to the passing scenery, and

Kimmy dozed intermittently along the way. Eventually, these views gave way to forest, and then increasing signs of population.

"I guess we're almost there," she commented, shaking off sleep as the car finally turned off the highway and slowed, approaching the resort town. They cruised through the tiny town center area and then out again, along a route shaded with huge pine and fir and cedar trees, passing driveways with glimpses of lodges and chalets. Their car turned down one of the driveways, then, and pulled up in front of a substantial peak-roofed chalet. *I'm not ready.*

But they were getting out of the car, and the driver unloaded their luggage as the front door opened and Sally and Crys rushed out to greet them with hugs and enthusiasm. "Hey, Dice, heard your interview on KTAB," Sally said at once. "You handled that like a boss. Also, happy engagement, you two. It's about time."

"Congratulations!" Crys chimed in enthusiastically. "I'm so happy for you – oh, what a lovely ring!" She gave Kimmy another joyful hug. "Isn't this the nicest thing to happen? A baby *and* a wedding to look forward to. Have you decided on a date yet?"

Angel appeared in the doorway, and at least he had a tolerant smile on his face in the moment. "Glad you got here," he said. "Welcome to our home for the next couple of weeks. Come on in."

Kimmy let out a silent huff of temporary relief and picked up her duffel bag and carry-on backpack that the driver had unloaded from the trunk, moving toward the door before she realized that Dice had frozen in the act of extending the handle of his rollaboard carry-on bag. For a moment, he just stayed there, bent over with his hands resting on the bag, his face set like he was trying to control some complicated feelings. Then he straightened up and looked straight at Angel without a hint of a smile on his face. "No congratulations, man?" he asked quietly, but his voice was hard.

Angel blinked at the unexpected challenge. Kimmy held her breath and waited to see what would happen. A few seconds of tense silence passed as Dice waited for a response and Angel seemed unable to process that his drummer had just called him out.

"Man, I don't know what you–" Angel began, seeming genuinely puzzled, but Kimmy thought his confusion had more to do with seeing a previously unknown side of the drummer than a real uncertainty about what he wanted. *She* recognized the assertive, determined, implacable side to her man, but hadn't been sure if it was something he could access in himself outside the bedroom.

Dice raised his eyebrows, not backing down.

Angel sighed. "Okay, congratulations on your engagement. Are we good?"

"As long as you mean it," Dice said. "As long as you can accept me for who I am now, not who I was ten years ago. I just – it's blindingly obvious that you're judging my ability to know what I want and when I've found love, and on top of all the other babysitting crap I get around here, it's too much."

"I don't know if I believe in love anymore," Angel said bitterly.

Sally's eyes widened, and she turned and headed inside, neither running nor stomping but a sort of angry combination of the two. Crys's face filled with dismay, and she said, "Oh, Angel..." before hurrying after Sally.

Kimmy didn't know whether to follow them and leave the two men their privacy or stay to support her fiancé if the situation got further out of hand. She hesitated, missed the moment to leave, and stayed.

But the anger in Dice's face had softened to concern at his friend's obvious distress. "You okay, Andy?"

"Fuck, no, but I'll survive. I always do." Angel shrugged, shaking off the bitterness and doubt that he'd revealed for a moment, resuming a detached mask that suddenly didn't fool Kimmy anymore.

"Look, I can see you're... going through something," Dice said. "But love exists. I'm feeling it. Blade's happier than I've ever seen him. Even Easy is in love, under his usual layer of mockery."

Angel grimaced in response, giving a short nod of acknowledgment.

Maybe that's the problem, Kimmy thought. If even the youngest band member, the one they'd all thought of as a little brother, had found love and happiness, where did that leave their front man?

Silence settled between them, there on the front steps of a luxury chalet in a gorgeous mountain resort in Western Canada, a perfect retreat for songwriting and creation... as long as there was harmony between the band members.

"I'm sorry, Dice," Angel said at last, and he looked worn and tired, older than he'd been. "I shouldn't shit on your happiness like that. Part of me can't help but see you as the fifteen-year-old kid from our street, still – I'll probably feel it forever, even when we're all old – and it's hard for me to believe you're going to get married and be a father."

For the first time, Kimmy noticed fine creases at the corners of the singer's eyes, the beginning of the crow's feet that would inevitably come. Maybe even in that regard, it could be hard for him to see Dice's slightly younger face, as yet unlined, still at the peak of youth. Still, lines gave a face character.

She could imagine Dice, a decade on, with the beginnings of that character starting to show – Jellybean would be in fourth grade – and a decade after that, when the etching would be deeper and strands of silver glitter would begin to emerge in his hair, and their baby would be... an adult... which didn't bear thinking about.

Shaking off these visions of the future, she said to Angel, "Could you try to be happy for us? Your turn will come."

"Try to be happy..." Angel muttered, and his whole demeanor shifted gear. "Try to be happy," he repeated in a more focused way, tapping a rhythm with his foot. "I'm trying to be happy..." He bobbed his head slightly, hearing something in his mind's ear.

Dice, catching on, perked up. He watched the twitching of Angel's foot for a moment, then began drumming a rhythm with his hands on his thighs. A song was forming. "Let's go find the others," he said gently, encouragingly. "Let's go write it right now."

Angel smiled – a little bit rueful, but a normal, real smile. "Might as well start what we came for," he agreed. "*So much romance around me,*" he sang, testing out an opening line. "*It eats me up inside. Might as well* be honest, right?" he added, switching back to a speaking voice. "That's what makes a song hit hard."

"It's going to be a good one." Dice punched Angel lightly on the arm, giving encouragement – a reversal of roles, because it was usually the other way around. "What if we weave in an ironic sample of the Mendelssohn *Wedding March* toward the end?"

Angel chuckled. "I can think of a few interesting things to voice over that, yeah." He turned to Kimmy. "Thanks for the inspiration, and honestly, congratulations. I guess I can't imagine Dice without you anyway, so you might as well marry the kid." His eyes creased with humor; he'd used the word *kid* on purpose.

"Hey," Dice said, but he was laughing, and when his eyes met Kimmy's, she knew everything would be all right.

The energy of a new song coming together so quickly infused the house with good feelings. Even Angel seemed happier at breakfast the next morning, as though letting his feelings out in music had combined with sleep and the mountain air to reframe things in a better light. He jokingly asked Kimmy if she was looking forward to her engagement photoshoot, and chuckled sympathetically at the reluctance on her face.

"It's not going to be a big deal, Kimmy. We'll just take a few pictures," Scott said kindly, his eyes crinkling at her with good humor. She'd known the Smidge photographer for years, and he hadn't changed much – his hairline had receded a bit farther each year and he'd buzzed what was left of his fair hair shorter and shorter in adjustment, and the lines in his plain-featured face had deepened a bit, but his inherent kindness and always-ready easygoing smile never altered. She'd seen many times how good he was at setting people at ease in front of the camera, though she'd never had cause to be that subject. Sure, he'd snapped some candid shots of her working over the years, but nothing posed.

"I know," she told him. "I don't mind. I've just never wanted to be the center of attention."

"Don't think of it like that," the photographer suggested. "The pictures are for you and Dice, for your memories. You don't even need to think about who else will see them."

Kimmy nodded, appreciating the perspective. "Okay. Then... I'm doing my own makeup and picking my own clothes for it, if it's truly for us."

"What were you thinking of wearing?" Crys asked. "Because I've got a small gift for you and maybe now's the time for it." The guitarist's wife got up from the table and hurried off, coming back with a folded cloth item in a sealed plastic bag. "Here. It's something I wanted so badly while I was pregnant, but I never thought of asking until it was too late, and then it took me this long to work out the design and logistics with the merch team. You get the first one, but it'll be available in Smidge's online shop soon, because pregnant fans shouldn't feel left out."

So Kimmy got her engagement photoshoot in jeans and a Smidge maternity t-shirt, with a purple leather choker and a touch of glitter eye makeup and her hair spiked up, and Dice wore a grey Henley and his jeans and Vans, with his hair tied back the way he liked to wear it when he wasn't being a rock star.

They'd been planning to backdate the photos to a week before Dice and Kimmy's brothers had gone viral, but the beautiful mountain scenery was so spectacular that it didn't seem worth taking pictures inside and wasting the location.

"It's not like we'd have taken professional pictures on the day of our engagement anyway," Dice pointed out – and then shared a secret grin with Kimmy, the two of them remembering their extraordinarily unprofessional, partially dressed, never to be shared pink unicorn bedroom selfie.

"So, when's the big day?" Scott asked during the photo shoot.

"Well, I'm due at the end of October," Kimmy said, looking down at her baby bump, which was unmistakable at this point, though she didn't yet feel enormous as she'd been told would happen. "I'm hoping to avoid a c-section or induction, though, so we won't know for sure until it happens. I don't *want* to need to know until it happens."

"Our due date is technically the 24th," Dice added, "but everyone keeps telling me that's just a guess and there's a window of like a month..."

Scott laughed. "I meant your wedding," he clarified. "Have you set a date yet?"

"Oh, that." Kimmy grinned back at him. "We're not in a rush. Sometime after Jellybean is born." Dice's dragon ring on her finger and not needing to hide or hold back her feelings for him was enough for now; she didn't feel any urgency to rush into the ceremony. She'd wanted to have a baby, and she was doing that, and it made sense to her to complete that journey before launching into a wedding.

"We can put the baby in your wedding photos, then," Scott suggested, snapping off another few photos as he spoke. "No, keep your hand on your bump there, Kimmy. Dice, move slightly behind her and put your hand over hers. Like that... good..."

Kimmy turned her head to look back at Dice as she felt him move in close behind her, and his hand came around to cover hers. It turned out to be her favorite one of the pictures.

Later, when it was just the two of them in their bedroom, she asked Dice if he thought his parents would mind them waiting for the wedding ceremony until after the baby was born. Not that it mattered, but she liked family harmony.

"Won't be a problem," he said at once. "I won't lie, they'll be glad we *are* getting married, but that's about it." He hesitated, then asked, "Would you... would you hate getting married in a church, Kimmy? We don't have to, it's not a big deal, but I know my dad would like to officiate, if..."

The way he said *it's not a big deal* made her think it actually was and he was holding back his preferences to make sure hers were accommodated. "I think it would be lovely to have your father marry us," she told him. "But more importantly, you don't need to tell me things aren't a big deal when they *do* clearly matter to you. Basic communication, right? It matters to me when you want something, and if a church ceremony is important to you for its own sake, you don't have to pretend to me that it's just for your family."

"I never want to impose my faith on you," he explained, his cheeks reddening. "I wasn't lying, just... trying not to push."

"I know," she said. "You're always so sweet to me. And I want you to have the church wedding of your dreams, with all the incense and organ music and prayers you could wish for."

♥

After two weeks of intensive songwriting and rehearsal, the band left their Whistler retreat, moving to the nearby city of Vancouver to begin the recording process. They didn't re-record "Band on the Road" since the original release had been so well received, but everything else was newly recorded for the album, which would be called *Reaching for Starlight*. Three of the songs, including the title track, had been written the year before but never recorded, since Smidge had collectively refused to give any more material to Arleigh Hayward Music. This was their first opportunity to record those songs for Valancy Records.

Once recording was completed, the band had a couple of festival commitments during the rest of June and July, but otherwise they were able to relax and enjoy not being on the road. Since Easy and Nell already had a house in Seattle, Crys and Blade were talking about buying in the area as well, and it was only a three-hour drive from where three-quarters of the band had grown up and Angel's parents still lived. Kimmy and Dice agreed that it would make sense to have a permanent base in the same city as the others.

"You don't mind living away from your family?" he asked her. "We don't have to live on the West Coast if you'd rather not."

She hugged him for his thoughtfulness. "I haven't really lived near them in years, being on the road and all. I can make the trip to see them whenever I need to. I'd like to have somewhere to go home to between tours, somewhere that's ours."

"Home," he said, with the wide, sweet smile she loved. "I like the sound of that. How many bedrooms d'you think we'll need?"

♥

They closed on the house in mid-October – four bedrooms, in the end, because the extra two could be a guest room and a music room unless or until they were needed for future occupants. Smidge was back to touring by then, but neither Kimmy nor Dice had a lot of possessions to move in, so it was just a matter of getting the keys delivered.

The decisionmakers at Valancy Records couldn't pause the tour altogether – the new album had to be promoted, after all – but they'd thoughtfully arranged the schedule from mid-October through November so the concert dates weren't too tightly booked, just a couple of shows a week, mostly in the Pacific Northwest, not too far from home. "We don't want Dice torn between his stage commitments and family commitments," Mr. Stirling said at a meeting before the *Reaching for Starlight* tour was officially launched at the end of the summer.

Jed approved of this. He told them that he hadn't liked Crys being forced into so much air travel toward the end of her pregnancy, since he'd have had to cope alone if she'd gone into labor on a flight. A commercial airline wouldn't have let her on board after 35 weeks but with private air travel, the band's old label and production company had no such restrictions to keep them in check. Jed said he was glad for everyone's sake that Kimmy wouldn't have to do so much flying toward the end of her pregnancy.

October 24th came and went. "Don't worry," Dr. Bev told Kimmy. "Lots of first-time moms go a bit late. We'll talk about induction if you get as far as November 6th, but your body knows what it needs to do. Relax, walk as much as you can."

They had shows booked for Seattle and Vancouver, then nothing after the 27th until November 2nd, when they would be in Portland.

"We have Halloween off, for once in our lifetimes," Easy said, looking at the schedule taped to the wall of their tour bus. "We should have a house party."

They were rolling back to Seattle after the Vancouver concert at two in the morning, along with the rest of the tour convoy. Dice had offered to stay with Kimmy at a hotel – they'd all been willing to make it an overnight stay for her – but she wanted to get home. She didn't want to risk going into labor without her mom nearby, and that currently meant the furnished apartment in Seattle the Baker parents had taken for October and November, leaving both the bakery and the garage in the hands of their sons.

Dice lit up at Easy's suggestion. "Could Kimmy and I host it? Now that we have a house, I mean?" Then he paused and glanced at Kimmy, a touch of concern in his face. "If you're okay with that, I mean. If it wouldn't be too much."

I'm enormous, I'm not sleeping, and I'm exhausted all the time, but sure. She smiled at him, loving his enthusiasm as always, and appreciating that he thought to check in with her. Why not go for it, if it would make him happy? "I won't be much help, but okay."

"We can make it a combination housewarming and Halloween party," Sally suggested. "We'll all help. Don't worry, honey," she said to Kimmy, "I'll make sure everything is taken care of. You can just chill."

"What if the baby comes before then, though?" Kimmy asked.

"Then we'll move the party to our place," Nell assured her, as though it was the most obvious solution in the world. Which... maybe it was. Crys and Blade and baby Luke were already staying with them, plus Camillo, who shared the second guest room with Ryan the bodyguard. The rest of the band and crew were at an extended-stay hotel for the moment, while Angel searched for a house large enough to accommodate everyone.

"I'm sorry we're not set up yet to have more people staying with us," Dice said, not for the first time. He and Kimmy were lucky they'd managed to acquire a bed of their own, even, and apart from the baby things in Jellybean's room, there was barely any furniture in the house. Aidan, who'd insisted on sticking with them, had an air mattress in one of the spare rooms.

"This is why you need a housewarming, dude," Erva pointed out.

♥

The morning of Halloween came, crisp and clear. "Good trick-or-treating weather," Kimmy said to Dice as she looked out the curtainless window from their bed. If the weather was as nice in Michigan, Polly and Tim and Bethany would be ecstatic.

"We need to get curtains," Dice grumbled. "Maybe if I crawl under the blankets, I could eat you without scandalizing the neighbors?"

Kimmy's belly felt tight and achy and her back hurt. She didn't want penetration, but a nice orgasm might help, and Dr. Bev had said sexy time could possibly hurry things along. So she stuck her tongue out at him and rolled over to prop herself against the pillows, leaning back and parting her knees in invitation. "Be gentle, drummer boy. I'm kind of fragile this morning."

Without hesitation, he crawled under the blankets and wriggled into position, his hands gently spreading her thighs farther. For a moment, the warmth of his breath was all promise and teasing, then his tongue caressed her with painstaking gentleness. He paused. "When we have curtains," he said, muffled but distinct, "I'm going to tie your wrists to the posts of this extremely excellent bed." A firm swipe of his tongue in just the right spot made her gasp. "Is that good, Kimber? You like it like that?"

She did. The mental image of being tied to the bedposts combined with the gentle demands of his fingers and mouth got her where she needed to be in no time at all. It triggered some deep cramping for a minute or two, but the relaxation was worth it. "Thank you," she murmured as he emerged from under the blankets. Then a thought struck her and she laughed. "Peter, Peter, Pumpkin Eater. Though I like you better as a knight."

Kimmy had found the perfect costume for herself in a maternity consignment store – a pumpkin, orange velvet from midriff to upper thighs, round and pumpkin-y to accommodate even the biggest almost-done belly, with a soft flannelette inner lining that wouldn't irritate sensitive stretched skin. The jack-o'-lantern features on the front of the belly were lit with LEDs to glow like the baby was a candle inside. The upper part of the costume, bra cups and straps in shimmery green satin made to look like leaves and vines, showcased the pregnant voluptuousness of her breasts while also providing support for them. It was the closest she'd come to feeling cute and sexy in a while.

Dice had admitted, a day after she found her costume, that he couldn't think of anything to go with a pumpkin as a couple's costume – the old *Hello, my name is Peter!* nametag was a tired joke, and none of the potential variations on *spice* or *patch* or *pie* had much appeal. In the end, he put together a simple knight's costume, a silvery chain mail shirt with a dark green tabard and a wide leather sword belt over it. A knight could pair with a pumpkin; they didn't have to do some cutesy goes-together thing.

A big bowl of candy waited by the front door in case any little children came knocking, and as party guests arrived throughout the day, the kitchen counters filled up with food.

Home. There still wasn't much furniture, but a dozen assorted folding chairs had showed up from somewhere for the party, plus an inflatable armchair that someone probably thought would be comfortable for Kimmy – a kind thought, but she could only imagine how much it would hurt her back, and there was a good chance she'd need divine intervention or a crane to get out of its embrace if she sat for a moment. The hardwood floors and open spaces would be perfect for dancing, if only she felt like dancing... She'd been crampy and achy all day, when she wanted so much to enjoy this first party in her own place. *Their* own place. *A house.* In all her wildest wishes for the future, she'd never imagined so much permanence.

Sally had arrived as an '80s pop star with a chaotic number of balloons, an enormous cake, and an assortment of glitter-infested decorations that were already shedding their sparkly contamination onto every surface. Angel was also doing the '80s for his costume, but the furthest possible thing from the music industry – he'd dressed as a preppy, complete with boat shoes and a baby pink polo shirt with a popped collar.

Erva surprised everyone by showing up in a tuxedo, drop-dead elegant, with expensively realistic vampire fangs and just an artful trickle of fake blood at one corner of her mouth. She brought deviled eggs, saying a party wouldn't be complete without them, plus something she called million-dollar dip and a tray of bourbon pecan brie bites.

Compared to all that sleek elegance, Kimmy couldn't help second-guessing her choice to be a pumpkin – not that anything would hide her baby bump at this point, but the cheerful pumpkin orange drew attention to it. Sighing, she slipped away from her guests in the kitchen to look out the front window for a moment. It was starting to get dark, and a group of very young trick-or-treaters were already visiting the houses down the block. *We need to light the pumpkin.*

She went looking for Dice, and the moment his eyes met hers, he crossed the room to her without hesitation. "Time to light the pumpkin?" he asked with a smile, seeing the darkening sky. "I'll take care of it. How are you doing?"

"Bit rough," she admitted. "I'm having a lot of cramping and I keep wondering if it's contractions. I mean, I'd know, wouldn't I?"

"Probably? Look, let me get you a chair, then I'll go deal with the pumpkin and–"

"No, I'll come with you. Our first pumpkin." She didn't want to miss any of it.

So they went outside together and lit the tealight candle that sat ready in the pumpkin they'd carved. The group of trick-or-treaters she'd spotted earlier were at the next house over now – neighbors they had yet to meet. "We're supposed to go inside so they can ring the doorbell," Dice pointed out.

As the two of them waited behind the door, a much stronger cramp gripped Kimmy's belly, making her hunch over with a gasp.

The doorbell rang, its cheerful chime echoing around her as the pain gripped her.

She felt Dice's strong hands grip her shoulders, steadying her. "Kimmy! Talk to me, what's wrong?" His voice sounded worried, and she wanted to reassure him.

"Maybe... a contraction?" she managed to say, panting. "Door... Trick-or-treaters." He didn't move.

"Breathe," he reminded her.

"I'm okay," she told him, straightening up and forcing a smile as the tightness in her abdomen subsided. "But you have to do the Halloween thing for us. I need to sit." She shuffled to the nearest folding chair and sank down onto it, feeling a bit wobbly.

With an overwhelmed nod, he opened the door, smiling, apologizing for the wait and praising the children's costumes. He put generous handfuls of candy into the little buckets they held and called out "Happy Halloween!" with a cheerful wave. But he dropped the act the moment he'd closed the door, striding over to her, his smile fading. "Talk to me, Kimmy. That *was* a contraction, wasn't it?"

"I think so."

"Is it... time?" He dropped to one knee in front of her, peering into her face, his expression an adorable mix of excitement and concern. In his knight's costume, with his silky hair loose, he looked like he'd tumbled from the pages of a historical romance book.

And I'm a pumpkin. Another contraction gripped her, and she breathed through it, trying to smile reassurance at him.

"Those are coming close together," he muttered – to himself or to her, she couldn't be sure. "And that lasted a full minute. You want me to phone Dr. Bev?"

"She's not on call this weekend," Kimmy said when she could speak again. "There's a maternity number for the hospital. And I want to call my mom, but I've put my phone down somewhere..."

Dice nodded. "It's okay, I'll find it."

He left, and must have said something to the others, because the next thing she knew they were all gathered around her. This was definitely the real thing now, no more wondering whether it was more Braxton Hicks or general third-trimester discomfort. "Okay, time to go," Jed said.

"I should get changed," she muttered, getting up. "We'll go as soon as Mom gets here."

Jed laughed. "You need to go *now*, Kimmy. Those are long, strong, and close together. Your mom can meet you there."

"But–"

"Now. Unless you want me to deliver the baby here..." he said, in a tone that suggested he wasn't joking. Another contraction came on and she closed her eyes, breathing. "Where's her hospital bag?" she heard him asking Dice. "I don't want to tie up an ambulance for something that's not an emergency, but–"

"Take my truck," Easy's voice broke in. "It's out front. I've had a few drinks, so someone else better drive."

"Come on, Kimmy. I've got your bag." That was Dice. "Time to go."

So Kimmy ended up in a labor and delivery suite at the hospital wearing her pumpkin costume, which fortunately unsnapped at the crotch because they got there just in time, with no chance to change into a gown or anything. Her memory of how everything unfolded was a bit hazy, first racing through the nighttime streets high up in Easy's crew cab pickup with a towel underneath her, then blinking in the bright lights of the hospital and being rushed down a hallway in a wheelchair, with someone saying urgently, "Don't push yet!"

The obstetrician had a scrub cap printed with candy corn.

It all happened so fast, in a blur of fiery internal pain and waves of intense effort, her body caught up in an inexorable process. There wasn't time for any of the things she'd hoped for in her birth plan.

Mostly she remembered Dice's voice, strong and comforting, assuring her that she could do this, that she was doing great, that it would be over soon.

And then it was.

Jellybean was a girl.

"Healthy little lady right here," the pediatrician said, but the infant wail was more reassuring, a small voice protesting the cold world as she was checked over. Kimmy, looking on in awe, wrung out from intense effort, barely registered what the obstetrician was doing to her beyond the words "placenta" and "stitches" since all of it hurt less than delivery, or maybe she'd moved past the point of feeling anything. She was completely transfixed by her tiny daughter's bright eyes, wide open to observe the world. Then Dice – still in his knight outfit – and the delivery nurse helped ease the pumpkin costume up over Kimmy's head and put a clean hospital gown on her instead, and at last she held her baby in her arms.

♥

Soft fussing woke Kimmy from an exhausted sleep, and after a moment of disorientation she remembered. *Hospital. Baby.*

In the half-light, she could see Dice standing by the bassinet, cuddling their daughter against his shoulder and bouncing gently, trying to soothe her with barely audible endearments under his breath.

"I'm awake," Kimmy called softly. "I can take her. What time is it?"

"Just after four," he said, coming close and handing Jellybean over. "I tried changing her diaper and snuggling her, but I think she wants you."

"Yeah. Hi, Jellybean!" she crooned. She fumbled to open the front of her hospital gown with one hand – it theoretically unsnapped at the shoulder – and he helped her.

"There you go."

"Thanks." She looked down as their baby latched on to nurse, and smiled. "This girl needs a name so she doesn't get stuck with Jellybean forever. You still okay to go with Caroline?"

"Carrie for short," Dice said, then hesitated before asking, "Baker or Satwyn?"

"I thought we might hyphenate it," Kimmy suggested softly. It was always going to be Baker in her mind, before. But suddenly she wanted her child to have both names.

A nurse opened the door, startling them. "Everything all right in here? Oh good, I see you're nursing. Back in a bit, then."

"No privacy in this place," Dice muttered, but he was grinning. "Caroline Baker-Satwyn. My dad'll want to give her a saint's name for a middle name."

It would probably be something dreadful. "We'll see," Kimmy said, laughing softly.

the end

Acknowledgments

PREGNANCY DIDN'T HAPPEN IMMEDIATELY FOR ME; I knew the stress of hoping for two lines on the test for too many months before it happened, both times, so Kimmy getting hers in just a couple of tries was a bit of wistful imagination. I don't think I could have written this book as I did without some of my real-life experiences in those years – not just the pregnancy tests, but the *oh foo what I have I done I'm not ready for this* feeling on getting a positive test (even after two years of trying), the stages of pregnancy, and having my husband by my side for all of it. We met in 1996, and from that moment on, he has always been supportive and encouraging about my writing, my parenting once the moment came for that, and everything I want to be. This book would not exist if I didn't have him in my life.

My daughter, who was a baby in a stroller when I started writing the first draft of *Rock Star's Heart*, is now applying to college. She gave me the title for *Rock Icon Ready*. It gives me immense pleasure that we can sit at the kitchen table writing and cheering each other on, and she finished the first draft of her first novel last summer while I worked on this book. My son is a teenager now too and gives me hugs when I need them, which is an important part of my author support system. They were lovely babies, but they've grown into even better people.

This book has been a long time coming – turns out, pandemics aren't good for my creativity or productivity. The first chapter went through several iterations but never started to flow until my writing buddy Andy suggested I was possibly starting it in the wrong place, which I absolutely was. His continued encouragement has meant a lot to me.

My dear friend Emily Bell was my first beta reader and has given me the most helpful feedback at multiple stages, and she let me borrow Ferndale for Kimmy with so many excellent details. I also got valuable feedback from professional beta reader Jennifer at Romance Rehab, and Tiffany John helped me solve a key issue at the beta stage as well.

I deeply appreciate the expertise of my sensitivity readers. Sienna St. Cyr was kind enough to advise me regarding kink aspects of the book. Meghann Robern provided feedback for demisexual representation. Donnie Martino, also known as Carmella Tafani, looked over the drag show for me and shared some helpful thoughts.

I'm grateful to Marnie for commenting on a Facebook post one day that drummers bang harder – my writer brain said *yes, yes they do*, and that's how Dice ended up with dominant tendencies.

I can't imagine publishing a book without my editor, Tanya Oemig. Once again, she did a superlative job of finding solutions to problems and reining in my semicolons and the embarrassing overuse of really and actually.

Any errors are mine.

Thank you to our cover model Hunter, who was a perfect Dice for the camera, and appreciation also goes to Rufus Drum Shop for letting us do our photo shoot inside and outside the shop and play with an exceedingly nice drum kit. My gratitude as always goes to Tiffany for the excellent photography, and to Deseré who was our assistant for the day.

Finally, thank you to my Sweethearts – my street team and book chat group – who have never given up on me. The encouragement and support and advice means everything to me.

I couldn't do this alone. You're all the absolute best!

♥

About the Author

KELLA CAMPBELL CAN USUALLY BE FOUND IN Vancouver, Canada.

She writes mostly romance, because love and relationships are what she finds most interesting about life and in fiction.

She likes tea and chocolate and happily-ever-after endings.

kellacampbell.com

www.ingramcontent.com/pod-product-compliance
Lightning Source LLC
Chambersburg PA
CBHW021645110726
47902CB00007B/1826